MEET SOME O...
OF THE GALAX...

...pern Trevagg, a ruth... ...alien he'd love to bed and a legendary j... ...d y kill.

Figrin D'an and the Modal Nodes, Jabba's full-time musicians who'll dare to break their exclusive contract for one dazzling gig . . .

Muftak, a daring spy who plots the biggest heist of his life— the plunder of a hundred worlds—but risks a one-way trip to the Great Pit of Carkoon.

Wuher the Bartender, a surly human who dreams of pleasing Tatooine's most evil crime lord by concocting the perfect brew . . .

Momaw Nadon, an exiled Ithorian priest who plots to destroy a vicious Imperial lieutenant—even if he must break his most sacred vows to do it.

Kardue'sai'Malloc, the flesh-shredding Devish who dares to trick none other than Jabba the Hutt . . . for the sake of a song.

Davin Felth, a raw recruit in the Emperor's armed forces who is thrust into a situation never covered in basic training . . .

Dannik Jerriko, an assassin who takes pleasure in his job . . . one victim at a time.

THEY'RE LOOKING FOR VICE AND SPICE AND ENTERTAINMENT . . .
THEY'LL BE LUCKY TO GET OUT ALIVE

TALES FROM
THE MOS EISLEY
CANTINA

edited by
Kevin J. Anderson

SPECTRA ™

BANTAM
New York   Toronto   London   Sydney   Auckland

Tales from the Mos Eisley Cantina

A Bantam Spectra Book / August 1995

SPECTRA and the portrayal of a boxed "s" are trademarks of
Bantam Books, a division of Bantam Doubleday Dell Publishing
Group, Inc.

Cover art by Stephen Youll.
Cover art copyright © 1995 Lucasfilm Ltd.
Interior illustrations by Michael Manley, Aaron McClellan, and
Al Williamson. Courtesy of West End Games. Copyright © 1995
Lucasfilm Ltd.

ISBN 0-553-56468-4

Published simultaneously in the United States and Canada

Bantam Books are published by Bantam Books, a division of
Bantam Doubleday Dell Publishing Group, Inc. Its trademark,
consisting of the words "Bantam Books" and the portrayal of a
rooster, is Registered in U.S. Patent and Trademark Office and in
other countries. Marca Registrada. Bantam Books, 1540 Broadway,
New York, New York 10036.

PRINTED IN THE UNITED STATES OF AMERICA

OPM   10 9 8 7

TO BILL SMITH
of West End Games

*who has been a wealth of information and ideas,
providing the character backgrounds and starting points
for many of these stories.*

Mos Eisley Spaceport. You will never find a more wretched hive of scum and villainy. We must be cautious.

—OBI-WAN KENOBI

I'm ready for anything.

—LUKE SKYWALKER

CONTENTS

CONTENTS ✧ x

TALES FROM
THE MOS EISLEY
CANTINA

We Don't Do Weddings:
The Band's Tale

by Kathy Tyers

Jabba the Hutt's cavernous, smoky Presence Room stank of spilled intoxicants and sweaty body armor. Guards and henchmen, dancers and bounty hunters, humans and Jawas and Weequays and Arcona lay where they'd toppled, crumpled under arches or piled in semiprivate cubicles or sprawled in the open. The inner portcullis yawned open.

Just another all-nighter at Jabba's palace.

That portcullis bothers me—what if we want to leave in a hurry?—but it keeps out the worst of the riffraff.

Let me rephrase that. The worst of the riffraff, Jabba himself, paid us well. Crime lord, connoisseur, critic; his hairless, blotchy tail twitched in rhythm when we played. Not our rhythm. His.

We are Figrin D'an and the Modal Nodes, members in good standing of the Intergalactic Federation of Musicians, and we are—or were—Jabba's full-time resident entertainers. I've never spotted his ears, but Jabba appreciates a good swing band. He also likes controlling credit and inflicting pain, and he finds either more therapeutic than our music.

Huddled on the back of the stage, we put away our horns while Jabba's guests snored. My Fizzz—you symphonic ridgebrows would call it a Dorenian Beshniquel, but this is jizz—slips into a thin case in less time than it takes to roll an Imperial inspector and check his pockets for credit vouchers.

We are Bith. Our high hairless craniums manifest a superior evolutionary level, and our mouth folds pucker into a splendid embouchure for wind instruments. We perceive sounds as precisely as other species perceive color.

Our band leader, Figrin Da'n, was wearily swabbing his Kloo Horn (there's a joke there, but you'd have to speak Bithian to get it). It's a longer double-reed than my Fizzz, richer in pastel harmonics but not so sweet. Tedn and Ickabel were arguing over their Fanfar cases. Nalan had started disconnecting the horn bells from his Bandfill, and Tech—we look alike to non-Bith, but you might've picked out Tech by the glazed gleam in his eyes—sat slumped over his Ommni Box. Plaster chips from a midnight blaster skirmish littered the Ommni's reception dish. (The Ommni clips our peaks, attenuates the lows, reverbs and amps the total sound. Playing it takes even a Bith's full genius. Tech hates Figrin. Figrin won the Ommni last season in a sabacc game.)

"Hey, Doikk." Figrin's head glistened. It was going

to be a typical Tatooine scorcher, and Jabba's temp exchanger needed repair.

I cinched down my Fizzz. *My* Fizzz. "What?" I had a shot "lip," as humans call it. I was in no mood for foolishness.

"Time for a friendly hand of sabacc?"

"I don't gamble, Figrin."

Figrin brushed the sheen off his head with one knobby hand. "You're thermal, Doikk."

And you're compulsive. "All musicians are thermal."

"You're thermal for a musician. Who ever heard of a bander that didn't gamble?"

I'm the band's inside outsider, the straight man. I've carried that sweet little Fizzz through six systems. I peg it when it cracks and lube it when the keys click. I carve my own reeds. I wasn't betting it on any sabacc match. Not even to placate Fiery Figrin Da'n, a bandleader who criticizes every missed note, owns everybody (else)'s instruments, and isn't shy about giving orders.

"I don't gamble, Figrin. You know th—"

A smoky silhouette rolled in through the main arch. "Figrin," I mouthed, "turn around. Slowly."

The droid's wasp waist, huge shoulders, and squared-off head had scalded my memory shortly after Jabba gave us our exclusive contract: his vintage E522 Assassin. Eefive-tootoo had saved my neck when one of Jabba's human sail-barge tenders accused me of munching out of Jabba's private snack tank of live freckled toads. Luckily for me, Eefive-tootoo gave me an alibi. I'd vowed never again to have more to do with humans than necessary.

But Jabba'd been hot to feed someone to the rancor. Justice would've suggested throwing in my human accuser, but Jabba and Justice are not on speaking terms. They dropped Eefive, liberally smeared with meat juice, through the rancor's trapdoor in front of Jabba's throne. By the time Jabba's huge, slavering mutant spat him out, he was beyond repair.

Or so I'd thought. Was he back for revenge?

He wore no restraining bolt. Rolling around a

blaster-scarred column, he headed toward us. Frantically I looked around. Nobody showed signs of waking up to rescue us.

The droid raised his upper limbs. Both ended at elbow joints. Somebody'd disengaged his business parts —but that didn't leave him helpless. Assassin droids carry backup.

"Figrin Da'n?" he asked in a brassy green treble.

"What would you do . . . if you found him?" Figrin sidled closer to me, trying to sound colorless. I've never carried a blaster. I wished I had one then, for all the good it would've done.

"Message delivery," honked the droid. "Do not fear. My assassination programming has been erased, and as you can see, my weapons are gone. My new employer saved me from deconstruction by using me this way."

"He doesn't remember us," Figrin whispered in Bithian. "His memory's been erased, too."

As I slowed my breathing, my longstanding attitude about assassin droids resurfaced: *Never worry about one you can see.* He hadn't fired before we spotted him, so we were safe. And I've always gotten along better with droids than with most sentients. Particularly humans.

But as for stripping Eefive of his weapons, that would be like . . . like saving my life by cutting off all my fingers.

"Who's your new owner?" I asked.

The droid hissed, shushing me with white noise.

I dropped my voice. "Who?" I repeated *sotto voce.*

The answer came softly. "Mistress Valarian."

Oh, ho. Val to her friends, Jabba's chief rival in the spaceport town of Mos Eisley, a tusk-mouthed Whiphid recently arrived on Tatooine. Gambling, weapons running, information for sale, the usual . . . but she'd thrived. No wonder she sent a recycled envoy.

Now that I'd processed the lack of immediate risk, I leaned back against the stage. "What does she want?"

"She wishes to hire your services for a wedding, to be held in Mos Eisley at her Lucky Despot Hotel."

I'd heard of the Lucky Despot. Figrin puckered his lip folds. "We don't do weddings," we answered in unison.

Please understand. A wedding gig wastes two days (three days, with some species, plus the time it takes to learn new music). You're treated like a recording, told to repeat impossible phrases and lengthen the usual processional, and ordered to play a final chord as the nerve-wracked principals arrive center stage . . . if they arrive. Someone always brings a screaming neonate. Then the reception, where they inebriate themselves until no one hears a note. All this for half pay and full satisfaction: You've helped perpetuate a species.

Eefive swiveled his flat head toward Figrin. Obviously his recognition circuits still functioned. "Mistress Valarian procured a mate from her home world," he declared.

Good thing I wasn't drinking. I'd've choked. The only thing uglier than a Hutt is a Whiphid. I tried to imagine another gargantuan, rank-furred, yellow-tusked Whiphid arriving on Tatooine. Valarian had probably promised luxury accommodations and good hunting. Wait'll *he* saw Mos Eisley.

The droid continued. "This job is for their reception only. Mistress Valarian offers your band three thousand credits. Transport and lodging provided, and unlimited meals and drinks during your stay. Also five breaks during the reception."

Three thousand credits? With my share, I could start my own band—live in the finest habitats—

Figrin hunched forward. "Sabacc tables?" he asked.

Too late, I recovered from my greed attack. Jabba had given us an exclusive contract. He wouldn't like our performing for Valarian, and when Jabba frowns, somebody dies. *No, Figrin!* I thought.

"Except while performing, certainly," the droid answered.

I buzzed my mouth folds for Figrin's attention, but

his sublime vision didn't deal me in. Figrin set down his deck and commenced negotiating.

We flew into Mos Eisley during first twilight, with one of the suns dipping behind a dull, murky horizon. Our cramped little transport skimmed through the decaying southern sector, chauffeured by an orange service droid. He, like the former assassin, wore no restraining bolt, which predisposed me to like their owner. Sentient shadows slipped into darkening corners as we drove past. The byword in Mos Eisley, which looks like a cluster of populated sand dunes, is camouflage. If nobody sees you, nobody shoots you. Or testifies against you in what passes for local courts.

Three stories above one of Mos Eisley's nameless streets, twin beacons blinked like ship lamps, and brilliant yellow beams glowed out of a wide-open entry hatch. The droid maneuvered us closer. A long curving ramp and straight stairs swooped up from street level to the elevated main entry. Beneath the stairway, I spotted the hotel's most notable feature: three large portholes.

A group of investors crazy enough to sink their credits on Tatooine had towed a beat-up cargo hauler here and sunk a quarter of it under the sand. Debris blown in by a recent dust storm lay clumped along its near side, which had been starboard. Antenna-cluster wreckage drooped over what must've been the cockpit. I mentally saluted the Lucky Despot with the spacer's traditional appraisal of somebody else's ship: *What a piece of junk.*

Our speeder settled at the foot of the long ramp. "Disembark here, gentles," droned the droid.

We unloaded our gear from the airbus's cargo compartment onto a repulsor cart. We'd only brought one change of clothes and our performing outfits, and left the rest of our belongings at Jabba's palace. Mos Eisley's odors—ship fuels, rancid food, low-tech industrial

haze, and the sheer desensitizing smell of hot sand—
hung in sullen air.

Once inside the lobby, we blinked while our eyes
adjusted. An orange-suited human security guard
slouched at one corner. No sign of Lady Val. Mentally I
recategorized her. She might trust droids, but she
equated musicians with kitchen help.

"This way." Our droid led us past an extremely attractive front-desk person, species unknown to me,
whose multifaceted eyes glistened prettily. A long, vast
room filled a third of the ex-ship's top deck. Reflective
black bulkheads and a shiny black floor enveloped several dozen sparsely populated tables, but more than
one table tottered over damaged legs, and here and
there white strips showed through the peeling black
bulkhead. In here—the famous Star Chamber Cafe—
we set up and started a number to get the room's
acoustics. Early diners clapped, clicked their claws, or
snapped their mandibles. Satisfied, we repacked our
gear and grabbed an empty dinner table. Within minutes, the show began. A comet whizzed past Figrin's
head. Constellations appeared beneath the ceiling and
reflected in my soup.

Holographic sabacc spreads flickered into existence
over several tables. Now I remembered the rest of what
I'd heard: Jabba had made sure the Despot never got
her gambling license from local Imperial bribemeis-
ters, so Valarian had to hide her gaming equipment
until dark. Reportedly Jabba warned Lady Val of
planned police raids . . . for a price.

Figrin ate rapidly, pulled out his deck, and wandered
away. Tonight he would lose. On purpose. My other
comrades joined a low-stakes Schickele match.

I found a bored-looking Kubaz security guard and
struck up a conversation. Kubaz make excellent security staff. Their long prehensile noses discern scents
the way Bith distinguish pitch and timbre, and a
Kubaz's greenish-black skin blends into every shadow.
In exchange for my personal stats, which he probably
knew anyway, and a mug of mildly intoxicating lum, I

found out that the green-caped Kubaz's name was Thwim, that he was born on Kubindi, and that Mistress Valarian's prospective bridegroom, D'Wopp, was an expert hunter—common enough profession on their homeworld.

I also spotted a familiar triangular face. Not friendly, but familiar. Kodu Terrafin pilots Jabba's courier run between palace and town house. He's Arcona: Dressed in a spacer's coverall, he looks like a dirt-brown snake with clawed legs and arms and a large, anvil-shaped head.

I kept up my conversation with Thwim as Kodu minced from table to table, swiveling the anvil head. I watched sidelong. Abruptly I spotted the yellow-green glitter of his eyes.

Immediately he slithered in my direction. *He's got me mixed up with another Bith,* I thought wearily. Thwim pushed back, lifting one edge of his cape, and made room for Kodu.

"Figrin, ihss it?" The bulbous scent organ between Kodu's faceted eyes twitched.

"Not quite," I mumbled.

"Oh, Doikk. Hssorry." At least he knew my voice. "Information for hssale. Want to find Figrin?"

I glanced toward Figrin's glimmering holographic sabacc table. Our leader hunched crookedly over his cards, feigning intoxication. Not a good time to interrupt. (*Who made Doikk Na'ts the band manager?* I wondered.)

Kodu pushed closer. "I don't want to hsstay," he hissed. "Do you want to buy? You'd hbetter." He smiled smugly.

"Ten," I offered. Figrin would cover that, if the news was worth hearing. Thwim watched the Uvide wheel studiously. His prehensile nose quivered as a cluster of Jawas hurried by, jabbering rapidly.

"A hhundred," Kodu answered without hesitation. Within three minutes we'd settled on thirty-five. He aligned his cred card with mine and we effected the transfer.

"Jabba." Kodu clicked his fingerclaws. "He'ss angry."

"Angry?" I glanced around. "Who, this time? Why?"

"You hsskipped out on your contract."

My stomachs knotted around each other. "We got another band to cover for us! Not as good as we are, but—"

"Jabba notissed."

It was the worst compliment imaginable. Who'd have guessed the big slug paid attention? "What'd he do?"

Kodu shrugged. "Fed two guardss to the rancor and promissed . . ." He shrugged again, skinny shoulders rising along his brown neck.

Promised to pay well if someone hauled us back to the palace. Good-bye, IFM retirement home. "Thanks, Kodu." I tried to sound as if I meant it. I'd left a sentimental mother at the bubbling pink swamps of Clak'dor VII. She missed her musical son.

Kodu touched his blaster. "Good-bye, Doikk. Good luck."

Luck. Right. Either we slipped out of Jabba's range fast, in which case Kodu wouldn't see me again, or . . .

I weaseled through the crowd to Figrin's table. Fortunately, Figrin had just lost big-time. A Duro shuffled the sabacc deck, scattering and regathering card-tiles with a deft gray hand. I tugged Figrin's collar. "Finish up. Bad news."

He excused himself droopily and arose. It takes twice as long to cross a room when you're looking over your shoulder every other step. Jabba pays well for mayhem.

We found an empty spot at the bar. "What?" Figrin's eyes seemed to have shrunk: spicing already, or faking it well.

I dropped the news on him. "We've got our instruments and two changes of clothes," I finished.

"But I'm losing. I'm behind."

I flicked my mouth folds. We would also need this gig money to buy food till we could get another job—

or Jabba recovered from his temper. I explained that to Figrin.

Barlight reflections wobbled back and forth on his head as he shook it. "We'll get offplanet," he said.

"What about your . . . stash, back at Jabba's?"

"Nothing irreplaceable. We'll leave tomorrow afternoon, after the wedding. I'm ready for bigger crowds again."

I agreed. "Even if gigs aren't so regular, out there in the competition." We've always had a following, but you can't eat "esoteric."

"Richer tables, too," he added, gilding his voice. "Somebody'd better stay awake tonight. Did I hear you volunteer?"

So the spicing act was just that . . . an act. "I'll take the first shift," I said.

Our band set up bleary-eyed the next morning in the Star Chamber Cafe. After breakfast, wedding guests started prancing, oozing, and staggering into the Lucky Despot's lounge. Waiting in the cafe, we tuned. I tried to imagine a Whiphid wedding (Did they osculate, lock tusks, or shout battle cries at the climactic moment?). I'd spotted two turbolifts, a kitchen entry, the main entry, and a small circular hatch that must've once been an emergency airlock. My caped, long-snouted friend Thwim staunchly held up one end of the bar. Around ten banqueting tables, Lady Val's staff laid out food, programmed bartend droids, and hung garlands, making the Star Chamber as classy as it could be, given its state of disrepair.

Beyond the big tables lay a dozen little ones. I could almost feel Figrin's mouth folds twitch, anticipating a wealthy crowd in the mood to celebrate.

A red-raucous cheer erupted in the lounge. "They must be married," Figrin mumbled. Beings streamed out into the cafe. Figrin swung into our opening number. Before we finished, I'd started to sweat . . . and not from the heat. Several of Jabba's toughs had ridden the wave of that stream into the cafe. Were they invited guests? Or had Jabba set us up a one-way trip to the Great Pit of Carkoon?

One more time, I looked around at Valarian's security. Eefive-tootoo stood beside her back hatch, gleaming new blasters and needlers retrofitted for the occasion . . . and a shiny new restraining bolt dead center on his massive chest. Evidently she only trusted droids so far.

A young human tottered up to our stage, wearing clean, unpatched clothing and a slouch. "Play 'Tears of Aquanna.' " He tugged Figrin's pant leg where it gathered above his boot. Figrin pulled his leg free. The human repeated his request, then headed toward me.

I didn't want my pants stretched. "Got it," I said toward him, then took a fast breath and hit my E flat entrance.

How were we to know that a local gang had adopted one of our numbers as their official song? The slouch and several friends huddled at the foot of our stage and caterwauled lyrics they'd obviously invented.

Several other humans lurched toward the stage, glaring. I elbowed Figrin. He took an unorthodox cut to the coda. We finished playing before the gang finished singing. Several of them glowered.

One newcomer, a darkly tanned female, shoved a nonsinging bystander aside. "Now play 'Worm Case,' " she growled in a voice that matched the shade of her skin. "For Fixer and Camie."

"Got it," said Figrin. I have a six-bar intro into "Worm Case." I cut it to four.

When you've played a piece six hundred times from memory, you lose track of where you are during the six hundred and first. This time through, it became a crazy game of cut-and-patch. I don't remember having so much fun with that moldy jump tune. This group didn't try to sing.

Thwim and another security guard accompanied both gangs away. I rechecked Jabba's toughs. They'd gathered near the bar, just killing time . . . for now.

At the end of that set, Figrin headed for a sabacc

table. I lingered onstage, up out of the congealing smokes and odors.

One of the ugliest humans I'd ever met, with a diagonal sneer for a mouth, sauntered over carrying two mugs. "You dry?" he asked in a surly black tone. "This one's lum, that one's wedding punch."

"Thanks." Despite my distaste, I seized the mug of punch and put down half of it.

"You're welcome." My plug-ugly sat down on one edge of the reflective bandstand, then stared out over the crowd. Not wanting to turn his back. Probably a native. I wondered if he'd consider it polite to ask his name, or if he'd take a swing at me. "Good band," he muttered. "What're you doing on Tatooine?"

I set down my mug beside the Ommni. "Good question," I said stiffly. "We've played the best palladiums in six systems."

"I believe it. You're excellent. But you haven't answered my question."

I began to warm toward him. "You're looking at it." I nodded down toward Figrin's gaming table. "We were passing through and got stuck. You work around here?"

"Yah." Sounding blue-gray, he picked up my mug. "I tend bar up the street. Rough living, but somebody's gotta keep the droids from taking over."

I hissed softly in a range humans find inaudible. Droids *improve* life. I was getting ready to remind him when he said "Keep your reed wet, my friend," and hustled away.

Was he one of the rare, approachable types? Had that been a warning? I looked for Thwim by his green cape and twitching snout, but I couldn't spot either.

Soon Figrin rejoined us on the bandstand. "Losing?" I murmured as he plugged in his horn.

"Naturally. Give me an A." We swung back to work. At the table just below us, something changed hands with infinitesimal, micron-per-minute movements: a normal Mos Eisley business deal.

Something else—something huge—lumbered into

view. Two gargantuan Whiphids—two and a half meters of tusk and claw and pale yellow fur, lashed together with a garland of imported greenery—danced
toward our stage with their long furry arms draped
around each other. I stood on a platform, but their
heads towered over mine.

D'Wopp stared rapturously into the broad, leathery,
tusk-bottomed face of his bride. Without seeing the
surreptitious traders already occupying the closest table, the Despot's owner and her professional hunter
sank onto empty chairs. They started untwisting greenery.

I held my head at an angle that made it look as if I
were staring out over the dance floor, but actually, I
was watching one of Jabba's toughs, an anemic, gray-
skinned Duro, glide in our direction . . . alone.

A trio of Pappfaks twirled past, entwining their tur-
quoise tentacles in something that looked like a pre-
nuptial embrace of their own. They nearly tripped over
a mouse droid wheeling toward Lady Val. Seeing the
droid, our hostess bride excused herself from D'Wopp
with a fond pat of his lumpy head. She followed the
droid toward her kitchens.

The Duro's red eyes lit. He edged along the dance
floor, approached D'Wopp, paused, and bowed. "Goo-
ood hunting, Whiphid?" Jabba's Duro shouted, gar-
gling through rubbery lips. He extended a thin,
knobby hand.

D'Wopp's massive paw closed on the Duro's arm,
dangling a ribbon of leaves. "Explain that remark,
Duro, or I shall serve your roasted ribs to my lady for
breakfast."

"No-o, no-o." The Duro rocked his head, cringing.
"I do not signify your lo-ovely mate. I *am* addressing
D'Wopp, bounty hunter of great r-repute, am I not?"

Placated, D'Wopp released the gray arm. "I am he."
He tilted his head back. "Is there someone you want
splashed, Duro?"

I breathed a little easier, too. Playing by memory

means occasional boredom and backflashes, but sometimes it saves your neck. I kept listening and playing.

"Has the lovely br-ride offered any game yet?" asked the Duro.

D'Wopp flicked one tusk with a foreclaw. "What is your point?"

I strained to hear the Duro answer. "There is a bigger-r boss on Tatooine, excellent one. Lady Valarian pays *him* protection money. A Whiphid who truly looves the hunt doesn't settle for small bait. My employer just offered a r-record bounty. You're probably not looking for work at the moment, but opportunities like this come r-rarely."

So the toughs were baiting Lady Val through her bridegroom—and not us! Goggle-eyed, I hit a string of offbeats and reminded myself that Jabba had plenty of time to come for us.

D'Wopp clenched his paws over the table. "Bounty? Is it a fierce bait?"

The Duro shrugged. "His name is Solo. Small-time smuggler-r, but he made the boss big-time mad. Jabba has man-ny more enemies than Lady Valarian has, reputable D'Wopp." The Duro's red eyes blinked. "May I sponsor-r you to the mighty Jabba?"

The Whiphid's leathery nose twitched. "Record bounty?"

At last the Duro dropped his voice. I missed the numbers that clinched the deal, but D'Wopp sprang up. "Tell your employer that D'Wopp will bring in the corpse. I shall meet him then."

Solo . . . Figrin had mentioned him as a tolerable sabacc player, for a human. Now he was my fellow bait on Jabba's short list. The Duro whined, "Ar-ren't you staying for the celebration?"

"Later," said D'Wopp. "My mate and I shall celebrate my glorious return. She is Whiphid. She will understand."

Lady Val reappeared out of the crowd. Jabba's Duro melted back into it like an ice cube on a sand dune. I held my breath. Figrin counted off another song, one I didn't know so well. I had to concentrate. Something rumbled at the foot of the stage. A deep voice shouted "fickle" in Basic. A gruffer one called "dishonorable."

My reed squeaked. Two bellows boomed out in an unidentifiable language. Our loving couple attacked each other tusk and claw, right below the bandstand. I stepped back and almost tripped over Tech's Ommni. Figrin missed tipping the Fanfar by millimeters.

A crowd gathered instantly. Mos Eisley being what it is, and with Jabba's brutes cheerleading, this brawl would spread like a sandstorm. I took advantage of a five-beat rest and blurted out the danger signal. "Sundown. Sundown, Figrin."

"I'm still losing," Figrin hissed. "We can't leave yet."

At the foot of stage left, Lady Val careened sideways into a knot of onlookers. Regaining her balance, she dragged three of them back into the multicolored melee. D'Wopp whistled twice. Two young Whiphids charged in. Jabba's toughs stampeded their side of the onlookers from behind. Lady Val shrieked. Every off-planet gangster in town, and every passerby who'd had too much of Jabba, rushed in on Lady Val's side. Chairs flew. One crashed into the bulkhead, offstage left.

Figrin bent over the Ommni. "End of set, thank you very much," he announced vainly over the bedlam. Tech, wide awake for once, broke down the Ommni. I couldn't find my Fizzz case. Glancing frantically around, I spotted white armor at the grand entry.

Stormtroopers? Not even Valarian could've called in Enforcement that quickly! All sabacc projectors shut down simultaneously, but the gang at the uvide table got caught with its wheel spinning. Just this once, I guessed, Jabba hadn't tipped off Lady Val. I'd've even bet that he sent the stormtroopers himself, but I don't gamble.

"Back door!" Figrin leaped off one end of the stage, barely missing a bulky human's murderous backswing. We followed Figrin along the bulkhead, clutching our instruments—our livelihood. I spotted my new friend

Thwim bashing heads. "Help us! We're unarmed!" I shouted.

His nose swiveled toward us. He leveled his blaster into the midst of us and fired. Tedn shrieked and dropped his Fanfar case. Appalled, I ducked. "Get the instruments!" Figrin cried. Nalan dove into a scrum and emerged carrying one arm at an odd angle—and two Fanfar cases. I grabbed Tedn's unwounded arm and pulled him closer to the hatch, mentally promising anything and everything to any deity listening, if only I could escape with my fingers unbroken and my un-cased Fizzz undamaged.

Eefive stood his post, calmly blasting every being that approached him. Figrin stopped running so suddenly that Tech almost bowled him over.

I glanced back over my shoulder. No use heading that way. Imperial and unlicensed weapons popped off all over the Star Chamber Cafe.

Well, I reminded myself, *I've always had better relations with droids than with sentients.* I marched straight toward Eefive.

"Doikk!" Figrin cried. "Get back here! Get away—"

Eefive didn't shoot. Just as I'd figured, he still had us on his recognition circuits. "Let us out," I pleaded. Something whizzed over my head from behind.

"Shut the hatch behind you," he honked.

"Go!" I shouted at Figrin, motioning him past me.

Figrin ducked under my arm and cranked the hatch open. I stood rearguard. As daylight appeared through the hatch, beings of all shapes and sizes charged at it. I spotted the slash-mouthed human bartender among them.

I hesitated. If nothing else, I owed him for a sweet mug of punch. "Come on!" I shouted, then I ordered Eefive, "Don't shoot that human."

Eefive may have recognized me, but he didn't take my orders. He pointed his needler straight at the bartender. Plug-ugly dropped to the floor, surprisingly agile for such a *big* human. "High register," he cried. "Do a slide!"

It sounded crazy, but I raised my uncased Fizzz and let out a squeal, pushing it higher with all the breath I could muster. Somewhere along the squeal, I must've hit the control frequency for that brand-new restraining bolt. The droid shut down.

The barman sprang up and rushed past me. We squeezed into the airlock together. "Stinkin' droids," he muttered, wiping blood off his nose. "Stinkin', lousy droids."

I emerged on a narrow duracrete ledge, three stories up. The bartender leaned back, sandwiching my Fizzz between his gray-belted bulk and a pitted bulkhead. "Careful! That's my horn!" I cried, teetering as I glanced down. Figrin jumped off the foot of a precipitous steel escape ladder and dashed away, dodging filth and leaping sandpiles.

An anvil-shaped Arcona head poked out the airlock. Clutching my Fizzz in one hand, I backed down the ladder. The human almost stomped my head in his hurry. "Come on," he grumbled. "Move." The ladder swayed from his weight. I barely held on, wishing I'd never met the guy. As more escapees piled on, the ladder's sway became a terrifying oscillation.

I kept dropping. Once down, I spotted another half-dozen stormtroopers trotting up the main ramp in formation.

Another hot morning in Mos Eisley.

Ignoring the trickle of escapees behind us, we ran. "Now what?" wailed Nalan, cradling his arm against his chest. "Without the credits from that job, how are we going to get offplanet?"

"Three thousand credits," Tech moaned, wagging his large, shiny head. "Three thousand credits."

I glanced down to examine my Fizzz. It looked undamaged. "Not only that, but Figrin gambled away our reserves, seeding the table so he'd win today. Didn't you, Figrin?"

The barman changed directions without even slowing down, and I almost got left. "This way," he called.

"We can't pay you for a bolt hole." I hustled to catch up. "Thanks, but we're broke."

"This way," he repeated. "I'll get you a job."

He led us up street and down alley. I followed, thinking, *I'll do anything—shovel sand, polish bantha saddles—but I won't work for humans!*

But his boss wasn't human. The cantina owner, a beige and gray Wookiee named Chalmun, offered us a two-season contract.

No, I thought across the Wookiee's office at Figrin. *It's too public, and that's too long. Jabba will find us for sure.*

"Sounds good," Figrin answered. In Bithian, he added, "Once we find a way offworld, the Wookiee can *keep* our severance pay. Say yes."

I almost walked back down the back stairs, but loyalty is loyalty.

We found crash space at Ruillia's Insulated Rooms. We emerge daily to play in the cantina where my only human friend, Wuher, tends bar. Solo beat Figrin at sabacc yesterday, so *he's* still alive, but D'Wopp was shipped home in pieces. Lady Val is single again and looks to stay that way.

And every time we tune up, I check the crowd. Just now, I spotted Jabba's swivel-eared green Rodian . . . Greedo. He's not bright, but he's armed.

I'm watching him.

A Hunter's Fate: Greedo's Tale

by Tom Veitch and Martha Veitch

1. *The Refuge*

"Oona goota, Greedo?"

The question, spoken fearfully, was answered by the mocking cries of luminous bo-toads hidden in the mountain cave in the dripping green jungle. Pqweeduk scratched the insect bite on his tapirlike snout and made a brave hooting noise. He listened as the sound echoed with the wind in the dark hole that had swallowed his older brother.

Pqweeduk's spiny back shivered. He flicked on his hand-torch and the suckers of his right hand fastened tightly to the shiny hunting knife Uncle Nok had given him for his twelfth birthday.

Pqweeduk stepped into the yawning cave.

But the cave in the jungle was not a cave, and a few meters in, the rocks and packed earth ended at an open steel door!

Pqweeduk leaned through the rectangular opening and flashed his torch upward. He was in a dome that filled the inside of the mountain. The young Rodian saw three great silvery ships squatting silently in the vastness.

"Greedo?"

"Nthan kwe kutha, Pqweeduk!" That was his brother's voice. Pqweeduk saw Greedo's hand-torch signaling and he walked toward it. His bare feet felt a smooth cold floor.

Greedo stood in the open hatch of one of the big ships. "Come on, Pqweeduk! There's nothing to be afraid of! Come on inside and check it out!"

Their bulbous multifaceted eyes, already large, grew even larger as the two green youths explored the interior of the silver vessel. Everywhere were strange and unfamiliar metallic shapes that glittered and flashed in torchlight or presented dark angular silhouettes full of hidden purpose. But there were also places to sit, and beds to lie on, and dishes to eat from.

Greedo had a funny feeling he'd been here before. But it was only a feeling, without any memories attached.

Indeed, the only memories he possessed were of life in the green jungle where his mother harvested Tendril nuts and his uncles herded the arboreal Tree-Botts for milk and meat. About two hundred Rodians lived together under the grand Tendril trees. They had always lived here, this was the only life he knew, and all his fifteen years Greedo and his younger brother had run wild in the forest.

The Rodians had no enemies in this place, except for the occasional Manka cat, wandering through on its way to the distant white mountains during Manka mating season.

The younger Rodians stayed close to home during that part of the year. The Mankas' savage roaring warned everyone of their coming, and the Rodian men would take weapons out of secret keeping places, and stand guard at the edge of the village, waiting for the Mankas to pass in the night.

During Manka season, Greedo would hear the guns scream, as he lay in bed, unable to sleep. The next morning the carcass of a big Manka would be hanging for all to see, from cross-trees in the village center.

Except for the Manka-killing, the Rodians led a quiet self-contained existence. The olders never spoke of any other life—at least not in front of the children. But Greedo overheard them, when they thought he was asleep, talk of things happening out among the stars.

He heard the olders use words like "Empire," "the clan wars," "bounty hunters," "starships," "Jedi Knights," "hyperspace." These words made strange images in his mind—he couldn't make sense of them at all, because the only life he knew was the jungle, the trees, the water, and endless days of play.

But the olders' secret talk filled him with feelings of unexplainable longing. Somehow he knew that he didn't belong to this green world. He belonged somewhere else, out among the stars.

The silver ships were the proof. He knew with uncanny certainty that these were the "starships" he had heard his mother and uncles speak about. Surely his mother would tell him why the ships were hidden under the mountain.

Pqweeduk isn't old enough to know . . . but I am.

•   •   •

Greedo's mother, Neela, was sitting on the ground in front of their hut, by firelight, peeling Tendril nuts. Her hands moved rapidly, slitting the thick husks with a bone knife and peeling them back. She hooted quietly to herself as she worked.

Greedo crouched nearby, carving a piece of white Tendril wood into the shape of a silver starship. When the ship was finished he held it up and admired it, making sure his mother could see it. "Mother," he asked abruptly, "when are you going to teach me about the silver ships in the mountain?"

The rapid movement of his mother's hands stopped. Without looking at her son, she spoke, in a voice that betrayed emotion. "You found the ships," she said.

"Yes, Mother. Pqweeduk and me—"

"I told Nok to fill in the opening in the mountain. But Nok loves the past too much. He's always sneaking up there to look at the ships." She sighed and resumed peeling the leathery skins off the big nuts.

Greedo moved closer to her. He sensed that she was ready to tell him things he wanted to know . . . things he *needed* to know. "Mother, *please* tell me about the ships."

Her moist faceted eyes met his. "The ships . . . brought us to this place . . . this world . . . two years after you were born, Greedo."

"Wasn't I born here . . . in the jungle?"

"You were born out there"—she pointed at the evening sky, visible through the tall Tendril trees, where the first stars were appearing—"on the world of our people, the planet Rodia. There was much killing then. Your father was killed, while I was carrying your brother. We had to leave . . . or die."

"I don't understand."

She sighed. She saw she would have to tell him everything. Or almost everything. He was old enough now to know the facts.

"Our people, the Rodians, were always hunters and fighters. The love of death was strong in us. Many years ago, when the meat-game was gone, we learned to raise all our food. But our people began to hunt each other, for sport."

"They . . . killed each other?"

"Yes, for sport. For deadly sport. Some Rodians thought it was foolishness, and refused to participate. Your father was one of those. A great bounty hunter was he . . . but he refused to join the foolish gladiator hunts."

"What is a bounty hunter, Mother?" Greedo felt a chill in his spine, waiting for the answer.

"Your father hunted criminals and outlaws . . . or people with a price on their heads. He was highly honored for his skills. He made us very wealthy."

"Is that why he died?"

"No. An evil clan leader, Navik the Red, named for the red birthmark that covers his face, used the gladiator games as an excuse to make war on the other clan leaders. Your father was murdered. Our wealth was taken, and our clan, the Tetsus, were nearly wiped out.

"Fortunately, some of us were able to escape the killing, in the three silver ships you've found."

"Why did you never tell Pqweeduk and me about the ships . . . and about our people?"

"We have changed. There was no need to dredge up the dark past. We have become peaceful here. The guns are only brought out when the Manka cats are prowling. We made a vow, in our council, that the children should not know of the terrible past, until they were full grown. I am breaking that vow now, in telling you these things. But you are . . . almost as tall as your father now."

His mother's eyes seemed to envelop Greedo. He loved the way she looked at him. Her skin exuded a pleasing perfume, a strong Rodian scent. He gazed at her wonderingly. Suddenly there was so much more to know. He wanted desperately to learn . . . everything.

"What is the Empire, Mother?"

She frowned and wrinkled her long flexible snout. "I've told you enough, Greedo. On another day perhaps I will answer all your questions. Go to bed now, my son."

"Yes, Mother." Greedo touched his hand suckers to his mother's in the traditional all-purpose greeting and good night. He went to his straw-filled bed in their little hut, where his brother was already asleep.

Greedo lay for hours, thinking of silver ships, of his father the bounty hunter . . . and the greatness of life among the stars.

2. *Red Navik*

A month and a day after Greedo and Pqweeduk found the silver sky ships, Navik the Red, leader of the powerful Chattza clan, found the Tetsus.

Greedo and his brother were climbing high in the Tendril trees when they saw a bright flash in the sky. They watched with quiet curiosity as the flash flowered and became a glittering red shape that grew larger and larger, until they could see it was a sky ship, twenty times larger than the small silver ships in the cave.

Anxious voices called from below. Greedo hooted with excitement and began to slide rapidly down the smooth tree, using his suckers to skillfully brake his descent. His brother was right behind him.

Below they could see the people coming out of their huts and pointing at the big sky ship. Uncle Nok and Uncle Teeko and others were running to get the weapons. Greedo sensed their fear.

"C'mon, Pqweeduk!" Greedo shouted, as his feet hit the ground. "We have to save Mother! We can't let them kill her!"

"What are you talking about, Greedo? Nobody's killing anybody!" Pqweeduk dropped to the ground and obediently followed his older brother.

As they ran through the trees, the red ship swooped lower, uncoiled its landing gear, and settled in a cloud of fiery smoke at the edge of the village.

Twin hatches hissed open. Greedo stopped and turned and gaped in awe as armored Rodian warriors poured out of the giant ship—hundreds of them, each wearing bright segmented armor and each carrying a vicious-looking blaster rifle.

The sight of these killers transfixed the young Rodian. It was a full minute before he felt his brother tugging fearfully at his sleeve. And then he heard his mother's voice, urging him to *run*. The last thing Greedo saw, before he turned his face to the forest, was the figure of a tall, imposing Rodian with a bloodred mark that stained most of his face. The marked warrior shouted an order, and the others raised their weapons.

The scream of laser fire mixed with the dying shrieks of the people, as Greedo and his brother and mother fled into the jungle.

Uncle Nok and Uncle Teeku and twenty others made it to the cave ahead of them. There was a great grinding noise and the roar of a landslide, as the top of the mountain opened, throwing off its burden of earth and stones.

Greedo caught his breath as the three silver ships gleamed in the light of the midday sun. Powerful engines already whined awake.

Uncle Nok greeted Greedo's mother as he urged everyone to get aboard as fast as possible. "Neela—*now* you know why I was always visiting the ships! I was keeping them in repair for this very day!"

Greedo's mother hugged her brother Nok and thanked him. Then they all rushed aboard, followed by a stream of refugees coming out of the forest.

Two of the silver ships lifted easily on columns of repulsor energy, their fission-thrust engines whining up so high that the sound vanished beyond the range of Greedo's hearing. The third ship was waiting for the last stragglers . . . the last survivors of the massacre.

A portly Manka hunter named Skee charged out of the forest, screaming that everyone behind him was dead—"Leave! Take the ships away, while you still have a chance!"

The third ship never got its hatch closed. A single bolt of ion energy fused its stabilizers into a molten mass, and a split second later a powerful laser blast blew the power core.

As the first two ships shot skyward, a bright sphere of fusion fire blasted back the jungle, mocking the midday sun. The third ship was no more.

Greedo never heard the explosion. He was in the cockpit of *The Radion,* gawking at the starlines, as Uncle Nok's silver ship vaulted into the unknown.

3. *Nar Shaddaa*

Planning for this emergency, Nok had programmed the Rodian ships to jump to a heavily trafficked region of the galaxy, where the survivors of his little tribe could lose themselves among the myriad alien races engaged in interstellar commerce.

So it was they came to Nar Shaddaa, a spaceport moon orbiting Nal Hutta, one of the principal worlds inhabited by the wormlike Hutts.

There was a continual buzz of space traffic between Nar Shaddaa and the far-flung systems of the galaxy: mighty transgalactic transports and bulk cargo vessels, the garish yachts and caravels of the Hutt ganglords, the battle-scarred corsairs of the mercenaries and bounty hunters, the pirate brigantines, and even the occasional commercial passenger liner, packet starjammer, or massive migration arks. And, of course, the ever-present star cruisers and sleek patrol vessels of the Imperial Navy.

The surface of Nar Shaddaa was an interlocking grid of miles-high cities and docking stations, built up over thousands of years. Level upon level of freight depots and warehouse and repair facilities were linked by gaudy old thoroughfares that spanned the globe, bridging canyons that reached from the upper strata, swarming with life, to the glowing depths where several forms of subspecies thrived on the refuse that fell continuously from the towering heights.

Greedo and his brother and mother and all the pilgrims on those two silver ships came to Nar Shaddaa, merging with the life of the great spaceport moon, finding a home in the huge sector controlled by Corellian smugglers.

The Corellians kept things reasonably under control in their part of the moon. Gambling was an important source of income for them. All races were invited to wander the brightly lit avenues and gawk and eat and drink and throw away money in the sabacc joints. A gun duel or a bounty killing now and then was to be expected, and petty thievery was largely overlooked. But there was an unwritten law in the Corellian Sector, enforced by Port Control: If you want to make big trouble, do it somewhere else.

The Rodian refugees merged with the denizens of the dingy warehouse districts on Level 88. Over the next months they found work as freight handlers and house servants, and went about their lives.

Nok ordered everyone to stay away from the public levels, the thoroughfares, and the casinos, on the chance they'd be recognized by a Chattza hunter. Nok assured them their stay on Nar Shaddaa was a temporary one, until he could locate another jungle world where they could dwell in peace.

For the adult Rodians it was not a happy time—they deeply missed the lush green world they had left behind. But for Greedo and Pqweeduk, a whole universe of excitement began to reveal itself.

Four years later Greedo's people were still on Nar Shaddaa, working and surviving. Greedo was nineteen, his brother was sixteen. The green youths had merged with the boundless spectacle of the Galaxy.

4. *Bounty Hunters*

"Jacta nin chee yja, Greedo!"

Greedo leaped back as three repulsor bikes whipped

past, jumped a broken retaining wall, and disappeared into one of the crowded concourses that had been declared off-limits by Uncle Nok.

He watched his brother and friends swerve their bikes among the landspeeders, antique wheeled cabs, Hutt floaters, skillfully dodging the strolling gamblers, alien pirates, spice traders, street hawkers, ragtag homeless . . . and bounty hunters.

"*Grow up,* Pqweeduk!" Greedo slouched against a wall, waiting for his friend Anky Fremp, a Siona Skup biomorph who had taught him the secrets of the street.

Greedo, on the edge of adulthood, had left the games of childhood behind. He'd traded his repulsor bike for a fine pair of boots. He had stolen a precious rancor-skin jacket. He had learned how to strip therm pumps and shield regulators off Hutt floaters while the local crimelords were lounging in the Corellian bathhouses, making deals with their interstellar counterparts.

Anky Fremp had shown Greedo the ins and outs of the black market—who paid the most for stolen hardware . . . and who had the best price on glitterstim, skin jackets, and Yerk music cubes.

Fremp and Greedo were a team, and had been a team for two years. Pqweeduk was still a dumb kid, playing mindless street games with his pals.

"Ska chusko, Pqweeduk!" Grow up, Pqweeduk!

While he waited for Fremp, Greedo watched the street. Every kind of life, human and alien, passed through Nar Shaddaa. Maybe half were legitimate traders and freight haulers, working for one or another of the great transgalactic corporations. The rest were operating somewhere beyond the outer edges of the law.

One group that fascinated Greedo didn't seem to be chasing gold and excitement, and you almost never saw them on the street. They were the so-called Rebels—political outsiders who had taken a stand against the despotic rule of Emperor Palpatine and his cruel military dictator, Darth Vader.

There were Rebels on this spaceport moon—Greedo knew. They hid out in an old warehouse on Level 88, the same level where the Rodian refugees lived. The Rebels were stashing all kinds of weapons there—weapons that arrived hidden in exotic cargos of precious metals and spice . . . and left in the darkest hours of the night, on blockade runner ships destined for far-flung outposts among the stars.

I'll bet the Empire would pay a lot to know what the Rebels are doing on Nar Shaddaa. But how would I give the Imps that information? I don't know anybody who works for the Empire.

Just then Greedo heard the shrill sting of laser shots and he instinctively ducked, crouching down behind the crumbling retaining wall his brother had repulsor-jumped a few minutes before.

Peering carefully over the top of the wall, he saw a man in the distinctive green uniform of an Imperial spice inspector emerge from the shadows and run through the crowded thoroughfare. More laser shots echoed, and the crowd began to rapidly disperse into the surrounding alleys and gambling saloons.

Greedo saw bright bolts of energy smashing off buildings and vehicles. The running man was hit and went down, not three meters from Greedo's hiding place.

Two imposing figures stepped out of the shadows onto the brightly lit concourse. With deliberate steps they approached the fallen man.

The larger of the two figures, who was dressed in a rusted skull-shaped helmet and full Ithullan armor, nudged the victim with his boot. "He's dead, Goa."

The shorter figure bent over to inspect the victim, and Greedo got a glimpse of a mottled brown wide-beaked face squatting on a disarrangement of leather and iron and bandoleers. "Too bad, Dyyz," said the short one. "I only tried to wing him. He was worth twice as much alive."

Bounty hunters, thought Greedo. *They've taken their prey . . . now they'll be collecting the reward. I'll bet it's a lot. I'll bet they're rich.*

The big one, whom the other called Dyyz, bent over and picked up the dead spice inspector and slung him easily over his shoulder. "All in a day's work, hey, Goa? I gave this scum a bribe or two myself, over the years . . . but when the Imps put a man on the bounty roster, there's only one way to go! Let's bag and stash him and go for a drink."

"Fine with me. I'm thirsty as a Tatooine farmboy."

Greedo noticed for the first time that the one called Goa had an oversized blaster rifle slung on his back. He'd never seen a blaster that large. It was cased in scrolled black metal and layered with tubing and electronics. *A custom job,* Greedo thought. *Look at the sights on that thing! I'll bet that's one bounty hunter who* always *gets his man.*

Greedo expected the two bounty hunters to disappear back the way they came, but instead they walked straight toward him.

The closer they got to the retaining wall, the more frightening their appearance became. The big one, Dyyz, wore a corroded parasteel helmet that covered his entire head. The face mask—narrow eyeslits in a stylized death's-head—communicated deadly, inexorable *threat.* This one wore the armor of the extinct Ithullan race—Greedo knew the warlike Ithulls had been wiped out hundreds of years ago, their civilization crushed and annihilated by another, equally warlike race, the Mandalore. From the looks of his armor, thought Greedo, he must have stolen it from an Imperial museum!

The other bounty hunter, Goa, was outfitted in a hodgepodge of gear that suggested he never changed it or took it off—he had simply added new pieces over the worn-out ones, until he became a walking collection of military costuming and equipment.

The most fascinating aspect of Goa was his head: obviously an intelligent species of bird—or descended from birds. Mottled brown leathery skin, featherless, with tiny intense eyes buried behind a broad scarred beak.

Dyyz and Goa reached the retaining wall and Greedo ducked down. The next thing Greedo heard was a third voice, rasping and cruel:

"Well, well, if it ain't Dyyz Nataz and Warhog Goa—where ya been, boys? You should know better'n ta stiff an' old friend!"

"Ease up, Gorm. You'll get your share. Fact is, Warhog and me are takin' in this blacklisted spice inspector. The Imps'll pay us plenty and we'll be more than happy to cut you in on the deal!"

"Hell we will, Dyyz." That was Goa's voice. "There's two of us and one of Gorm. He can wait for the credits we owe him."

"One of me is worth *six* of you cage cleaners—"

Blaster fire spanged and red bolts of energy shot over Greedo's head. He ducked lower and the sounds of a fierce struggle came to his ears. Suddenly Goa's big blaster rifle came flying over the wall and clattered on the pavement next to Greedo.

As he impulsively reached out to touch the weapon, Greedo heard the one called Gorm directing the one called Dyyz to hand over the body of the spice inspector. "Give 'im up . . . and I'll let ya live another day—"

Finding the courage to again peer over the wall, Greedo saw a most awesome figure, two heads higher than Dyyz Nataz, clothed in heavy plated armor and full helmet. The eyes of the face mask were glowing red electronics. *Must be a droid,* Greedo thought. *I've heard of renegade assassin droids taking up the bounty trade. Or maybe it isn't a droid . . .*

Greedo suddenly had an idea. Taking the huge blaster rifle in trembling suckers, Greedo hefted the weapon as quietly as he could into firing position. He checked for a safety switch—found it and armed the gun.

Then, surreptitious as Uncle Nok waiting for a

Manka cat, he hoisted the nose of the rifle over the edge of the retaining wall. It pointed straight at the back of *Gorm*.

Greedo saw Goa's eyes go to the rifle and then flick away. Greedo squeezed the trigger.

The weapon whistled and roared and the bounty hunter called Gorm toppled forward with a grunt, a blackened blaster hole in the center of his back.

As Greedo stood up, Goa emitted a maniacal cackling noise and lunged for the rifle. But Greedo swung the barrel at Goa's head.

"Whoa, kid! Easy there! That's a hair-trigger yer pinching!"

Dyyz snorted and laughed. "Thanks, kid. You saved our skin. We're eternally in your debt. Now if you'll just give my partner back his weapon, we'll be on our way."

Greedo clambered carefully over the wall, keeping the blaster rifle trained on Goa. Moving closer to the prone figure of Gorm, he looked into the hole he'd made in the big bounty hunter's back. Fused wires, exploded electronics. "Is he a droid?" asked Greedo.

"You might say that," said Goa. "Now about the gun —how about we cut you in on the reward for this inspector? You've earned it."

"I've got a better idea," said Greedo. "I think I can help you guys make a *lot* of money."

5. *The Smuggler and the Wookiee*

"Spurch Warhog Goa?" Why do they call him Warhog?

Anky Fremp, Greedo's street friend, sat on the edge of a parking platform, with his short legs dangling over a miles-deep city canyon. Anky was a Sionian Skup, a near-human race with small closely spaced eyes, hair as brittle as glass, and skin the color of dianoga cheese. Anky pitched one bottle after another into the abyss.

The distance from the spaceport's highest tower to the surface of the Nar Shaddaa moon was so great, they never heard the bottles hit. But sometimes the bottles collided with a cab or freighter repulsing up the shaft, and that was fun.

"What you doin' that for?" Greedo said with disdain. "That's the kind of stupid game my kid brother plays. If Corellian Port Control catches ya, we can be conscripted to work on an ore hauler."

"Yeah . . . you're right. I'm gettin' too old for this stuff. Oh well, there goes the last one."

A hangar scow emerged into the shaft seven levels down, and Fremp's missile hit the scow pilot square on his protective helmet. The man looked up, screaming, and shook his fist.

When the scow lifted rapidly toward them, Greedo and Fremp decided they'd been edge-sitting long enough, and began walking fast toward Ninx's garage —one of their favorite hangouts.

"Okay, so tell me the deal, Greedo. These bounty hunters you met are going to make you rich?"

"Yeah, I told 'em about the Rebels runnin' guns through Level 88. The Empire pays a *big* bounty for that kind of information. Dyyz and Warhog said they'd cut me in on the take."

"Wow. Will ya share it with *me?*"

Greedo sounded superior. "Yeah . . . I'll throw a few credits your way, Fremp. But most of it I'm going to use to buy me my own *ship*. Ninx has got a cute little Incom corsair he'll let me have for fourteen thousand. All she needs is new power couplings."

"That's nothing. We can *steal* the couplings!"

"Right. *I* can steal the power couplings." Greedo gave his eager friend the Rodian's version of a condescending look, as they arrived at the secret door to Ninx's garage. *Fremp doesn't need to think any part of my new ship is going to belong to him.*

Shug Ninx's assistant was an ambidextrous Corellian hyperdrive mechanic named Warb. Warb recognized the two youths on the entry monitor.

"Hey, Anky . . . Greedo. Got any hot therm pumps for me today?"

"Sorry, Warb. Tomorrow we'll have something."

"Okay, see ya tomorrow. Shug ain't around and I'm busy."

"I want to show Anky that little Incom corsair I'm going to buy."

"Hmmm . . . okay. C'mon in. But if any tools show up missin' I'm gonna know who to vaporize."

Warb buzzed them into Ninx's garage and went back to work helping a smuggler overhaul the lightdrive on a beat-up YT-1300 freighter he'd won in a sabacc game.

The cavernous repair shop was a confusion of dismembered ships and the greasy clutter of a lifetime—parts everywhere, whole assemblies hanging from lifts and cradles—and bright flashes of ion flow welding from technician droids working high on scaffolding surrounding a massive Kuat Starjammer-IZX fast freight hauler that seemed to take up half the garage.

Greedo and Anky wandered through a maze of packing crates to where the Incom Corsair sat on her landing skids, gleaming like an Arkanian jewel. She looked almost new!

"There she is," said Greedo proudly. "I'm going to call her *The Manka Hunter*. Nice, huh?"

Anky gulped. "Only fourteen thousand credits for this? I don't believe it! Shug's probably going to substitute some broken-down *clunker* once he's got the money."

"Not my pal Shug. He knows I'm going to be a bounty hunter. He knows a bounty hunter has to have a good ship."

"*You're* going to be a bounty hunter?"

Greedo puffed out his chest. "Yeah. My friend Warhog Goa said he'd teach me the trade. He said some of the best bounty hunters are Rodians."

Anky became an instant believer. "Do you think he'd teach me to be a bounty hunter, too?"

Greedo hooted. "I don't think the *Skups* were ever known to do much in the way of bounty killing."

Anky looked crestfallen. The Sionan home world was noted mostly for the master *thieves* it had produced.

"Come on, Anky. Let's look at the inside of my ship."

But the Corsair's hatch was locked. Since Shug wasn't around, they'd have to ask Warb to unlock it. They made their way back through the packing crates and clutter and headed toward the YT-1300 where Warb and the smuggler were working. They were almost to the freighter when Greedo spotted a pair of Dekk-6 power couplings sitting on a workbench, next to Shug's milling machine.

Greedo knew right away they were Dekks. Dekk-6's were the best. Modog couplings used to be the best, but starship technology was advancing very rapidly, thanks to the Empire and its insatiable military needs.

Fremp spotted the Dekks too, and both youths stopped to admire the gleaming components. A pair of Dekk-6's could cost twenty thousand credits—that's how advanced they were.

"I'll bet Warb is planning to put these in that junk heap he's workin' on," said Greedo. "He's going to have to mill the casings, to fit the converter flanges on that old freighter."

"These are just what we need for your new Corsair," said Anky, fingering the expensive hardware. "They'll drop right in."

Yes. Greedo had already felt an impulse to steal the Dekks. They were brand-new, they were beyond beautiful, and he would never find their like stripping Hutt caravels.

A bounty hunter needs a fast ship. My ship will be the best. I will replace every part of my ship with the most advanced components I can buy or steal. No one will outrun The Manka Hunter.

Greedo looked around casually and scanned the garage. Warb and the smuggler were floating a heavy power cell up the gangway of the YT-1300. They disappeared through the hatch.

No one was watching.

Greedo slipped off his rancor-skin jacket and wrapped it around the fist-sized couplings.

"Come on, Anky. Let's go. I gotta meet Goa in twenty minutes."

"Right. Let's go."

Suddenly Greedo felt powerful shaggy paws grip him around the waist and hoist him into the air. He dropped the skin jacket as he kicked and struggled, and the Dekk couplings clattered onto the floor.

"HNUUAARRN!"

"Te kalya skrek, grulla woska!" Put me down, ya hairy heap!

The Wookiee turned Greedo with his paws so he could look into the snouted green face. "NNHNGR-RAAAGH!" Greedo saw bared teeth and angry eyes, and he wilted. Anky Fremp was already heading for the door.

"What's goin' on, Chewie?" The tall Corellian smuggler appeared, with Warb at his side. The smuggler had his right hand on a holstered blaster.

"HNNRRNAWWN." The Wookiee's groans were just terrifying noise to the youth, but the smuggler seemed to understand them perfectly.

"Stealing our Dekk-6's, huh? Great. What kind of shop you guys running, Warb? Do you know what I had to pay for these Dekks?"

"Sorry, Han. I told Shug I didn't trust these street kids, but he took a liking to the green one . . . You know the rules, Greedo. I'm goin' to have to tell Shug about this. If you know what's good for ya, you'll get out of here and never come back . . . that is, if the Wookiee don't break yer neck first!"

The big Wookiee was still holding the terrified Rodian a meter off the floor, as if waiting for a signal from his friend the smuggler.

"Wait a minute," said the smuggler. "Don't hurt him, Chewie. I'm going to teach the little sneak a lesson . . . Where'd you put those burnt-out Modogs, Warb?"

The Wookiee lowered Greedo to the floor, but kept

his hairy paw on him as Warb fished around in a big trash barrel next to the workbench. A second later Warb emerged with two blackened and corroded Modog power couplings. He gave them to the smuggler and the smuggler handed them to Greedo.

"Here. The kid wants power couplings, he can have these. I took 'em off the *Millennium Falcon*. They've got a real pedigree, kid. And all I want for 'em is this rancor-skin jacket. What do you say? Even trade?"

The smuggler grinned and the Wookiee squeezed Greedo's shoulder.

"T-te jacta." I'll get you for this.

"Did he say what I think he said?" asked the smuggler.

"He said it's a deal," laughed Warb.

"Good. The kid knows a bargain when he sees one." The smuggler held out his hand for a handshake, but Greedo ignored it. Instead he made a popping noise with his hand-suckers and threw the burnt couplings on the floor. Then he turned and ran for the door.

"HWARRNNUNH."

"Yeah, Chewie, I was probably a little rough on him. But you got to set punks straight while they're still young. Otherwise no telling where they'll end up . . . Here, Warb, ya want this jacket? It's a birthday present."

"Thanks, Han. How'd you know today's my birthday?"

6. *The Teacher*

Spurch Warhog Goa was sitting by himself, counting a pile of credits, in a corner of the Meltdown Cafe. He waved his arm when he saw Greedo come in. "Hey, kid —over here!"

Greedo was still nursing his anger and resentment, but he tried to look like a seasoned spacer as he moved through the noisy gathering. He started to feel better when one grizzled old Twi'lek actually jumped out of his way.

"Hello, Spurch."

"Have a seat, kid. Ya want somethin' to drink? . . . Don't sit too close. You Rodians don't smell right to a Diollan."

Greedo took a place opposite his new mentor. Goa ordered up a bottle of Tatooine Sunburn for Greedo.

"T-that's a lot of money, Spurch." Greedo eyed the pile nervously. He hoped Ninx would still sell him the Corsair, after what happened.

"Call me Warhog, kid. I don't care for that other name. My mother thought it was cute 'cause it means 'brave bug catcher' in our language." Goa snorted. He took a stack of chits off the pile in front of him. "Here, kid. For you. Thanks for the tip about the Rebels. It paid off . . . big-time."

"Cthn rulyen stka wen!" Wow, that's great! Greedo picked up the bills and flipped through them. They were small denominations . . . far less than he had expected. Visions of piloting his own fast Corsair began to evaporate.

"Uh . . . two hundred credits . . . uh, thanks, Warhog."

"Whatsamatter, kid? You look disappointed." Goa surveyed his new protégé with a bright bird eye.

"Uh . . . I thought there would be more, I guess."

"Hey, kid. You want to be a bounty hunter, right? Didn't I say Rodians make the *best* bounty hunters? Didn't I?"

Greedo nodded solemnly. *I do want to be a bounty hunter. But a bounty hunter needs a ship.*

"Now, you think I train bounty hunters for *free*? Huh? Do ya? . . . Drink your Tatooine Sunburn, kid, it's delicious."

Obediently Greedo picked up the bottle and swallowed the thick fluid. It tasted bitter. He felt embarrassed. Warhog was right. "Uh . . . I guess I . . . uh, never thought about that," he said.

"Right. It never crossed your greedy little mind. Goa gets *paid* for teaching young punks how to hunt! Now look here—" Goa reached into one of the many pouches strapped to his body and pulled out a much larger roll of credits. "This is all yours, if you want it—twenty thousand. That's one-third of what the Imps paid for the intelligence on the Rebels."

Greedo's eyes watered, and a profound hunger rippled in his guts as he stared at the mound of credit notes. Visions of *The Manka Hunter* started to re-form.

Goa leaned forward and fixed Greedo with his beady eyes. "But if you take this money, that's *it*, ya understand? I never want to see you again. You gotta make up your mind, kid. Do you want to learn the trade from an expert . . . or do ya want a few nights on the town and the down payment on a hot rod you'll probably crash in a week? Warhog Goa can make you the galaxy's second-greatest bounty hunter, kid . . . Warhog Goa being the *first*."

Greedo let Goa's words roll around inside his head for a minute, and they connected with his deepest desires. He wanted that Corsair more than anything, but he felt a deeper need to *hunt* . . . a need to be like his *father*. And the trade of bounty-hunting was a way of making *lots* of money. A rich bounty hunter might own his own moon and lots of ships—sloops, cruisers, cutters . . . even *warships*.

"You'll really teach me the secrets?" asked Greedo diffidently.

"Teach ya? I'll shove the stinkin' secrets down your stinkin' throat! We got a deal, kid? Believe me, I wouldn't do it for anybody. But you saved my life. You cut me and Dyyz in on your first capture . . . and by the Cron Drift, you're a *Rodian*. I tell ya, Rodians are *born* bounty hunters."

Greedo felt waves of pride sweep over him. Born bounty hunter. Rodians are born bounty hunters. *Yes, I can feel it, I've always felt it. My father was a bounty hunter. I will be a bounty hunter. I am a bounty hunter.*

"*Deal*, Warhog." Greedo hooted and held out his hand.

Goa looked at the suckered fingers and a look of disgust crossed his face. *Even the kid's hand smells funny.*

He carefully touched Greedo's hand with his own. *"Deal,"* he said. "C'mon, I'll buy ya another Sunburn at the bar . . . introduce ya to some of the boys."

Fool kid fell for it, thought Goa, as he pushed his way toward the bar. *I get to keep his share, and all I got to do is tell him a few "secrets" and most likely he'll get himself aced in a month or two . . . Anyway, who knows, maybe he will make a good bounty hunter . . . 'Tho I never saw a Rodian good for anythin' except killin' unarmed Ugnaughts!*

7. Vader

Fifteen thousand kilometers out from the spaceport moon, in the shadow of the luminous Hutt planet, the starry void cracked open and a mighty triangular warship emerged from hyperspace.

Star Destroyer.

As the massive vessel moved into stationary orbit over Nal Hutta, Imperial shocktroops answered the assembly klaxon, buckling on white body armor and pulling energized blaster rifles from charging sheaths.

The troopers' boots resounded in the main launch bay as they ran to formation next to the two camouflaged Gamma Assault Shuttles that would carry them to the spaceport moon.

High above, on the quarterdeck of the Star Destroyer *Vengeance,* the Mission Commander received final instructions from an imposing figure entirely encased in black armor. The figure's deep voice resonated through an electronic breath mask.

"I want *prisoners,* Captain. Dead Rebels won't tell me where they're shipping those weapons." The menacing hiss of the grotesque breath mask underscored the threat implicit in the voice and the words.

"Yes, Lord Vader. It shall be as you request. The incident on Datar was unfortunate, sir. The Rebels fought us to the last man."

"We had lost the element of surprise, Captain. Vice Admiral Slenn paid with his life for that mistake. This time there *won't* be a mistake. This time the Rebels *won't* know we're coming. Are the assault shuttles ready?''

"Yes, Lord Vader. I've had them camouflaged as light freighters, sir. Our agents have obtained the necessary priority docking codes from Port Control. We're free to enter the Corellian Sector of Nar Shaddaa at any hour of our choosing."

"Good. Leave at once, find the enemy enclave, and capture as many Rebels as you can. I will follow the moment the situation is secure."

"Very good, sir. The mission will launch immediately."

When Rebel SpecForce sentinel Spane Covis saw the two weatherbeaten stock freighters drop past him down the flight shaft and enter Level 88, he didn't think anything about it.

From his post in a rented viewroom in Port Tower One, Covis was supposed to alert his cadre commander if any unusual ship traffic entered the vicinity. It was a boring job. Nothing out of the ordinary happened. Covis's attention was operating at about thirty percent.

Then it hit him: The sheathing's all wrong. The cargo doors are too small. The cooling towers are in the wrong place. *I've never seen freighters configured like those.*

Covis grabbed his comlink and yelled. "Stardog One, this is Dewback!"

"Go ahead, Dewback, what's the problem?"

"Watch your tail, Stardog. Two rancors in the house!"

"Got it, Dewback."

Twenty Rebel commandos had already taken up positions inside the warehouse, their surveillance sensors scanning the street, when the camouflaged Gammas rumbled into view.

In the rear of the cavernous building, other

SpecForce infantry loaded the hold of a massive Z-10 transport, clearing the warehouse of as much ordnance as they could before the firefight began.

In the very center of the warehouse, behind a heavy blast shield, a C4-CZN ion field gun was rolled into position.

The element of surprise the Imperials hoped for was gone.

The firefight on Level 88 was very fierce and it happened *very* fast.

Greedo's mother Neela heard a shuddering roar and ran to the window of the reconstructed ventilation flue where she and her sons lived, in the warren of structures crammed into one end of the warehouse district.

At that moment one of the Gamma Assault Shuttles transformed into flaming vapor, becoming a sphere of light and energy that expanded in a flash, igniting both sides of the street. The green fireball seared Neela's large eyes, and she turned and bolted screaming into the back of the apartment.

The other Gamma unleashed twin turbos, and the front of the Rebel warehouse shattered and split. The shuttle crew ramps came down. Imperial shocktroops emerged blasting.

Another round from the C4 ion gun, and the second Gamma was history. A rain of blaster shots were exchanged, sixty shocktroops went down, and the fight was over. The rest surrendered.

Greedo was hanging around with Goa and Dyyz and a bunch of other bounty hunters on Level 92. The hunters had news that a wanted list had been released by a top Hutt ganglord. The Hutt was assigning collection jobs on a first-come basis, complete with signed contracts.

Suddenly emergency sirens began to blare and

Greedo saw Corellian firefighting scows plunging down the flight shaft, red strobes flashing.

"Looks like the Imps got our *message*," said Warhog, giving Greedo a knowing wink.

Greedo tried to sound nonchalant. "Yeah—maybe so. Could be just another fire started by the Gloom Dwellers." Then smoke began to pour up the shaft and Greedo started to worry.

It hadn't occurred to Greedo until after he'd told Goa and Dyyz about the Rebel gunrunners that there might be danger for his people. The Rodian refugees lived and worked on Level 88—they'd be in the path of any attack by Imperial stormtroopers.

"Uh . . . guess I'll . . . uh, see ya later, Warhog. You too, Dyyz. Got some business to take care of."

Goa raised an eyebrow. "Sure, kid. Me and Dyyz are most likely jumpin' to Tatooine tonight—so if I don't see ya, good luck!"

Tatooine! The Hutt contracts! Greedo walked away feeling angry and betrayed that Goa hadn't invited him to go with them. So far Goa had given him very little training. *And he took my share of the reward.*

Greedo started to turn back, to beg Warhog and Dyyz to take him to Tatooine. Then his mother's screaming face suddenly flooded his mind. Instead of turning back, Greedo began to run for the nearest repulsor lift.

Greedo stepped into the lift and hit the stud marked "88." The lift dropped like a stone, stopping smoothly a few seconds later at Level 88. An alarm sounded and the lift door refused to open. Automatic sensors had locked out the lift at this level.

Looking through the transparent door, Greedo saw why—the street was a mass of smoke and flame. The Corellian firefighting scows were working the blaze with chemical sprays, and making rapid headway.

Greedo tried to peer through the smoke to see if his family's dwelling complex was on fire. The Rodians lived back near the refuse core. Greedo couldn't see that far, but he guessed everything was okay. Only the

Rebel warehouse and the buildings across the street were burning.

Greedo relaxed and began to enjoy the scene before him. He recognized Rebels helping the firefighters, and he began to wonder exactly what had happened here. The only stormtroopers visible were lying on their backs, helmets shattered.

Just then Greedo heard the sound of rending metal and he saw the firefighters all turn toward the flight shaft, which was out of his line of vision. The firefighters' faces changed to fear, and a second later a massive black war machine hovered into view, spewing laser fire from ten different points on its convoluted surface.

The machine was a monstrous engine of death, shaped like a crab, with ripping claws left and right, a phalanx of blast weapons fore and aft, and a command cockpit secured behind heavy shielding in the center, about where a crab's mouth would be. It floated on repulsor energy, it moved very swiftly, and it killed *everything* in its path.

Greedo pounded on the lift door. It still wouldn't open. Part of him was glad it wouldn't open. Part of him wanted to leave. That part of him punched the button for Level 92. *My family will be okay. Only the Rebels are going to die.*

As the lift rose away from the carnage, Greedo got a last glimpse of the Death Engine as it spewed a thick stream of white-hot energy into the Rebel warehouse. Then he was moving between levels and his vision was blocked.

A moment later the whole sector shook as if it had been hit by an asteroid.

Greedo stumbled out onto the Level 92 thoroughfare and promptly fell on his face. The street heaved and shook, and a terrifying rumble filled the air. People ran or grabbed onto vehicles as they careened past, heading for the flight shaft.

As he dragged himself to his feet, Greedo saw the

bounty hunters moving together toward the reserved parking platform where they had all stashed their ships. He saw Dyyz Nataz, but he couldn't make out Warhog Goa.

A gloved hand grabbed Greedo's shoulder. He looked up into the broad-beaked face of his friend.

"If ya know what's good for ya, kid, you'll come with me and Dyyz. The Imps are in a *bad* mood about somethin'. I think the Rebs gave 'em more of a fight than they expected."

"My folks . . . I can't leave my family . . . my people."

"Don't worry about the family, kid. If you're goin' to be a bounty hunter, you're going to have to kiss off the family, sooner or later. Now's as good a time as any . . . Besides, they'll probably be okay."

Warhog Goa gave Greedo a questioning look and then walked away, following Dyyz toward their ship.

Greedo stood and watched Warhog go, trying to make up his mind, trying to decide what he really wanted.

He wanted to be a bounty hunter.

The sleek cruiser *Nova Viper* lifted with the swarm of bounty-hunter craft that headed out of port, lining up for jump clearances.

No clearances came. Port Control was preoccupied. So the ships jumped anyway.

The last thing Goa and Dyyz and Greedo saw was the collapse of an entire quarter of the Corellian Sector, floor upon floor, with a magnificent flash and rumble and roar.

"Wheez! Musta took out twenty levels!" shouted Dyyz. "A lot of good people just *died*, Goa."

"And we're alive . . . right, Greedo?"

Greedo didn't answer. He just stared at the swelling conflagration, the succession of fireballs, the billowing black clouds.

The navicomp clicked in for Tatooine.
They jumped.

8. Mos Eisley

A massive armor-plated figure stood in the entrance of
the dim and noisy cantina, surveying the motley crowd
with glowing red electronic eyes.

"Hey—ain't that Gorm the Dissolver? What's he
doin' here? I thought we *killed* him!"

"Sure . . . my buddy Greedo decimated his mo-
tivator. But there's biocomponents from six different
aliens in Gorm. The only way to *kill* him is to vaporize
the whole assembly."

Dyyz Nataz groaned. "Why didn't ya tell me that,
Goa? I would have *finished* him. Now we got to worry
about him hittin' us for the *credits* we owe him!"

"Take it easy, Dyyz. Jodo Kast just told me Jabba gave
Gorm the sweetest hit on the wanted list—fifty thousand credits to bring in *Zardra*."

"You're kiddin'. Zardra's a *bounty hunter*. What's
Jabba got against her?"

The three were sitting in the smoky shadows of the
Mos Eisley Cantina, sipping green Pica Thundercloud
and watching the bounty hunters drift in from around
the galaxy: Weequays, Aqualish, Arcona, Defels,
Kauronians, Fneebs, Quill-heads, Bomodons, Alpher-
idians—and the inevitable *Ganks*. Greedo even saw a
couple of Rodians. They nodded in his direction, but
he didn't return the greeting. He'd learned long ago
that unknown Rodians could be dangerous.

A cocky Corellian and a big Wookiee entered and
stood on the lobby steps for a minute, surveying the
crowd. Greedo recognized the smugglers he'd come
up against in Ninx's repair barn on Nar Shaddaa. He
felt hatred roil up inside him at the sight of the two.

Then the Corellian turned and left the cantina, and
the Wookiee followed him. Dyyz Nataz snorted: "Right,
Solo. You're in the *wrong* place, buddy."

"*Han Solo?* Is he here?" Warhog Goa swung around in his chair and looked around the room.

"Yeah. Solo and his Wookiee pal Chewbacca came in and looked around and *left*. Solo's on Jabba's list, ya know. If I was him, I'd make like a space frog and hop to some other galaxy!" Dyyz took a deep swallow of Thundercloud. "Now, what's this about Zardra? What did *she* ever do to be worth fifty to ol' Jabba?"

Goa turned back to his two companions and hoisted his glass. For a bone-dry planet, Tatooine sure brewed some of the best beverages in the galaxy—*expensive*, but very tasty. "Here's to Zardra," he said, and he drank, then wiped his mouth with his gloved hand.

"Zardra and Jodo Kast were on a hunt in the Stenness System, lookin' for a pair o' spicejackers named the Thig Brothers. The Thigs were armed to the gills with Imperial blasters they'd stole from a military supply depot. Jodo says to Zardra, 'Why don't we split up? I'll put the word around the ports that I'm following the Thigs . . . and you stay out of sight. The Thigs will be itchin' for a fight—I know those guys. They'll come lookin' for me, I'll stage a little face-off, and you sting 'em from the shadows. Just stun 'em, you know. We'll take 'em alive.'

"Jodo knew he could count on Zardra. She's as fearless as they come—and a crack shot with a stun-laser."

"Yeah. I've seen her in action. The best. So then what happened?"

All this time Greedo wasn't saying anything. He was savoring Dyyz's remark that Solo was on Jabba's list. Half-formed images of revenge flickered through his mind. He was content to sit and listen to his friends and watch the crowd of bounty hunters. *I'm one of them,* he thought. *I'm a bounty hunter. Spurch is going to take me to meet Jabba . . . Jabba needs good hunters right now . . . lots of 'em. Jabba needs me.*

Just then Gorm the Dissolver stood up at his table and scanned the room with his electronic red eyes. Greedo ducked and shielded his face with his hand. Squinting between two suckered fingers, he watched the big bounty hunter turn and swagger toward the lobby.

"There goes Gorm," said Greedo, alerting his friends.

"Oh . . . yeah? Good riddance, I say. He'll be on his way to find Zardra. I hope she melts him ta slag!"

"Maybe we ought to warn her, Warhog."

"Don't worry, she knows. She's got a lot of friends in our line of work. I'll wager a good krayt steak Jodo's already told her."

"You're probably right . . . So what's the rest of the story? *Why is Jabba the Hutt payin' Gorm fifty thousand to kill Zardra?*"

"Easy. She killed a *Hutt*, that's why! When the Thig Brothers came lookin' for Jodo, they found him waitin' in the Red Shadow—that's a bistro on Taboon, a slag heap of a planet where nobody but 'Nessies would ever live. Trouble was, a Hutt named Mageye was passin' through, on his way ta cut a deal with ol' BolBol, another Hutt who practically *owns* the Stenness System."

"Oh, I get it. Mageye gets caught in the crossfire?" Dyyz made a yawning noise under his blastmask.

"Worse. Mageye is carried into the bistro on a palanquin, ya see, by these five strong Weequays. The excitement starts, the Thigs are shootin' at everything that moves, two Weequays get hit, they drop the palanquin, and the worm rolls off . . . right on top of Zardra!"

"Hah! Poor Zardra!"

"Poor Mageye. Zardra's wearin' full armor, but she's still gettin' crushed and the slime and stench is about to suffocate her . . . So she pulls a gauge-six thermal detonator out of her pocket and pops it into the Hutt's mouth!"

Goa paused for effect, letting his listeners form an image of what happened next. Greedo made a soft hooting noise. Dyyz emitted a choking sound. Goa picked up his Thundercloud and swallowed.

"It took 'em a month to clean up the mess, boys." Goa swigged more Thundercloud, and his foam-covered beak made a satisfied clacking noise.

"Uh . . . great. Good story, Warhog," said Dyyz, laughing. "So when's our turn to meet with Jabba?"

Goa looked at his chronometer. "Actually, we're late," he said. "Let's get moving."

9. *Jabba*

Jabba the Hutt, gangster preeminent, was receiving petitioners at his Mos Eisley town house, a short walk from the cantina.

A violent windstorm brewed in the surrounding desert, whipping clouds of grit over Mos Eisley. The narrow streets of the spaceport were dust-choked and dim. The three bounty hunters pulled protective cloaks across their faces as they hurried to their audience with the notorious Hutt.

"Don't know how they can keep droids functioning on a place like this," said Dyyz. "My visor's already got three centimeters of sand under it."

"Moisture farmers use up a lot of droids," said Goa. "Sand seizes joints and clogs cooling fins, and the 'tronics burn out. Half the population thrives off the *junk* that's the main product of this hot and dusty planet."

Two stout Gamorrean tuskers blocked the heavy iron grid that protected the courtyard of Jabba's town house. The piglike brutes made threatening grunts and brandished battle-axes as the bounty hunters appeared out of the darkening streets. But Warhog Goa didn't hesitate, roaring out the password he'd been given earlier. The Gamorreans immediately stepped back.

The spear-tipped gate rose with the grinding of hidden gears, and Goa sauntered under the menacing points with a cocksure gait. Dyyz and Greedo held back, waiting to see what happened to their friend. Goa turned and cackled. "What's the matter, Dyyz? You afraid of ol' Jabba? He's the hunter's *friend*! C'mon, Greedo, I'll show you how to get *rich*!"

Suddenly four vicious-looking Nikto emerged from

the shadows of the courtyard and leveled blaster-prods at Goa. "Nudd chaa! Kichawa joto!" one of them shouted.

"What do you know—we're just in time! Jabba's ready to see us!" Goa ignored the prods and strode fearlessly toward the glowing aperture of Jabba's domicile. The Nikto lowered their weapons and snarled something unintelligible.

Dyyz and Greedo followed, cautiously.

The raucous babble of the galactic riffraff that crowded Jabba's audience chamber was deafening. Alien and human, a hundred different species, faces contorted with greed and depravity, wearing a motley assortment of spacers' costumes and military gear.

All eyes turned to the three newcomers. Greedo surveyed the grotesque gathering and wondered—it seemed as if he recognized only a few species from his years on Nar Shaddaa. "Are these all *bounty hunters*?" he shouted to Goa.

"Nah. Maybe about half of 'em. The rest are just the slimy bottom feeders that enjoy being around Jabba's stench and corruption."

Goa wasn't just kidding. Greedo noticed a rancid odor permeated the room, and in a few seconds he guessed its source: the great worm himself, Jabba the Hutt, ensconced on a platform to his right, puffing on a convoluted water pipe.

Greedo had seen many Hutts in the streets of Nar Shaddaa. But he had never been in a closed space with one. His stomach churned and twisted at the sight and smell of the miasmic mass of the great gangster, fawned over by unctuous Twi'leks and Squidheads and . . . *Rodians*. Yes, the two Rodians they'd seen in the cantina were before the great Jabba, bowing slavishly, like suppliants in the palace of a Paladian Prince. A silver protocol droid was translating their groveling remarks for malodorous Jabba.

"Maybe they're bending over to throw up," said Dyyz, reading Greedo's thoughts.

"How would a Rodian know the difference?" said Goa. "The green goons stink almost as bad as Jabba."

Greedo gave Goa a startled look. *Why did he say that? Am I just a "green goon" to him?* He decided Goa was trying to make a crude joke.

As the two Rodians faded back into the crowd, majordomo Bib Fortuna cast a suspicious eye toward the new visitors. With an almost imperceptible nod, he signaled for Goa, Dyyz, and Greedo to step forward.

The rabble quieted as the three hunters moved to position in front of the great worm. Everyone wanted to see if a death sentence was about to be executed. When it became apparent that these were just another team of rapacious bounty hunters, the hubbub resumed.

"Vifaa karibu uta chuba Jabba!" began Goa, speaking perfect Huttese. He knew that Jabba himself spoke many languages fluently, and used his protocol droid for the several million other forms of communication. But he wished to honor the crimelord in every way possible.

"Moja jpo chakula cha asubuhi!" rumbled the Hutt, apparently pleased to be treated with respect by scum.

"What did he say?" said Dyyz. "What did *you* say?"

"I told 'im he's the most disgustin' pile o' swamp sludge in the galaxy. He thanked me for groveling before his bloated slimy putrid body."

"R-really," whispered Greedo. "You said that?"

"Goa's pullin' yer snout, kid. We'd be rancor bait if he'd said any of that stuff."

Goa turned his full attention to the Hutt, hoping Jabba hadn't heard the whispered exchange.

If he had heard it, Jabba gave no sign. He proceeded to laugh quite jovially and popped a squirming sand maggot into his mouth. Greedo almost retched at the sight of the swollen tongue, dripping with slaver. At this distance, of not more than a meter and a half, the malignant smell of Jabba's breath was overpowering.

The Hutt's lardaceous body seemed to periodically release a greasy discharge, sending fresh waves of rotten stench to Greedo's sensitive nostrils.

"Ne subul *Greedo,* pombo gek fultrh badda wanga!" Goa put one hand on Greedo's shoulder as he introduced his protégé to the illustrious gangster. Greedo bowed nervously, as the huge eyes turned on him and reduced him to space dust.

Jabba and Goa exchanged a few more phrases, and then Jabba proceeded to deliver a long soliloquy that ended with the words ". . . kwa bo noodta du dedbeeta *Han Solo?*"

Goa turned to Greedo and Dyyz. "The worm has seen fit to offer us the opportunity of hunting one of his most *notorious* debtors—that pirate Han Solo. Solo claims he lost a load of spice when he got boarded by Imps. But Jabba thinks Solo sold the spice and kept the money. This is a collection job—*Jabba wants that money.*"

"I ain't messin' with Solo," said Dyyz. "He's got too many ways of gettin' revenge . . . even after he's dead."

"I can handle him," said Greedo. "He's just a small-time Corellian spicerunner who thinks he's big stuff. He stole a rancor-skin jacket off me. *I'll take Solo.*"

Warhog Goa looked at Greedo for a moment and then slapped him on the back. "Okay, kid. That's what I like to hear! This'll be a good assignment to cut your baby teeth on, 'cause Solo's on Tatooine! We saw him today in the cantina, remember? I'll even be able to give ya some backup. If he's got the money on him, you'll get it easy."

Dyyz snorted. "Great—you help the kid. I don't want nothin' to do with it . . . Now what about us? You gonna set up a couple of deals for us, or you gonna waste the whole trip on the kid?"

"Right. I got that covered." Goa exchanged a few more words with Jabba, and then Fortuna handed the bounty hunters three scrolls, the official contracts assigning them exclusive "hunting rights" for the period of two Tatooine months. The Solo scroll was for a much shorter period, due to the fact that Jabba was anxious to clean up a debt that had remained uncollected far too long.

On a signal from Fortuna, the three bounty hunters bowed ceremoniously and moved back to make room for the next team of job applicants—an unsavory human named Dace Bonearm and his IG-model assassin droid.

Greedo found himself separated from Goa and Dyyz, as they were swallowed up in the crowded audience chamber. Greedo made his way to an open spot in a corner, next to the bar. Without being asked, the Aqualish bartender slid a brimming glass his way. Greedo felt proud of himself as he leaned back against the wall and sipped the syrupy Tatooine Sunburn.

Across the room he could see Dyyz, standing next to a hunter named Dengar that Greedo remembered from Nar Shaddaa. They were both examining their scrolls and comparing notes.

Warhog Goa was deep in conversation with one of the Rodians. Greedo felt a twinge of jealousy, seeing his mentor talking to another Rodian bounty hunter.

I'm a bounty hunter, he thought. *I'm going to stalk my prey and I'm going to collect the reward and I'm going to start building a rep. I'm going to be the* toughest *Rodian bounty hunter that ever was.*

I wonder what that Rodian and Goa are talking about? He saw Goa look toward him and then the Rodian's eyes met his, and Greedo realized they were talking about him. At first he felt uneasy being noticed by the strange Rodian. Then Goa waved and the Rodian held up his hand, suckers out, in a gesture of brotherhood.

Greedo beamed with pride. *Okay, they're talkin' about me—Greedo the Bounty Hunter.*

10. *Solo*

"RRUUARRRNN!" The Wookiee slammed a shaggy fist down on the *Millennium Falcon*'s shield generator and pushed back his welding mask.

"Take it *easy*, Chewie. I wanna get off this dirtball as much as you do. But without deflectors we're easy game for spicejackers and nosy Imps."

"Hwuarrn? Nnrruahhnm?"

"Right. Jabba's throwing the biggest bounty-hunting bash in the sector—and you just *know* our names are gettin' bandied around over dessert. That's another reason to blow this joint. But like I say, if the ship had been undercover during the sandstorm, we wouldn't be in this mess."

Han Solo finished vacuuming sand out of the alluvial dampers and wiped his brow on his sleeve. *Why does a free and unfettered guy like me always end up on wasted planets like this, when he could be basking in the oceanside breezes of any gambling resort in the universe?*

Because I'm not very good at sabacc, he thought. *Lucky sometimes, yeah. But not that lucky. Unlike some people I know, I gotta work for a living.*

Chewbacca made a soft warning growl and Solo raised his head and looked around. Two bulbous faceted eyes were staring at him out of spiny green balls of flesh. The leather-garbed humanoid body beneath the head held a blaster in multisuckered fingers.

"Han Solo?" The voice from the long green snout spoke through an electronic translator.

"Who wants to know?" Han *knew* who wanted to know. A Rodian with a blaster is *always* a bounty hunter . . . or a bill collector.

"Greedo. I work for Jabba the Hutt."

"Greedo . . . oh yeah, I remember you—the kid who tried to steal my power couplings. Okay, good for you, so now you're workin' for Jabba. By the way, I understand Rodian, so you can turn off the squawk box."

Han jumped down from the scaffolding as casually as

he could and picked up a rag to wipe his hands. Hidden in the rag was a small Telltrig-7 blaster, carefully placed there for just this eventuality. Fortunately he didn't have to use it—his mouth was his best weapon:

"Listen . . . tell Jabba the *truth*—I came to Tatooine for only one reason: to *pay* him."

Greedo turned off the translator. Goa had suggested he use it to make sure the "client" fully understood the gravity of the situation. *But if Solo really understands Rodian, I'll be able to use untranslatable Rodian threats.*

"Neshki J'ba klulta ntuz tch krast, Solo." *Jabba doesn't believe dorsal-spine parasites tell the truth, Solo.*

"Yeah, well, what does that overfed vermiform know? Do you really think I'd come anywhere *near* this place if I didn't have the money?"

Greedo's hand tightened on his gun. He wasn't sure if insulting one's employer required special action on the part of a bounty hunter. What Solo said about being on Tatooine was logical, though. If somebody was after your hide, would you fly into his back pocket? *This is going to be easy.*

"Skak, trn kras ka noota, Solo." *All right, then give me the money, Solo.* "Vnu sna Greedo vorskl ta." *Then Greedo will be on his way.*

"Yeah, tell ya what, Greedo . . . tell ya what. It's not quite that simple. The loot is bolted into the frame of the *Falcon* here. Secret hiding place. Understand? Why don't you come back tomorrow morning and I'll hand it right over, easy as pie. How's that sound?"

"Nvtuta bork te ptu motta. Tni snato." *No, get it right now. I'll wait.*

I'm not letting this gulley fish slip out of my grasp, Greedo thought . . . *especially with Warhog watchin' me from the shadows.*

"I *can't* get it right now. Listen, if you can wait till tomorrow, I'll throw in a little bonus—a couple thousand credits just for you. How's that sound?"

That sounded good.

"Prog mnete enyaz ftt sove shuss." *Make it four thousand credits.*

"*Four* thousand? Are you crazy—? Oh, all right, ya got me over a barrel, pal. We'll do it your way. Four thousand for you, first thing in the morning. It's a deal."

Without another word, Solo turned his back on the bounty hunter and began cleaning a spanner. He palmed the little blaster, just in case the green kid changed his mind. But a minute later Chewie gave his "all clear" grunt and Solo relaxed.

"Great, Chewie. Can you believe the nerve of that guy? Now we got to finish prepping the ship *tonight*. When that punk comes around tomorrow morning, all he's going to find is a big grease spot on the hangar floor!"

Warhog Goa sipped a Starshine Surprise and glanced around the Mos Eisley Cantina. The bounty-hunter crowd was thinning out. A lot of hunters had gotten their contracts and jumped. Some of 'em were probably already stalking targets in the streets of cities a thousand parsecs away. "Solo doesn't plan to pay you," he said, looking at his protégé. "Don't you get it? It's a stall."

Warhog noticed the two Rodians sitting in the booth near the entrance lobby. They nodded to him and he nodded back. "You ought to meet those two Rodies, Greedo. They're good hunters. I'll bet they can teach ya stuff even I don't know. Want me to introduce you?"

Greedo looked down at his drink. *Goa wouldn't know about the clan wars. I never told him. He wouldn't know about the time the ships came, hunting the Tetsus refugees. Tetsus just don't talk to strange Rodians. He wouldn't know that, because I never told him.*

Yeah, but what's the point? I'm a bounty hunter now, that's the important thing. Bounty hunters hang together, drink together, trade war stories, help each other out of jams. So after I take my first bounty, after Solo pays me and I hand the money over to Jabba, after the word starts to get around . . . then I'll make friends with those guys. They'll respect me and we'll have a drink together and they'll tell me some great stories and I'll tell them about how I saved Dyyz and Goa by blasting Gorm right through his electronic guts.

". . . so, like I say, Greedo, there's two sides to every deal with Jabba. That's my lesson for today. If you collect the debt, you'll be in Jabba's good graces. But if you let Jabba down, you're as good as *dead*."

Greedo tried to sound scornful. "Don't worry, Warhog. Solo will pay. First we find out for sure if he's got the money with him. Then, if he doesn't hand it over, I'll kill him and *take* it. . . . You still going to work backup—in case the Wookiee tries anything?"

"Sure. That's the plan, ain't it?"

"Wknuto, Goa." Thanks, Goa.

Han Solo's ship, the *Millennium Falcon*, was still sitting in the docking hangar when Greedo walked in shortly after sunrise the next morning.

Han Solo was nowhere to be seen. Greedo tried to open the *Falcon*'s hatch, but it was code-locked.

Greedo and Goa finally found Solo and the Wookiee having breakfast at a little outdoor cafe behind the dewback stables.

Greedo kept his hand on his holstered gun, but didn't bother to turn off the safety because Goa had a rifle trained on the quarry from the alley across the street.

"Rylun pa getpa gushu, Solo?" Enjoy your breakfast, Solo?

Greedo tried to sound tough and relaxed, but in fact he was wound up tight. If Solo stiffed him today, he wouldn't know what to do. Jabba wouldn't be happy if he killed Solo without collecting the debt. The contract was for the money, not a corpse.

"Greedo! I've been looking all over for you! Decide to sleep in today?" Han chortled to himself and took another bite of dewback steak. Chewbacca raised an eyebrow and cocked his head. He had his bowcaster leaning against his leg, loaded and ready.

"Fna ho koru gep, Solo. Kras ka noota." *Don't be funny, Solo. Give me the money.*

"Sure. The money. Happy to oblige. You want something to eat first? You look like you could use a good meal."

Greedo realized Solo was putting him on, and sudden anger flared in his veins. Impulsively he reached down and grabbed Solo's shirt. "Ka noota! Grot pleno ka Jabba spulta?" *The money! Or would you like to explain to Jabba personally?*

"NNRRARRG!" Instantly Chewie was on his feet, one huge shaggy arm around Greedo's neck, the other gripping the bounty hunter's blaster hand.

"Nfuto—!"

"Thanks, Chewie." Han stood up and casually wiped his mouth with a napkin. He reached over and took Greedo's weapon, snapped open the chamber, and removed the power cell. He handed the useless blaster back to Greedo.

"You know, kid, I was almost starting to *like* you. Now I'm not so sure. Let me give you some sage advice. Stay away from slugs like Jabba. Find an honest way to make a living . . . Let him go, Chewie."

"Hnnruaahn!" Chewie released his grip, and Greedo tumbled forward. Han stepped out of the way and Greedo fell against a table, sending dishware crashing.

"Nice. Where does Jabba find these punks? What about the guy in the alley across the street, Chewie?"

"Hwarrun!"

"Disappeared, huh? Another half-baked bounty creep, probably. You'd think Jabba could buy the *best* to track a guy like *me*!"

"Hurrwan nwrunnh."

"Yeah, I agree. We're playin' with fire hanging around here. The *Falcon's* prepped—we could have jumped this morning if Taggart had kept his promise. If he doesn't show by tomorrow with that load of glitterstim he wants transferred, we're history, okay with you?"

"*WNHUARRN!*"

"I thought so."

Jabba the Hutt was not amused.

"Kubwa funga na jibo! You said this inexperienced slime-wart could collect from Solo! I ought to toss you both into my private dungeon and let you rot!"

Or words to that effect. The great worm huffed and rumbled and oozed foulness. On either side of his throne platform, Weequays and Nikto brandished their weapons ominously. As usual, Jabba's audience chamber was crowded with the dregs of a hundred galactic civilizations.

Warhog Goa was abject. He groveled shamelessly before the bloated drooling crimelord. As he did so, he regretted bringing Greedo back here without the prize. But he had to seek another audience, to persuade Jabba to let Greedo *kill* Solo without collecting the debt. That was the key. Now the words tumbled out in one breath—he had to say it all before Jabba pronounced *their* deaths!

"Oh, most incomparable Jabba, as you are well aware, Han Solo, that worthless piece of dianoga dung, is a very difficult customer. May I suggest that you allow my protégé to simply *kill* Solo, and take his *ship* as payment for the debt he owes you?"

Jabba grunted and puffed his water pipe thoughtfully. Then he seemed to brighten, if that were possible. "Ne voota kinja. Jabba likes your suggestion. He will spare the superfluous life of your protégé."

He looked straight at Greedo before he spoke again. At a signal from Jabba, the silver protocol droid, K-8LR, stepped up and translated Jabba's every evil word into the Rodian tongue: *You may bring me Solo so that I may kill him—or you may kill him yourself and deliver his ship's papers to me. Jabba has seen in his wisdom that this must be so.*

Greedo breathed a sigh of relief and bowed slavishly. "Thank you, great Jabba. Your wisdom is—"

"Na kungo! But you had better work fast! I now declare an open bounty on Han Solo. And I raise the price for his head to one hundred thousand credits!"

"One hundred thousand!" said Goa. "Every bounty hunter in the—"

"Yes. So true. If your protégé can't get Solo, somebody *else* most certainly will!"

Then Jabba leaned forward and once again fastened his malevolent eyes on Greedo. "And if *you* do not fulfill *our* bargain, *you* had better start running, little green insect. *Bring me Solo—alive or dead!*"

11. *The Cantina*

There was live music today. The patrons were in an ugly mood.

Greedo and Goa sat in the booth next to the lobby entrance. When Solo and the Wookiee came in, Solo pretended not to see them, but Chewbacca articulated a low growl as he passed Greedo.

"They know we're here, Warhog."

"Yeah. That's the idea. Are you ready to execute the plan?"

"Nchtha zno ta. Fnrt pwusko vtulla pa." I'm not sure. I'm getting a bad feeling.

"Well, if you're not ready, I suggest we head for hyperspace, before Jabba finds out. I've got work to do."

"Where's Dyyz?"

"He left this morning. Hitched a ride with 4-Lom and Zuckuss. Dyyz has a rich contract—a warlord who decided to evict the Hutts from the Komnor system."

"Sounds like a difficult job."

"Very difficult. But Dyyz Nataz is the man to do it. And *you're* the right hunter for the Han Solo hit, Greedo my boy. Are you *ready*?"

Just then there was a disturbance at the bar. Shouting, a scuffle, then the sudden flash and drone of a lightsaber. A dismembered arm flew through the air, landing near Greedo's chair. The music stopped.

Greedo and Goa had noticed the old man and the boy come in, and they had heard the bartender eject the droids. Goa had noted the quiet intensity of the old man, and the thought had crossed his mind: *He's old, but I wouldn't want to test myself against him in a blaster fight.*

The room was deathly silent. Greedo sucked in his breath and hooted softly. "Nice piece of work for an old man," he said.

"Must be a Jedi," said Goa. "I thought their kind were long gone."

Greedo had never seen a Jedi.

The room came to life again, the band resumed tootling, the bartender's helper removed the mutilated arm. Somebody ordered a round of drinks for the house.

"Check it, Greedo. The old man and the kid are talking to Solo and the Wook. You're going to have to wait your turn."

Greedo didn't respond. His veins were pumping excitement at the sudden carnage.

The two Rodian bounty hunters strolled in, and Goa motioned them over to the table. Greedo looked at his beer, concentrating on what he was going to say to Solo.

"Boys . . . I'd like you to meet Greedo . . . my apprentice. Greedo, this is Thuku and Neesh, two fine bounty killers."

Greedo looked up and saw two pair of huge eyes studying him with detached curiosity. Did he detect hostility glinting in those multifaceted orbs? The one called Thuku held out a suckered hand. "Wa tetu dat oota, Greedo."

"Ta ceko ura nsha," said Greedo, allowing his suckers to briefly engage Thuku's. The three Rodians entered into a short conversation, while Goa looked on, amused. Neesh told Greedo he'd heard that Jabba had awarded him Han Solo as a quarry. Neesh seemed impressed. Thuku warned Greedo that Solo "has already killed two of Jabba's bill collectors . . . Be careful, brother. *You* could be the next."

"Thanks for the advice," said Greedo, with bravado. "I'm not worried. I've got Warhog for backup, in case Solo or the Wookiee try anything stupid."

The two fellow Rodians exchanged glances with Goa, and Greedo thought he detected they were silently laughing at him. *Yeah, of course they think I'm a young fool. Well, that's the way it is when you're just starting out. I'll show 'em!*

Imperial stormtroopers entered the bar, and a minute later, when Greedo looked across the room, Solo and the Wookiee were sitting alone. The old man and the boy had disappeared.

After the Imps passed their table, Goa unhitched his blaster and placed it in front of him. "Okay, lad. This is your chance. If the Wook tries to interfere, I'll blast him to red smoke."

The moment had come. Greedo felt a mixture of fear and excitement. He closed his eyes and gathered his energies. Suddenly his mind filled with a bright image of a jungle world, dripping green neon leaves, a gathering of little huts and busy half-naked green bodies. He saw himself, and his brother Pqweeduk, running under the tall Tendril trees, running toward the village. He saw his mother standing in the clearing waiting for them. He saw himself and his brother run to her and she held out her arms and hugged them both. Then he was inside the vision, looking up into her huge eyes. She was crying. "What's the matter, Mother? Why are you sad?" "I am sad and I am happy, Greedo. I am sad because of what must happen. I am happy because you are coming home."

Greedo snapped out of his trance and a feeling like an electric shock went through him. *What was* that? he thought.

Goa was staring at him with an annoyed look. "C'mon, kid. Are you gonna make your move? Solo and the Wook are startin' to leave!"

The Wookiee, Chewbacca, passed their table and disappeared into the lobby. The perfect moment had arrived. Greedo stood up, hand on his blaster.

"Oona goota, Solo?" *Going somewhere, Solo?*

"Yes, Greedo, in fact I was just going to see your boss. Tell Jabba I've got the money."

"Sompeetalay. Vere tan te nacht vakee cheeta. Jabba warin cheeco wa rush anye katanye wanaroska." Greedo snickered. "Chas kin yanee ke chusko!" It's too late, you should have paid him when you had the chance. Jabba's put a price on your head so large every bounty hunter in the galaxy will be looking for you.

"Yeah, but this time I've got the money."

"Enjaya kul a intekun kuthuow." And I found you first.

"I don't have it with me. Tell Jabba—"

"Tena hikikne. Hoko ruya pulyana oolwan spa steeka gush shuku ponoma three pe." If you give it to me I might forget I found you. Jabba's through with you. He has no use for smugglers who drop their cargo at the first sign of an Imperial cruiser.

"Even I get boarded sometimes. You think I had a choice?"

"Tlok Jabba. Boopa gopakne et an anpaw." You can tell that to Jabba. He may only take your ship.

"Over my dead body."

Goa saw the blaster coming out of Solo's holster under the table. He relaxed and leaned back, sipping his Sunburn. Poor Greedo, he thought.

"Ukle nyuma cheskopokuta klees ka tlanko ya oska." That's the idea. I've been looking forward to this for a long time.

"Yes, I'll bet you have."

With a tremendous explosion of light and noise Solo's blaster propelled a bolt of energy through the wooden table. When the smoke cleared there was very little left of Greedo.

"Sorry about the mess," said Solo, flipping the bartender a coin.

Spurch Warhog Goa met with the two Rodians on Docking Bay 86, as he made ready to board his ship, the *Nova Viper*.

The tall one, Thuku, handed Goa a chest of newly minted Rodian coinage, pure gold, each coin embossed with the image of Navik the Red.

"The Rodians thank you, Goa. We would have killed him ourselves, but we can't let it be known we are hunting our own kind."

"His clan are all sentenced to die," said Neesh, making a snorting noise with his green snout.

Goa picked up one of the coins and watched it glint in the bright-hot Tatooine sun. "Yeah . . . but tell ya the truth, boys, this is one bounty I ain't too proud of. Least I didn't have to kill him myself. I knew Solo would take care of that."

Hammertong:
The Tale of the
"Tonnika Sisters"

by Timothy Zahn

"It's a dilemma, really, that's what it is," Dr. Keller-ing said in that precise Imperial Prime University voice of his that went so well with his young, upper-class-pampered face. And so poorly with the decidedly low-class tapcafe he and the two women were sitting in. "On the one hand there's the whole question of security," Kellering continued. "Especially with all the Rebel activity in this sector. And I can assure you that Dr.

Eloy and I aren't the only persons within the project who are concerned about it."

His forehead wrinkled in upper-class-pampered perplexity. "But on the other hand, Captain Drome is extremely hot-tempered in regard to what he considers his personal territory. If he knew I was even talking about this matter outside the compound, he'd be terribly angry. Especially with people like—well, like you."

Seated across the table from Kellering, Shada D'ukal took a sip from her cup, the wine carrying with it a hint of remembered bitterness and shame. Like most girls growing up on their war-devastated world, the Mistryl shadow guards had been the focus of all her hopes. They had been the last heroes of her people, the enigmatic cult of warrior women still fighting to force justice for her world from uncaring, even hostile, officials of the Empire. She had begun her training as soon as they would take her, studying and working and sweating her way against the odds until, at last, she had been deemed worthy to be called a Mistryl. Assigned to a team, she had headed out on her first mission.

Only to learn that the Mistryl were no longer the valiant warriors of legend.

They were mercenaries. Nothing more than mercenaries. Hiring out to useless, insipid people like Kellering.

She sipped at her wine again, listening with half an ear as Kellering prattled on, letting the memories fade. Now, a year and seven missions later, the shame had faded to a dull ache in the back of her mind. Someday, she hoped, it would be gone altogether.

Beside Shada, Team Prime Manda D'ulin lifted a hand, finally putting an end to Kellering's ramblings. "We understand your problem, Dr. Kellering," she said. "May I suggest that you've already made your decision. Otherwise the three of us wouldn't be sitting here."

"Yes, of course." Kellering sighed. "I suppose I'm still—but that's foolish. The Mistryl may be somewhat —but still, you certainly come highly recommended.

When my cousin was telling me about you, he said you had—"

"The mission, Doctor," Manda interrupted again. "Tell us about the mission."

"Yes. Of course." Kellering took a deep breath, his eyes darting around the crowded tapcafe as if wondering which of the humans or aliens at the other tables out there might be Imperial spies. Or maybe he was just wondering what he was doing outside his pampered little academic world. Consorting with mercenaries. "I'm connected to a research project called Hammertong," he said, his voice so low now that Shada could barely hear it over the background noise. "My superior, Dr. Eloy, is senior scientist of the group. A couple of weeks ago the Emperor's representative to the project informed us that we were all going to be moved to some new location. We're to leave in three days."

"And you don't think Captain Drome is handling security properly?" Manda asked.

Kellering shrugged uncomfortably. "Dr. Eloy doesn't. The two of them have had several arguments about it."

"So what exactly do you want from us?"

"I suppose—well, I really don't know," Kellering confessed, throwing hooded looks back and forth between the two women. "I suppose I thought we could talk to Captain Drome about you bringing in some people to help guard us en route . . ." He trailed off, apparently finally noticing the expression on Manda's face.

"Let me explain something about the Mistryl, Dr. Kellering," she said, her voice still polite but with an edge of chromed mullinine to it. "Your cousin probably told you we were just your standard group of fringe mercenaries. We're not. He probably told you we sell our services to the highest bidder, no questions or ethics involved. We don't. The Mistryl are the warriors of a forgotten cause; and if we hire ourselves out as temporary security to people like you, it's because our world and our people require money to survive. We will not work with Imperial forces. Ever."

Strong words. But that was all they were. There was a great deal of simmering hatred toward the Empire among the Mistryl, anger for their suspected complicity during the war and for their complete indifference since then. But with the remnant of their people living on the edge of survival, the simple cold truth was that the Mistryl couldn't afford to turn down anything but the most odious of offers from the most odious of people. Manda could sound as high-minded as she wanted to, but in the end she and the team would accept Kellering's job.

And as she had seven times before, Shada would do her best to help them fulfill the contract. Because the other simple cold truth was that she had nowhere else to go.

But of course, Kellering didn't know that; and from the look on his face, Manda might have just dropped a large building on him. "Oh, no," he breathed. "Please. We need you. Look, we're not really with the Empire—we're funded by them, but we're actually a completely independent research group."

"I see," Manda murmured, frowning thoughtfully. Making a show of the decision-making process, probably in hopes of stifling any protest on Kellering's part when she finally named her price. With an Imperial-funded project, that price was likely to be high.

It was. "All right," Manda said at last. "We can bypass your Captain Drome entirely and run you a forward screen net that should flash out the sort of ambushes the Rebel Alliance likes to stage these days. You said three days till departure; that'll give us time to bring a few other teams in. We should be able to field a minimum of ten ships in the screen, plus a two-ship aft guard in case the Rebels try something cute." She lifted her eyebrows slightly. "The fee will be thirty thousand."

Kellering's eyes bulged. "Thirty *thousand*?" He gulped.

"You got it," Manda said. "Take it or don't."

Shada watched Kellering's face as it went through the run of shock, nervousness, and discomfiture. But as Manda had pointed out, if he hadn't already made his decision they wouldn't be here. "All right," he sighed. "All right. Dr. Eloy can cut you a credit when we meet with him this afternoon."

Manda shot Shada a quick glance. "You want us to meet with Dr. Eloy?"

"Of course." Kellering seemed surprised by the question. "He's the one most worried about security."

"Yes, but . . . where would we meet him? Here?"

"No, at the compound," Kellering said. "He almost never leaves there. Don't worry, I can get you in."

"What about Drome?" Manda asked. "You said yourself he was pretty touchy on the subject of outsiders."

"Captain Drome isn't in charge of the project," Kellering said with precise firmness. "Dr. Eloy is."

"Such details seldom bother Imperial military officers," Manda countered. "If he catches us there—"

"He won't," Kellering assured her. "He won't even know you're there. Besides, you need to see how the Hammertong's been loaded aboard the ship if you're going to know how to properly protect it."

Manda didn't look happy, but she nodded nevertheless. "All right," she said, her hand curling into a subtle signal as she did so. "I have a couple of matters to attend to here first, but after that I'll be happy to come with you. Shada can go offplanet in my place and get the rest of the team assembled."

"Understood." Shada nodded. The team didn't need any assembling, of course—all six of them were right here in this tapcafe, with their two disguised fighters, the *Skyclaw* and *Mirage,* parked in separate docking bays across town. But it was as good an excuse as any for Shada to disappear from sight. Backups, after all, weren't supposed to be seen.

"Good," Manda said briskly. "Have the others here in Gorno by nightfall. In the meantime—" She gestured Kellering toward the door. "We'll go deal with a couple of details, and then go meet your Dr. Eloy."

"They're approaching the gate," Pav D'armon's voice murmured from one of the two comlinks fastened to Shada's collar. "Two guards visible, but I see movement in the gatehouse behind the fence. Could be as many as six or seven more in there."

"Copy," Shada acknowledged, stroking a finger restlessly across the side of her sniper's blaster rifle and wishing Pav wouldn't get so chatty on the air. Mistryl comlinks were heavily encrypted, but that wouldn't stop the Imperials from pinpointing the transmissions if they took it into their heads to do so. And this close to a major base, that was a distinct possibility.

The base. Lifting her eyes from the section of road winding through the hills below—the road Manda and Kellering would be traversing in a few minutes if they made it through the gate—Shada studied the waves of rolling hills that stretched into the distance beyond the innocuous security fence cutting across her view. It certainly looked like the agricultural test ground the signs on the fence claimed it to be, not at all like the weapons-bristling popular image of an Imperial military research base. But its strategic location, within fifty kilometers of the Gorno spaceport and four major technical supply and transport centers, made its true identity obvious.

Perhaps too obvious. Perhaps that was why they were moving everyone out. She wondered how they would handle it: subtly with freighters, or blatantly with Imperial Star Destroyers. Kellering had implied this Hammertong thing had already been loaded for transport; a look at the ship they were using should give Manda a clue as to how they were going to go about it. That would affect how their screen net would be put together—

"They're through," Pav reported. "Gate's closing. They're headed your way."

"Copy," Shada said, frowning. There was something in Pav's voice . . . "Trouble?"

"I don't know," Pav said slowly. "It all looks okay. But there's something here that feels wrong, somehow."

Shada tightened her grip on her blaster rifle. Pav might be a chattercase on the com, but she hadn't survived long enough to become Manda's team second without good combat instincts. "What do you mean?"

"I'm not sure," Pav said. "They got through just a little bit too quick—"

And abruptly, Pav's voice dissolved into an earsplitting shriek of jamming static.

With a curse, Shada ripped the comlink from her collar with her left hand, throwing it as far away from her as she could. So much for Kellering's naïve assurances of safety. In the split of a hair the thing had suddenly gone sour . . . and Manda and Pav were right in the middle of it.

With Shada herself about to come in a close third. Beyond the fence, from over the next line of hills, the gleaming white figures of a dozen stormtroopers on speeder bikes had suddenly appeared. Headed her way.

Shada cursed again, lining up her blaster rifle with her right hand as she groped for the switch on her backup comlink with her left. If they were lucky, they'd have a minute before the Imperials found that frequency and locked it down, too. She located the switch, flicked it on—

"—trap—repeat, a trap," Pav was saying, her voice tight. "They've got Manda—she's down. Probably. And they're coming for me."

"Pav, it's Shada," Shada cut in, squinting through the sight and squeezing off a shot. The lead stormtrooper's speeder bike exploded into a shower of sparks, pitching him to the ground and nearly doing the same to the two on either side of him. "I can be there to back you up in two minutes."

"Negative," Pav said. The tension in her voice was

gone, leaving a sad sort of resignation that sent a cold chill up Shada's neck. "They're already too close. I'll do what I can to keep them busy—you and Karoly had better get back to the ships and get out of here. Good luck, and good—"

There was a brief crinkle of sound, and then silence.

Ahead, the speeder bikes had shifted into evasive maneuvers. Shada fired four rapid shots, catching another of the stormtroopers with the third of them. "Karoly?" she called toward her comlink. "Karoly? Are you there?"

"They're gone, Shada," Karoly D'ulin said, her voice almost unrecognizable. "They're gone. The stormtroopers—"

"Snap out of it," Shada snarled, keying the Viper grenade launcher attached to her blaster rifle barrel. The recoil kicked the gun hard into her shoulder as the slender cylinder blasted out toward the approaching stormtroopers. "Can you get to your speeder?"

There was a short pause, and Shada could imagine Karoly's earnest face as she pulled herself together. "Yes," she said. "Are we retreating?"

"Not a chance," Shada said through gritted teeth, getting halfway to her feet and heading at a crouch toward the bushes where her speeder bike was hidden. "We're heading in. Get moving." The approaching stormtroopers, finally presented with a target, opened fire—

Just as the grenade hit the ground ten meters in front of them, exploding into a billowing cloud of green smoke.

"We're going *in*?" Karoly echoed in disbelief. "Shada—"

"I'm clear." Shada cut her off, slinging the rifle over her shoulder and kicking the speeder bike to life. Over the roar of the engine she could hear the thuds of her erstwhile attackers falling out of the sky as the specially formulated smoke burned into the speeder bikes' power connectors. "Call Cai and Sileen—tell them to bring the ships in for backup."

"But where are we *going?*"

Shada swung the speeder bike around. Manda and Pav were gone, and she knew that eventually the pain of that loss would catch up with her. But for right now, she had only enough room for a single emotion.

Rage.

"We're going to teach the Imperials a lesson," she told Karoly. Kicking the throttle to full power, she jumped the fence, curved around the edge of the green cloud, and headed in.

It was a little over ten kilometers from the outer fence to the main base area, and for the first eight of them Shada flew low over the rolling hills and wondered where in blazes the vaunted Imperial defenses were. Either they hadn't thrown this ambush together until Kellering's ground car pulled up at the gate, or else they'd assumed their quarry would run for it and had concentrated their forces out beyond the fence.

Or else they were concentrating on Karoly. Blinking against the wind pounding against her face, trying not to think about what she might have gotten her teammate into, Shada kept going.

She was two kilometers out when the Imperials seemed to finally wake up to the fact they had an intruder in their midst . . . and those two kilometers more than made up for the preceding eight. Three Mekuun hoverscouts rose from nowhere to meet her, bolstered by two more squads of speeder-bike stormtroopers. Off to the side, sections of two hills opened up, revealing a pair of what looked like Comar antiatmospheric guns. The air around her was suddenly thick with blaster and laser bolts, some missing, the rest deflected by shields that hadn't really been designed with this kind of all-out attack in mind. Clenching her teeth hard enough to hurt, Shada kept going, maneuvering and returning fire on pure reflex. Off to her left, she could see another whirlwind of Imperial activity near where Karoly should be coming in—

And then, suddenly, the hoverscouts and speeder

bikes seemed to scramble out of her path. The Comar guns shifted their aim away from her—

And with a screaming roar the *Skyclaw* shot past overhead, spitting a withering fire of laser blasts at the Imperials.

"Kan si manis per tam, Sha," Sileen's voice blared from the *Skyclaw*'s belly loudspeaker. "Mi nazh ko."

"Sha kae," Shada shouted back, shifting fifteen degrees to her left as per Sileen's instructions and permitting herself a flash of cold satisfaction. The Imperials might be able to jam comlinks and slice sophisticated encrypts, but she would bet starships to groundworms they wouldn't have the faintest idea what to do with Mistryl battle language. To her left, she could see Cai and the *Mirage* now, running cover for Karoly, and she made a quick estimate of their intersect point. Just over the next row of hills, she decided. Dropping a little lower to the ground, she braced herself for whatever Sileen had sent her toward.

She topped the hills; and there, nestled in a wide valley, was a complex of perhaps twenty buildings, ranging in size from flat office blocks to a single windowless structure the size of a capital ship maintenance hangar. The Hammertong base, without a doubt.

And lying in the middle of it all, dominating the scene by the sheer unexpectedness of its presence there, was the long sleek shape of a Loronar Strike Cruiser.

"Sha re rei som kava na talae," Sileen's voice boomed again from above her. Without waiting for an answer, both fighters veered off to the right.

A motion to her left caught Shada's eye, and she turned as Karoly's speeder bike slid into formation beside her. "You all right?" Shada called.

"Yes," Karoly shouted back. She still looked nervous, but at least she didn't look as if she were going to freeze up again. "What did Sileen say? I didn't catch it."

"More Imperials coming," Shada said. "She and Cai are going to intercept."

"What about us?"

Shada nodded toward the Strike Cruiser. "We're going to make the Imperials hurt a little. Bow hatchway's open—let's try to get there before they get it sealed."

They found out immediately what two of the smaller buildings on the periphery of the complex were for, as sections of wall fell away and four more Comar guns opened fire. But it was too little too late. Between the harassment from the two fighters and the small size and maneuverability of the speeder bikes themselves, Shada and Karoly made it past the hot drive nozzles at the Strike Cruiser's stern and into the relative shelter of its flank with no damage apart from burned-out shields.

"Pretty rotten security they've got here," Karoly huffed as they headed toward the bow hatchway. An instant later she nearly had to swallow those words as, from the ground beside the landing ramp, a dozen Imperials opened fire with blaster rifles. But the two speeder bikes had the edge in both firepower and targeting accuracy, and they'd covered no more than half the Strike Cruiser's four-hundred-fifty-meter length before that nest of opposition had been silenced.

"Now what?" Karoly asked as they braked to a halt at the foot of the ramp.

"We do some damage," Shada said, half standing up on her speeder bike and taking a quick look around. There was still some resistance, mostly from the Comars and the handful of speeder-bike stormtroopers that hadn't yet been blown out of the sky. She and Karoly should have enough time to make their way to the Strike Cruiser's bridge, drop a canister or two of their corrosive green smoke where it would do the most good, and get the blazes out again.

And then, over the distant hills ahead, a new group of Imperial forces appeared, burning through the air toward them like scorched mynocks. "Uh-oh," Karoly muttered. "I take it back about their security. Maybe we'd better get out while we still can."

Shada took a deep breath, her last views of Manda's and Pav's faces floating up from her memory. "Not until we've hurt them," she said, swiveling around and pointing her speeder bike at the ramp. "Stay here long enough to give me a two-minute warning, then you can take off."

Karoly hissed between her teeth. "Get moving," she gritted out as she dropped her speeder bike into the limited protection of the ramp and unslung her blaster rifle. "I'll cover you. Make it fast."

"Bet on it," Shada agreed tightly, trying to visualize the standard Strike Cruiser layout as she headed up the ramp. She would have to go forward about ten meters along the exit corridor, then starboard to the central corridor, then forward another twenty meters to get to the bridge. Standard Strike Cruiser complement was something over two thousand crewers; if there was even a fraction of that number aboard who felt like getting in her way . . . but she would just have to do what she could. She reached the top of the ramp, swerving to the side as she passed under the hatchway arch to avoid the exit corridor bulkhead—

And lurched to an abrupt halt. "Mother of—"

"What?" Karoly's voice snapped from the comlink on her collar. "Shada? What is it?"

For a moment Shada was too stunned even to speak. Stretched out in front of her, where the command rooms, crew quarters, and combat stations should have been, was a vast cavern of open space, three hundred meters long and nearly fifty in diameter, running all the way from the bow to the main drive section. A heavily reinforced deck had been built across the bottom of the huge room, connected to the outer hull by an intricate spiderwebbing of support lines and bracing struts.

And extending down the center of the chamber for at least three-quarters of its length was a three-meter-diameter cylinder studded with thousands of pipe connections and multicolored power and control cable linkages. Carefully wrap-protected, just as carefully static-fastened to the deck, all ready for travel.

The Hammertong.

"Shada?" Karoly called again.

Shada swallowed, glancing around. The chamber seemed to be deserted, its crew or workers probably those who'd been shooting at them from the foot of the ramp. To her left, at the far forward end of the chamber, the standard Strike Cruiser bridge had been replaced by a simplified freighter-style cockpit, also unmanned. And from the looks of the status displays—and the way those drive nozzles had been humming when she and Karoly had passed them—it looked as if they'd been running an active status check on the flight systems when the Mistryl attack had interrupted them.

Which meant the ship should be pretty much ready to fly . . .

"Change of plans," she told Karoly, swiveling around and gunning the speeder bike forward toward the cockpit setup. "Get in here. And seal the door behind you."

She was running the start-up procedure at the Strike Cruiser's helm by the time Karoly joined her. "Mother of space and time," Karoly breathed, backing up to the copilot's seat, her eyes goggling at the room behind them. "Is *that* the Hammertong thing Kellering was talking about?"

"I don't know what else it could be," Shada said, mentally crossing her fingers as she eased in the repulsorlifts. A ship this size wasn't really designed to come this deep into a gravity well . . . but it seemed to be lifting okay. The Imperials must have added more repulsorlifts while they were gutting the interior. "Get the comm adjusted to our frequency, will you?"

"Sure." Still keeping half an eye behind them, Karoly sat down and busied herself with the comm. "What's the plan?"

"The Imperials went to a lot of work to build that thing and modify a ship to transport it," Shada said, giving the displays a careful scan. For all their arrogance, the Imperials weren't stupid, especially when it came to hardware as impressive as the Hammertong. If their ground defenses had been low-profile, they were bound to have some heavy space-based weaponry nearby to back it up.

But if it was there, it wasn't showing up on the displays. Hiding around the horizon? Or could the Mistryl counterattack have caught the whole bunch of them by surprise?

Either way, there was no percentage in waiting around for them to get their seats under their rears. "You got Cai and Sileen yet?" she asked Karoly.

"Almost," Karoly said, her hands busy on the board. "I'm running a split-freq mix . . . there we go."

"Shada? Karoly?" Sileen's voice came over the speaker. "What in blazes are you doing?"

"We're giving the Empire a bloody nose," Shada said. The Strike Cruiser had cleared the boundary of the base now and was starting to pick up speed, leaving what was left of the speeder-bike force behind them.

"Shada—look, we're all upset about Manda and Pav," Sileen said carefully. "But this is just crazy. You're going to bring the whole Imperial fleet down on top of us."

"They need to know they can't just go around killing Mistryl," Shada retorted. "Not without paying dearly for it. Karoly and I can handle it ourselves if you want to leave."

There was a hissing sigh from the speaker. "No, we'd better stick together," Sileen said. "Anyway, what can the Empire do to us that hasn't already been done?"

"I'm in, too," Cai said. "One small question: Now that we've got the Hammertong, what are we going to do with it?"

Shada glanced back at the long silent cylinder behind her, the enormity of what she'd gotten them into belatedly starting to sink in. What *were* they going to do with the Hammertong? She and Karoly could nurse the Strike Cruiser along for a short flight by themselves, but that was it. Anything beyond that—fancy maneuvering, combat, even basic running maintenance—was out of the question. "We'll have to ditch the ship," she told the others. "Someplace close by. Find a way to hide it, then see if we can disassemble the Hammertong into pieces we can put aboard one of our own freighters."

"Sounds tricky," Karoly said. "You got someplace in mind?"

"We've got company," Sileen cut in before Shada could answer. "Imperial Star Destroyer, coming out of hyperspace aft."

"Got it," Karoly said, swiveling around to the sensor section of the board. "Confirm one Imperial Star Destroyer. Launching TIE fighters."

"The base probably called for help," Shada said, keying the navcomputer. This was it: no second thoughts, no chance of grounding the Strike Cruiser and escaping aboard the fighters. They were committed now. "Cai, Sileen, here comes your course feed—code Bitterness. Make the jump to lightspeed as soon as you can; we'll be right behind you."

There was a brief pause. "You sure this is where you want to go?" Sileen asked.

"I don't see us having a lot of choices," Shada said. "It's close, it hasn't got much of an Imperial presence, and the locals don't ask a lot of questions." She could imagine Sileen gazing out at the Strike Cruiser and wondering just how far the locals' indifference was going to stretch. But—

"All right," was all Sileen said. "You want both of us to come with you, or should I head out and try to scare up a freighter?"

"That's a good idea," Shada agreed. "Go ahead. Cai and Karoly and I can handle this end."

"Okay. Good luck."

The *Skyclaw* flickered with pseudomotion and vanished into hyperspace. "Here we go," Shada muttered, keying in their course and hoping fervently that the Imperials hadn't torn the hyperdrive apart as part of the ship's preflight check. Those TIE fighters back there were getting uncomfortably close, and there wasn't much margin for error here. "Everything set there, Karoly?"

"Looks like it," Karoly said, checking over her own board. "You going to let me in on the big secret of where we're going?"

"No secret," Shada said, reaching for the hyperdrive levers. "Just a useless little hole in space. Called Tatooine."

It was not so much a landing as it was a marginally controlled crash; and by the time the Strike Cruiser had skidded to a halt against one of the rippling sand dunes, it was clear to Shada that the ship would never leave there again. Not without a great deal of assistance.

"Terrific landing," Karoly commented, her breath coming a little heavily as she shut down the drive. "I presume it's occurred to you that we stick out here like a Wookiee wearing landing lights."

"Not for long we won't," Shada said, checking the displays. "That cloud to the west is the leading edge of a sandstorm. Another hour and no one's going to find us. Come on, let's go take a look at our new toy."

They had the wrap-protection off the first couple of meters of the Hammertong by the time Cai joined them. "Any trouble?" Shada asked.

"Not really," Cai said, stepping up to the Hammertong and peering closely at it. "I'm not sure they even picked me up coming in. They sure didn't hail me."

"Usually no one bothers with ships that aren't coming into the spaceport at Mos Eisley," Shada said. "A lot of contraband comes through Tatooine, and everyone pretty much looks the other way."

"I'm glad one of us keeps up with these things," Cai said dryly. "So this is the Hammertong, huh? Any idea what it is?"

"Not yet," Shada said. "How's your astromech droid doing these days?"

"Deefour? Erratic but functional. You want me to go get him?"

Shada nodded. "We'll want to get a technical readout at the very least. Is the *Mirage* ready for that sandstorm?"

"As ready as it's going to be," Cai said, heading back toward the hatchway. "I tried to position it to keep a passage clear to both ships, and we can put the hatchway deflector shields up just to make sure. I'll be right back."

The full force of the sandstorm hit about ten minutes after Cai and the droid returned; and it took less than ten minutes more for Shada to wonder if this whole idea might not have been a big mistake. Even through the thick hull they could hear the drumming of the sand against the ship, a drumming that was growing louder with each passing minute. The plan had been to hide the Strike Cruiser from probing Imperial eyes; it would be a rather costly victory if they all wound up entombed inside it.

Cai was apparently thinking along the same lines. "That's all the bolts down there," she said, climbing out from under the Hammertong and handing her hydrospanner to Karoly. "I'm going to go check on the storm. Make sure we're not getting buried too deep."

"Good idea," Shada said, returning her attention to her own line of bolts. She finished them, waited as Karoly finished hers, and then together they eased the massive access panel off.

The Hammertong's inner workings weren't nearly as complex as the number of pipe and power connections poking through the surface would have suggested. Most of the power and control cables seemed to run to a series of multihelix prismatic crystals and a group of unlabeled but identical black boxes; the piping seemed mostly connected to coolant lines and sleeves. "Maybe it's some new kind of power core," Shada suggested. "It's a modular design—see how the pattern of connectors repeats every five meters down the side? We ought to be able to take it apart at those spots."

"Maybe," Karoly said, prodding thoughtfully at one of the black boxes with the end of her hydrospanner. "Deefour, see if you can find a place to tie in. Might as well start pulling a technical readout—we're going to want everything we can get on this thing."

"Hey!" Cai called from the cockpit area. "Shada, Karoly—you'd better come see this."

She was hunched over the main display, fiddling with the fine-tuning, when the other two reached her. "What is it?" Shada demanded.

"I'm not sure," Cai said. "Hard to tell through all the sand, but I think there's a battle going on up there. An Imperial Star Destroyer against something about the size of a bulk freighter."

Shada leaned over the display, heart pounding. If Sileen had been unexpectedly fast at bringing in transport for them . . . "Can you scrub the image any more?" she asked.

"I'm at the limit already," Cai said. "It's the sandstorm—wait a minute, there's a break. It's a Corellian Corvette."

Shada let out a quiet sigh. Not one of the Mistryl's ships, then. "I wonder what's going on."

"I don't know," Cai said slowly. "Wait a minute. Two more Star Destroyers coming in from hyperspace."

"That's a lot of firepower for a planet like Tatooine," Karoly said. "They only had one Star Destroyer guarding the Hammertong."

"Unless one or more of these were supposed to have been there, too," Shada suggested. "Could be they got pulled away to help chase that Corellian."

"Either way, the Corellian must be pretty important to them," Cai said. "We could be in the middle of something really big here."

Shada looked back at the Hammertong and the diminutive droid working alongside it. Cai was right . . . and suddenly she was feeling very short on time. "Cai, do you think we could get one of those modules off the Hammertong?"

"We could try. Probably take a couple of days with just the three of us and Deefour. Why?"

"I don't think we're going to be able to wait for Sileen to bring back a ship," Shada said. "If she hasn't made it in by the time we get one of those modules off, we'd better take what we've got and get out of here."

"You'll never get one of those modules into the *Mirage*," Karoly objected. "It's way too big."

"I know," Shada said. "That's why, if it comes to that, you and I will go to Mos Eisley and hire ourselves a freighter. Come on, let's get started."

"Over there," Shada said, pointing toward a dilapidated building across the sandy Mos Eisley street and double-checking her datapad. "That's the cantina."

"Doesn't look like much," Karoly said, swinging the *Mirage*'s antique speeder over toward it. "You really think we're going to find a good pilot in there?"

"Someone in the Mistryl thought so." Shada shrugged. "It was the top name on the contingency list for Tatooine."

"I doubt that's a really telling recommendation," Karoly grumbled, letting the speeder coast to a stop. "I don't like this, Shada. I really don't."

"Brea, not Shada," Shada corrected her. "And you're Senni. Don't forget that inside or this whole thing could fall apart."

"It's got a good chance of doing that all by itself," Karoly shot back. "Look, just because a couple of stormtroopers on traffic duty bought this charade"— she gestured sharply at the slinky jumpsuit and hived-hairdo wig she was wearing—"doesn't mean anyone who actually knows the Tonnika sisters is going to fall for it. They're not."

"Well, we certainly can't use our own names and IDs," Shada pointed out, trying to hide her own nervousness about this masquerade. "This place is crawling with stormtroopers already, and if they haven't got listings on us yet, they will soon. The Mistryl have been running this camouflage prematch system for a long time now, and I've never yet heard of it failing. If it says the two of us can pass as Brea and Senni Tonnika, then we can."

"Looking like them and acting like them are two very different things," Karoly countered. "Besides which, pretending to be a couple of criminals is not my idea of keeping low."

She had a point, Shada had to admit. Brea and Senni Tonnika were professional con artists—good ones, too—who were said to have separated an impressive amount of wealth from an equally impressive list of the galaxy's rich and powerful. Under normal circumstances, borrowing their identities would indeed not be a smart way to stay inconspicuous.

But the circumstances here were far from normal. "We don't have any choice," she said firmly. "Complete strangers automatically draw attention, and a place like Mos Eisley is always crawling with informants. Especially now. Our only chance of keeping the Imperials off us is to look as if we belong here. To everyone." She looked out at the cantina. Karoly was right; the place didn't look very inviting. "If you'd rather, you can stay out here and watch the door. I can find a pilot by myself."

Karoly sighed. "We're going to have to talk someday about these sudden surges of recklessness. Come on, we're wasting time."

Shada had held out the hope that, like certain other criminal dens she'd heard of, the cantina's interior would be a marked improvement over its exterior. But it wasn't. From the dark, smoke-filled lobby and flickering droid detector to the curved bar and secluded booths along the walls, the cantina was as shabby as some of the less choice tapcafes on their own world. Karoly had been right: Being number one on Tatooine wasn't saying much.

"Watch the steps," Karoly murmured beside her.

"Thanks," Shada said, catching herself in time not to trip over the steps leading down from the lobby to the main part of the cantina. She hadn't realized until then just how much her eyes were having to adjust from the bright sunlight outside to the dimness of the interior. Probably deliberately designed to give those already inside a chance to check out any newcomers.

But if any of the patrons were overly curious about her and Karoly, they weren't showing it. Around the room, humans and aliens of all sorts were sitting or squatting at the tables and booths or leaning against the bar, drinking a dozen different liquids and chatting in a dozen different languages and not paying the least bit of attention to the new arrivals. Apparently, the Tonnika sisters were familiar enough to the clientele to be known on sight.

Or else minding one's own business was the general rule here. Either way, it suited Shada just fine.

"What now?" Karoly asked.

"Let's go over to the bar," Shada said, nodding to an empty spot against one side. "We can see the room better from there than from a table or booth. We'll get a drink and see if we can find anyone from our listings."

They made their way through the general flow of bodies to the bar. Across the room, a Bith band was belting out some bouncy but otherwise nondescript tune, the music not quite able to drown out the mix of conversations. Partway around the bar a tall not-quite-human was smoking from an oddly shaped loop pipe and gazing off broodingly into space; beyond him, an Aqualish and a badly scarred man were drinking and glaring around at other customers; beyond them, another tall human was holding a quiet conversation with an even taller Wookiee.

"What'll you have?" a surly voice asked.

Shada focused on the bartender standing there in front of them. The expression on his face matched his voice; but there seemed to be some recognition behind the indifference in his eyes.

Enough to risk an experiment. "We'll have the usual," she told him.

He grunted and busied himself at the bar. Shada glanced at Karoly's suddenly aghast expression, winked reassuringly, and turned back as the bartender put two slender glasses in front of them. He grunted again and walked away.

Shada picked up her glass, willing the tension to flow out of her. "Cheers," she said, lifting the glass to Karoly.

"Are you crazy?" Karoly hissed back.

"Would you rather I had ordered something way out of character for us?" Shada asked, taking a careful sip. Some kind of Sullustan wine, she decided. "Let's get started."

Still glowering, Karoly pulled the slender cylinder of their spies' scanner/datapad from her jumpsuit and flicked it on. "All right," she muttered, glancing back and forth between it and the cantina's patrons. "The fellow with the loop pipe . . . never mind, he's an assassin. Those two Duros over there . . . no listing here for them."

"Their flight suits look too neat for smugglers, anyway," Shada said. Across the bar, an old man with white hair and beard and dressed in a brown robe stepped up to the Wookiee and his tall companion. There was a short conversation between the two humans, and then the tall human gestured to the Wookiee and wandered away. "What about that Aqualish over there?"

"I was just checking him," Karoly said, peering down at the end of the scanner. "Name's Ponda Baba, and he's definitely a smuggler. That scarface beside him—"

"Hey!" the bartender barked.

Shada stiffened, her hand reaching reflexively for her hidden knife.

But the bartender wasn't looking at her. "We don't serve their kind here," he snapped, gesturing sharply.

"What?" came a voice from behind her.

Shada turned around. At the top of the steps stood a boy about her own age, dressed in loose white clothing and frowning in puzzlement at the bartender. Beside him were two droids, a protocol droid and an astromech unit similar to Cai's Deefour model. "Your droids," the bartender growled. "They'll have to wait outside—we don't want them here."

The kid spoke briefly to the droids, who turned and scurried back out. Continuing down the steps alone, he moved over to the bar and gingerly wedged himself in between the Aqualish and the old man in the brown robe.

"The scarface is named Dr. Evazan," Karoly said. "I've got ten death sentences listed here for him."

"For smuggling?" Shada asked, frowning at the brown-robed old man. There was something about him; some sense of quiet alertness and self-control and power that set the hairs tingling on the back of her neck.

"No," Karoly said slowly. "Botched surgical experiments. Yecch."

"We'll keep him in mind as a last resort," Shada said, her eyes and thoughts still on the brown-robed man. Whoever he was, he definitely didn't fit in with the rest of the clientele. An Imperial spy, perhaps? "That old man over there—do a check on him," she told Karoly. The kid was still standing on his other side, gawking around like a tourist. Were they together? Grandfather and grandson, maybe, in from the countryside to see the big city?

And then, abruptly, the Aqualish gave the kid a shove and snarled something at him. The kid looked at him blankly, then turned back to the bar. Stepping away from the bar, smiling rather like a predator preparing himself for lunch, Dr. Evazan tapped the kid on the shoulder. "He doesn't like you," he said.

"Sorry," the kid breathed, starting to turn away again.

Evazan grabbed a handful of the kid's clothing and yanked him back around. "*I* don't like you, either," he snarled, shoving his mangled face close to the kid's. Around them, conversations came to a halt as heads turned to look. "You just watch yourself," Evazan continued. "We're wanted men."

"Uh-oh," Karoly said quietly.

Shada nodded silently. The kid was in for it now—she'd seen enough tapcafe fights to know a setup when she saw one. "We're staying out of it," she reminded Karoly.

"But if they get arrested—"

Shada cut her off with a sharp gesture. Smoothly, gracefully, as if he'd been fully aware of the situation from the start, the old man had turned away from his conversation with the Wookiee. "This little one's not worth the effort," he said soothingly to Evazan. "Come, let me get you something."

It was, Shada realized, as neat a face-saving gesture as she'd ever seen. Evazan and the Aqualish could now accept a drink, maybe snarl and posture a little more, and then move on with whatever passed for personal honor intact.

But unfortunately for the old man, Evazan wasn't interested in a peaceful settlement. For a split second he glared at the old man, his predator look hardening into something ugly and vicious. Conversation at the bar had all but ceased now, every eye turned toward the violence about to break. From their alcove the band played on, oblivious to what was happening.

And then, with a roar, Evazan shoved the kid violently to the side to crash into one of the tables. His hand swung up, a blaster gripped in it. Beside him, the Aqualish also had his blaster out, an urgent "No blasters—no blasters!" from the bartender going completely unnoticed. The weapons swung up, targeting the old man.

They never got there. Abruptly, the old man's hand exploded into brilliant blue-white light, a flickering hard-edged fire that slashed with surgical precision across his two attackers. There was a blaster shot that ricocheted into the ceiling, a scream and gurgling roar—

And then, as abruptly as it had begun, it was over.

Evazan and the Aqualish collapsed out of sight beyond the bar, their moans showing they were at least temporarily still alive. From where she stood, Shada could see the Aqualish's blaster lying on the floor, still clutched in a hand no longer attached to its owner.

For another moment the old man remained as he was, his glowing weapon humming, his eyes flicking around the cantina as if assessing the possibility of more trouble. He could have saved himself the effort. From the casual way the other patrons were turning back to their drinks, it was obvious that no one here had any particular affection for the downed smugglers. At least not enough to take on the old man over it.

And it was in that second's worth of pause that Shada was finally able to identify the weapon the old man had used against his attackers.

A lightsaber.

"You still want to know who he is?" Karoly asked dryly from beside her.

Shada licked at her lips, a fresh tingle running through her as the old man closed down his weapon and helped the kid back to his feet. A Jedi Knight. A real, living Jedi Knight. No wonder she'd sensed something odd about him. "I doubt he's for hire," she told Karoly, taking a deep breath and forcing her mind back to the business at hand. If the Jedi Knights of the Old Republic had still been in power when their world was destroyed . . . "Well, that eliminates Evazan and the Aqualish," she said to Karoly. "Keep looking."

They spent the next few minutes sipping their drinks and surreptitiously scanning the room, then spent a few minutes more talking to three of the most likely prospects. But to no avail. Two of the smugglers were already under contract, though one of them offered with a leer to take them along as passengers if they were nice to him. The third smuggler, an independent, was willing to talk, but made it clear that he wasn't planning to move his ship until this sudden Imperial focus on Tatooine had calmed down.

"Great," Karoly grumbled as they returned to their previous spots at the bar. "Now what?"

Shada looked around. A few new faces had come into the cantina since they'd begun their search, but most of them had the look about them of men who didn't want to be disturbed. She looked in turn at each of the booths lining the walls, wondering if they might have missed someone.

And paused. There, right behind them, were the Jedi Knight and the kid. Talking to the Wookiee and a man she hadn't seen come in. "Check him out," she said, nodding toward the latter.

Karoly peered at the scanner readout. "Name's Han Solo," she said. "Smuggler. Does a lot of business with Jabba the Hutt—"

"Put it away," Shada interrupted her, looking toward the cantina lobby. "Quick."

Karoly followed her gaze, and Shada felt her stiffen. Striding down the steps toward the bar, heavy weapons held at the ready, were a pair of stormtroopers. Who clearly weren't here for a drink.

"I wonder if there's a back door out of here," Karoly murmured.

"I don't know," Shada said, running a finger along her slender wineglass as the Imperials summoned the bartender over. Thrown against the face of a stormtrooper helmet, it ought to slow him down long enough for her to slide her knife blade into a critical junction . . .

The bartender pointed somewhere behind them. Shada frowned, then understood. "They must be asking about the Jedi Knight," she said, turning to look at the booth. A knot of aliens brushed past, momentarily blocking her view. They continued on—

The old Jedi was gone. So was the kid. The stormtroopers stepped up to the booth, eyed Solo and the Wookiee a moment, then moved on. For a moment, as they looked around, their armored masks seemed to pause on Shada and Karoly. But they said nothing, and continued on their way toward the rear of the cantina.

Karoly nudged her. "Now's our chance," she said. "Let's go talk to him."

Shada turned back. Solo and the Wookiee had left the booth now, Solo heading for the lobby while the Wookiee went in the direction the stormtroopers had gone. Probably where the back door was, which would explain how the Jedi and the kid had disappeared. "Right," Shada agreed, taking one last sip from her glass and putting it back on the bar. She turned again—

To find that Solo was no longer walking toward the lobby. He was, instead, backing into a booth at the wrong end of a blaster held by a dirty-looking Rodian. "Uh-oh," Shada said. "Friend of his?"

"Doubt it," Karoly said, palming the scanner. "Hang on . . . his name's Greedo. He's a bounty hunter."

For a long moment Shada stared at the quietly tense discussion in the booth, trying to decide what to do. Taking action would jeopardize her cover as Brea Tonnika, and certainly there was no shortage of smugglers in the cantina. But there was something about the way Solo carried himself that she liked. Or maybe the fact that he'd been talking with the Jedi Knight . . .

"I'm going to take him," she told Karoly. "Get ready to back me up."

She reached for her knife; but before she could draw it, Solo solved the problem on his own. From the booth came a flash of muffled blaster fire, and the Rodian slumped over onto the table. Warily, Solo slid out of the booth, holstered his blaster, and continued on toward the lobby, flipping a coin to the bartender as he passed.

Karoly let out a breath. "Good thing we weren't interested in Greedo. This isn't a very healthy place to hang around."

"No kidding," Shada said. "Let's go catch Solo before he gets away."

And then, from behind her, a sweaty hand closed on

her wrist. "Well, well, well," a voice said. "What have we here?"

Shada turned. The sweaty hand belonged to a sweaty Imperial colonel, his uniform streaked with sandy dust, a maliciously pleased look on his face. Behind him were the two stormtroopers who'd come through earlier. "Brea and Senni Tonnika, I do believe," the colonel went on. "How nice of you to drop back into sight again. You can't imagine how brokenhearted Grand Moff Argon has been since your departure. I'm sure he'll be pleased to see you again." He lifted an eyebrow. "*As well as* the twenty-five thousand you stole from him."

Smiling sardonically, he gestured to the stormtroopers. "Take them away."

The police station cell was cooler than the cantina had been, but that was about all it had going for it. Small, sparsely furnished, streaked with Tatooine's ubiquitous sand, it had all the charm of a used transport crate.

"Did you catch when they'd be moving us out?" Karoly asked, leaning against a wall and gazing dolefully at the door.

"Didn't sound as if it would be anytime soon," Shada said. "The colonel said something about finishing up the search before getting us transferred to his ship."

Karoly's lip twitched. Clearly, she was also appreciating the irony here: The Imperials' search had already ended, only they didn't know it.

Or maybe they did know it. Maybe the colonel was just playing along with the masquerade while he sent out for the proper interrogation equipment.

Shada looked around the room. A single bunk, a reading lamp fastened to the wall over one end, primitive refresher facilities, a barred door, and a one-way observation window opposite it. Limited resources, and no privacy to use them.

Which left only their combat training. And the possibility that the Imperials still didn't know they were dealing with Mistryl. "I just hope they feed us before then," she commented to Karoly. "I'm starving."

Karoly's eyebrow twitched. "So am I," she said, looking around. "Maybe I should beat on the bars and see if I can get someone's attention."

"Go ahead," Shada said, stretching out on the bunk and letting her hand rest idly on the reading lamp above her head, examining it with her fingertips. It was fastened to the wall over the bunk, but a little work with her belt buckle ought to get it off. Behind it would be power cables . . . "On second thought, you might want to try that mirror instead," she said to Karoly, nodding back at the spy window. "Someone's probably watching it."

"Okay," Karoly said. She stepped over to the window and pressed her face against it, blocking the view into the cell. "Hey! Anyone there?"

Quickly, Shada pulled off her buckle and got to work as Karoly kept up the noise. She got one of the three fasteners loosened; did the second; started on the third—

"Shut up the noise!" someone snapped.

Shada paused, palming the buckle, as a man in a faded uniform appeared at the door. "We're hungry," she complained.

"Too bad," he growled. "The meals come in two hours. Now shut up or I'll have you strapped down and muzzled."

"Two *hours*?" Shada repeated. "We'll never make it that long. Can't you get us something to tide us over?"

"Please?" Karoly added, smiling encouragingly.

The guard's lip twisted; and he was just opening his mouth for what would probably have been a memorable comeback when a young man in civilian clothing stepped into view. "Problems, Happer?"

"Always," the other growled. "I thought you were off till tonight."

"I am," the younger man said, peering thoughtfully at Shada and Karoly. "Heard you were drowning in prisoners; figured I'd come in and take a look. Who do we have here?"

"Brea and Senni Tonnika." Happer threw a glower at the two women. "Very special prisoners of Colonel Parq. And none of our business, if you ask me. If the Imperials want to lock up half of Mos Eisley, the least they could do is provide their own holding tanks."

"And do their own ID checks?"

"Don't remind me." Happer grunted. "I've got fifteen of them running right now, with about thirty more in the hopper." He glared again at the prisoners. "Look, Riij, do me a favor, will you? Go down to Stores and pull a couple of ration bars for these two. I've got to go down to the check room—the sifter's been needing a lot of babysitting today, and those stormtroopers are starting to get snotty."

"I'll handle it," Riij assured him. "Have fun."

Happer grunted again and disappeared down the corridor. "So," Riij said, gazing at them again. "Brea and Senni. Which is which?"

"I'm Brea," Shada said carefully. There was something about the way he was looking at her that she didn't at all care for.

"Ah," he said. "I'm Riij—Riij Winward. You know, I could have sworn I heard you two had gotten on a transport heading out toward Jabba the Hutt's three hours ago."

Shada's heart seemed to seize up inside her. The Tonnika sisters were *here*? On Tatooine? "We came back," she said through suddenly dry lips. "I guess we shouldn't have."

"I guess not." Riij paused. "I heard something else interesting too, just after this big Imperial droid search came down all over Mos Eisley a couple of days ago. It seems the Empire's also put out an urgent search-and-detain order for a stolen Strike Cruiser."

"A Strike Cruiser?" Shada repeated, putting as much scorn as she could into her voice. "Oh, I'm sure. People steal Strike Cruisers all the time."

"Yeah, I thought that sounded pretty strange myself," Riij agreed. "So I went over and talked to a pal of mine at the control tower to see if that was even possible. You know what he told me?"

"I'm dying to hear."

"He said he'd picked up something sneaking in toward the Dune Sea an hour or so before that Star Destroyer showed up and all these Imperials dropped in on us. Something just about the size of a Strike Cruiser." Riij lifted his eyebrows. "Interesting, wouldn't you agree?"

"Tremendously," Shada said, fighting to keep her sudden dread out of her voice. So they had spotted the Strike Cruiser, after all. And Cai was in big trouble. "Were the Imperials pleased to hear this?"

"Actually, he hasn't told them yet," Riij said, eyeing her closely. "He was going off duty at the time and didn't feel like holding a question session with a bunch of stormtroopers. 'Course, once they came down in force and took over the tower, he was even less inclined to remember stuff like that. That happens on Tatooine."

"I see," Shada murmured. They were still in trouble, but at least they still had a little breathing space. "You'll forgive me if lost Imperial property isn't high on my list at the moment. We have more pressing problems of our own."

"I'm sure you do," Riij said solemnly. "Number one being how to get out of here before Happer finds out you aren't Brea and Senni Tonnika."

Shada felt herself tense up again. She'd suspected he knew, but had been hoping fervently that she was wrong. "That's ridiculous."

"It's all right," Riij said. "The microphones in this cell haven't worked in three months. I popped out the circuit fuse a few minutes ago too, just to make sure."

Shada glanced at Karoly. She looked as puzzled as Shada felt. "All right," she said, looking back at Riij. "Fine. Let's cut through the smoke here and tell us what you want."

Riij seemed to brace himself. "I'll let you out," he

said. "In exchange for some of whatever's in that Strike Cruiser."

Shada frowned at him. "What are you doing, running a smuggling service on the side?"

"Not smuggling." He shook his head. "Information. To certain interested parties."

"What parties?"

"It's not important." Riij smiled faintly. "On Tatooine, one normally doesn't ask that question."

"Yes, well, we're new here," Shada countered, thinking hard. This could be an Imperial trick, she knew: a way to get her and Karoly to tell them where they'd hidden the Hammertong. But somehow that seemed a little too subtle for people who owned interrogator droids and normally had no compunction about using them. "All right," she said. "But only if you can find us a freighter that can handle something three by five meters."

Riij frowned. "Three by—?"

"Hey, Riij!" Happer's voice called from down the corridor. "Gotta go—something big brewing over at Docking Bay 97. The Imperials have called the whole duty force in to run backup. Can you watch things here a while?"

"Sure, no problem," Riij assured him.

"Thanks."

Happer ran off, his footsteps cut off by the boom of a closing security door. "Well?" Shada prompted.

"I can get a freighter," Riij said, forehead wrinkled in thought. "The problem's going to be getting it fast enough. There's a sandstorm sweeping in across that part of the Dune Sea—a big one. It'll hit in a couple of hours, and there's a good chance it'll bury your ship for good."

"Then we haven't got much time, have we?" Shada said. "Get us out of here, and let's go."

The wind was already picking up across the sand dunes as Riij set the transport ship awkwardly down at the

edge of the makeshift tunnel leading to the Strike
Cruiser. "How long have we got?" Shada asked, shouting to be heard over the wind as the three of them half
walked, half slid their way down the sand to the hatchway.

"Not long," Riij called back. "Half an hour. Maybe
less."

Shada nodded back, keying the panel open and stepping inside. On the deck just inside the hatchway lay
the segment of the Hammertong they'd removed, its
loadlifters still attached. Across the huge empty room
Deefour was warbling to himself as he poked around
the rest of the huge cylinder, searching for any last-
minute bits of data he could add to his extensive technical readout of the device. There was no sign of Cai.
"Cai?" Shada called. "Da mala ci tri sor kehai."

"Sha ma ti," Cai replied, emerging from hiding behind one of the support struts and holstering her
blaster. "I was starting to think you weren't going to
make it back in time."

"We may not have," Shada said grimly. "We've got
another sandstorm breathing down our necks. There's
a transport outside—you and Karoly get that Hammertong segment aboard."

"Right," Cai said. "Karoly? Grab the lifts on that
end."

Together they got the Hammertong segment off the
floor and out the hatchway as Shada went forward to
the Strike Cruiser's cockpit. As it had before, the flying
sand was interfering with the sensors, and she had to
adjust the fine-tuning several times before she was able
to get a good view. As far as she could tell, there were
no longer any Star Destroyers over Tatooine. They
must have assumed their escaped prisoners had already
made it offplanet. Keying off, she headed back to
where Riij was crouched beside the end of the Hammertong cylinder, his face pressed close to one of the
openings. "So there it is," she said. "What do you
think?"

He looked up at her, his face pasty-white. "Do you

know what you have here?" he whispered. "Do you have any idea?"

"Not really," she said warily. "Do you?"

"Look here," he said, pointing to a plate. "See? 'D.S. Mark Two. Module Seven, Prototype B. Eloy/ Lemelisk.' "

"I see it," Shada said. "What does it mean?"

Riij straightened up. "It means this is part of the prototype superlaser for the Death Star."

Shada stared at him, a shiver running up her back. "What's a Death Star?"

"The Emperor's latest grab for power. Like nothing you've ever seen." Riij looked back along the Hammertong's length. "And we've got a piece here of its main weapon."

"A *piece?*" Shada frowned, following his gaze. A solid two hundred meters of laser— "You mean this isn't all of it?"

"I don't think so," Riij said. "Module Seven, remember?" He looked at Shada sharply. "I've got to have that piece you cut off. It's absolutely vital."

"Forget it," Shada said. "If this really is a weapon, my people can find a better use for it than you can."

"We'll pay you anything you want."

"I said forget it," Shada said again, brushing past him. Cai was going to need help—

And abruptly, she was spun back around by a hand on her arm. Reflexively, she reached up to break his grip—

She froze, staring at the blaster that had appeared from nowhere in Riij's hand. "Is this how you keep your bargains?" she demanded.

"You have to let us have it," he said, his voice low. "Please. We need to know everything we can about the Death Star."

"Why?"

He swallowed hard. "Because we're likely to be its first target."

Shada stared at him. Tatooine was going to be the first target? Ridiculous.

And then, suddenly, it fell into place. "You're with the Rebel Alliance, aren't you?"

He nodded. "Yes."

Shada focused on the blaster in his hand. "And this thing is important enough to you to kill me in cold blood?"

He took a deep breath, let it out in a hissing sigh. "No," he conceded. "Not really."

"I didn't think so," Shada said. "Mish kom."

And in the blink of an eye, it was all over. Cai, coming in from behind the Hammertong, had Riij's blaster. And Riij. "What do you want me to do with him?" she asked, handing the blaster to Shada.

Shada looked at Riij, half bent over in Cai's grip. "Let him go," she said. "He can't stop us now. Anyway, he's sort of on our side."

"If you say so," Cai said, releasing her hold on his arm. "We're ready to go as soon as you are."

"All right." Shada pursed her lips. "Riij, can you beat the storm in that airspeeder you had aboard the transport?"

He nodded. "If I can get going in the next few minutes."

"Fine. Cai, get it unloaded. And then you or Karoly get Deefour aboard and get the ships ready to fly."

"Got it." With one last look at Riij, Cai headed for the hatchway.

Riij was still standing there, looking at Shada. "I'm sorry the deal's fallen through," she told him, trying to ignore the pang of guilt twisting through her stomach. He'd risked a lot for them, and it looked as if he were going to wind up with nothing. "Look, if you can get back in here after the storm, you're more than welcome to what's left of the Hammertong."

"Let me make you a counteroffer," Riij said. "Join us. You've already said we're on the same side."

Shada shook her head. "We're barely making it ourselves. We don't have the time or the resources to take on the galaxy's problems. Not now."

"If you wait too long, there may not be anyone left to fight with you," he warned.

"I understand," she said. "I guess it's a chance we'll have to take. Good-bye. And good luck."

The sand was shaking the transport's hull by the time Shada finished double-checking the Hammertong's restraints and made it back up to the bridge. "We all set?" she asked Karoly as she strapped herself in.

"Yes. Riij get off all right?"

Shada nodded. "Looks as if just in time, too."

Karoly threw her a sideways look. "I'm not sure it was such a good idea to let him go."

"If we start killing anyone who gets in our way, we're no better than any other mercenaries," Shada said. "Besides, he doesn't like the Empire any more than we do."

The comm pinged. "I'm ready," Cai's voice came.

"Same here," Shada told her. "Is Deefour all settled in?"

"Deefour?" Cai echoed. "Didn't Karoly take him?"

"I thought *you* had him," Karoly said.

For a long moment she and Shada just stared at each other. Then, with a muttered curse, Shada jabbed at the comm panel. "Riij? Riij, come in."

There was a hiss of sand-driven static; and then the other's voice came faintly over the speaker. "This is Riij," he said. "Thanks for the loan of your droid. I'll leave him with the Bothan shipping company on Piroket; you can have him back when you return the freighter."

Another crackle of static and he was gone. "You want me to go after him?" Cai asked.

Deefour, with a complete technical readout on the Hammertong . . . "No," Shada told her, smiling in spite of herself at Riij's ingenuity. "No, it's all right. We owe him that much. And if he's right, he and his friends are going to need all the help and information they can get."

Her smile faded. "D.S. Mark 2" the plate on the

Hammertong had said. Death Star, Mark 2, perhaps? A second generation of this thing Riij was so afraid of?

It could be. And if so, the Mistryl might have to seriously consider that offer to join up with the Rebel Alliance.

And if not all of the Mistryl, perhaps Shada would do so on her own. Maybe there she would find something she could truly believe in.

But in the meantime, she had a package to deliver. "Fire up the repulsorlifts," she told the others. "Let's go home."

Play It Again, Figrin D'An: The Tale of Muftak and Kabe

by A. C. Crispin

Muftak whiffed the chilly, moist air with his short, tubular proboscis, testing it, trying to determine whether it was safe. As he sniffed, the huge four-eye searched the street for infrared afterimages with his night-eyes, the larger, lower pair in his furry visage. Here, in the older part of Mos Eisley spaceport, the darkness was nearly absolute, only lightened by the tiny gray half-moon scuttling overhead.

Gesturing to his small companion, Kabe, to stay be-

hind him, the shaggy giant crept forward to a better
vantage point behind a large garbage receptacle. As he
scanned, his four black ball-bearing eyes gleamed in
the darkness of his face. Automatically, his olfactory
organ filtered out the stench of the rotting garbage,
the rankness of unwashed bodies, both alien and human, and the sharp, musky scent of his Chadra-Fan
friend and accomplice.

No one here recently. He waved a massive, fur-cov-
ered paw at his companion. "Come on," he rumbled,
"the sandtroopers are gone."

Kabe scampered out, her fanlike ears and little snout
twitching indignantly. "I could have told you that long
ago!" she scolded, in her squeaky, double-time voice.
"You are so cursed *slow*, Muftak! Slower than a bantha,
that's for sure. We'll never reach home before day-
break! And I'm *tired*."

Muftak gazed down at her, patiently enduring her
tirade. Kabe, despite all her streetwise sophistication,
was still a child. He'd adopted her when he'd found
the baby Chadra-Fan wandering the streets. "We must
be extra cautious," he reminded her. "Imperial troops
are everywhere. The sooner we reach home, the safer
we'll be. Let's go."

Kabe subsided sulkily, and started after him.
"Why're they here, that's what I'd like to know. Do you
know, Muftak?" She didn't wait for a reply, and the
four-eye held his peace. Muftak knew a great deal
about the comings and goings in Mos Eisley, but generally, he only divulged what he knew for a price. "Ships
landing all night!" she complained. "What the hell is
going on, anyway? The Hutt's hiring them, that's what
it is. He's going to cut us out completely. And if he
won't take us back, we'll have to beg!"

Muftak emitted an exasperated buzzing sound. "The
Bloated One isn't part of this. This is Imperial business."

Kabe's sharp little face blazed in Muftak's infrared
vision, and he saw her expression change. "Can't we
go to the cantina today?" she demanded, changing the

subject. "Spacers go there, drunk spacers with fat pockets. Last time we were there we ate for a week on what I lifted. Please, Muftak?"

"Kabe." Muftak sighed, a faint humming noise in the stillness. "I'm not so stupid as all that. I know you never miss a good pocket, but the real reason you want to go to the cantina is for juri juice." Absently, the four-eye inspected the twisty alleyways that opened onto the street. "Two cups and I'll have to carry you home . . . the way I always do."

Kabe's only response to this truism was an audible sniff.

Dawn came rapidly on Tatooine, and the desert sky was already taking on the faint silver sheen that presaged the rising of the suns. Muftak lengthened his strides, tempted to pick Kabe up bodily and really hurry. It was his fault they were so late.

Expert thieves though they were, neither Kabe's skill with electronics nor Muftak's great strength had prevailed against the new time-lock devices that all the Imperial hangars now bore. Worse, one of the sandtroopers had spotted them . . . but humans had very poor night vision, and, to them, all exotic aliens tended to run together. In the dark, Muftak hoped, he could've been mistaken for a Wookiee or one of the other large bipeds. Kabe was about the same size as a Jawa.

Stealing Imperial property was extremely risky—but these days, there was little else they could do. Any payoff would have justified their effort, given them the wherewithal to buy back their burglary franchise (lost due to an ill-advised bit of pickpocketry by Kabe) from the Hutt. Everything of value that didn't belong to the Empire either belonged to or had been declared off-limits by Jabba—and *nobody* was crazy enough to cross the Hutt crime lord.

In order to reach "home"—a tiny cubicle in a section of abandoned tunnels beneath Docking Bay 83—they had to pass through the marketplace. Risky, but they had no choice.

Kabe bounced as she walked, half skipping, her restless energy undepleted despite their night's labors. Muftak shuffled rapidly, though he felt almost too weary to place one huge, padded foot before the other. Suddenly, the tops of the whitewashed domes gleamed; moments later, everything was splashed with gold. The first sun was rising. Muftak instinctively switched over to his day-eyes, obscuring some details, revealing others. They passed a street vendor setting up for the day, then another.

Mos Eisley was a hellhole at best, and recent changes made survival even more uncertain. The increasing Imperial presence added an unpleasant new dimension to Jabba's corrupt regime. Muftak's and Kabe's lives had never been easy; the two of them had scrabbled for years to eke out a living. Now, with the Senate's inaction, things were growing worse. Previously, the four-eye had shared his little friend's indifference to politics, not caring who was in power, as long as they let him alone.

But the sandtroopers were even worse than the Hutt's thugs. Cold, cruel, brutal, they were like killing droids. Hundreds—maybe thousands—had been arriving during the last two days to enforce the will of that ancient, rotting Emperor who lived far, far away. *Tightening the Empire's grip on my world* . . .

Bzzzzz. Muftak's remote laughter echoed in his head like a dancing bee. *My* world? Ridiculous! Bzzzzz . . .

Since there were no other creatures on Tatooine even remotely like him, Muftak knew only too well that this was *not* his home world. When he'd awakened that day long ago, standing beside his shredded cocoon, he'd figured that his people had originated on another world—which one, he had no idea. He'd spent a lifetime searching for information about himself, and, in the process, had learned much about Tatooine, its deserts so different from the lush paradise of his dreams. Knowledge, the four-eye found, was power, of sorts. Denizens of Mos Eisley knew that if you wanted information about almost any activity or person on Tatooine, you went to see Muftak.

Since he'd "adopted" Kabe, an orphan like himself, the big alien's hazy dream-memories had receded into the background. For all practical purposes, Tatooine *was* his world.

The second sun was rising as they made their way through the main square of the marketplace. It was already getting hot, and Muftak felt his dew-wet, diaphanous fur drying out. Reaching the main street, the pair turned west, toward their little burrow, trying to hurry without looking suspicious. The fences were setting up quickly and efficiently, displaying freshly stolen booty. Muftak glanced nervously at several blasters, priced well beyond his means, trying to look as though he had nothing better in the world to do than shop. Kabe skittered about, muttering to herself, whiffing the air, then squinching up her muzzle with disdain. "Look at that trash." She snorted. "If you'd let me rob Jabba's town house, I'd give them some real stuff to fence. It'd be a snap, and we'd be set up for life."

This was such an old argument Muftak didn't bother to reply. The Hutt was currently occupying his desert palace, but his residence in Mos Eisley was still fully guarded. The four-eye lengthened his stride. Sanctuary lay just ahead . . .

Suddenly a mechanical-sounding voice barked, "You there, Talz, halt!" The voice belonged to an Imperial soldier.

Hastily, Muftak obeyed, then turned, slowly and ponderously, to face the sentry. As he did so, he was careful to conceal Kabe's small form with his huge body. Knowing the plan, she darted off and ducked behind a public dew collector. Signaling to her behind his back to stay out of sight, Muftak faced the white-armored human.

Only then did it strike him . . . the word the trooper had used. "Talz." What was a Talz? Slowly he felt the truth sink in, like moisture in the desert. The Imperial trooper must have recognized his species!

The word "Talz" reverberated through Muftak's mind, his heart. Talz . . . yes! It was part of the meaningless vocabulary he had found in his brain after his "birth." *Talz means* me. *I am a Talz!*

Muftak shook his head, pushing this revelation to the back of his mind. There was a more immediate dilemma to face. The sandtrooper, blaster drawn, was staring at him, waiting. Muftak let the air filter out slowly from his proboscis, humming a little. "Yes, Officer. What can I do for you?"

"We are looking for two droids, one bipedal and the other wheeled, traveling unaccompanied. Have you seen them?"

Not looking for us, no, by the Force, not looking for us. Looking for those two droids, like all the others . . . "No, sir. I haven't seen any droids this morning. But if I do, Officer, I'll let you know."

"See that you do. All right, Talz, on your way." As the trooper began to turn away, curiosity overcame Muftak's caution. "Excuse me, sir," he began, scratching his head nervously. "I noticed that you seem to recognize—"

There was a whooshing sound and an aircar appeared from around a corner. As it approached, Muftak saw two Imperial troopers, one dressed in the blue uniform and short-billed cap of an officer. The Talz took a cautious step back, but resisted the urge to run.

The sentry snapped to attention as the aircar stopped.

The officer, a pale, sagging man with a supercilious air, inclined his head briefly and commanded, "Your report, Trooper Felth." His words sounded lifeless, barely different from the mechanically filtered voice of Felth.

"Nothing to report, Lieutenant Alima. It's been very quiet, sir." Muftak tensed. He recognized that name. His friend Momaw Nadon had told him about a Captain Alima, the butcher who'd decimated the hammerhead's home world. Could this be the same man? His rank was different, but . . .

"Interrogate everyone you see, Felth. Don't take any chance with this local scum . . . and keep your blaster ready. These bastards will as soon kill you as look at you."

"Yes, Lieutenant."

"What about that one?" Alima drew his pistol and pointed it at Muftak. "An ugly bug . . . has he seen the droids?"

"No, sir."

Muftak gathered his courage. Things were becoming *very* interesting. Worth a little risk. "Sir, respected representative of our beloved Empire, I am well connected in the more . . . shall we say, obscure . . . sections of Mos Eisley. It would be my pleasure to uncover this information for you, if I can."

The officer's eyes were very dark as he stared hard at the Talz. "See that you do, four-eyes. Now get on about your business. Don't dawdle . . . off with you!"

Kabe was only a little distance away, still hiding behind the dew collector, and Muftak walked in that direction without looking back. As he passed, the little one joined him, chattering happily. "They let you go! I thought they had us, didn't you? What happened?"

"They weren't looking for us, Kabe. Just two unlucky droids. But something very . . . important happened. A chance encounter. That trooper knew who . . . what . . . I am. I am a Talz! Kabe . . . this may be the clue I've been looking for."

The Chadra-Fan looked up at Muftak, squinting her little eyes against the morning sun. "But, but . . . you're not going away, now, are you? You can't go. We need each other. We're partners, aren't we?"

Muftak gazed down at his friend, feeling a strange emotion, a distant tugging that he had never felt before. Gigantic hanging purple flowers filled his mind's eye. He scraped a claw across his domed forehead. "Don't worry, little one. I'd never leave you alone. Right now, we're going back to get some sleep. Then I

have some inquiries to make . . . and before evening,
I must go to Momaw Nadon's house, find out if he
knows anything about the race called the Talz. And
perhaps . . . give him some information in return.''

"But what about the cantina?" Kabe wailed. "You
promised, Muftak!"

The Talz ignored this palpable untruth. "You will
get your wish, little one. We'll go tomorrow."

Chalmun's cantina was, as always, bursting with disreputable life. Momaw Nadon was already at their usual
spot, and Muftak took the seat opposite, against the
wall. The hammerhead pushed a drink across the table. "Welcome, my friend." From the position of his
eyestalks and the tone of his grayish skin, Muftak de-
duced that the Ithorian was glad to see him, but also
apprehensive—not unexpected, in view of their meeting yesterday.

The Talz picked up his drink, a polaris ale appropri-
ately tepid, and thrust his proboscis into the liquid,
drawing deep. "Things are going well, Momaw. Last
evening I planted the seed that you desired. Alima now
thinks you know the whereabouts of the droids."

"Planted the seed." Momaw Nadon blinked slowly.
With his eyes squinched shut, all semblance of a face
vanished. "A good way to express it. If all goes as
planned, the 'seed' will come to fruition before this
day is over." One eyestalk swiveled. "Did Alima pay
well?"

Muftak buzzed with amusement. "Five hundred.
The Imperial chit he issued proved worthless, of
course."

"Not surprising," Nadon said.

Muftak ran a claw through his hair, scratching nervously. "Momaw . . . what will become of you? Alima
is ruthless. Now he's looking for you."

"He has found me," Nadon admitted, his dual voice
a harsh whisper. "Do not worry, my friend. All is un-
folding as it must."

The Talz took another sip of ale, reluctant to pursue this depressing subject.

"No matter what happens today," the Hammerhead continued, "things here in Mos Eisley are changing. Yesterday you learned the name of your species. Soon you will discover the name of your world, and where it is located. Then . . . what? Will you go home?"

Muftak let out a tiny buzz, rising in pitch. "Home. It is such a simple word. In my native language, the word is 'p'zil.'" He paused, unwilling to reveal such intimate details even to a friend. "If I have dreamed truly, it is a cool, wet world, with wide, rich jungles beneath a deep indigo sky. My dreams are full of huge flowers shaped like giant bells, all colors, hanging high in the lush foliage. I climb to those flowers, treading along a strong ridged petal. Deep in the center darkness lies a rich reservoir of nectar. I drink, marvelous rippling flavors . . ." He sighed. "This ale is only a pale reflection."

The Ithorian bobbed his eyestalks in understanding. "Those dreams are true, my friend. Racial memories, no doubt, to guide you when you emerge from your cocoon. Just as you were born with a knowledge of your native language. I have never heard of such a people as the Talz, but they are obviously unique and of great value. You must return and join your essence with that of your people. It is the Law of Life."

"I haven't thought that far, I'm afraid," said Muftak. "I don't have the credits to pay for such a trip. And . . . what about Kabe? The galaxy is in turmoil. Even if I could obtain safe passage for us, I can't trust her. She only thinks of herself. How can I take her with me?"

Momaw Nadon closed his eyes for a long moment. "I may not live out the day, so I cannot help you. But you will think of something. Let us drink—"

Suddenly Kabe bobbed up at Muftak's side. "He won't serve me again!" she sputtered angrily. "Damn that Wuher. And damn Chalmun! I'll feed the Sarlacc with them both. They won't sell me any juice, Muftak.

My credits are good, damn it! Damn them all! You know that I—''

Muftak interrupted her with a loud buzz. "Calm down, little one. What did Wuher say?"

"He said he wanted no tipsy Ranats robbing his customers. Me, a Ranat! Muftak, can you go talk to him? Please?"

Muftak stroked his proboscis slowly, thinking. "His reaction isn't surprising, considering what happened last time we were here, Kabe. But . . . I'll speak to him." He raised his glass to Momaw Nadon. "After all, this is a celebration . . . of sorts."

Kabe's ears twitched with distaste as Figrin D'an's sextet swung into yet another off-key, off-tempo number. The little Chadra-Fan's hearing was as sensitive as Muftak's sense of smell, and this "music" was particularly jarring. But Chalmun's cantina was the cheapest source of juri juice around, so she endured it. She guzzled the dregs from her cup, feeling the pleasant rush of the liquor.

Licking the last drops from her whiskers, she held up her tumbler. "More, Wuher. More juri juice! I'm thirsty!" The bartender glanced across the room at Muftak, muttered something under his breath, then grudgingly took the glass and refilled it with the ruby brew. Kabe grabbed it eagerly.

Suddenly, the bartender straightened, scowling angrily. Was he getting ready to summon the bouncer? Kabe stood poised, ready to run to Muftak, but all Wuher did was order some moisture boy to get his two droids out of the cantina.

Relaxing, Kabe studied the customers closest to her, scanning expertly for pockets to pick. With a little juri juice in her, she was twice as fast and twice as clever. No one was safe.

The identity of the two customers on either side of her gave her pause; Dr. Evazan and Ponda Baba weren't good prospects. It was one of Kabe's secret prides that she'd once managed to pick both their pockets, dropping a few trinkets from the good doctor's purse into Baba's pocket at the same time—but they'd been very juiced then . . . which they weren't at the moment. High, perhaps, but not enough to tempt her. The risk wasn't worth it.

The two prospects beyond Evazan were definitely more promising. The grungy moisture boy who'd been dumb enough to bring the droids in was standing on her immediate right. The man he'd entered with was an old fellow with a beard the color of Muftak's fur, wearing a coarse brown cloak with a hood—no doubt made by a Jawa tailor, Kabe thought, amused. She recognized neither of them, which meant they weren't from Mos Eisley. Good! Wide-eyed desert dwellers usually presented easy pickings. Beyond them was the contraband runner Chewbacca, but she dismissed him without a second thought: Not only did he not possess pockets to pick, but everyone knew it wasn't wise to upset a Wookiee.

Muftak was still in deep conversation with Momaw Nadon. *Damn him, too. Suppose he finds his home world, what then? He'll probably want to go there . . . and then, by the Force, where'll that leave me?* Kabe had a brief vision of herself, stuck in Mos Eisley, with no one to make Wuher serve her juri juice . . . no one to protect her from outraged victims when her fingers weren't quick enough . . .

She'd be all alone. Kabe took a deep draft of juice, thinking of her small, secret hoard—so secret that even Muftak didn't know about it. It wouldn't last long . . . a tenday, maybe. And then what? No doubt about it, trouble was coming, unless she found a way to distract the Talz.

A tall, thin humanoid down the bar was puffing away on a hookah. Expertly, she located his credit pouch. Easily accessible . . . but something, she wasn't sure what, held her back. Ears twitching, she strained to pick up his vibrations. For some reason she couldn't define, he *sounded* wrong. When his gaze brushed hers, the fur on the back of her neck crawled suddenly, as if someone had draped something limp and dead across her shoulders.

Not him, Kabe thought, shuddering. *Definitely not him.*

The boy, she decided. He was obviously nervous, but not really alert. And then the old man. There was something about the old man that betokened a quiet competence, despite his shabby clothes. She'd have to be extra careful with that one.

Suddenly Kabe sensed movement on her left from Ponda Baba. She ducked back, barely in time to avoid a vicious elbow as he deliberately shoved the boy. "Out of my way, human excrement!" he bellowed in Aqualish. *Oh no,* she thought, *here we go again.* Whiskers twitching, Kabe scurried behind the old desert dweller, then peeked cautiously out, carefully putting her half-empty glass on the bar.

The boy obviously didn't understand the big alien's language. He glanced up, startled, then silently moved away and went back to his drink. Kabe poised herself for action; when Evazan and Ponda Baba's newest victim lay charred and smoking, she'd have only a moment to snag his purse before he was dragged away.

Maybe, she thought, *now would be a good time to do the old one.* His attention was fixed on Ponda Baba. Perfect. Now, if she could only find his purse . . . "I have the death sentence on twelve systems!" Evazan's loud voice hurt her ears. Hmm. That was a promising little bulge. Just a little closer . . .

The old man stepped forward—and his pocket slid away from her fingers. Cautiously, Kabe followed. There was a sudden exodus away from the bar, and Kabe realized the fight was about to start—but she was determined to snatch the credits before she too retreated.

"This little one isn't worth the effort," the old human was saying, his soft, pleasant voice carrying an undercurrent of true authority. "Come, let me buy you something."

Ponda Baba roared in inarticulate rage, Evazan let

out a bellow, and the young human flew past her, landing in an ignominious heap beneath a nearby table.

"No blasters! No blasters!" screamed Wuher.

There was a sound like tearing silk, and Kabe shrank closer to the old desert dweller, cowering until she was almost covered by his cloak. Ponda Baba shrieked, Evazan howled with pain, and something dropped to the floor with an ominous thud.

Kabe peered out, to see that the thing on the floor was Ponda Baba's arm, fingers still twitching as they tried without success to fire the blaster again. The old man stepped back gracefully, and the searing blade of light that was his weapon (a weapon Kabe had never seen before) flicked out. Abandoning all thought of robbery, she scampered back. As the old man helped the youngster up, the boy staggered, staring in disbelief at the still-twitching arm . . . and his heel crunched down on Kabe's toes.

She squeaked shrilly at the sharp pain. *Damn! Humans are heavy!* Whimpering, limping, Kabe retreated into the darker recesses of the room, waiting for them to clean up. Luckily, they hadn't spilled her juri juice . . .

"You mean you'll help me?" Kabe stared up at her friend, amazed.

Muftak nodded. "There'll never be a better time to take the town house. The Hutt is away at his palace and the city is in chaos."

The little Chadra-Fan gazed at him goggle-eyed, the aftereffects of juice slowing her thoughts. Suddenly, she dropped her half-eaten falotil fruit to the dusty floor of their lair, jigging ecstatically. "I knew you had it in you, Muftak!"

He nodded, wishing he were as confident. The Hutt's vengeance would be terrible indeed if they were caught, but the store of treasures in Jabba's town house, deliberately displayed to tempt the greedy, would be easy pickings if Kabe's "secret" entrance panned out. The Talz had made his decision on the way home from the cantina, carrying the unconscious Kabe in the crook of his arm.

Muftak looked around the dwelling they'd shared for almost five years. Kabe's little nest, his sleeping perch, a trunk holding their few possessions. Nothing, really. And the future would only be worse.

"We'll be able to leave this dump," said Kabe, as if she'd read his thoughts. "Maybe buy our own cantina. Live in real style." Disdainfully, she scratched a crumbling wall, sending a little avalanche of dirt onto the floor. "The credits will be worth a little risk, you'll see."

The Talz scratched his head, buzzing softly. "There's no sense in waiting. Tonight."

Kabe nodded happily.

Nighttime. Muftak, surprisingly agile for his size, pulled himself over the lip of the roof, until he was crouched on the main dome of Jabba's town house. Cautious as always, he drew his ancient blaster, scanning the rooftop for signs of life. The moon was heading down, losing its luster among distant clouds, leaving them in near-total darkness.

Ahead of him, Kabe was already halfway up the dome, moving quickly. She stopped suddenly, and Muftak made out a large, crescent-shaped orifice just below the dew-collector array. Replacing the weapon in the sling across his back, he climbed, claws scrabbling, up the rough pourstone surface.

"See, Muftak," the Chadra-Fan whispered, knotting the climbing rope she'd carried to the dew-collector base, "it's just like I said. It hasn't changed since I discovered it. Just the standard security net. Hear that? Air currents singing along the edges of the metal door. One good shove, and it'll give."

Muftak crouched beside the portal. "Hard to believe," he said. "Can you hear anyone inside?"

Kabe listened, ears twitching. "Just snores on another floor. No one moving around."

"Then here goes." The Talz got a good hold on the sill and pushed. The access portal slowly gave, bending inward, then the hinges broke and the metal fell away. A muffled clank sounded from somewhere below.

"The vibrations haven't changed," Kabe exulted. "What'd I tell you, Muftak? This'll be a cinch for sure!"

Before Muftak could stop her, Kabe swung herself over and down into the darkness. The Talz heard her chittering quietly as she climbed, and knew she was listening for echoes. "Nothing unusual so far," she reported. "I'm almost dow—" Hearing her break off, Muftak flung himself down, head through the hole, straining his night-eyes. Below him, Kabe dangled, spinning slowly, a paw's length from the floor.

"Kabe, what's happening? Why'd you stop?" Muftak demanded.

"Shhh." As he watched, Kabe changed position, turning upside down, then lowering her head until her ear was just above the carpet. She chittered again. "Oh, bantha dung . . ." he heard her mutter.

"What is it?"

"A noise, below the floor . . . something down there. The air has to go around it, and it hums . . . metal, probably." Suddenly she let out a terrified little squeak. "Don't come down yet! It's some kind of trap! There's a spring actuator . . ."

Muftak watched as she clicked, trying to gauge the structures below the floor. "Standard joists over here . . ." she muttered, a few seconds later. With a couple of vigorous wiggles, she swung back and forth, then dropped her pry bar as a test.

"No change!" she cried, then leaped off herself. "Just land right here . . ."

When Muftak was down, they left the dome room, and crept down the dark stairway. At the bottom, Kabe heard the distinctive electronic hum of an alarm.

Quickly, the little Chadra-Fan located and deactivated it.

To their right, an archway led into a large room, a lounge of some sort, outfitted with luxurious, plush furniture. One wall held an open curio cabinet filled with small golden statues and bejeweled antique weapons. Muftak gasped softly . . . the plunder of a hundred worlds—theirs for the taking!

Cautiously, they entered. Working with feverish haste, they began stuffing valuables into the sacks they'd brought.

"We'll be out of here before you know it," Kabe whispered, sliding a particularly ornate pipestand into her bag. "Now aren't you sorry you didn't—"

Two lights winked on in the lounge's anteroom. A droid, turning itself on. Kabe froze in terror. Muftak drew his blaster.

"Oh, forgive me for interrupting you," said the droid in a melodious tone. "I've been waiting for . . . by the way"—its tone changed—"what are you doing here at this time of night? I know that Master Jabba's friends are a little . . . unusual, but . . ."

Muftak took a step toward the machine. "We belong here. Your illustrious master asked us to fetch some of his possessions to transport to his palace."

The droid took a few mincing steps into the room. "That explains it then. Bzavazh-ne pentirs o ple-urith feez?"

Muftak did a double take. His language. "Where did you learn that?"

The droid tilted its head, and its illuminated eyes seemed full of satisfaction. "Oh, friend Talz, I am conversant in the languages and customs of your planet, Alzoc Three, and four thousand nine hundred and eighty-eight other worlds. I am Master Jabba's protocol droid, Kay-eight Ellarr. Master Jabba couldn't do without me. Admittedly, I've never had a chance to use my Talz module before. I'll just check with Master Fortuna to see if you are telling the truth."

Kabe, under control now, was moving slowly toward

the droid, trying to look pleasant. She uncoiled her climbing rope. "We're telling the truth, droid. You don't have to check."

"Oh, but I do, friend Chadra-Fan, k'sweksni-nyip-tsik. You have no idea what trouble I'd get into if I didn't—" Suddenly Kabe sprang and wrapped the rope around its limbs. "The restraining bolt, Muftak!"

"My friends, please don't—" K8LR was moaning like a Jawa street beggar. "Oh! Master Jabba will punish you—" It began to fight, but the Talz loped forward, and with a single motion collared it and grabbed the bolt affixed to its chest. K8LR was struggling, trying to free itself of the ropes around its body, but Muftak was desperate. With a quick wrench, he ripped the bolt free.

When the bolt came off, the droid stopped struggling.

"Oh, thank you," it said. "You have no idea how much better that feels. I never liked working here. Never. That Jabba . . . so uncouth! And the rogues that work for him! Things I've seen would curl your proboscis, friend Talz. Now, if you don't mind, I think I'll be leaving. Could you untie me?"

"Be quiet, droid!" Kabe pricked up her ears, listening intently. When she detected nothing, they began gathering loot again. K8LR, still half trussed, followed them about, complimenting them on their selections in a metallic whisper.

"Kay-eight Ellarr," Muftak said, stuffing a tiny figurine carved from living ice into his furry abdominal pouch, "if you really are grateful, tell us where the Hutt keeps his most valuable treasures."

The droid stopped, appearing to think. "There are Corellian artifacts on the walls of his audience chamber that are beyond price, if my memory banks are correct. And a shapework from the earliest days of human civilization."

"Take us there!"

·   ·   ·

As Muftak and the droid headed for the door, talking in low voices about the location of Alzoc III, Kabe hastily pried a large fire-gem from the eye of a sculpture. She stuffed it into one of the myriad pockets of her robe, joining the other small valuables she'd secreted about her person. *I'll never have to pick pockets again,* she thought.

They followed the droid back into the hall and to the right. As they tiptoed along, Kabe's ears twitched at a noise so soft no one else could have heard it. Breathing. Agonized, rasping . . . and aware. She halted before the third door. "Who is in this room?" she demanded of K-8LR. "Whoever is in here is awake."

K-8LR stopped. "It is one of my former master's victims, I'm afraid. A human courier. They have been torturing him for days with a nerve disruptor."

Muftak motioned her on, but Kabe hesitated. "Do you know how much Valarian would pay for a nerve disruptor?" she whispered to the Talz. "Droid, can you open it?"

"Certainly, madam." K-8LR interfaced with the lock and the door swung open.

Muftak shifted nervously, scratching his head. "Kabe, let's not get involved with this. It stinks in there."

The Chadra-Fan ignored her friend, marching into the room. Reluctantly, Muftak followed.

A naked, frail, sallow man with an air of infinite sadness lay strapped onto a bunk, moaning. As they entered, his eyes fastened on them. The nerve disruptor, a small black box mounted on a tall tripod, stood by the bed. Kabe went over and, resolutely ignoring the human, began to disconnect it.

"Water," the man pleaded in a ghastly husk of a voice. "Water . . . please."

"Be quiet," Kabe snapped. Even as her fingers moved, deftly unscrewing little components, she remembered the days before Muftak had found her, when she'd wandered the streets of Mos Eisley, hungry . . . and nearly crazed with thirst. Unable to stop herself, she looked up at the human. Their eyes met.

"Water," rasped the man. "Please . . ."

Kabe's fingers slowed, then, cursing under her breath, she pulled a small flask from her belt and held it out. "Here's water. Now leave me alone." With his arms restrained, the human could only gaze at the flask longingly.

"I'll give it to you, sir," said K-8LR, coming forward. He raised the human's head, and held the water to his lips.

The nerve disruptor was finally detached. Kabe stuffed it in her sack. "This alone will buy us enough juice for a lifetime!" she said triumphantly.

The human finished the water and licked his cracked, impossibly rough lips. He eyed them carefully. "You two . . . are interested in credits. How'd you like to earn thirty thousand, quick, without risk?"

Muftak, restless, was keeping a lookout on the hall. Kabe, already turning to leave, halted. She regarded the man suspiciously. "What d'you mean, human?"

"My name is Barid Mesoriaam. Remember that name, because it will be your password. If you deliver a datadot to a certain Mon Calamari who will be in Mos Eisley for the next few days, the credits are yours."

Kabe considered. "A datadot. Thirty thousand? But where'll you get it? How do we know—"

"You'll just have to trust me. As to the location of the dot . . ." Mesoriaam closed his mouth and worked his tongue against his teeth. When he opened it, there was a tiny black circle visible on the tip of his tongue. Kabe plucked the datadot off.

Muftak, who'd returned to the bedside in time to hear most of the exchange, stared wide-eyed at the man. "What is on this dot that is of such value?" he asked.

Mesoriaam tried to raise himself, but he was too weak. "That is not for you to know. Tell the Mon Calamari it is for General Dodonna's eyes only."

"Barid Mesoriaam is a participant in the Rebellion

against the Empire," said K-8LR smugly. "They wish to restore power to the Senate, as I understand it. No doubt the datadot has something to do with Rebel plans."

The Talz stroked his proboscis, thinking. "Here, Muftak, put this in your pouch," Kabe ordered, holding out the datadot.

Muftak complied. "Rebels," he repeated meditatively. "Kay-eight, what was Jabba trying to get out of him? Was he under Imperial order to do this?"

"My former master does not play favorites," replied the droid. "He sells to the highest bidder. Unfortunately for him, no matter how Mesoriaam was tortured, he revealed nothing."

"Since you know what I am and what this dot contains," said Mesoriaam, "there is nothing to stop you from selling the information to the Prefect. But, if you do, remember that there is no place for nonhumans in the Empire. In the proud days of the Republic, all beings had equal status. Look around you and tell me if that is still the case."

Kabe scowled impatiently. "If your friend'll give us thirty thousand, I don't care what he—" She whirled around abruptly. "What was that?"

Lights came on in the hall. "Oh, no," said K-8LR. "This doesn't seem to be a very promising turn of events."

Muftak drew his blaster. "Let's get out of here. Now."

The Talz held his breath as he reached the hallway, brandishing his blaster, but no one was in sight. Kabe followed, trying to fit one more prize in her already full bag. "Jabba's audience chamber, Muftak. That shapework must be worth millions!"

Muftak gaped at her, incredulous. "Kabe, are you crazy? We've got to—"

From out of the lounge sprang two burly, porcine Gamorreans brandishing axes, grunting obscenely.

Muftak shoved Kabe behind him, and they backed away from the newcomers. The Talz triggered his blaster—but nothing happened. "Shoot them, Muftak!" Kabe shrilled.

Muftak emitted a frustrated hum. "I'm trying!"

Encumbered by his sack, he examined the weapon as best he could, backpedaling all the while. The Gamorreans squealed at each other, evidently making plans. Desperately, Muftak wiggled the power supply into better contact, saw the ignition coil begin to glow hot. Got it. Aiming, he fired at the nearest guard. The weapon spat, and the bolt of energy caromed off the guard's axhead, which it was using as a shield. The Gamorreans dived for cover, just as a tiny Jawa appeared from another door, firing its blaster. Muftak coaxed out a few more shots, sending the Jawa scurrying back into hiding.

"This way!" Kabe was heading past the main entrance, a reinforced blast door big enough to admit the enormous Hutt. One glance told Muftak it was electronically locked.

The Chadra-Fan scurried in the direction of the audience room. "There's another exit in here—hold them off while I get it open!"

"Hold them off?" Muftak cried. "How?" He followed Kabe, and they dashed into the huge, circular audience chamber. Dominating the far end of the room was the Hutt's ornate wooden dais; over it hung a gigantic tapestry depicting a grotesque scene of Hutt family life.

Just as Kabe had promised, there *was* another, smaller door—but it too bore an electronic bolt. "Now what?" Muftak gasped. "We're trapped!"

"Maybe I can get it open . . ." Kabe said uncertainly. "But I'll need time . . ." Pulling out the nerve disruptor, she set it on the floor, pointing at the doorway, then turned it on. "I'll use this to block the entrance!"

Time was against them—they'd only gotten halfway across the chamber before more Gamorreans charged through the door, howling like Tusken Raiders. One was armed with a blaster. Lethal bolts ricocheted behind them as Muftak grabbed Kabe and dashed across the chamber, taking cover behind Jabba's audience dais.

The blaster bolts halted abruptly, and the two thieves peered out to see the four Gamorreans staggering in the entranceway, yowling with pain and fury. Sighting carefully, Muftak cut three of them down with well-placed shots. The fourth escaped back into the hall.

Kabe started crawling for the door. "I'll open—"

All hell broke loose. Ten guards of various species appeared at the doorway, each of them loosing a barrage of blaster fire. Kabe's disruptor held them back for the moment, but the two friends were pinned down behind the dais.

"We can't hold out much longer like this." Muftak grunted, sighting and firing into the gaggle of guards jammed into the entrance. "Sooner or later one of their shots will hit the disruptor—and then they'll be in here."

Kabe's only response was a terrified squeal. Muftak peered over the dais, searching for a good target, and glimpsed chalky-white albino features at the back of the crowd. Bib Fortuna . . . Jabba's Twi'lek major-domo, who was doubtless directing the battle from the safety of the hallway. A whistling snarl from overhead attracted his attention, and he glanced up to see a huge net hanging from the ceiling, large enough to cover the entire middle of the audience chamber. Word had it that the net contained kayven whistlers, flying carnivores with appetites as large and sharp as their teeth. Jabba used the kayven to "influence" recalcitrant business associates into deals favorable to the Hutt.

Aiming at a hulking Abyssin's torso, Muftak squeezed off another shot, and was rewarded when the being went down with a scream. "Muftak, what are we going to *do*?" Kabe bleated. He glanced down at her, saw her huddled, quivering, against his side.

"If we could only get that door open," the Talz muttered, half to himself. But it was too far away . . .

Another blaster shot sizzled overhead, so close that Muftak threw himself over Kabe, almost mashing her flat. A crackling filled the air; the tapestry behind them was now burning in one spot and smoldering in several others. *That's it . . . we'll never get out of here alive,* he thought. *I'll never get off this sandy hell, never see Alzoc III . . . never taste the nectar of those flowers—*

"Get off me!" Kabe squeaked beneath him. Muftak levered himself up, gasping and gagging on smoke. Kabe stared at the fire round-eyed. "Muf-tak . . ." she wailed.

The Talz squinted against the smoke tendrils, trying to aim. He fired at a Gamorrean, but blurred vision made him miss. Return fire caromed off the furniture. One blaster bolt struck the nerve disruptor, shattering it.

Now they'll be all over us! Muftak thought, but the guards still held back. Evidently they hadn't realized that the entrance was now clear—either that, or the smoke deterred them. *Maybe Bib Fortuna ordered them to stay back, figuring the fire will get us,* he thought. *That way he doesn't risk losing any more guards.*

Without warning, the exit door swung open.

Fresh night air rushed in, fanning the flames, sending the smoke eddying in billows. Muftak grabbed the two sacks of loot, shoving them into Kabe's hands. "Run for it!" he ordered. "I'll cover you!"

The Chadran-Fan hesitated. "But what about you?"

"I'll be right behind you!" he lied. Someone as small and quick as Kabe might be able to make it out the door, under the cover of his fire, but Muftak, with his lumbering bulk, didn't have a chance. But at least Kabe would live. With the wealth in those sacks, she'd be set for life . . .

"Go!" he cried, literally booting her out from behind the dais. He fired at the guards, catching a glimpse of her scuttling through the smoke out of the corners of his left eyes.

A hail of fire forced him down again, but not before Muftak was rewarded by the sight of Kabe vanishing through the door. *Thank the Force for that.* He settled back, his blaster scorching his paw as he prepared to sell his life dearly . . .

Gasping, choking, Kabe staggered out the exit and into the night. The heavy sacks of loot weighed her down, but she'd sooner have cut off her arm than lose them. Ducking through a gate and into a walled garden, she sagged against a life-size sculpture of Jabba, gulping air. Behind her she could hear blaster bolts whining. Where was Muftak?

Peeking through the gate at the exit from the audience chamber, the Chadra-Fan watched as clouds of smoke billowed. With each passing second, the pain in her pounding heart and straining lungs eased. Still no Muftak. Kabe glanced up the street, hearing the distant sounds of firefighters and water sellers converging on the Hutt's town house from all directions.

Where in the name of the Force was Muftak?

Kabe winced at the sounds of more blaster fire from the audience chamber. Smoke darkened the night, obscuring the stars. The entire room must be ablaze . . . Muftak!

Grimly, the little Chadra-Fan realized that her friend had never intended to follow her. He'd given her the chance to escape at the price of his own life. Slowly, she picked up the two laden sacks. She'd be crazy to throw away the Talz's last gift to her . . . Muftak *wanted* her to get away—with the loot.

Kabe took a step toward the gate on the other side of the garden, heading for the alley. Images flashed before her eyes, of herself, starving, whimpering in alleys, too weak to run, almost too weak to walk. Muftak had picked her up, tucked her under his arm, and carried her home to his den . . . had bought water for her, and food . . .

Kabe took another step . . .

The sacks slipped from the Chadra-Fan's fingers, thudded to the sandy ground near the sculpture's stone tail. Kabe kicked them viciously, knowing they wouldn't last two seconds out here, no matter how she tried to conceal them. "Damn you, Muftak!" she squealed—

—and, turning, raced back into the audience chamber.

Chittering loudly, Kabe could pick up Muftak's presence by his vibrations, even through the engulfing smoke. The Talz was still where she'd left him, but the room was now filled with advancing guards. Muftak was returning fire, but the power pak in his blaster was clearly running low—the beam flickered as she scuttled across the floor of the audience chamber.

Eyes watering, coughing as she tried to sense vibrations, Kabe picked up a shape in front of her. A Rodian. She leaped, fastening her sharp teeth in the guard's leg. He shrieked, dropped his blaster and turned, trying to club her away with his fist. The Chadra-Fan let go, grabbed the blaster, and shot the guard at point-blank range. "Muftak!" she shrilled. "Come on! I'll cover you!"

Somehow, despite the melee, he heard her. Kabe chittered wildly amid the chaos of smoke, flame, and scuttling bodies, and was rewarded with the sound of the Talz crawling out from behind the dais.

Crouching down, she made herself as small a target as possible, all the while firing wildly at anything moving. She could see Muftak; he was lumbering toward her, knocking aside guards as though they were children, using his enormous bulk to flatten anything in his path.

"Over here!" Kabe called. "The door!"

Muftak headed toward her—only to be confronted by two Gamorreans, grunting and squealing threats. Kabe took careful aim, and shot one in the back. His partner whirled toward her, and Muftak kicked him aside.

Suddenly a new voice called out. "Friend Talz!

Friend Talz—stand away from the center of the room, please!"

Kabe glanced up, through the smoke, to see K-8LR leaning out of a window halfway up the wall of the dome. Muftak obeyed, changing the direction of his charge just in time to avoid a huge net that tumbled down from the apex of the dome, engulfing most of the guards.

Shrieks and squeals from the guards mingled with the savage hootings of kayven whistlers. The net heaved wildly.

One long stride later, Muftak reached the Chadra-Fan, scooped her up without pausing, then raced out the open door.

"Put me down!" Kabe squeaked, the moment they were clear of the town house. Quickly, she hurried over to the shadow of the statue, but, of course, the sacks were gone.

The Chadra-Fan's shoulders sagged. "Bantha dung!"

"Kabe . . . you came back . . ."

It was Muftak, and he was regarding her incredulously, his eyes still clouded with smoke. "I thought you'd be halfway home by now."

Kabe kicked the crumbling garden wall disgustedly. "Muftak, you're so cursed *stupid*! Of course I couldn't leave you in there, when you're too dumb to get out of there by yourself. You'd have been bantha fodder for sure!"

The Talz regarded her quizzically, then, suddenly, he buzzed with soft amusement. "Kabe . . . you saved my life. You and Kay-eight. You came back to save me."

The Chadra-Fan put both hands on her hips and glared at him. "Well, of course I did, you idiot! We're *partners,* aren't we?"

Muftak nodded. "That's for sure, Kabe. Partners. Come, let's get out of here."

The two began skulking along, automatically moving in shadows, avoiding passersby. Behind them, the blaze was spreading. "The walls won't burn," Muftak observed, "but the interior is going to be gutted, at this rate."

"Jabba's so rich he'll fix it up, no problem," Kabe said truthfully. "Muftak . . . one thing puzzles me. Who opened the door?"

"It must have been the droid," the Talz replied. "I only hope that Bib Fortuna didn't see it helping us out. If he did, there's no hope for Kay-eight Ellarr."

"Where will we go now?" Kabe, ever-practical, asked.

"Momaw Nadon's house. He'll hide us . . . if he's alive. And there were no reports of his death, so he must have managed to outmaneuver Alima somehow."

"But we can't stay here . . ." Kabe wailed. "Our lives won't be worth Sarlacc spit if Jabba finds out who messed up his house!"

Muftak gave her a long look. "You're right . . : we can't stay here. We're getting out of Mos Eisley and off Tatooine before anyone can inform on us."

"How, Muftak? We lost almost all of our loot!" Which wasn't quite true . . . Kabe could feel the small bulges of half a dozen gems in her robe.

"Have you forgotten the datadot?" Smugly, the Talz patted his furry belly.

Kabe stared at him, wide-eyed, then began to chatter happily to herself. "Thirty thousand! And it will all be ours! And you didn't even want to go into that room . . . I practically had to drag you! I told you you'd never regret this night, Muftak, didn't I? Didn't I?"

Silently, the big Talz nodded agreement.

Two nights later, in the secret hiding place beneath the roots of the Ithorian's carnivorous vesuvague tree, Muftak faced the Mon Calamari that Momaw Nadon had conducted there to meet him. "Barid Mesoriaam said this was to be for General Dodonna's eyes only," the Talz said.

"I understand," the fish-being said, holding out a finned hand. "The datadot, please?"

"First, our payment," Kabe piped up. "Do you think we're stupid?"

Silently, the Mon Calamari produced credits from a pouch that made the Chadra-Fan's eyes gleam avidly. Muftak hastily counted it. "There is only fifteen thousand here," he complained. "We were promised thirty."

"I have something better than credits, to make the rest of the payment," promised the Rebel contact, reaching into his pocket.

"What could be better than credits?" scoffed Kabe, openly contemptuous.

"These—" the spy said, holding up two official-looking stamped and sealed documents. "Two letters of transit, signed by Grand Moff Tarkin himself. With these, you can go anywhere!"

Muftak stared at the documents, all four eyes huge. Letters of transit! With these they'd be able to reach Alzoc III—and then, perhaps, Chadra, Kabe's world of origin.

"But obtaining passage out of Mos Eisley is still no easy task . . ." Muftak said, taking the precious documents and stowing them, along with the credits, in his pouch. Gravely, he handed over the datadot.

"Passage has been arranged, my friend," Momaw Nadon said, stepping out of the shadows. "You leave tonight. Perhaps, now that you have those . . ."—the Ithorian cocked one eyestalk in the direction of the letters of transit—"you will one day be able to aid the Rebellion again."

"Don't count on it, Momaw," Kabe squeaked. "We're in this for ourselves, not for any Rebellion, right, Muftak?"

The Talz scratched his head, and didn't answer.

Kabe craned her neck to peer out the porthole of the small freighter, gazing down at the golden world below them, turning lazily in the light of its double suns. "I never thought I'd see Tatooine from here," she chirped, a little uneasily. "I could use a drink, Muftak."

"Not while we're in space, little one," the Talz said. "We don't want you getting sick. But on Alzoc . . . ah, there is the finest of nectar to sip!"

"What about juri juice?" she demanded, taken aback. "Don't tell me they don't have any juri juice, Muftak!"

Muftak hummed softly. "I have no idea, little one," he said gently. Every time the Talz moved, he could feel the letters of transit in their place of concealment. *First Alzoc III*, he thought. *Then, perhaps, Chadra . . . and from there? Who knows? The Rebellion has been far more charitable to us than the Empire ever was or would be . . . perhaps, after we have seen our home worlds, it will be time to think once again of the Rebellion.*

Kabe was still gazing out the porthole, muttering disgustedly to herself about the lack of juri juice. But suddenly she glanced up at her large friend, her little eyes twinkling. "I've just thought of one more reason I'm glad to leave Mos Eisley, Muftak."

"What is that, little one?"

"At least I'll never have to listen to that . . . that *noise* Figrin D'an makes again! Especially his rendition of 'The Sequential Passage of Chronological Intervals.' That one *really* hurt my ears . . ."

Muftak stroked his proboscis, buzzing softly with amusement.

The Sand Tender:
The Hammerhead's Tale

by Dave Wolverton

The cantina was crowded now that the afternoon suns beat down on Tatooine, yet even sitting with his friend in the crowded cantina, Momaw Nadon felt somehow alone. Perhaps it was because Nadon was the only Ithorian—or Hammerhead—on the planet. Or perhaps it was the news that his longtime friend Muftak bore.

Muftak the hairy white four-eye drank a cup of fermented nectar, slurping with his long proboscis, and said with palpable excitement, "Talz is the name of my species—at least that is what the stormtrooper called me, and as soon as he said it, I recognized the word. Have you heard of the Talz?"

Nadon had a perfect memory. "Unfortunately, I have never heard of your species, my friend," Nadon answered, the words from his twin mouths cutting through the room in stereo. "But I have contacts on other worlds. Now that we know your species, we may be able to learn where your home lies."

Muftak got a faraway look in his eyes as he sipped his drink. "Home."

"These Imperial stormtroopers that questioned you," Nadon asked, "what were they after?"

"I have heard," Muftak said, "that they are searching for two droids who evacuated a Rebel ship and dropped into the Dune Sea. The Imperials are conducting a door-to-door search, even now."

"Hmmm . . ." Nadon considered. He couldn't tell what the Imperials were really after. Often they would visit a planet, pretend to investigate a minor infraction as an excuse to bully the locals, then leave a garrison of gunslingers to "ensure the peace." A small force of stormtroopers had been onplanet for some time. Now it looked as if the Empire were raising the stakes on Tatooine. At this very moment, all over the planet, residents of the underworld were scurrying to hide illegal drug shipments, forging documents. Nadon saw worried faces in the crowded bar. There was no telling how long the new Imperial forces might stay or what direction their investigations might take.

Muftak laid a heavy claw on Nadon's arm in warning. "There is something more that I must tell you, my old friend. The Imperials that stopped us were led by a commander named Lieutenant Alima, an older human from the planet Coruscant."

At the mention of Alima's name, Momaw Nadon's blood went cold and the muscles of his legs tightened, preparing him to run. "It would be a great favor," Nadon said, "if you could discover if this man once led the Star Destroyer *Conquest* in its attack against a herd-ship on Ithor."

"I have already begun asking around," Muftak answered. "I noticed that the men in Alima's command did not respect him—they looked away when he gave orders—and even his subordinates retained a healthy distance from him."

"Which means?" Nadon asked.

"This Alima is an outcast among his own men—probably recently demoted, on his way down in the ranks. There is a good chance that he is the one who betrayed your people. If he is, what will you do?"

Nadon stopped his digestive processes for a moment, sending extra blood to his brains as he considered. Alima was a vicious man. Contacting him would be dangerous, but Nadon knew he could not resist confronting the man who was responsible for his exile. "I don't know what I will do," Nadon said. "If this Alima is my old foe, tell him that you know of an enemy to the Empire who may be harboring the droids. Sell him my name. . . . And make sure he pays you well." It was an ironic moment. For years now, Nadon had spied for the Rebellion and had sought to hide this affiliation. Now he was asking a friend to sell him out.

"One more thing," Muftak said with a note of warning. "This Alima was brought in by Lord Vader as an interrogator. Word from the desert is that he's already killed fifty of our citizens."

"I know the type of man I am dealing with," Nadon said heavily.

That evening, as the lavender- and rose-colored suns of Tatooine dipped below the horizon, Nadon felt restless. His sympathies for the Rebellion were widely known, and he did not doubt that the Imperials would soon come to question him—probably even torture him.

Over the years, Nadon had used his share of his family fortune to invest in farming ventures on a hundred worlds. His investments were paying such handsome dividends that he had gained a fortune, and usually at this time of night he would have been hard at work, managing his wealth. But tonight he was ill at ease.

To calm himself, Nadon decided to engage in an ancient Harvest Ceremony, so he took his hovercar to a nameless valley in the mountains north of Mos Eisley. There, Nadon had planted leathery, shade-giving Cydorrian driller trees. With their far-reaching root systems, the driller trees had quickly formed a thriving grove.

Nadon went to the healthiest specimen and pulled a series of thin golden needles from a pouch at his belt, then inserted the probes into the tree bark so that he could harvest gene samples. As a part of the gene-Harvest Ceremony, he talked softly to the tree as he worked. "With your gift, my friend," he told the tree, "I will splice the DNA for producing your long root systems into the native Tatooine hubba gourd. The hubba gourd serves as the staff of life to Tatooine's wild Jawas and Sand People. And so, because of this little pain I have inflicted, many people will be served. For this harvest I thank you. And I thank you for the greater harvests to come."

When he had collected his samples, Nadon lay back on the warm sand, watched the stars burning in the night skies, and remembered home. Nadon had a flawless memory, so he replayed incidents in his mind, and as he remembered, the sights and smells and emotions all came to him new again so that he was lost to the present. He relived the time that he and his wife Fandomar had planted a small, gnarled Indyup tree to commemorate their son's conception. For a moment in his memory, Nadon knelt beside his wife digging beneath a sun-splattered waterfall in the steaming Ithorian jungle, then cocked his head to listen to an arrak snake that burst into song from the heights of a nearby cliff.

Then he recalled being a child, gently inhaling with both mouths the sweet smell of a purple donar flower.

After the rush of memories, Nadon felt frail, wasted. Home. Nadon could not go home. Once, he had been revered among his people as a great High Priest, an Ithorian renowned for his knowledge of many agricultural ceremonies. But then Captain Alima had come with his Star Destroyer and forced Nadon to reveal the secrets of Ithorian technology to the Empire.

Nadon's people had banished him. As his punishment, Momaw Nadon had chosen to live on this dreary world of Tatooine—the equivalent of an Ithorian hell. Where once he had led his people in caring for the vast forests of Ithor, Nadon now tended the barren sands of Tatooine. As penance for his crimes, he struggled to develop plants that could thrive in these deserts, hoping that someday Tatooine would become a lush and inviting world.

Nadon replayed his first memories of Alima, captain of the Imperial Star Destroyer *Conquest*. Alima had been a young man with dark hair, a craggy face, and fierce eyes. Nadon had been newly married, High Priest of the *Tafanda Bay*.

On his native Ithor, Nadon's people lived in immense floating cities called herdships, which used repulsorlift engines to constantly sweep over the forests and plains, and the *Tafanda Bay* was the largest and finest of Ithor's planetary herdships. Inside each herdship, hundreds of biospheres were painstakingly reproduced down to the microscopic flora and fauna of the topsoils. The Ithorians harvested plants from the biospheres of the ships, but particularly on their huge groundships, they also harvested from the abundant forests of Ithor—taking nourishment from fruits and grains, creating medicines from saps and pollens, using plant fibers to create fabrics and ultrastrong porcelains, harvesting minerals and energy from otherwise unusable roots and stems.

The study of plants and their uses was the lifework of most Ithorians, and the greatest of the students became priests who guided others, prohibiting the people from harvesting plants that could think or feel.

Only those plants that slept, those that were not self-aware, could be harvested, and then only under a rigid law: For every plant that was destroyed in the harvest, two must be planted to replace it. This was the Ithorian Law of Life.

As a High Priest, Nadon had spent decades in the service of life, until Captain Alima came seeking excuses to board the *Tafanda Bay*, then demanded to know the secrets of Ithorian technology. At first Nadon had refused to reveal his secrets, until Captain Alima trained his Star Destroyer's blasters on the sentient forests of Cathor Hills. Thousands of the Bafforr died, trees that had been Nadon's teachers and friends in his youth. Neither the trees nor the Ithorians had the weapons to fight the Empire.

When the forest was destroyed, Captain Alima had turned his weapons on the *Tafanda Bay* and ordered Nadon to surrender. In a last-ditch effort to save his own people, Nadon had no choice but to relinquish the secrets of Ithorian technology to Alima.

As punishment for revealing the Ithorian agricultural ceremonies, Nadon could still hear the elders' judgment ringing in his ears, "We banish you from Ithor and from our mother jungles. Go and consider your evil actions in solitude."

Home. Nadon found himself both envying Muftak and feeling gratitude that perhaps the hairy creature would find joy.

Nadon was interrupted from his reveries by a comlink call on his personal channel.

"Nadon," Muftak said over audio, "I just sold your name to this Lieutenant Alima. You had better get home to meet him. Be careful, my old friend."

"Thank you," Nadon said.

When Momaw Nadon reached Mos Eisley, his house was quiet. With the suns down, many of the townspeople were on the streets, enjoying the cool evening. Out across the Dune Sea, winds raced over the sand, raising clouds of dust. Static discharges in the dust clouds made the night growl with the sound of distant dry thunder.

Nadon unlocked his door, checking the doorjamb for any sign that someone might have forced their way in before him. The air in his house was rich with the smell of water, and dreeka fish chirped among the reeds of the pond in his living room. Everywhere in the dome, creepers climbed the pourstone walls toward the skylights. Small trees shivered under the weight of a breeze produced by fans.

Nadon made his way over a paved trail into one of his many side domes, to a small grove of Bafforr trees that glowed pale blue in the starlight under black leaves. Nadon knelt before them and wrapped his long leathery gray fingers around the trunk of one tree. The bark was smoother than glass.

"My friends," Nadon whispered. "Our enemy Captain Alima is coming. I do not know how to admit this, but I wish to kill him."

The bark hummed under his touch, and a pure and holy feeling enervated him, as if light entered his every pore. The soothing mind-touch of the sentient trees nearly overwhelmed him with its beauty, but the trees were displeased by his confession. Above him, the black leaves trembled, hissing the words, "Noooo. We forbid it."

"He slew the Bafforr of Cathor Hills," Nadon said. "He is a murderer. And he killed your brothers so that he could gain greater prestige among evil men. His every intent was impure."

"You are a priest of Ithor," the woods whispered. "You have vowed to honor the Law of Life. You cannot slay him."

"But he killed your kin," Nadon reasoned. He did not know if the Bafforr understood him. Each tree in itself had limited intelligence, but through their intertwining roots they were connected and thus formed a group intelligence. A large forest grew wiser in lore than any other being, but these few trees were not a great forest. Still, Nadon had not come for their counsel, only for their permission.

"Our kin would have died in time," the Bafforr reasoned. "Alima only hurried their end."

"Just as I wish to hurry Alima's end," Nadon said.

"You are not like Alima." The trees sharpened the focus of their mind-touch, and Nadon gasped at the beauty he felt as rivers of light cascaded through him. The profound peace that settled in his bones was meant both as a reward and a warning. While he basked in the glow, he dreaded the moment when he would have to leave the sacred grove and return to the mundane world. "If you break the Law of Life," the Bafforr said, "we will no longer be able to tolerate your touch."

"I would not kill him myself," Momaw Nadon pleaded. "I would command the vesuvague tree to strangle him, or I would have the alleth consume him or the arool poison him."

"All of these are lower life forms than us," the Bafforr said, "and they respond to your command as if they were common weapons. But once again, we warn you, you cannot break the Law of Life."

The mind-touch of the Bafforr withdrew abruptly, and Nadon choked out a sob as he was suddenly excluded from the group mind. He fell to his face and began to weep.

"Fancy meeting you here," an unfamiliar voice said. Momaw Nadon turned.

Beneath a glow globe that shone like a moon stood an aging human in an Imperial uniform. Emerald-winged moths fluttered about the globe, and for a moment the human eyed their bright green wings.

Alima's face was fatter than when Nadon had last seen him, and his voice had grown hoarser with age. His cheeks had sagged and his hair was graying, but Nadon recognized him. He would have recognized that face anywhere. "I see you are still a priest, crying over your sacred trees," Alima said. He waved a blaster toward the grove.

"And I see that you are still a servant of evil," Nadon said, "though somewhat fallen in rank."

Alima chuckled. "Believe me, my old friend," he countered, "my fall from grace was carefully orchestrated. Only a fool would want to be captain of Lord Vader's flagship: The mortality rate is phenomenal. Still, Vader finds uses for me even as a lowly lieutenant —which is why I'm here. So, tell me—enemy of the Empire—where the droids are. I paid good money to learn the name of one who was said to be harboring them."

"Then you wasted your money," Nadon retorted, hoping that Muftak had extorted plenty. "I don't know the location of any droid."

"But you are an enemy of the Empire, serving the Rebellion," Alima whispered dangerously. "I'm sure of it!"

"I know nothing about any droids," Nadon answered softly. He checked Alima's location. The warrior stood close to an arool cactus. Nadon could command it to strike, but in order to get within range of its stinging spines, Alima would have to move a couple of steps farther down the path.

Nadon got up from the forest floor, stepped onto the path, and backed away from Alima, hoping to lure him a meter.

Alima followed Nadon's eyes, glanced at the arool. "Do you really think I'm so stupid as to walk into your traps, Priest?" Alima asked.

Alima raised his blaster and pointed it at Nadon, then abruptly swiveled and fired into the grove of blue-glowing Bafforr. A tree exploded into flame, its trunk splitting under the impact. Black leaves rustled and waves of pain rippled from the woods, battering Nadon's senses as if they were mighty fists.

"You will devote all of your resources to finding those droids," Alima said. "Look to your friends within the Rebellion. If you do not have a location on the droids by tomorrow evening, I will sew your eyes open and make you watch as I take a vibroblade and slice each limb off your precious Bafforr trees, one at a time. Then I'll drop a thermal detonator in your living room and fry the rest of your damned vegetable friends. Believe me, if your family were here or if I thought there was anything that you loved more in life, I would gladly destroy it, too—"

"I'll kill you—" Momaw Nadon shouted, his stereophonic voice ringing through the dome surprisingly loud.

"You?" Alima asked. "If I thought you had it in you, I'd have brought a squadron of men. No, you'll cave in to my demands, just as you have in the past!"

Alima turned and walked away, unconcernedly, and Nadon could do nothing but watch helplessly even though rage burned within him.

When Alima had left, Nadon went to his grove to see if he could save the wounded Bafforr, but the pale blue sheen of its glasslike trunk was already turning black in death.

He reached out for the trees with his mind. Nadon fell to his knees in the mossy turf under the dark leaves and pleaded, "Now? Now may I kill him?"

The leaves of the living Bafforr trees circling him rustled dimly in response. "What? What happened? Who touches us?"

Momaw Nadon listened to the trees' voices. Their number had been reduced from seven trees down to six—just below the number needed for the grove to achieve true sentience. He could not tell how much they might understand. "Momaw Nadon, a friend, touches you. Our enemy killed a member of your grove. I wish to punish him for his act."

"We understand. You cannot break the Law of Life," the Bafforr whispered with finality. "We forbid it."

Nadon backed away without closing his eyes in the traditional sign of acceptance. Perhaps the Bafforr were willing to die for their principles, but Nadon could not sit by quietly and let them.

He considered his options. He *could* search for the droids, give in to Captain Alima's demands.

The thought was so revolting that it caused Nadon physical pain, made his eyes feel gritty and itch. Nadon rubbed his forehead between his eyes with his long thin fingers, physically stimulating a pleasure-inducing gland along the ridge of his brow so that he could think clearly again.

If the Empire wanted those two droids so badly, then it was imperative that the Empire *not* get them.

No, Nadon had to fight. Lieutenant Alima was a dangerous man—as vicious as they come. He would leave a trail of charred and mutilated victims behind in his search for the droids, and sooner or later, someone would tell him what he wanted to know.

As much as Nadon detested violence, he knew that Alima was a monster, someone who must be destroyed. It would be a small loss to the Empire, an ineffectual blow, but Alima represented a constant, undeniable threat to the Rebel Alliance.

Just as importantly, by letting Alima live, Nadon would be allowing the man to kill more plants, more people. Nadon couldn't allow Alima to live.

In another room a sprinkler system softly hissed to life, and Nadon took that as a signal to leave. He checked his utility belt for some credit chips, then went out the front door.

Down the street, he spotted three stormtroopers on guard, standing together talking. They didn't hide the fact that they were watching his house. Nadon had to walk past them. The flashing red lights on their blaster rifles testified that the rifles were set to kill. As Nadon passed, one of the stormtroopers peeled away and followed at a discreet distance.

The streets were crowded now that full night had hit and the blistering temperature had fallen to a comfortable level. Nadon passed through the markets and had no trouble losing the stormtrooper.

Nadon made his way to Kayson's Weapons Shop. The gruff human who owned the shop had been in business forever, but Nadon had never set foot on the premises. It took less than five minutes to buy a heavy blaster and a holster that could be concealed under Nadon's cloak, then the Ithorian was back out the door.

He wandered the streets aimlessly for nearly an hour, without any kind of plan. He simply hoped to spot Lieutenant Alima, pull his blaster, and shoot the human. Nadon knew that nothing much would be accomplished by such an action. He would kill the human, but in the end he would forfeit his own life. The precious Bafforr trees in his home would be uprooted by whoever took over his house, and one way or another he would never be able to speak with them again. But at least they would not be tortured by the likes of Alima.

He set the blaster to kill, then searched the streets until he heard the scream of fire sirens in his own neighborhood. For a moment he was struck with horror, fearing that Lieutenant Alima had already come to burn his house, but as he ran up the streets, Nadon saw that some trader's home was a roaring blaze.

Firelight reflected from the column of smoke, lighting the streets and alleys in a dull red.

From every home, people were running toward the house with foam canisters. Water was so precious on Tatooine that the authorities would probably let the house burn rather than waste the water used in the foam extinguishers, but if the hapless owner of the home was in the vicinity, he might purchase enough canisters—at inflated prices—to rescue his valuables.

From the corner of his eye, on a side street, Nadon glimpsed the dark uniform of an Imperial officer with its billed cap. He turned just in time to recognize Lieutenant Alima walking steadfastly up the hill toward the fire.

Nadon rushed up the street parallel to Alima's path, then turned down the next alley, running toward Alima. He pulled out his blaster, fumbled with it momentarily. The gun was not made to accommodate an Ithorian's extraordinarily long, thin fingers, and Nadon could hardly get his finger into the trigger guard. He found that his hearts were racing, thumping wildly in his chest like a pair of Jawas in a struggle.

Nadon huddled against a wall, and checked the side streets in three directions. He could not see anyone. Good. There would be no witnesses.

Alima walked into the open not a meter away, and Nadon shouted his name, pulled the blaster up level to Alima's face.

Alima turned and looked at the Ithorian calmly, glanced at the blaster.

"Come here, into the alley!" Nadon commanded. His mind was racing, and he could not think what to do. He thought of pulling the trigger, but he wanted to talk first, to tell Alima why he felt he had to do this. Perhaps, Nadon thought, he will even repent. Perhaps he will turn away from the Empire. Nadon's legs cramped, aching with the desire to run, his species' preferred response for coping with danger.

Alima laughed. "You can't kill me with a blaster set to Stun," he said. Nadon knew he had set the blaster to Kill, but feared that perhaps it had been knocked off the setting by accident. Nadon glanced down in horror at the indicator lights on the blaster, saw the red flashing lights of the Kill setting. Just as Nadon realized his mistake, Alima dodged from Nadon's line of fire and pulled his own blaster.

A blue bolt tore through the darkness, slamming Nadon between his stomachs, knocking the big Ithorian into the stone wall at his back. For a moment, it seemed that a white sun blazed before his eyes, and then Nadon found himself lying on the ground in a dark alley, and someone was kicking his right eyestalk. Blood oozed from the wound. Nadon reached up with his long arms, trying to cover his eyestalks, and he moaned loudly.

His attacker stopped kicking, apparently more from being winded than from any desire to offer mercy. "You pacifist species are so pathetic in battle," Alima said, standing over Nadon, panting. "You're lucky that *my* blaster *was* set to Stun!"

Nadon groaned, and Alima waved two blasters in his face. "Find me those droids! You have until sunset tomorrow!" He pointed his blaster between Nadon's eyes and pulled the trigger again.

Nadon woke with a throbbing ache in his eyestalks. It was nearly dawn, and a pale light washed through Mos Eisley, turning the pourstone buildings to golden domes. Nadon wiped the blood from his face with his cloak, then managed to crawl to his knees. He felt as if he stood in a whirling fog that threatened to sweep him away, and he leaned against the side of the building for support.

Stupid. I was stupid, he realized. For one split second, Nadon had had the opportunity to kill Lieutenant Alima, and he had failed to do so. Even though Nadon understood intellectually that the Empire could only be overthrown by violence, his Ithorian nature had not allowed him to kill.

Nadon closed his eyes, tried to blink away the pain. He glanced up. A thin smoke hung over the city, and people were already beginning to scurry for cover from the morning heat.

Nadon got up and wearily headed for home, his ears still ringing. He shook his head, tried to clear it. He went into his house, sat beside a pool and washed the blood from his eyestalk. During the cool of the night, moisture had condensed at the top of the dome. Now it sometimes fell like droplets of rain. Above his head was a large gorsa tree, a stout flowering tree that used phosphorescent flowers to attract night insects for pollination. Now that morning had come, the pale orange phosphorescent flowers were folding in on themselves.

In Mos Eisley it was rumored that Momaw Nadon's house was filled with carnivorous plants. Nadon encouraged the rumor in order to keep out water thieves. Besides, the rumors were true, but those who walked through the biospheres under the High Priest's protection did not have anything to fear.

Nadon went to a side dome where vines and creepers hung from a large, red-barked tree that stood beside a pool. Nadon said, "Part your vines, friend."

The tree's limbs quivered, and the vines parted, exposing the trunk. In the dim light of morning, four human skeletons were revealed hanging from the limbs near the trunk of the tree, each with a thick creeper wrapped around its neck—hapless water thieves.

Nadon fumbled beneath some thick grass near the tree's trunk, pulled at a handle until a concealed door jerked upward. A light flipped on below him, showing the ladder leading down.

Nadon had secreted many a Rebel in the room below, and for a long moment he considered climbing down himself, hiding. Perhaps in this concealed chamber, he would be able to disappear from view for a while. Alima could ignite a thermal detonator in this room, but there was a chance that Nadon could ride out the firestorm intact, remain hidden.

He had enough food stored here to last for weeks. And Nadon was sorely tempted to climb down.

But he couldn't. He couldn't let Alima kill his plants. One last chance, Nadon thought. When Alima comes this evening, I might be able to kill him yet.

Nadon got up, strolled through his biosphere, touching the limbs of trees, stroking the gentle fronds of ferns, tasting the scent of moisture and undergrowth, the life all around him.

There was no other way, Nadon realized.

He would have to remain and fight, though it cost him all. In the evening, Alima would come. Nadon knew that Lieutenant Alima would be true to his word. He would sew Nadon's eyes open and make him watch as he slew the Bafforr. It would gratify Alima's little Imperial heart to know how he had tortured an Ithorian, leaving Nadon alive to bear witness to the Empire's cruelty. Alima would then incinerate the house.

Momaw Nadon considered what that would mean.

All of his plants would be destroyed, all of his notes. Years of work would be wasted. Nadon considered the plants, decided that he would take some containers outside, saving the specimens that showed the best hope of improving the ecology of Tatooine.

The Bafforr would die—they could not be uprooted —but the Bafforr had accepted their fate, and Nadon realized that now he must accept his.

For years Momaw Nadon had hidden on this rock, seeking cleansing, trying to overcome the anger that insisted he should fight back against the Empire. The elders of Ithor had balked when he suggested that the Empire was a weed that needed to be destroyed. His elders would have let the Imperials destroy the Bafforr forests of Cathor Hills, trusting that some shred of decency left in Alima would make him stop short of genocide against an entire species. His elders would have forgiven the Empire.

But in all his years seeking spiritual cleansing, Nadon had never been convinced that he was wrong. He believed that he had been right to try to save what he could.

Nadon was not above killing an insect to save a tree.

So, Nadon had to resist the Empire the best he knew how. Even if that meant he had to watch the Bafforrs be destroyed. Even if it meant he himself was destroyed. He could not just let the Empire crush him.

Nadon was exhausted, but could not sleep. He decided to calm himself by continuing his Harvest Ceremony. He went to his laboratory on the east wing of the house, opened the fruit of a large Tatooine hubba gourd, and removed some pale, transparent seeds. Using tiny robotic manipulators, he carefully opened four young seeds and removed the zygotes.

Using his genetic samples from the Cydorrian driller trees, he put the DNA into a gene splicer. Nine genes controlled the drillers' root growth. Nadon took these genes, spliced them into the hubba gourd zygotes, then returned the gourd's zygotes to a nutrient mixture so that they could grow.

The whole painstaking ritual calmed Nadon immensely, even though he knew that soon most of his work would probably be destroyed. The task took nearly twelve hours, and when Nadon looked up from his work, he saw by the shadows on the wall that nightfall was approaching. Soon, Alima would come.

Time to say good-bye, Nadon whispered. At this time of the day, his good friend Muftak would be trying to cool himself off at Chalmun's cantina—a difficult task considering the thickness of the four-eye's furry white pelt.

Nadon went to the cantina, thinking furiously, wondering how he might best lure Alima into the dangerous depth of his own personal biosphere.

The cantina was as busy as usual—bustling with disreputable aliens. It was a tough place, frequented by cruel beings.

Sure enough, Nadon found Muftak sitting alone at a table, sipping polaris ale while his partner in crime, the little thief Kabe, chittered and wandered about in the darkness, begging Wuher the bartender for juri juice and eyeing the pockets of the cantina's inhabitants.

Nadon spoke to Muftak of inconsequential things— the price that Muftak had gained for selling Nadon's name, Muftak's dreams of home. Always, Nadon tried to accentuate the positive, to leave his friend uplifted, but Nadon's own thoughts were dark, and when they drank a toast, Nadon found himself offering comfort that he himself could not receive.

Suddenly there was a disturbance in the cantina: A hideously scarred human named Evazan and his alien sidekick Ponda Baba were picking a fight with some wide-eyed local moisture boy. "I have the death sentence on twelve systems!" the scarred human warned. Nadon looked at the small group. The moisture boy was unfamiliar, some farmer from the desert who had come in only moments earlier with the old mystic Ben Kenobi. Nadon had seen Ben only once before, when he'd come into town to shop. Nadon had noticed the pair because the barkeep Wuher had shouted for them to leave their droids outside. Evazan and Ponda Baba were regulars, had been hanging around the spaceport for weeks.

Suddenly, Ponda Baba swung a clawed arm, bashing the moisture farmer across the face, sending the boy crashing against a table. Ponda Baba then pulled a blaster free just as Wuher shouted from behind the bar, "No blasters!"

Old Ben Kenobi whipped out an ancient lightsaber. It hummed to life, flashing blue as he slashed off Ponda Baba's arm, sliced Evazan's chest. Then he flipped off his lightsaber and cautiously backed away with the young moisture farmer in tow.

Nadon followed Ben Kenobi with his eyes as the music went silent. The bloodshed nauseated Nadon. Old Ben Kenobi took his young friend to the back of the cantina, and together they spoke with the Wookiee smuggler Chewbacca, then retired to a private cubicle with Chewbacca's partner, Han Solo.

"I think I should be going," Nadon said to Muftak. "Things are getting hot in here."

"Please," Muftak said heavily. "One last drink for old times. I'm buying."

This was such an unusual offer that Nadon didn't dare refuse. They ordered another round, and Nadon sat talking for a few more moments with Muftak, said his good-byes. A moment later, Ben and his moisture boy got up from their table at the back of the bar, and a seed of thought sprouted in Nadon's head. He wondered what business the old mystic from the Jundland Wastes might have in town with smugglers, especially bringing a moisture farmer in tow.

Then he remembered the droids that Ben Kenobi had with him, and Momaw Nadon saw the truth: Ben Kenobi was trying to smuggle the droids off Tatooine.

In that one second, Momaw Nadon's hearts beat wildly and he saw his salvation. Nadon knew exactly where to look for the droids, and if he told Alima, then the lieutenant would spare his life.

But as old Ben Kenobi passed him, the mystic

glanced calmly into Nadon's eyes, and somehow, Nadon suspected that Kenobi knew what he was thinking. Ben and the moisture boy walked past, yet Ben said nothing to Nadon.

"Did you see the way he looked at you?" Muftak asked. "Like a Tusken Raider staring down a charging bantha. What do you think that was all about?"

"I have no idea," Nadon said. Yet he looked down at the table, ashamed even to have thought of sacrificing someone else in an effort to escape his own pain.

Nadon fell silent for a moment, glanced around the room. Certainly, if Nadon could figure out what was happening here, others might also. Yet Ben Kenobi was not a regular in town, and few in the cantina would have recognized him. No one followed the old mystic out.

Muftak laid a hairy paw on Nadon's smooth gray-green arm. "You are afraid, my old friend. Your worries weigh on you. Is there anything that I can do?"

Blaster fire erupted from a cubicle at the back of the cantina, and Han Solo stepped out, holstered his blaster. He puffed out his chest in false bravado, threw a credit chip to Wuher as he left.

Muftak put a hairy paw to his head and scratched.

"I think I had better be leaving, too," Momaw said. "I don't want to be here if the Imperials come to investigate."

Momaw hurried out, looked up at the suns dropping toward the horizon. Time for the torture to begin.

He glanced up in despair, wishing that he were like Han Solo, wishing that he could kill someone who merited death, then walk away calmly. But he couldn't. Even in his deepest rage, he could not harm another. And so, there was nothing left to do but save what he could.

Momaw Nadon breathed deeply for a moment, then hurried home and began carrying the most valuable of his plant samples and setting them outside the back door in the hope that they would escape the fire.

The streets were nearly deserted, except for a few stormtroopers that watched the house.

When this is done, Nadon promised himself as he worked, I will go home. I will repudiate the elders and their foolish traditions. I will bear the limbs of the burned Bafforr trees in my arms, and I will show the elders my scarred eyes, and then they will see how monstrous the Empire has become, and they will know that we must fight.

Nadon chuckled to himself. Somehow, his spiritual eyes had been sewn open long ago. He'd seen the evil, known he had to fight it. But when Alima came and made the act physical, then Nadon's scars would bear witness to his people. The Ithorians were not a stupid species. They were not as hopelessly pacifistic as Lieutenant Alima and his Empire believed. Though they might never go to war themselves, they could still help fund the Rebellion. Perhaps this one small evil act could turn against Lieutenant Alima in the long run. The Empire's evil will betray itself, Nadon told himself.

As he considered the possibilities, Nadon felt a strange rush of hope. Perhaps his suffering would be worth something after all. Perhaps he could end this seclusion, return to his wife and his son and the vast forests of Ithor.

And as Nadon considered the possibilities, he realized that his loneliness and suffering here as an outcast on Tatooine did not hurt so much. His deepest regret, he found, was not the pain he had endured, but that his work here—his plant samples—would be destroyed. On Ithor, the people had a saying: "A man is his work." Never had the saying felt more true. By destroying the results of Nadon's labor here on Tatooine, Alima would destroy a part of Nadon.

Nadon stood gazing down at his little plants sitting in the sunlight outside the door, decided to carry them across the street, give them a better chance of survival.

The muted explosions of blaster fire punctured the air and began echoing from buildings. Nadon looked up from his labors. Down the street, stormtroopers that had been guarding his house all began running toward the spaceport. Nadon looked up in time to see Han Solo's old junker, the *Millennium Falcon,* blasting into the sky.

So, Nadon realized, old Ben Kenobi's droids made it off Tatooine. He watched the ship for several moments to make sure that none of the planetary artillery fired on the *Falcon*. When he was certain that the ship had gotten away, he found himself running behind the stormtroopers toward the docking bays.

Outside the bays, some Imperial captain stood before dozens of stormtroopers and port authorities, shouting in a frantic rage: "How could this happen? How could you let all four of them get away? Someone must be held accountable, and it won't be me!"

There at the back of the crowd, Nadon saw Lieutenant Alima standing nervously, staring toward the ground. No one was stepping forward to claim responsibility for Solo's breakout, and the frantic look in the captain's eye suggested that he needed a scapegoat.

The evil of the Empire will turn against itself. A man is his work. You cannot break the Law of Life.

Nadon realized what he must do. He could never kill a man, but he could stop Alima. He could sabotage the man's career, get him demoted even further.

Nadon called out to the Imperial captain: "Sir, last night I informed Lieutenant Alima that a freighter owned by Han Solo would be blasting out of here with two droids as its primary cargo. I suspect that your lieutenant's negligence in letting Solo escape goes beyond ineptitude, and should be considered criminal in nature."

Nadon looked at Alima, wondering if he could make such charges stick. Nadon had a perfect memory. He would never get tangled in a snare of his own lies, so long as he chose those lies carefully.

"No!" Alima shouted, giving Nadon a pleading look that betrayed profound horror. The Imperial captain was already fixing Alima with a dark stare. Stormtroopers stepped aside, clearing a path between the two men.

The captain glanced back at Nadon. "Would you swear to this under oath, Citizen?"

"Gladly," Nadon said, seeing ways that he could make his false testimony stand up in a military tribunal. The two had met alone in Nadon's house. Surely Alima had listed his meeting with Nadon in his personal logs. Nadon knew that as Ithorians—a race of peaceful cowards—his people were known as easy targets for intimidation. Nadon could claim that Alima had tortured the information from him. Certainly, with the bruises and bloody eyestalks, he could show that he'd been tortured. There was a good chance that Alima would be demoted—perhaps even imprisoned.

The captain glanced back at Alima and said, "You know what Lord Vader would do if he were here." Before Nadon had time to blink, the captain pulled his blaster and fired into Lieutenant Alima three times. Blood and gobbets of roasted flesh spattered across the courtyard.

Nadon stared in shock, realizing belatedly that the captain had not wished to convene a tribunal. He simply needed a scapegoat.

"I will expect your testimony to be recorded," the captain said. Momaw Nadon stood blinking, unable to move, and the suns seemed to have gone cold. He wavered, feeling faint. The stormtroopers all began walking away, apparently heading toward a transport so they could leave Tatooine. The Law of Life kept running through Nadon's mind like a litany. "For every plant destroyed in the harvest, two must be cultivated to replace it."

Nadon knew that his act would require penance. The blood of a man was on his hands, and such a stain could not easily be removed. But surely the Bafforr would understand. Surely they would forgive him.

At last, before the Imperial medics could arrive, Nadon forced his legs to move. Numbly, he went to the warm corpse, leaned over, and took two golden needles from his belt. He inserted the needles and removed the genetic samples. On Ithor were cloning tanks that would allow him to create duplicates of Alima. For his penance, Nadon would nurture Alima's twin sons. Perhaps in their day, they too would grow wise and kind, serving as Priests on Ithor, promoting the Law of Life.

Nadon packed the needles in his utility belt, then headed toward his biosphere. There would be so much to do before he left Tatooine—depositions to give the Imperials, plants to be uprooted in preparation for the move, hubba gourd seeds to be sown in the wilds.

A stiff wind kicked up, and stinging sand blew in from the desert. Nadon closed his eyes against it, and allowed himself to become lost for a moment in the memory of his wife's final embrace as he was banished from Ithor, and in the memory he relished the scent of his young son. "I will be waiting here for you if you ever return," she had said. And for the first time in ages Momaw Nadon walked free and his steps felt light. He was heading home.

Be Still My Heart:
The Bartender's Tale

by David Bischoff

On his way to work, Wuher, after-double-noon shift
bartender at the Mos Eisley Spaceport Cantina,
was accosted. To make matters worse, the accoster was
his least favorite of the many things that congregated
in this most egregious of congregations of intergalactic
scum.

An extensor whipped from the pale shadows of the
alley, wrapping around his ankle lightly, yet with
enough strength to detain him. Automatically, Wuher
reached to the back of his belt for his street-club. A
weapon of some kind was always a necessity for those
who strode the byways of a haven for cutpurses and
cutthroats like Mos Eisley. However, the pathetic voice
from the juncture of walls and garbage cans gave him
stay.

"Please, sir. I mean you no harm. I humbly request
asylum."

Wuher blinked. He rubbed his grimy sleeve over his
puffy eyes. He'd drunk too much of his own barbrew
last night and overslept. He had a faint growl of hang-
over nagging him; he was in no mood to deal with
riffraff begging for shelter or alms.

"Get off me," he snarled. "Who the hell are you?"
Wuher was a surly sort who preferred to keep his

thoughts to himself. He also had a rather aggressive
curiosity sometimes, though. This was a trait that his
employer, Chalmun the Wookiee, found to be a re-
source in the chemical experimentation aspects of
Wuher's work, but claimed would ultimately cause him
grief.

"I am Ceetoo-Arfour," squeaked the voice, accompanied by a curious blend of whistles and clicks. "I
have escaped from the Jawas, who intend to utilize me
for spare parts, despite extreme functional utility if I
am left in one piece—to say nothing of the value of my
consciousness. Through sheer good luck, the Jawas
used a corroded restraining bolt, which fell off, allowing me to escape."

Wuher moved farther into the shadows, his eyes adjusting farther away from the ambient, anguished
brightness that was one of the planet Tatooine's
charming qualities. There, amongst the stacked refuse
and plastic and metal containers, squatted one of the
oddest things that Wuher had ever laid eyes upon. And
Wuher had laid eyes upon far too many of these scuttling tech-rats for his taste.

"You—you're a blasted *droid*!" he spat.

The metallic creature released what little tension was
left in the extensor and cringed back with the vehe-
mence of Wuher's accusation.

"Why, yes sir, I am indeed. But I assure you, I am no
ordinary droid. My presence on Tatooine is a mistake
on a veritable cosmic level."

The droid's body was low and rounded, similar to
the streamlined contours of R2 units. However, this
was where the similarity ended. Bulbs and boxy ap-
pendages hung like balconies on the robot's sides,
amidst an array of two whiplike metal extensors and
two armatures invested with digits. In the very middle
of its sensor-node "face" was an opening with a grill,
set with what appeared to be jagged, sharp teeth. The
whole affair looked cobbled together, as though the
droid had indeed begun its life as an R2 unit, but had
been sent onto other paths with the help of a de-

mented mechanical mind owning a half-baked electronic and welding talent.

"Wait a minute. You look like a souped-up Artoo unit, but you sound like one of those pansy protocolers!"

"My components include aspects of both units, as well as several more. However, my specialties include meal preparation, catalytic fuel conversion, enzymatic composition breakdown, chemical diagnostic programming, and bacterial composting acceleration. I am also an excellent blender, toaster oven, and bang-corn air-popper, and can whip up an extraordinary meal from everyday garbage."

Wuher goggled at the plasteel contraption in disbelief.

"But you're a *droid*. I *hate* droids."

"I would be of extraordinary use!"

Wuher wondered why he was even giving the droid the time of day. Damned curiosity, that must be it. He needed a blasted brain scrub, that's what *he* needed. "Look, machine excrement. I despise your kind, as does my boss, for good reason. Even the lowliest Jawa knows what tribe he's from, even if he's stabbing that tribe in the back. You droids—who knows who you are or where you're from. You look like bombs, and nine times out of ten you blow up in the face of your owners, doubtless just to spite them." Wuher lifted a foot, planted it squarely on the thing's head. "Now get out of my way. I have work to do!" He gave the thing a shove. It rolled back, beeping, into the recesses of its corner as Wuher proceeded on his way.

"Sir! Kind sir! Forgive my offense! Reconsider! I shall be here all day, recharging my batteries. I dare not emerge in sunlight, for the Jawas will find me. Grant me asylum, and you will not be sorry, I swear."

"Pah! The word of a droid. Useless!" the man snarled in contempt.

With grand, elevated disgust, Wuher hurried away. Just one more proof that he should not be so free about strolling through alleys to save a scant few seconds. He avoided the darker, cooler ones, since they tended to attract crowds. This one, though, was lighter and Wuher had thought it would be a safe shortcut.

The normal byways of Mos Eisley were a dusty cloud through which double suns beat beat beat hot radiation upon ugly buildings and hangars. Occasionally a roaring beast of a spaceship would propel itself into the brightness of the sky, or descend shakily to hunker down in hiding. The place smelled even more strongly of its usual blend of noxious space fuels and heated alien body effluvia, touched with the occasional whiff of exotic spice, or rather more mundane rot or urine. Wuher noticed amidst the urban burblings a larger number of speeders than usual, as well as a discomfiting percentage of stormtroopers.

Something odd was afoot, that was certain.

Oh, well. It just meant that maybe he'd be busier at the cantina today. Another shuck, another buck, as Chalmun so eloquently stated.

Still, as the human bartender bustled through the busy streets, sun hood up, squinting, he was bothered by that droid who had accosted him. Wuher was well aware that droids were essentially harmless. To hate them was like hating your latrine or stove or moisture vaporator if they'd somehow been overlaid with innocuous consciousness. True, droids tended to be essentially faithless, with no ethical or racial structure. So were a lot of biological aliens that Wuher had met. The truth, the bartender knew, was that droids were an easy target.

Wuher had been abandoned on Mos Eisley in early youth, a human amidst peoples who disliked humans. He'd been kicked about and spat upon all his squalid, hard life. His boss hated droids essentially because they didn't drink and thus took up necessary room in the cantina that might be occupied by paying customers. Wuher hated everyone, but droids were the only creatures he could actually kick with impunity.

He was a bulky, middle-aged man, Wuher, with a constant late-afternoon-shadow beard, dark bags under his eyes, and a surly attitude from the top of his greasy head to the depths of his low stony voice. His eyes were hard and dark, and it was impossible to see anything but quotidian amoral stoicism in them. However, a small fire flickered in his heart, a dream that he kept alive with hard work through years of drudgery. At night, shuffling back to his grimy hovel, often as not a little tipsy from his own spirits, Wuher would gaze up at the night stars in the blessed cool and it would seem possible to actually reach up and touch them, possible to live out his fantasy.

Perhaps then, when that dream was achieved, he would no longer have to kick helpless, imploring droids to bolster his own pathetic self-esteem. Perhaps then he could give something to lesser creatures than he.

The lumpy mushroom shape of the cantina billowed before him. Wuher stumped around to the rear entrance. He took out his ID card, unlocked a door, and walked carefully down dark steps. He turned on lights. It was not dank down here in the cellar. There were no dank basements on a world like Tatooine. However, a dry, earthy smell was the foundation for all the other scents that fought for attention here, smells that hung upon the rows of laboratory equipment, barrels and tanks and vats that rose from tables and the floor like ridges of metal, plastic, and glass mold.

Chalmun imported a minimum of drinking materials, the cheap bastard. The rest of what the Mos Eisley Cantina served was either made in the city, or down here.

Wuher had little time. His shift topside started soon. Nonetheless an urgent sense drove him to a small alcove in the rear section, a portion of the large basement where the other employees seldom ventured. He turned on a small light there, revealing a machine consisting of coils, tubings, dials, and glass beakers. In the largest of these beakers, a small amount of dark green fluid had collected. Wuher examined the dials detailing gravity and chemical composition. A kind of acrid effluvia hung over the enclosure, like moldy socks. Sweet music to Wuher's nostrils! And the dials and digital readouts—why, they displayed almost exactly the ratios of contents that Wuher had calculated was necessary. A shiver of excitement passed over him. This could be the stuff. His elixir! His perfect liqueur, suited expressly to the biochemical taste buds of no less a personage than Jabba the Hutt, for all intents and purposes lord and slave master of the criminal element of Tatooine.

Wuher contained his trembles, took a deep breath, and found a sterile dropper tube. He lifted the stopper of the beaker, inserted the tube, and sucked up a minuscule amount. Carefully, he withdrew the jade treasure.

Ah! If this distillation was the right stuff, the drink that Jabba the Hutt deemed to be the perfect liqueur, then what else could Jabba do but name him his own personal bartender, distiller, brewer, winemaster? Thus elevated in position, the lowly Wuher might gain reputation and monies that would allow him to ship off this anal juncture of a desert snotworld to some bright, pristine bar on a paradisal planet.

Wuher brought the tube toward his mouth. A dangle of fluid sparkled diamonds in the amber light. He let a touch drop to his tongue. A flash and sizzle. A sliver of gas slithered off. The pain was immediate, but he bore it. He allowed the flavoids to creep upon his palate like death marchers with cleated boots. He winced and cringed and endured. Rotwort. Skusk. Mummergy. Bitter and fiercely aromatic with a kicker alcohol afterburst.

Damn it, though. Not quite right. His bioalchemist instincts, having studied carefully Jabba's other favorite drinks, had synthesized a theoretical perfect amalgam, a liqueur that would delight the huge wormthing.

This was not quite it. A certain element was lacking. A certain gagging whisper of illusive yet ineffably attractive decadence.

Damn.

The bartender went to get his apron, and to trudge wearily up the stairs to where his smoky den of work awaited.

"Water!" demanded the green alien in its annoying language. "Bottled distilled water, bartender, and make no mistake! I've got the credits for the real stuff. This nose can tell if it's anything more or less!" The alien touched its absurd proboscis with one of its green digital members.

Wuher's nose twitched. Was it him, or was the stench in this pangalactic hole worse than ever? "Well, buddy. It's your call, but you look as if you could use something a little stronger."

The alien's jewellike eyes glittered with fury and its ears seemed to flap indignantly. "How dare you call me by a familiar name, you piece of human trash. Believe me, I am a valiant drinker of all manner of manly, powerful drinks. However, I make it a rule to accept such only from *real* bartenders."

A mangled face pushed itself across the underlit bar and into the conversation. "Actually, this guy makes some damn fine drinks for a lousy dung-eating native. Take it from me—Dr. Evazan. I've had many drinks in all twelve systems in which I've obtained a death sentence and these drinks here pass muster!"

Wuher nodded surly thanks. However, the arrogant alien would have none of it. This guy was a Rodian, Wuher knew—and a bounty hunter from the boastful affront of him. A particularly egregious combination.

"Nonsense," said the Rodian, tiny satellite addenda atop his head turning back and forth as though searching for some television channel. Disdain dripped from his tone. "Humans don't have what it takes to be a proper bartender. The two terms are mutually exclusive!"

This was the song that Wuher heard all too often. From the very first day that he'd graduated from his chemistry kit to a taste for interesting drinks and had parlayed that knack into a successful application to a sleazy but effective bartender correspondence school, he'd been dumped upon for wanting to take on the duties of serving drinks to an array of peoples from different planets, biomes, ecologies, what have you. Bartenders in these sorts of places, frequented by different and unique biochemistries, were more xeno-alchemists than simple pourers of drinks. You had to pay attention to what you were doing. Wouldn't do at all to serve up a nice glass of the variation on sulfuric acid that Devaronians enjoyed to, say, a Gotal. Likewise, a simple beer could make a Jawa shrivel up like a slug. It really wasn't that humans couldn't handle the challenge, it was generally that most of them didn't care to bother. Indeed, there were a few in old xenophobic Republic days who used the opportunities to slowly poison enemies.

"Hey, greenie," snarled Wuher defensively. "You go to Chalmun's office. My certification is right on his wall."

"I shall! And I shall make every effort to have you fired from this post. Your kind doesn't belong here." The Rodian leaned over the bar with its wide orby eyes and stared directly into Wuher's: his species very confrontational mode for expressing supreme contempt. Wuher's nostrils were immediately assaulted by a stronger dose of the odor he'd noticed before. He cringed backward.

"Pah. Coward!" The Rodian spat on him. "And be it known to you, 'bartender,' that I, Greedo, am highly valued in my employ by none other than Jabba the Hutt. I shall also make my complaint to him, after I take care of the business I have come to this lice-ridden cantina to deal with. Now. My bottle of pure water, please. And snap to it before I have to come and get it myself."

The odor was so strong that Wuher was momentarily stunned. Even as he reached down, pulled up a bottle of water, clicked off the top, he was in a fog.

That smell . . . Something about that smell . . .

Pheromones, surely. But unique pheromones, unlike any other that Wuher had sniffed. The bartender had a big nose, with highly trained and sensitive olfactory capabilities. This was one of the reasons he was such a good bioalchemist. Something about this Greedo—

The Rodian snatched the bottle away, contemptuously dumped a handful of credit chips on the counter, and marched away into a dark corner booth. Even though he'd had this kind of treatment before, it still stung Wuher. He felt like a pile of womp rat guano, and the fact that he could do absolutely nothing to avenge his slighted feelings made it all the worse. This, mixed with that smell. He could smell that smell to the corns on the soles of his feet. It touched him to the very core of his being, and he was not entirely sure why.

For the next moments, he was in a kind of reverie as he went about his work, serving. He worked up some nice drinks for the band, whose music had actually helped make working in this dump bearable. He served an Aqualish and the Tonnika sisters. He whipped up a gaseous delight for the blues-loving Devaronian. All the while in a sensory smog of anger and confusion.

He barely noticed the new arrivals until his assistant tugged on his tunic.

"Wuher. We've got a positive on the droid detector."

Alarm swept away the mental images as Wuher turned away and looked down at the little Nartian creature, two of his four arms still busy washing glasses.

"Thank you, Nackhar."

Wuher turned his attention to the entranceway, to where an old man and a young towheaded fellow were making their way into the light-speckled smoky darkness of the tavern, followed by a sparkling, mincing protocol droid and a rolling R2 model.

"Hey!" called Wuher in his best gruff voice. "We don't serve their kind in here."

There was some confusion.

He had to make his position clear. "Your droids. We don't want them here."

The droids left.

He got particular satisfaction from booting the droids out. It was one of the only exercises of power that Wuher truly felt comfortable with—it was a clear and free area in which he was sure he would offend no one else. Nonetheless, even as he watched the droids leave, something bothered him. The memory of that lone droid, stranded in that alley, pleading for assistance. Somehow, the pang of that memory merged with the strong scent of Greedo's pheromones to create a jarring unease and yet odd excitement in the bartender.

A young man in desert duds shook him and asked for some water. It took a couple of shakes to get a reaction out of Wuher, but finally the drink was served and Wuher went about his business, serving yet another squeaky ranat.

He was so immersed in his own particular funk that it took him a while to realize that an altercation was building. Wuher looked over to see that Dr. Evazan seemed to be having a confrontation with the young man. The older man stepped in and spoke. The next thing Wuher knew, there was a blinding flash.

Alarmed, he cried out. "No blasters! No blasters!"

A light sword swashed through the air. A chop, a flop —and the gun arm of Evazan's Aqualish companion separated from his body.

The old man and young man stepped away and after a moment of silence, the band struck up again.

"Nackhar," said Wuher to his assistant. "Please clean that up. I have work to do."

Even though the doctor had stood up for him, Wuher felt no kinship. The man was an ugly, bent, and demented creature. Nonetheless, there was no reason to litter the floor with blood and groans of the doctor's associate for an overlong time.

The Nartian scurried away.

Wuher went back to work.

A day's shuck, a day's buck.

Business as usual at the Mos Eisley Cantina.

Too bad Chalmun wasn't around. His imposing figure usually discouraged these kinds of shenanigans. That Wookiee that had been talking to the old man looked a bit like his employer, only taller and younger. He'd been hanging around before, with that larcenous smuggler Han Solo. The spacer had burbled something yesterday about the Wookiee being his first mate. Dangerous profession, that. Perhaps there were worse things in the universe than being dumped on by Rodians in the Mos Eisley Spaceport Cantina.

Still, it rankled, and Wuher could feel his anger and hatred roiling and coiling like a stepped-on sandsnake.

The next thing he knew, a pair of stormtroopers had come through the doors and immediately stepped to the bar.

"We understand there's been a ruckus here," said one in a muffled electronic voice through his white skull-like helmet.

"You bet," said Wuher. He looked around, saw the backs of the perpetrators at a table at the far end of the establishment. Curiously enough, sitting across from them were none other than Han Solo and his Wookiee first mate. "The old guy and the young guy over there."

He pointed. The sooner these troopers got out of here, the better. They made him nervous. The place had plenty of trouble enough as it was. Besides, stormtroopers were *terrible* tippers.

Wuher's mind dipped back into his musing as he went on automatic pilot, making up barium frizzes and frosty sulphates and even serving the odd shot and a draft. He even poured himself some of his own homebrew ale, to take some of the edge off the mild headache that sulked at the back of his skull. However, during all this he was still haunted by two things: that smell that still clung to his nostrils, and that squeaking droid. What was going to happen to it? Why should he care? And what did it say its specialty was?

His musings were suddenly interrupted by a loud blast.

All heads swung toward its origin, the table where Han Solo sat. The jaunty smuggler was rising up and walking toward the bar, sticking his gun back into its holster.

Wuher could not believe what he was leaving behind.

"Sorry about the mess," Solo said, flipping a two-credit chip toward Wuher. Normally, Wuher would have immediately slapped a palm down onto the coin to prevent its appropriation. However, he was far too stunned by what he saw to think about money.

There, flopped over at the table, was none other than Greedo the Rodian bounty hunter, a shred of smoke rising up from a blasted abdomen.

Greedo, dead as a starship rivet.

A kind of chill satisfaction moved through Wuher, a transection of reality and dream that did not occur often enough. True, creatures got killed in here all the time, and it would have given Wuher far more satisfaction to have actually been behind the trigger of that blaster, seen its power rip through that obnoxious, smelly—

A kind of transcendental realization flashed through the bartender. Thought processes meshed thunderously in his head, and it was as though the heavens had opened and the light of Cosmic Wisdom poured down upon him.

That droid . . . that odd, frightened droid . . .

He had to get it out of harm's way. He *had* to save it!

"Nackhar!" he called.

The little creature scuttled up. "Did you see that, sir? I say that Chalmun should take all guns at the door. I say—"

"Are you going to be the one to do the body searches, Nackhar?"

The assistant bartender was stunned speechless at the notion.

"Take over for me. There's an urgent task I must attend to. I shall be back soon. In the meantime, do not allow the body of the Rodian to be moved a centimeter. Don't let those Jawas trying to bag it take it out of here. Do you understand?"

"Yes. Of course—but if the police—"

"They can examine it all they want to, and there's no question about who did it. However, claim it in the name of Chalmun. It's officially our property now."

"But why can't you—where are you going?"

"I am embarking on a mission of mercy!"

Thus saying. Wuher left.

The droid was not amongst the refuse cans.

Alarm filled Wuher. The thing had said that it would be here until nightfall. Its absence could only spell foul play.

Wuher bent and examined the sandy floor. Sure enough, tracks. Fresh tracks, leading down the alley in the other direction. Without a further thought, either for caution or self-protection, the bartender hurled himself after them.

The droid must be saved.

He puffed through the twisting alleys, following the tracks. The ground told the story clearly enough. Droid tracks. A pair of small shoe tracks. A Jawa had scoped the metal being out, as it had feared. As he moved along, Wuher removed the club from the back of his belt. Within moments, he heard the telltale beeping and chitter: the sounds of the droid and its new master.

Wuher slapped himself against a wall, peered around the corner. Sure enough, there they were, waddling along. The Jawa had clamped a restraining bolt on the odd-looking droid. They were within yards of a main thoroughfare.

He must move quickly.

Without hesitation, Wuher the bartender leaped out from his concealment, ran up behind the Jawa, and fiercely and conclusively brought down his club upon the back of its hood. Thunk. The Jawa went down like a bag of smunk roots. Speedily, the bartender dragged the hooded creature back to a darker part of the alley, trailing a slight seepage of blood.

He went to the droid, examined its body, and found the restraining bolt. He pulled it off and tossed it after the downed Jawa.

The droid came alive.

"Sir! You have saved me. You have delivered me from my enemies!"

"That's right, Ceetoo-Arfour."

"You have undergone a change of heart. I knew it, I knew it, I could tell that deep within you there beat a heart of gold. That is why I risked my encounter with you. Why, this is marvelous. This is what they write stories about! A hard soul, changed for the better. Thank you, kind human. Oh, thank you!"

"You're welcome, Ceetoo-Arfour. Yes, I realized that you were a wronged droid. The squalor and sadness of my life made me realize that I should do something good and worthwhile for once." Wuher smiled. "However, we shouldn't just stand here and banter. There are doubtless more Jawas about. We should get you back to where it's safe."

"Oh, my lucky stars shine this day. Sir, you have redeemed my faith in the true pure spirituality of the human soul. For you see, we droids, though of metal, possess consciousness and thus spirituality as well."

"Oh, good. I'm sure we've got a lot of philosophy that we can discuss. First, though, we should hurry on," said Wuher solicitously. "Is there anything that I can do to ease your path?"

"You already have, kind sir. And here I was thinking myself the poorest, most bereft soul in Mos Eisley. There is indeed room for growth in the purity of the human soul."

"Yes, I have had a complete turnabout in my attitude

toward droids," said Wuher. "I am bringing you back to the cantina. I will hide you in the basement, where there are no droid detectors."

"Oh, oh!" said the droid, clearly enraptured by this stunning turnabout. "Finally, I experience the milk of human kindness."

"Oh," said Wuher, with a wry grin. "I don't think I'm particularly interested in *milk* today."

The drop depended, a jewel of promise.

Dropped.

The usual pain, of course. Too bad, but that was the price you paid for system incompatibilities. Still, Wuher bore it stoically, even gladly, awaiting the news his taste buds would bring. Already, his quivering nostrils were behaving in a positive fashion as the familiar wisp of steam rose to tickle them.

Around Wuher, as though hovering expectantly, were all the trappings of his experimental alcove, along with its two new additions . . .

Yes, yes, this was new!

He detected a hint of bergamot!

Better, something more. . . . and it struck him with such tremendous power, it was as though someone had kicked him in the head.

The taste of two bloody aliens arut in a tangle of erupting spice pods and mud mushers.

He fell off his stool, a spasm racking him.

"Master! Master!" cried Ceetoo-Arfour. "Are you all right?"

Wuher shivered.

He shuddered.

He arose, a silly smile on his face.

"Wow!"

He looked over at his still, at the larger beaker, already almost half full of this deadly elixir, and with so much more still bubblingly in the works in the coils and guts of his makeshift lab.

"It's even better than I'd hoped," he said. "This is exactly the liqueur that will appeal to Jabba the Hutt."

"Jabba the Hutt, Master?" said the droid. "Is he not the criminal gang lord of this territory?"

"Nonsense," said Wuher. "He is wronged by his enemies. He will not only be *my* benefactor, but ultimately yours as well."

"Indeed!"

"Yes. Of course. We're going into business together, Ceetoo-Arfour. First we shall work for Jabba the Hutt. Then we shall shake the miserable dust of this detestable planet from our heels. Greatness, Ceetoo. We are destined for greatness!"

The rough bartender beamed at his new collaborator.

Ceetoo-Arfour stood in the very center of the alcove. Below a new item that extruded from his barrel side—a spigot—was a small bottle full of an emerald-gray liquid. Just a few small drops of this stuff had been sufficient to give Jabba's liqueur its new and wonderful kick into the territory of greatness. Wuher, bioalchemist extraordinaire, was going to be able to keep Jabba the Hutt happy a very long time.

From the droid grill-jaw extruded a naked green alien foot, pausing for a moment before it too was processed to remove every last bit of precious juice in Ceetoo-Arfour's excellent chemical extractors.

Hanging on a spike by the bubbling still was the other new occupant of Wuher's bioalchemical alcove: the head of Greedo the Rodian. Nackhar had had to fight hard with those Jawas to procure the body. It had cost him several rounds of free drinks, but it had been worth it.

"Here's to your pheromones, Greedo," said Wuher the bartender, hoisting his dropper in toast. "Han Solo did both Rodian females and yours truly a vast favor."

The head glared back blankly.

"I must say, the creature was a gnarly, gristly thing," the droid said. "I'm afraid that my grinders shall be needing a sharpening after this arduous effort."

Wuher grinned and winked. "Nothing's too good for you, Ceetoo. Believe me, this is the beginning of a beautiful friendship."

For, indeed, now Wuher the bartender had an entirely new attitude toward droids.

Nightlily:
The Lovers' Tale

by Barbara Hambly

"Madam, I am most sorry." Feltipern Trevagg switched off the computer screen above his desk with the air of being anything but. "If you don't pay your water impost there isn't anything I can do about your water line being shut. I don't make the taxes."

As it happened, he *had* made this one, or at least made the suggestion to the City Prefect of the Port of Mos Eisley that the water impost be raised twenty-five percent. But, Trevagg reasoned, rubbing his head cones as he listened once again to the Modbrek female's frantic plea for more time, she probably wouldn't have been able to come up with the original impost, so it didn't really matter. What mattered was that now, through proper go-betweens of course, he'd be able to offer her a few thousand credits for her dwelling compound—which she'd be glad to accept, after going without water or food for a couple of days —and rent it out by the room. Provided, of course, he could arrange it with his go-betweens before the Prefect heard about it and outbid him.

The Modbrek female's distress irritated him. Coming from another of his own species—another Gotal— it might have evoked pity, though Trevagg had been less ready than many of his compatriots to yield to emanations of wretchedness and fear. But Modbreks were in Trevagg's opinion only semisentient, wispy ephemeral beings, hairless as slugs save for the grotesque masses of blue mane that streamed from their undeveloped heads, with huge eyes, and tiny noses and mouths in pointy pale faces. This female and her daughters, sending forth waves of anxiety, reacted on him as a kind of screechy music.

"Madam," he said at last, sighing, "I'm not your father. And I'm not a charity worker. And if you knew you couldn't pay your water imposts—which I assume you did know, since you've been in arrears for two months and neither you nor your daughters have troubled to find decent-paying work—you should have gone to your family or some charity organization before this."

He nudged a toggle on the control board of his desk. A human deputy in a rumpled uniform came in and showed the three females out. Trevagg could sense the man's pity for them, and also, much to Trevagg's disgust, the fact that the human found the insubstantial creatures physically attractive, even sexually interesting.

Of course, Trevagg had always had difficulty understanding how humans found *each other* sexually interesting. Wan, flabby, squishy, they lacked both the Gotal ability to transmit a range of emotional waves, and the contrast between strength and weakness so necessary to pleasure. How could anyone . . . ?

He shrugged, and turned back to his desk to tap through a call. Behind him he heard a step on the threshold, felt the heat of a body—no closer than the threshold, and human range—and recognized the electromagnetic aura as that of Predne Balu, Assistant Security Officer of Mos Eisley. Felt too like a smoky darkness the man's weariness, the bitter tang of his disgust.

"You couldn't have let her have another month?" Balu's raspy voice sounded tired. The heat of the Tatooine suns seemed to have long ago baked out of Balu the savagery, the enthusiasms so necessary to a hunter. Trevagg despised him.

"She's had two. Water's expensive to import."

A message flickered across the black screen of the receiver: PYLOKAM 1130. Trevagg moved a finger and the pixels wiped themselves away as if they had never been. He turned in his chair, to face Balu: a heavy man, slope-shouldered in his wrinkled dark blue uniform, hair black, eyes black, but the pitiful stubble of what humans called beard was thickly shot with gray. A head like a melon. Trevagg never could look at humans without feeling contempt and a little amusement. He knew they had other types of sensory organs than head cones, but even after many years on the space lanes—as bounty hunter, Imperial bodyguard, and officer of ship security—Trevagg had never gotten over how silly, how ineffectual, beings looked who didn't have cones. On Antar Four, though everyone knew in their heart of hearts that the size of one's cones didn't affect their ability to pick up sensory vibration, Gotals whose cones were undeveloped frequently resorted to falsies.

He simply, instinctively, had no respect for a being without them.

"Be ready with your deputy to close the water lines to her compound tomorrow."

Balu's mouth tightened under heavy cheeks, but he nodded.

"I'm going out. I should be back within the hour."

Walking through the marketplace of Mos Eisley always filled Trevagg with a sense close to intoxication. A hunter by upbringing as well as by blood, he had quickly found his current position as a tax official a disappointment. What had been represented to him as an opportunity for acquiring vast quantities of credits had turned out to be little more than a clerical stint.

Yet he sensed, he knew, that there were credits here to be made.

In the marketplace of Mos Eisley, the hunter stirred again in his blood.

Awnings flapped overhead in the baked breeze, the solar coats casting black rectangles of hard shadow, the cheaper cotton and rag staining the faces of those beneath them with red and blue light. The harsh sizzle of bantha burgers and much-used fritter grease swirled from a hundred little stands wherever some enterprising Jawa or Whiphid could find room to set up a solar-power stove. Races from every corner of the galaxy wandered the banded shadows of this makeshift labyrinth. In one place a corpse-faced Durosian was holding up strings of opaline "sand pearls" and sun-stained blue glass for a couple of inquisitive human tourists; in another, a nearly nude Gamorrean belly dancer was performing on a yellow-striped blanket to the appreciative whistles of a couple of Sullustans, who were among the many races to find Gamorreans attractive.

But more than anything else, it was the air of danger that filled the place, the edginess, the watchfulness, that soaked Trevagg's cones like drugged wine. After a walk in the marketplace he always came away wondering if he shouldn't pack in the Imperial service and go back on the hunt.

But as always, he looked around him a second time, and saw how many of these people were dressed in castoffs or shabby desert gear. He stroked his new jacket of deep green yullrasuede, his close-fitting trousers tailored for his form and no other, and thought again. He might not have made his fortune on this blasted piece of rock, but at least he could make a little.

And the opportunity would come.

Had come.

His pulses quickened at the implications of the vibration he'd sensed two weeks ago, walking through this very market. All he needed to do, he told himself, was be a hunter, and wait. The chance of his lifetime had come, and if he waited, it would come again.

If things went right.

Jabba the Hutt's go-between, an enormously obese Sullustan named Jub Vegnu, was waiting for him by Pylokam's Health Food booth. Pylokam, an aged and fragile human in trailing dirt-colored rags and a garish orange scarf, had been optimistically peddling fruit juices and steamed balls of vegetable gratings for years now, surrounded on all sides by a dripping banquet of dewback ribs and megasweet fritters—no sugars, no salts, no artificial additives, and no customers. Even Jabba had given up trying to get a percentage of his nonexistent takings.

Vegnu was leaning on the counter eating a caramelized pkneb—something Pylokam would never have stocked—the juice of it running down what chin he possessed; Trevagg bought a sugar fritter from a nearby stand and joined him. At Pylokam's they could be assured of being completely uninterrupted.

"I need to set up a go-between and a loan deal," grated Trevagg in his harsh, rather monotonous voice. "Immediate takeover in three days, complete secrecy from everyone. Ten percent to Jabba of all subsequent take."

They haggled a little about the percentage, and about what the deal was, Trevagg knowing full well that if word got to the Prefect—or indeed, to several other members of the Imperial service that he knew about—he'd be very likely outbid before the widowed Modbrek even decided she had to sell. In time Trevagg got guarantees of secrecy, for what they were worth, but at the cost of another four percentage points. At that rate, he thought bitterly, it would take him a year to make back his investment . . .

"Is that it, then?" the Sullustan inquired, licking his stubby fingers of the last traces of caramel and grease.

Trevagg hesitated, and the go-between—with almost Gotal sensitivity—tilted his head, waiting for what would come next. Seeming to feel, Trevagg thought, how big the coming deal was.

"Not . . . quite."

There was no need to scan the marketplace visually. Trevagg knew the hint he'd gotten, the buzzing, shivering sense he'd picked up in passing through two weeks ago, was nowhere around. And he didn't know when it would return, when the person—the creature—that had caused it would next pass through Mos Eisley.

But it was as well to be ready.

"I will need a go-between on another deal," he said slowly.

"For what?"

"I can't say." He held up his hand against Vegnu's impatient protest. "Not yet. But I need someone to act for me in a situation where, as an employee of the Imperial government, I would be expected to perform as a part of my duties."

"Ah." Vegnu leaned back against the counter. "But a civilian, performing the same task, would be rewarded?"

"*Well* rewarded," said Trevagg, his pulses stirring again at the thought of just how well rewarded. "And it's a task well within, say, your capabilities."

"How much?"

"Twenty percent."

"Gaah . . ."

"Twenty-five," said Trevagg. "And that five is for secrecy, for absolute secrecy, at the time."

"About you?"

"And about the . . . nature of the task."

The nature of the task, thought Trevagg, threading his way swiftly through the blazing slats of dust and shadow, heading back toward the government offices a few minutes later. *That is, after all, the delicate thing about this deal.* A simple task, informing the Imperial Moff of the Sector about someone . . . someone for whom they had been looking for a long time.

The sense that had come to him here in the market two weeks ago had been like finding a jewel in the dirt; the vibration itself like a sniff of perfume, scented once in other circumstances but never forgotten. The trick would be, of course, to keep his go-between from taking that jewel—that one piece of information, that name—and turning it in himself.

Trevagg the Gotal knew he would have to be very careful with this one, whose reward could get him the foundations of real wealth.

Passing through the market two weeks ago, he had picked up the unmistakable vibrations of a Jedi Master.

"Lady to see you," reported the operations clerk in the next cubicle as Trevagg reentered the office. After the blast furnace of the noon street the prefecture seemed shadowy and cool as a cave—the solar deflectors on the roof didn't really start having trouble until two or three hours past noon. Were it not for the shelves jammed with boxes of datadisks, the dust-yellowed hard copy drooping from overstuffed storage boxes stacked along one wall—were it not for the almost palpable atmosphere of defeat, of grimy hopes and petty spites—the offices themselves would be pleasant to enter after a time outside.

Only so long, thought Trevagg, as he strode toward his office. *Only so long will I have to put up with this place.* It was no place for a hunter to be, no place for a true Gotal.

Just until he could accomplish his final hunt, trap his final quarry. Until he could turn over to the Empire information about this Jedi, whoever he was . . .

It hadn't been a passer-through, that much Trevagg knew. After losing the sense of the Jedi's vibrations in the marketplace—the thick, strange buzzing in his cones that he had been told long ago was the concentration of the unknown Force, the magic of the Jedi— he had gone at once to the docking bays, ascertained that no vessel had taken off for the past several hours. As collector of imposts he had access to passenger lists, and had made it his business to personally check each traveler.

And in two weeks of roving every corner of Mos Eisley, he had never sensed that particular reaction again.

So it must be someone on the planet, but not in the town. Someone who had come to do marketing, for instance.

Trevagg was a hunter. He would wait.

His mind was full of this, rather than whoever this tedious female was and what she wanted of him, when he stepped through the office doorway—and fell in love.

The vibration of her filled the room, before she even turned at his entrance. It was an intoxicant, a heady compound of milky warmth that he could feel almost through his skin, of trembling vulnerability, of an electrospectrum aura like a new-blown pink teela blossom, and of an innocent and unself-conscious sexuality that almost lifted Trevagg off his feet.

She turned, putting back the white gauze of her veil, to reveal an alien loveliness that stopped his breath.

What race, what species she was, he didn't know. It didn't matter. Skin blue-gray as desert's final twilight molded over the proud jut of cheekbones any woman on his home planet of Antar would kill to possess, double, treble rows of them blending softly into the fragile ridges of the chin. More ridges led the eye into the graceful curve of proboscis, a feature Trevagg had always considered striking in such races—like the Kubaz or the Rodians—who possessed them. Eyes wide, green as grass, and fringed with ferny lashes peered timidly from beneath a deep splendor of brow ridge, like the eyes of a rock tabbit too frightened to flee a hunter's step.

But above the brow was what drew Trevagg's eyes. Half-hidden by the cloaking gauze of the veil, the skull rose into four perfectly shaped, exquisite conelets, their smallness, their smoothness seeming to invite the touch of a male hand, the breath of male lips.

Of course they couldn't really be cones, thought Trevagg the next moment. She was no Gotal, but some-one of the dull-minded and insentient lesser races . . . But the imitation was perfect, and it was enough.

He wanted her.

He wanted her badly.

"Sir . . ." Her voice was halting, but of a beautiful, even key, modulated like a deep-toned flute through the proboscis. Her three-fingered hands, skin tailored over jewellike knobs, seemed to cling to the edges of the veil she had just laid aside, as if for protection. "Sir, you must help me. They said I should come to you . . ."

Trevagg found himself saying, "Anything . . ." Then, quickly correcting himself, for he was, after all, an official of the Empire, he added, "Anything in my power to assist you, miss. What seems to be the trou-ble?"

"I have been put ashore." Distress and fear blos-somed from her in trembling waves. "They said there was something wrong with my papers; there was a pas-sage tax."

Trevagg knew all about the passage tax. That was something else he'd come up with.

"I . . . I had to budget very closely in order to visit my sister on Cona, I . . . my family is not wealthy. Now I've lost my seat on the *Tellivar Lady*. But if I pay the passage tax I won't have enough to return to my mother on H'nemthe.'' The name of her home world came out like a dainty sneeze, unbelievably entrancing. The vibration of her sorrow was like the taste of blood-honey.

"My dear . . .'' He hesitated.

"M'iiyoom Onith,'' she supplied. "The m'iiyoom is the white flower that blossoms in the season of trine, the season when all three moons give their light. The nightlily.''

"And I am Feltipern Trevagg, officer of the Empire. My dear Nightlily, I shall go investigate this matter at once. It grieves me to be unable to offer you better quarters to wait in, but this city is not a savory one. I shall return within moments.''

Balu was in the outer office, boots on desk, drinking a fizzy whose bulb sweated in the stuffy heat. He cocked a dark eye at the Gotal as Trevagg closed his office door. "Give the child back her seat, Trevagg,'' he grunted. "You don't need the seventy-five credits. You run, you can catch the *Tellie* before she lifts.''

Trevagg leaned across the officer and tapped a key on the board. The screen manifested the schedule. Unlike many Gotal, Trevagg had mastered computers quickly, once those in the prefecture had been properly shielded. The *Tellivar Lady* lifted at 1400, and he knew Captain Fane was punctual.

But an hour wouldn't be enough.

"Trevagg . . .'' The officer's voice halted him as he reached for the door. Trevagg turned, mostly from a desire to legitimately waste time—he'd have to walk very slowly indeed to actually miss the *Tellivar Lady*'s lift. "You're a hunter. You ever hear of the Force?''

Trevagg went absolutely cold inside. He only said, "No.''

"It's supposed to be some kind of magic field . . .'' Balu shook his head. "The old Jedi were supposed to have it.'' He lifted a hand to indicate the Imperial communiqué, tacked to the discolored plaster of the wall behind him, offering fifty thousand credits for "any members of the so-called Jedi Knights." Ten thousand for information leading to the capture of.

Unless, of course, it was the captor's or informant's job to capture or inform. Then they just got their salaries. And a nice letter of commendation from the local Moff.

"I heard rumors the Jedi have been seen on Tatooine," said Balu. "I've had a watch on Pylokam's stand—figuring the one place a Jedi might show up. Someone's got to drink that herb tea. But I wondered if you'd run across anything—strange."

"Only what Pylokam serves at that stand of his," grumbled Trevagg, and made a far more precipitate exit than he'd planned.

It still took him a great deal of dawdling on the way to reach Docking Bay 9 too late to stop the liftoff of the *Lady*.

Nightlily was dazzled to be taken to luncheon at the Court of the Fountain, the closest thing to a high-class restaurant Mos Eisley boasted. It occupied one of the sprawling stone-and-stucco palaces that dated from Mos Eisley's long-ago boom days; reflective solar screens had been stretched over the many courtyards where fountains trickled and gurgled among exotic plants and gemlike tiling. It was small, of course, and catered mostly to the tourist trade, but Nightlily *was* a tourist, and she was enchanted. Jabba the Hutt—because, of course, Jabba owned the place—boasted that there wasn't an appetite in the galaxy that couldn't be catered to by his personal chef, Porcellus.

Porcellus, who only operated the Court of the Fountain during those few hours not spent in preparing the Bloated One's gargantuan repasts, knew perfectly well that he'd be fed to Jabba's pet rancor if the Hutt ever grew bored with his menus, so he was an enthusiastic chef, indeed. And, in a way, he took great pride in his work. The filet of baby dewback with caper sauce and fleik-liver pâté was the best Trevagg had ever eaten, and when Nightlily hooned, with modestly downcast eyes, that virgins of her people were only permitted fruits and vegetables, Porcellus outdid himself in the production of four courses of lipana berries and honey, puptons of dried magicots and psibara, a baked felbar with savory cream, and staggeringly good bread pudding for dessert.

And a great deal of wine, of course.

"Nothing is too expensive for you, beautiful one," responded Trevagg, to her hummed protest about the expense. "Or too good. Have another glass, my darling." He would definitely, he thought, have to have a chef who could cook dewback like this when he collected his reward. "Don't you understand that fate has brought us together, fate in the form of a stupid ruling by a venal official?" He took her hand in his, loving the satin texture, the smooth eroticism of the way the knots on its back tightened and swelled at his touch. "Don't you understand what I feel for you? What I felt for you the moment I entered the office, the moment I heard your voice?"

The moment I sensed in you the ultimate prey, the most beautiful of conquests to be vanquished?

She turned her face aside, confused. The long silver serpent of her knife-pointed tongue ran nervously out to pick at the remains of the bread pudding in a gesture he found almost unbearably sexual. It had to be muscled to those three sets of cheekbones on the inside—what could he not persuade her to do with that tongue!

He wasn't sure exactly what inner vibrations he should transmit to convince her of his overwhelming desire for her—she obviously didn't have the civilized sensitivity of a Gotal, maybe couldn't pick up anything at all and was operating entirely at the face value of his words. Judging by her conversation, she was either barely sentient or truly stupid, and in any case, Trevagg had very little interest in females' thoughts or desires.

He cradled the side of her face with his hand, reveling in the daintiness of the cheekbones under his clawed strength. He felt her timidity, and with it, a dawning wonderment, a surge of glowing excitement in her heart.

"Don't you understand that I need you?"

"Are you proposing . . . marriage?" She stared up at him, awed, dazzled, halfway to surrender.

Softly he nuzzled the side of her face. Stupid as a brick, he thought. But he'd get this one into his bed before the day was through.

"Trevagg, leave the girl alone." Balu spoke in a low voice, so that Nightlily, in the outer office, would not hear. The security officer slouched in the doorway of Trevagg's cubicle while the Gotal keyed through a credit transfer and ticketing information on the *Starswan*, leaving early tomorrow morning. The least he could do, he reflected, was give the girl passage out of here—third class, naturally—to wherever the hell she was going. Besides, once he'd had her he certainly didn't want her hanging around under the impression that he was actually going to go through with *marrying* a semisentient alien bimbo, wondrous though she might be between the sheets.

"Leave her *alone?*" Trevagg turned around disbelievingly, staring at the human. He kept his voice quiet, still excluding Nightlily, who was just visible through the doorway past Balu's shoulder, sitting at an empty desk with her head bowed in shy ecstasy and her veils half drawn about her face. "You can be anywhere within four meters of that—that love morsel, and you say leave her alone?"

Balu turned his head to consider her. Trevagg could tell from the man's temperature and the vibration of his pulses, even at this distance, that he found her no more sexually stimulating than he'd have found a Jawa. Disgust flooded him at the sheer, galling insensitivity of humans.

"Trevagg," said the officer, "most species—most civilizations—ostracize members who bear hybrid children. If you find her attractive there's probably enough enzyme compatibility for you to *get* her with child. You'd be ruining her for life."

Trevagg emitted a sharp, barking laugh. "I can't believe you. You're within two meters of *that,* and you're talking to me about *enzyme compatibility*? Man, grow some gonads! If she was worried about that she shouldn't be traipsing around the galaxy in that flimsy little head-veil in the first place."

Balu put his hand on Trevagg's arm warningly, and the Gotal halted in surprise. Balu seldom showed any disposition to care about anything, but there was a definite threat in his dark eyes.

Patiently, Trevagg promised, "All right. I'm only taking her out for a walk. She can always say no."

But after three drinks at the Mos Eisley Cantina, he reflected, as he entered the outer office again and took Nightlily's arm—not to mention the prospect of marriage that seemed to push every switch on her board— it wasn't at all likely that she would.

"I can't believe that you would . . . would truly love me enough to wed," crooned the girl, as they crossed the brazen burnish of dust and sunlight in the street. "The males of my species . . . fear that commitment. That giving of all for love."

"The males of your species are fools," growled Trevagg, gazing deep into her eyes and drinking in the heady perfume of her sexuality. As far as he was concerned that went for the females too, but he didn't say so. He glanced back from the shadows of the buildings opposite, just in time to see a flicker of dusty robes, the trailing brightness of an orange scarf . . .

Pylokam the health-food seller. Crossing the street to the government offices.

The Gotal's mind seemed to click, all things falling into place with a hunter's cutting instinct. Balu. Pylokam had seen the Jedi.

His first reaction was sheer annoyance. He'd already told Nightlily he'd booked passage for her on the *Starswan,* and she'd flung her arms around him, asking if he had booked his own passage, to come to H'nemthe to marry her with due ceremony before her mother and sisters. He'd gotten out of that one by promising to embark within a few days—"I am an official of the Empire, you know. I can't just leave everything all in a moment, though, believe me, I will be counting the days." But it meant that there was no putting her off.

There was no reason for Pylokam to come to the impost offices other than to report to Balu, and he knew Balu, for all his world-weary slovenliness, was not one to waste time. He'd investigate—and he'd report.

And that meant Trevagg would have to find someone to assassinate Balu this afternoon.

Ordinarily, of course, he'd have gotten in touch with Jub Vegnu, set up a meeting, made an appointment with Jabba the Hutt, and arranged for payment . . .

But of course he knew—everybody knew—that freelance assassins were ten for a half-credit in Mos Eisley and most of them were supposed to hang out in the Mos Eisley Cantina. It couldn't be *that* difficult to meet one. The encounter would presumably be short and sweet—that's what assassins were for, to make life easy for those who had other things to do—leaving him plenty of the afternoon and all of the evening to conclude an encounter of another kind with Nightlily in the Mos Eisley Inn.

If entering the government offices from the noon street was like passing into a (more or less) cool grotto, transition from the late-afternoon dust and glare into the near-darkness of the cantina was comparable to being swallowed by a bantha with indigestion. Trevagg's hunter eyes switched almost instantaneously from day vision to night as a great drench of vibration hit him: overlapping electrospectrum fields, personal magnetic auras buzzing like a hive of bees, halos of irritation and annoyance swollen by the proximity of strangers and exacerbated by every sort of psycho- and neural relaxant known in the galaxy.

It was like the marketplace, only more sinister, without the bright spiciness of making a living. The thoughts and emotions swirling through the gloom were darker, more dangerous, against the brassy twirling of the little dark-clothed, insectoid band. "Are you sure it's safe?" hummed Nightlily, clinging once more to his arm, and Trevagg patted her hand. Her fear reacted on his hunter's instinct as her anxiety and distress had earlier—prey signals that read as an invitation to conquest. He felt an almost overwhelming desire to crush her in his arms.

Instead he cradled the back of her exquisite coned head in one hand, said, "With me, you're safe, my blossom. With me you'll always be safe."

They took one of the small booths to the left of the raised entry vestibule, Nightlily gazing around her, fearfully marveling. In addition to being a virgin, she had confessed to Trevagg over lunch, she had never been away from her home planet before, had never seen anything like this. As well she hadn't, thought the Gotal, amused at the way she relaxed under the influence of Wuher the barkeep's drinks computer. In another booth a completely illegal card game was in progress between a ghoulish Givin, a giant one-eyed Abyssin, and a big fluffy white thing of a species even Trevagg had never seen; in another a shaggy, ferocious-looking Wolfman sipped his drink alone. While Nightlily sighed, and giggled over her second drink, and asked him, "Are you truly sure, beloved? Mating is such a solemn thing, such an awe-inspiring thing . . ." Trevagg was searching the crowd with his eyes and, more importantly, with his cones, seeking out the vibrations of danger and blood, the vibrations of another hunter, as he had once been.

"It is as nothing," Trevagg said. "No sacrifice is too great for what I feel for you." The fact that she couldn't even detect him in a lie—that she didn't have that much sensitivity to the vibrations of his mind—only redoubled his contempt for her. *So desirable—so innocent—so* stupid . . . *No wonder they don't let virgins travel off her planet.* She'd told him that, too. *They'd never make it home.*

Not as virgins, anyway.

Meantime, his hunter senses roved the dark forms, seeking another hunter.

The two tall human females drinking by the bar were a maybe: They sparkled with danger, a flamelike brightness that some assassins had. But the color of their aura wasn't quite right. The Rodian at another card table, with his small earlike antennae swiveling nervously in the noise of the room—yes. Definitely a killer, though Trevagg wasn't certain he could take on Predne Balu. The Wolfman, yes; he looked big enough, tough enough, to take on the human and win. The brown-haired human talking quietly with an enormous Wookiee at another booth—maybe. The edge was there, but not the darkness. The thin man smoking a hookah at the bar—absolutely. His aura was dark, terrible, but there was a coldness about him that made Trevagg wonder if he could be approached at all. That was one, he thought, who killed for a huge sum . . . or for his own pleasure. Nothing between.

For the rest, they were locals: the foul Dr. Evazan and his disgusting Aqualish friend were well known to Trevagg, dangerous but not for hire; the horned and sinister-looking Devaronian swaying his fingers dreamily to the music of the band was much less dangerous than he appeared. The old spacer in most of a flight suit Trevagg recognized as a smuggler who worked for the monastery, probably involved in something illegal —like most of the religious brothers of that organization —but he would stop far short of murder.

And then he felt it. The rushing, buzzing sensation in his cones, the strange humming confusion, almost like the presence of a high-energy machine . . .

And the Jedi came into the cantina.

He was a nondescript old human, his beard gone white as the hair of humans did with age, his robes shabby with wear and desert dust. He was trailed by a human youth—a back-desert moisture farmer, by the look of his clothes and the way he stared around him, as Nightlily had, awed by what he thought was the Big

City—and by a couple of much-battered droids whose
power cells made Trevagg's cones prickle. Wuher the
barkeep swung immediately around. "Hey, we don't
serve their kind here!"

"What?" said the boy, and the taller of the droids, a
dented C-3PO, looked as disconcerted as it was possible for a droid to look.

"Your droids. They'll have to wait outside. We don't
want them here."

Trevagg, sitting only a few feet away, heartily con-
curred. It was difficult enough to think in here, to determine what he should do, with Nightlily so soft and
vulnerable and giggly on one side, and the dark vibrations of the assassins on the other.

"Listen, why don't you wait out by the speeder," the
boy said quietly—an unnecessary courtesy, in Trevagg's
opinion. A C-3PO only looked human, and an R2-D2
didn't even do that. "We don't want any trouble."

The old man, meanwhile, had gone to the bar, and
was deep in murmured conversation with the elderly
monastic spacer in the flight suit; Trevagg stretched his
hearing to pick up their words, but over the music of
the band it was not easy.

Even less easy was it to hear something besides
Nightlily's soft voice, slightly flown with unaccustomed
substances, asking yet again, humbly, how he could
truly love her so much.

"Of course I do, of course," said Trevagg, watching
the old Jedi move into conversation with the towering
Wookiee. He looked safe for a moment, and Trevagg
turned back to Nightlily, grasping the smooth dark
ivory of her hands. "Nightlily, you mean . . . Everything. Everything to me."

She said "Oh . . ." while staring up into his eyes.
"Oh . . . Oh, Trevagg. That we should have met like
this—that you should have come into my life like
this . . ."

He wondered if he could slip away for a moment,
summon the city police . . . But he needed a go-between if he were to get the money. Slip away and con-

tact Jub Vegnu—first speak to one of the assassins, in case Balu had tracked the old man here himself.

He felt the flare of emotions, of irrational rage and drunken aggression, before the yelling started. Swinging around in his chair, Trevagg saw, to his horror, that the sinister Dr. Evazan had decided to pick a fight with the farm boy, throwing him sprawling into a table while Wuher ducked under the bar yelling desperately "No blasters! No blasters!" and someone else grabbed for a sidearm . . .

The roar of the Force in Trevagg's cones peaked like the drumming of a high-desert gravel storm. The old man, in what seemed like a single smooth gesture, somehow had a glowing stalk of light in his hand. A lethal slash, a severed limb leaking blood on the floor, Nightlily's terrified hoot, and silence—a silence less shocked than cautious as everyone reevaluated the situation.

Then the band started up again. So did the conversations. The wounded would-be combatant was taken away. So was the arm, by Wuher's small helper Nackhan recognized as operating a fast-food stand in the marketplace. The old Jedi picked up his young companion, moved off with the Wookiee to the booth where the brown-haired smuggler with the scar on his chin waited. Trevagg became aware that Nightlily was clinging to his arm, and his every instinct told him now was the time to move in on her.

Unfortunately, now was also the time to listen, to stretch out his hearing, to key and sharpen his hunter's awareness of every word they said. Trevagg disengaged his arm from the trembling girl, stated "You need something to calm you down, my blossom," and moved over to the bar, listening over the jumble of the music, the murmur of the crowd. Lingering by the bar, he heard the words "to the Alderaan system," and felt the swift rush of hunter's adrenaline in his veins. It was, indeed, now or never.

Then, a moment later, he heard the old man say,

"Two thousand now, plus fifteen when we reach Alder-aan . . ."

Trevagg breathed a sigh of relief. That meant a delay here, while they raised the cash. Probably they'd sell the speeder the boy had mentioned, or the droids, or all three. That only left the question of Balu.

The brown-haired human and the Wookiee were obviously not for hire as assassins. Judging by such of the conversation as he could hear, Trevagg guessed they were only smugglers anyway. The Wolfman was engaged in a sharp altercation with a lampreylike thing beside him, whose vibrations caused Trevagg to back quickly away, and, nearby, the hookah smoker felt too eerily dangerous, too deadly. That left the Rodian . . .

"Docking Bay Ninety-four," he heard the smuggler say, and the old man repeated it, "Ninety-four," as Trevagg returned to his booth with his own drink and Nightlily's, double-strength and dosed with a Love-Wallop pill Trevagg had had the foresight to slip into his pocket before leaving the office. He knew how much Wuher charged for them. There would now, he knew, be plenty of time.

Riches, he thought, and the beautiful creature leaning on his arm, crooning softly, "Oh, my love, my love." Maybe he'd even spring for a first-class ticket for her. It was, after all, the least he could do.

He wasn't surprised, or particularly upset, when the stormtroopers showed up. He even felt a kind of scorn for them as they looked around, for of course the old man and the boy had vanished. So, incidentally, did several other patrons, including the hookah smoker. The Rodian didn't, Trevagg observed, and slipped one hand from Nightlily's soft waist to feel in his belt pouch for the money he'd brought. A hundred credits, he had been told, was the current going rate for the down payment on a man's life.

He would be glad, he thought, to get this annoyance out of the way. To make sure Balu was not going to cheat him out of the reward that was rightfully his.

Unfortunately, just as Trevagg was rising to go to the

Rodian's table, the Rodian himself got up, with a shift in aura that told Trevagg that this was indeed a hunter, closing in on his own prey. That prey, it turned out, was the brown-haired smuggler, who after a prolonged altercation shot the Rodian neatly with a blaster drawn under the table.

Nightlily shrieked again and clung to Trevagg's arm; Wuher's helper ran to guard the remains even as the smuggler and his Wookiee companion tossed the barkeep a couple of credits and took their leave: "Sorry about the mess." After a momentary pause, the band took up its tune without missing a bar.

Disgusted and annoyed—because the Wolfman had also left by this time—Trevagg gathered the flustered and languishing Nightlily on his arm. So much, he thought, for trying to shortcut middlemen. When he contacted Jub Vegnu to arrange information to the City Prefect about intercepting the old man and the boy at Spaceport Speeders, he'd mention the need to dispose of Balu for an extra hundred creds. That should take care of any competition for the reward for the old man's hide.

And in the meantime, thought Trevagg, slipping his arm around the trembling bundle of aromatic sensuality that fate had dropped into his lap, there was the matter of this girl, and getting a room at the Mos Eisley Inn, to consummate what she thought would be the start of a wonderful marriage—the more fool she!— and what was, in actuality, merely the more delectable of the two hunts upon which he had engaged today.

Really, Trevagg thought, as he guided Nightlily's tipsy steps along the gold and shadow of the street outside, he might have retired from the trade, but he was still quite a passable hunter after all.

What with the commotion of Imperial troops coming into Mos Eisley to search for a pair of droids, the sudden rumors of a Sand People massacre on an outlying farm, and the firefight at Docking Bay 94 ending with a smuggling craft's illegal liftoff, nobody found Feltipern Trevagg's body until the following afternoon.

"Didn't anybody *tell* him?" demanded Wuher the bartender, brought over to the Mos Eisley Inn by Balu's deputy to view the body and give the security officer his deposition.

"Tell him what?" Balu looked up from jotting on his logpad. He'd never much liked the Gotal, but that kind of death—evisceration with what looked to have been a long, thin knife, skillfully wielded—was something he wouldn't have wished on anyone.

"About H'nemthe." When Balu continued to look blank, the bartender added, "The girl he was with. The H'nemthe female."

"Nightlily?" Balu was startled. The girl had looked too frightened by her surroundings—and too dazzled by Trevagg's charms—to have harmed a hair of the Gotal's head.

"Was that her name?" Wuher rolled his eyes. "It figures."

A small crowd had gathered. Of course, none of the Imperial stormtroopers and none of the Prefect's guard, either. A murder this small wasn't worth their time. Balu couldn't help observing Nackhar in the background slipping the coroner's deputy a few credits. For what, he decided not to ask.

"The m'iiyoom—the nightlily—is a carnivorous flower that feeds on small rodents and insects that try to drink its nectar," said the barkeep, hands on hips and looking down at the dark-stained sheet the coroner had laid over what was left of Trevagg. "After mating, H'nemthe females gut the males with those tongues of theirs—they're as sharp as sword blades, and a lot stronger than they look. Some kind of biological reaction to there being twenty H'nemthe males for every female. The males seem to think it's worth it, to achieve the act of love. I saw them together in the cantina, but I didn't think Trevagg was crazy enough to try to bed the girl."

"He was always bragging about being such a great

hunter," said Balu wonderingly, stepping aside for the coroner's deputies to carry the body out of the dingy and bloodstained room. "You'd have thought he'd sense it coming."

"How could he?" The barkeep tucked big hands into his belt, followed the officer back out to the street. "For her it was the act of love, too."

He shrugged, and quoted an old Ithorian proverb current in some sections of the spaceways: "N'ygyng mth'une vned 'isobec' k'chuv 'ysobek.' "

Which, loosely translated, means: "The word for 'love' in one language is the word for 'dinner' in others."

Empire Blues:
The Devaronian's Tale

by Daniel Keys Moran

I don't suppose it took us five minutes that afternoon to execute the Rebels, start to finish.

The Rebellion on Devaron stood no chance. My home world is sparsely settled even by Devaronians, and is politically unimportant; but it is near the Core. Near the Emperor, may he freeze.

I was Kardue'sai'Malloc, third of the Kardue line to

194

bear that name; a Devish and a captain in the Devaronian Army.

Kardue had served in the Devaronian Army for sixteen generations: through the Clone Wars, back into the days when no one dreamed the old Republic would ever fall. The army lifestyle suited me, and I the army; aside from the stress of dealing with the Imperium, and the detested necessity of placing Devaronian troops under Imperial command during the Rebellion, it was a tolerable life.

Sixteen generations of military service ended the afternoon after we overran the Rebel positions in Montellian Serat. It took me half a year to hang up the armor; but that was the moment.

Montellian Serat is an old city. Well, was; it dated back to the days before my people had star travel. That the Rebels chose to make a stand there was tactically foolish, but not surprising. I spent the night overseeing the shelling of the ancient city walls, and in the first light of morning stopped shelling long enough to offer the Rebels a chance to surrender. They accepted the offer, laid down their arms by the shattered walls at the city's edge, and came out in single file: man and woman they were seven hundred strong.

I herded them into a hastily constructed holding pen, and mounted guards. I had concern for a rescue attempt; half a day's march south, another group of Rebels were still fighting.

After they surrendered, we shelled the city into rubble. The Empire wanted to make sure no one made the mistake of sheltering Rebels again.

Our orders came just after noon. The Rebels were believed to be moving north; I was to take my forces and intercept them. I was not to leave any of my forces behind as guards for the captured Rebels.

The orders were no more specific than that . . . but they could not be misunderstood.

I had them executed in mid-afternoon. I pulled the guards back into a half circle, and had them open fire on the Rebels inside the holding pen. It took most of five minutes before the screaming stopped and I could be certain all seven hundred were dead.

There was no time to bury them.

We marched south to the next battle.

With one thing and another it took almost half a year for the Rebellion on Devaron to be put down. Rebellions are drawn-out affairs, even the failures. When it was over, I submitted my resignation. At first my superiors, humans all, could not decide whether to accept it and let my fellow "natives" kill me once I no longer had the protection of the Imperial Army, or to refuse it and execute me for treason for having made the request in the first place.

I recall I did not much care.

They let me go.

I vanished. Neither my Imperial superiors, nor the family or friends left behind, who lusted for my horns, ever saw me, or my music collection, again.

Time passed.

Halfway across the galaxy from Devaron, on the small desert planet of Tatooine, in the port city of Mos Eisley, in a cantina tucked away near the center of the hot, dusty city, I looked up from my empty drink and smiled at my old friend Wuher.

I gave him the polite one. Devish are more sharply differentiated by sex than most species. Men have sharper teeth than women, designed for hunting; Devish evolved from pack hunters. Women have canines as well, but also have molars and can survive on food that men would starve on. In rare cases, though, about one birth in fifty, a Devish man will be born with both sets of teeth. I'm one of them. In the old days it was a survival trait; Devish men with both sets of teeth were used as solitary scouts by the pack. They could range farther and survive in terrain where most males would starve. It may be cultural and it may be genetic, but there is no question that Devish with doubled teeth are less creatures of the pack than most Devish men.

I doubt most Devish could do what I've done, at that.

My outer row of teeth are female, flat and not at all threatening. The inner row, composed of sharp, needle-pointed teeth, is for shredding flesh. When I feel threatened or angry, the outer row of teeth retract. In those circumstances it's a reflex; but I can do it on purpose.

Sometimes I do it on purpose. It startles humans . . . well, it startles most noncarnivores, but humans are a special case, a whole species of omnivores. There are not many intelligent omnivorous species out there. I have a theory about them: They're food that decided to fight back. In the case of humans, tree munchies. They never quite get over their own audacity, I suspect, and they're a nervous lot because of it.

(A human once tried to tell me that *humans* were carnivores. I did not laugh at him, despite his molars and his pitiful two pair of blunted incisors, and a digestive tract so long that the flesh he ate rotted before it came out the other end. With a body designed like that, *I'd* take up leaf eating.)

Wuher gave me the usual scowl in response to my polite, flat-toothed smile. "Let me guess, Labria. The glass is defective."

Wuher is my best friend on Tatooine. He's a squat, ugly human with a bad attitude and none of the human virtues. He hates droids and doesn't care much for anything else. I like him a great deal. There is a purity to his loathing for the universe that is quite spiritually advanced. If I could free him from his love of money, he might well attain Grace. "Yes, my friend. It has ceased functioning. If you would fix it . . ."

"With?"

"Oh, the amber liquid, I suppose."

"The Merenzane Gold?"

"The bottle bears that label," I conceded.

"One Merenzane Gold, point five credits."

I dropped the half-credit coin on the bartop, and waited while he refilled my drink. Merenzane Gold is a sweet, subtle concoction, with many thousands of years of brewing tradition behind it. A single bottle goes for well upward of a hundred credits, depending on vintage.

I took a sip of my drink and smiled again. Proper. You could use it to clean thruster tubes, except it might melt the shielding. I wandered over to my favorite booth, as far away from the bandstand as I could get, and settled in with my ear plugs for the day.

I was the first customer in the door that morning. I could barely remember a time when I had not been.

Tatooine is a nasty, useless little planet. The only noteworthy things about it are Jabba, and the pilots it produces year after year. I don't have any idea why Jabba picked Tatooine as a base; maybe because it's so far from the Core that the Empire is less likely to bother him here. Doesn't matter, really.

As for the pilots, well, Tatooine's a desert, filled with moisture farmers north to south. A single farm takes up so much space that to visit with one another they must travel long distance by speedster; their children learn to fly at an early age. On most Tatooine farms it would take you a day to walk from one end to the other, and you'd likely die of thirst first.

I hate Tatooine. I'm still not sure why I stayed here. It was a temporary thing, I recall that. I was following Maxa Jandovar, the great—well, for a human, great—vandfillist. I kept *missing* her. She was one of the half-dozen surviving artists I hadn't seen live who was *worth* seeing. I spent half a decade following her around through the outback, hitting planet after planet weeks or days or, in one instance that gave me ample opportunity to demonstrate Grace, a mere half day after she'd left. She didn't leave an agenda; she couldn't, very well. The Empire wouldn't go to the trouble of hunting her, but if she'd announced where she was going next, she'd certainly have found a squad of stormtroopers waiting for her at the spaceport when she arrived.

The Empire doesn't trust artists. Particularly the great ones. Politics does not interest them, and they persist in speaking the truth when it is inconvenient.

They arrested Maxa Jandovar on Morvogodine. She died in custody. I was on Tatooine when I got the news, getting ready to head to Morvogodine.

Somehow I ended up staying.

Nightlily, the H'nemthe sitting down at the end of the bar, looked bored and horny. I felt sorry for *someone*.

"Hey, Wuher!"

Wuher looked at me from down the length of the bar. "Yeah?"

"Universal Truth Number One: You should never say 'Well, why don't you bite my head off?' to a female H'nemthe who is bigger than you are."

He didn't smile. Jerk.

In the booth next to mine, two humans were trying to talk a Moorin merc into helping them rob a bar over on the other side of Mos Eisley; I made a note to myself to call the bar's owner and sell him a warning about the men. Not that it looked as if the Moorin were going to help them; only one of the humans spoke the merc's language, his accent was horrific, and his syntax was occasionally hysterical. I could see the merc struggling to take them seriously. At one point the merc, Obron Mettlo, growled at them that he was a soldier, a fighter; he mentioned some of the battles he'd fought in. I'd actually heard of most of them—if he wasn't lying, he was a serious professional.

"Hey, Wuher!"

Wuher looked at me from down the length of the bar. "Yeah?"

"What do you call someone who speaks three languages?"

"Trilingual."
"Someone who speaks two languages?"
"Bilingual."
"Someone who speaks one language?"
He puzzled at it a second. "Monolingual?"
"Human."
He almost smiled before he caught himself.

The day passed slowly. They tend to. I drank enough to keep the world slightly out of focus, and waited for the suns to set. I moved around a bit, sat at the bar a few times, looking for conversation; I even bought two drinks for an off-duty stormtrooper, slumming. Wasted; he was more interested in women than in conversation, and I doubted he knew anything anyway. That is the nature of investments, though; someday he *might* know something, if such a thing were possible for a stormtrooper. And then he *might* think of his old friend and drinking buddy, Labria.

Brokering information is a chancy occupation, at best.

Can't say I'm any good at it.

Long Snoot showed up toward late afternoon. It had been a good day until then; Wuher didn't have musicians that day, and I hadn't had to wear my ear plugs even once.

Long Snoot wanted to sell *me* information.

I smiled at him, in my corner booth as far away from the stage as I could get. The sharp smile. "That's a new one. Pass."

Long Snoot's "name" is Garindan. I had a protocol droid do a search on the word once. In five different languages it meant "Blessed One," "burnt wood," "dust from a windstorm," "ugly," and "toast." None of the five languages were spoken by a species that looked anything like Long Snoot's.

Long Snoot's the most successful spy in Mos Eisley.

In a town with as many spies as this city has, that says something. He pays adequately for information; sometimes I give him information of value. Sometimes I even do it on purpose. "But Labria," he wheedled, voice low, "this is a subject of *particular* interest to you."

"Give me a hint."

He shook his head, trunk waving gently in front of my face. I suppressed an uncivilized urge to swat it with a sharpened nail. (I often have the opportunity to exhibit Grace in dealing with Long Snoot.) "Fifty credits, Labria. You won't regret it."

I thought about it. I took a sip of the acid gold and swished it around my back teeth for a bit. I could feel it helping keep them sharp. "Fifty credits is a lot. Resellable?"

He scratched under his snout, thinking. "I can't think to whom."

Something of interest to me, but not resellable . . .

I could feel my ears straighten. "Who is it?"

"Fift—"

"I'll pay. Who's onplanet?"

"Figri—"

I came up out of my seat. "Fiery Figrin Da'n is on *Tatooine?*"

He made an *urk* noise. "People . . . are . . . *looking.*"

I looked around. Some of them were, in fact. Odd, having all those eyes on me. I let go of Long Snoot, and they turned away. "Sorry. Bit excitable."

He rubbed his throat. "Your nails need trimming."

"I expect they do." He sat back down again, but I was too excited. "The band is with him?"

"Fifty credits."

A snarl rose in the back of my throat. I pulled out a fifty-credit note and dropped it into his outstretched hand, and tried to keep the growl out of my voice when I spoke. "Who?"

"They're playing for Jabba."

"All of them?"

"The Modal Nodes."

"That's them," I said, unable to keep the excitement out of my voice. "Doikk Na'ts on the Fizzz, Tedn Dahai and Ikabel G'ont on the Fanfar, Nalan Cheel on Bandfill, Tech Mo'r on the Ommni—"

"Yeah. Those are the names."

Oh, my.

The greatest jizz band in the galaxy was in town.

I left earlier than usual, as soon as it was dark outside. Wuher nodded at me on my way out. "Tomorrow, Labria."

I nodded at him and went outside into the hot night.

"Labria" is an extremely dirty word in my native tongue. It translates, roughly, as "cold food," though the basic phrase loses the flavor of it.

By my horns, I don't understand humans. I've lived around them close to two decades now. The things they swear by! Sex, excrement, and religion.

I'll never understand them.

There are four hundred billion stars in the galaxy. Most of them have planets; about half have planets capable of supporting life. About a tenth of those worlds have evolved life of their own, and about one in a thousand of those worlds have evolved *intelligent* life forms.

These are rough numbers. There are well over twenty million intelligent races in the galaxy, though. No one can keep track of them all, not even the Empire.

I have no idea how many bounty hunters there are in Mos Eisley. Hundreds of professionals, I'm sure. Tens of thousands who would turn bounty hunter without a moment's pause if the bounty were high enough, and if anyone knew of it.

The Butcher of Montellian Serat has five million

credits on his horns. But Devaron is halfway across the galaxy, and there may only be a dozen sentients on all of Tatooine who even know for sure what species I belong to. (There are two other Devaronians onplanet, Oxbel and Jubal. I rather like Oxbel; we pretended to be brothers once, during a rather involved scam that didn't work out the way we'd hoped. We don't look *anything* alike—his ancestors evolved at the equator, mine toward the north pole—but the humans we were trying to cheat couldn't tell the difference. I rather like Oxbel, but I don't come close to trusting him. He's been away from Devaron even longer than I have, and it's entirely possible that even *he* hasn't heard of the Butcher of Montellian Serat—but it's best to be safe.

(There are downsides to being safe, though. The closest Devish woman is on the other side of the Core. Just the thought makes my horns ache.)

Most bounty hunters are lazy. If they weren't, they'd be in another line of work.

And research is not their strong point.

I took the short way home.

A Reason for Living:

I keep a small underground apartment about twelve minutes' brisk walk from the cantina. It's been broken into twice since I've lived there. The first time I came back and found the deed done; the second time I surprised the burglar in the act. A young human. Turns out humans don't taste very good.

The lights come on automatically as I unlock and let myself in. The door leads down a flight of stairs to a cold, sweaty basement that costs an indecent amount to cool. The heat-exchange coils turn on automatically when I enter; I know from long experience I won't be able to sleep until they have been on for quite a while —and at that it will not be properly cold until I am done sleeping, and it's time to turn them off.

There's only one thing of value in the apartment; neither of my two thieves found it, fortunately. From the outer room you go into the sleeping cubicle, and from there into the bathroom. The sanitary facilities are human designed, but they suit me well enough. In the shower, you push back on the tiled wall, and it slides back enough to step through, sideways.

I step through and into a small eight-sided room. The walls are not perfect; they tend to reflect the higher frequencies and absorb the lower ones, so virtually everything ends up sounding brighter than it should. Some of that can be adjusted for; some of it I simply have to live with.

The wall behind me sighs shut. The room is already cool; it's the first part of the apartment to be cooled.

Along the walls are the chips.

Some of them are unique, I'm sure. Priceless. Copies of recordings that are preserved by no one else in the galaxy. Some of them are merely rare and very expensive.

I have everyone. Or, to be precise, I have *something* by everyone. I have music the Imperium banned a generation ago . . . by musicians executed for singing the wrong lyric, in the wrong way, to the wrong person, by musicians who simply vanished, by musicians who had the good fortune to die before the Empire came to power.

Maxa Jandovar is here, and Orin Mersai, and Telindel and Saerlock, Lord Kavad and the Skaalite Orchestra, M'lar'Nkai'kambric, Janet Lalasha, and Miracle Meriko, who died in Imperial custody four days after I saw him play *Stardance* for the last time. The ancient masters, Kang and Lubrichs, Ovido Aishara, and the amazing Brullian Dyll.

I have two recordings by Fiery Figrin Da'n and the Modal Nodes. Da'n may be the greatest Klooist the galaxy has ever seen. As for Doikk Na'ts . . . there's something about his playing that's always struck me as cautious, careful . . . but sometimes, sometimes the fire comes, and he plays the Fizzz as well as Janet Lalasha ever did.

Most of their backup players could play lead, in a lesser band.

I settle down in the seat, set just off center for the room, where the sound comes together most cleanly, open a bottle of twelve-year-old Dorian Quill, and wait for the music to start.

My people believe that to kill something, you must cherish it and love it as it dies. There is no barrier between you and the thing you are killing, and you die as you kill.

Music is the only thing I know that feels the same way.

The music surrounds me until I cease to exist.

I die as I kill.

It's what I live for.

I'm glad my fathers are dead.

In the morning I went to see Jabba.

He had me stand on the trapdoor, and his tail twitched as we spoke. That always bothers me. Part of me was frightened by it; even carnivores get eaten by bigger carnivores. Another part of me wanted to pounce on it.

He regarded me with those slitted ugly eyes, and laughed a rumbling, unpleasant laugh. "So . . . what information does my least favorite spy have to sell me?"

I made it good. I spoke to him in Hutt, which I normally try to avoid; it hurts my throat, and I have to use both sets of teeth to make some of the sounds. After a long conversation, the front row aches from being pulled up and then dropped down again quickly. "There's a mercenary in town." I'd learned what I could about him before heading over. It hadn't been much, but I'd been rushed. I wanted to move on this quickly—if Jabba didn't like Da'n and the Nodes, I might *never* get to see them play. Nor would anyone

else. "Obron Mettlo. A real professional, fought in dozens of battles, often on the winning side, looking for
employment. Moorin, has an attitude—"

He made a low, grumbling sound that might have
been interpreted as interest. Jabba had plenty of muscle, but not always smart muscle; and Moorin tend to
be bright as well as vicious.

I forged ahead. "If you like, I could get in touch with
him. Bring him by to meet you . . . for dinner, perhaps. Possibly some entertainment, some music—music is good with Moorin. Keeps 'em peaceable."

His eyelids drooped slightly; either he was bored or
he was thinking. Finally he gave me a slight chuckle,
and said, "Send him over."

I bowed and backed away as quickly as was polite,
getting off that trapdoor. "As you wish, sir. We'll be by
—would first dark be appropriate?"

He smiled at me and it made the fur on the small of
my back stand straight up. "Send *him* by," he clarified.
"You are not invited."

I stood frozen at the edge of the trapdoor, mind
refusing to function. Surely there had to be some way
to wangle—

Jabba made a sound. A familiar sound; I've heard
Devish make it, too—except that it takes a pack of Devish. It straightened my ears and made my front teeth
jump out of the way. "You can leave now."

I bowed and got out.

I spent the evening at the cantina, drinking myself into
a stupor.

I just *knew* Jabba would feed the Modal Nodes to the
rancor. He'd *never* had a decent band before, never,
not once. The closest he'd ever come was Max Rebo's
bunch, who could carry a melody if you gave them a
basket to keep it in.

But the next morning, I learned that Rebo was out
looking for work.

Jabba had a new favorite.

.   .   .

It came *this* close to killing me.

For four days I couldn't sleep for thinking about it. There they were, not a half part's speedster trip from Mos Eisley. Playing for *him*. It ate me alive thinking about it. I lost so much Grace in those days that if I had any shame left to me, I'd have to use some of it on that period.

Sometime on the fifth day I drank too much. I awoke lying facedown in the alleyway upstairs and behind the cantina, in darkness, with someone nudging my shoulder with his toe. I decided to take a chunk out of his calf—

Wuher knelt next to me. "Can you stand up?"

The cold gravel pressed against my cheek. I had bruises, cuts—the memories came back slowly. Several someones had beaten me—heavy wood or metal staffs, I vaguely recalled. Just a random robbery. My right arm wouldn't move at all. "I don't think so."

"Come on." My body is denser than humans'; he staggered, helping me to my feet. The strain sent a jolt of astonishing pain through my shoulder. "Where do you live?"

He half carried me to my apartment, and stood at the opening while I fumbled with the interlock. "Do you need medical help?"

I don't remember if I answered him or not. It was a stupid question. No doctor on Tatooine knew anything about Devish physiology—or if they did, I didn't want to know *them*.

I made it to the shower before I collapsed. I got the cold water turned on and sat in it until morning, trying to decide how badly I wanted to live.

By morning the apartment half reminded me of home. I stayed in it and did not go out, kept the heat-exchange coils running all day. Around midday I found the strength to pull a slab of womp rat the length of my arm from the freezer, heat it to blood temperature, and drag it into the shower with me. I sat under the water, nude, eating until my stomach bulged, and when there was nothing left but bones on the floor of the stall, turned the water off and staggered to my bedpit.

It took me some time before I felt safe going out in public again. Several times someone came to my door; I didn't open it. Some information travels Mos Eisley faster than light. Mos Eisley is like a living creature: It eats the sick and weak. I'd survived all these years without having to kill more than a few of my fellow residents. They'd have heard by now of the attack on me— the humans who'd robbed me might have boasted of it, in which case I'd have them in my freezer, whoever they were, before the month was out.

But in any event I dared not go back to the cantina until my strength was returned.

The arm took longest to heal; weeks later it was still stiff and it hurt when I moved it wrong. But I was almost out of food, so I had no choice. Early one morning I dressed, set my alarms, and headed for the cantina.

Wuher looked up and nodded at me when I entered. First one in the door. He put a glass on the counter and poured a shot of golden liquid. "On the house. Drink it before someone else comes in."

I looked at the drink, and then at Wuher, almost as much at a loss for words as I'd been when Jabba told me to send the merc over by himself. "Many thanks," I finally got out. He nodded and I lifted the glass—

And stopped. Predators have better noses than leaf eaters. There was something wrong with the alcohol. It was—

He poured himself a shot while I was staring at my glass, raised it to me, and knocked it back.

Merenzane Gold. The *real* stuff. Precious, pure, *real* Merenzane Gold.

Wuher corked the unlabeled bottle while I was still staring at him, put it away under the bar, and wandered away from me to finish opening up.

I took the glass to my booth, sat and drank it very slowly. I hadn't known there was a bottle of real Gold on all of Tatooine. I'd almost forgotten what it tasted like.

I wondered how many years he'd had that bottle down there without saying anything about it.

By the Cold, I'm a lousy spy.

That's something to be proud of.

I spent the morning listening to the talk throughout the bar. I'd been out of touch . . . and interesting things had happened while I'd been hidden away from the world. Last night an Imperial battle cruiser had fought in orbit with a Rebel spaceship, and today stormtroopers were looking all over Tatooine for someone, or something, that had escaped them.

And a piece of horrifically *bad* news: The damn mercenary I'd recommended to Jabba had picked a fight with a pair of Jabba's bodyguards and shot them both up before getting himself fed to the rancor. There was some rumor that perhaps the merc had been an assassin paid by the Lady Valarian, whose real target had been Jabba himself—

Maybe Jabba had forgotten who had recommended him.

And maybe Long Snoot would give me my fifty credits back.

It came to me in a vision.

Okay, that's not true, but it's close. Long Snoot stopped by and mentioned something interesting: The Lady Valarian was getting married. Max Rebo and band were going to play at the wedding.

I barely noticed when Long Snoot left. I stared straight ahead, through the noonday crowd come to escape the heat, not seeing them, not seeing the cantina. Just thinking.

"Wuher."

He turned away from a conversation with a pair of human females who looked like clones; the Tonnika sisters, they'd introduced themselves as. He did it grudgingly; they were attractive, by human standards. "Yeah?"

"How's business?"

He stared at me suspiciously. "It stinks. It always stinks."

"How would you like entertainment by *real* musicians?"

"Rebo? Can't afford him, and his bunch don't draw what they cost anyway."

I gave him the polite smile. "Figrin Da'n and the Modal Nodes. They're Bith. They're *good*, Wuher. I mean really, *really* good."

"What would they cost me?"

"Five hundred a week."

He gave me the suspicious stare again. If something sounds too good to be true, someone's being screwed. "Really. A band better than Rebo's will work here for less than his."

"I think I can arrange it."

"How?"

I told him. When I was done he said in a somber voice, "You are one twisted puppy, Lab."

"Is it a deal?"

He shook his head no, said "It's a deal," and wandered away, shaking his head and muttering to himself.

The Lady Valarian is the closest thing to competition that Jabba the Hutt has on Tatooine. That's not saying much; Jabba tolerates her because it keeps all the discontents in one place. She's a Whiphid, which means she's stupid, huge, ugly, has more muscle on her than I do, and smells worse than Jabba. I wouldn't eat her even after a long hunt.

I went to see her at her hotel, the Lucky Despot. The Lucky Despot isn't much of a hotel, truth told; just a spaceship that won't ever lift again.

"That's right," I said. "Modal Nodes. Lead is Figrin Da'n. I know you want the best for your wedding, Lady Valarian. This group makes music so glorious, your wedding will be the talk of this corner of the galaxy. People for dozens of light-years will speak with envy and longing of the entertainment provided at the wedding of the great Lady Valarian and her handsome consort, the daring D'Wopp, of the romantic mood set by the finest musicians this poor galaxy has ever seen."

She glared at me—well, I think she glared at me; with those mad little eyes Whiphids have, it's hard to tell—and said skeptically, "Better than Max Rebo? I *love* Max Rebo."

She would. And she deserved to have the ugly little runt play her wedding, for all of me. "Fair mistress, your taste is as that of your tongue, and none would dare say otherwise." I gave her the polite smile. "But Modal Nodes is currently Jabba the Hutt's favored entertainment. Would you have it said that the entertainment at your wedding was provided by the musicians Jabba deemed too poor to play for him?"

It took her a bit to work through it. I'd gotten a little carried away with my syntax; Whiphids have a working vocabulary of only about eight thousand words. "No! No, I won't have it! I want the Nodal Notes!" She looked briefly uncertain. "Do you think they'll come?"

"They'll be expensive, madam. They'll be braving Jabba's displeasure to play for you. It might cost . . . two, or three thousand credits, perhaps. If I can have the loan of a messenger droid, I would be most happy to begin making the arrangements . . ."

The morning of the wedding I called Jabba.

He laughed with, I think, real amusement on seeing me. "My least favorite spy!" he boomed. "Perhaps you should come visit me. We can have dinner together, and talk about the mercenary you introduced to me.''

''I have information, Jabba.''

''Hmmm.''

''Do you know your musicians are missing? Figrin Da'n and the Modal Nodes?''

''Hmmmph!'' He made a bellowing noise and rocked himself off camera. I heard shrieks, steel clanging, things breaking . . . I stood patiently in front of my comlink's pickup and waited for him to come back, if he was going to. After a bit he did. ''Hoooo,'' he muttered, shaking his head. ''Where are they, least favorite spy?''

''The Lady Valarian is getting married today. She's hired them to play at her wedding, at the Lucky Despot Hotel.''

The eyes narrowed to slits. ''And what does my least favorite spy want for this information?''

I spread my hands. ''Let us forget a certain unfortunate introduction . . .''

He looked at me through the slitted eyes for a second, and then gave the booming laugh. ''Least favorite spy, call me again sometime.''

He broke the connection.

Cold sweat trickled through the fur on the small of my back.

Wuher had dressed for the wedding. He'd changed his shirt.

The cantina was dark and silent; I'd never seen it like this before, except the first few minutes in the morning. I gave Wuher my invitation; the Lady Valarian had given it to me in gratitude for acquiring the ''Nodal Notes'' for her wedding, while hinting that, in the future, I might find it better business to share information with her rather than with Jabba.

Someone'll kill Jabba, someday, but it's not going to be Valarian.

"You're sure the wedding's going to be broken up," he repeated.

"I'm sure the Modal Nodes aren't going to want to go back to Jabba after this. All you have to do is offer them a place to lie low for a while, play a few gigs, pick up a few credits. They're going to be broke; Valarian won't pay them after her wedding is broken up."

He shook his head, tucking his shirt in again. "You think they'll go for it?"

"I think they'll jump at it."

Wuher stood there, studying me in the gloom. "Lab . . . if you put this kind of effort into anything else, you could be a wealthy being."

I shook my head, and said gently, "My friend, this is all that I want."

It's hard to outthink Jabba. Also dangerous.

I sat in the shadows of a building down the way from the Lucky Despot, watching the crowd arrive for the wedding. A scummy lot, all around. I recognized several of the "guests" as Jabba's people. I hoped there wasn't any shooting. I didn't see enough of Jabba's troops to make that likely; if he'd decided to wipe out Lady Valarian for her theft of his musicians, he'd have sent more soldiers. That was a good sign.

I could hear, so faintly that my ears twitched, a song that might have been "Tears of Aquanna." It was followed by what was, quite definitely, "Worm Case." Odd choices for a wedding. Maybe they were playing requests.

And then the bad news arrived.

Stormtroopers.

Two squads. They set down out of the night, quietly and with running lights doused, in full combat armor. One squad covered the entrance to the hotel, and the second squad went in. From the moment they set down I doubt it took them twenty seconds.

Oh, the noise was *awful*. From where I sat, I could hear it. Screams, blaster bolts, yelling, another round of blaster fire—one of the stormtroopers near the entrance went down. I lifted my macrobinoculars and watched the building through them. Windows opened and the scum of a dozen different races came squirming out through them. I moved the macrobinoculars up, scanning across the structure of the half-buried ship . . . Toward the top of the ship, three stories above the dirty sand, an emergency airlock clanged open. The first head through it was a Bith. I couldn't guess who: All Bith look alike, even when you're not looking through macrobinoculars. More Bith followed, and then the unmistakable squat form of my friend Wuher. They took off across the sand together, Wuher and the Bith, and ran straight by me in the darkness without pausing.

I'd never have guessed that Wuher could move that fast . . . and a moment later I saw why he was managing it. A pair of stormtroopers came charging after them, weapons at the ready. I shed a little Grace by tripping the one in the lead. The second stormtrooper tripped over him. I bent over them and picked up their rifles. I hadn't handled an assault rifle in—well, in a very long time, but they hadn't changed. I pulled the charge cages from them and handed them back to the two stormtroopers as they recovered their feet.

"You appear to have dropped these, gentles."

One of them immediately jumped backward, rifle pointing at me, and shouted, "Don't move!"

The other one looked at me, and then at his rifle, and then at me again.

"Come now," I said gently. "We're reasonable beings. You tripped and I helped you up again. No need for anyone to get upset. If you got injured in the fall, perhaps, I'd be more than happy to compensate you for it . . ."

I let my voice trail off and the three of us watched each other for a beat.

The one pointing the useless rifle at me said in a strained voice, "Are you trying to bribe us?"

I drew myself up to my full height and stared down

at them, and gave them the sharp smile. "Not," I said, "if you're going to be snotty about it."

In the morning, when I reached the cantina, I found the Modal Nodes already there, setting up.

Wuher scowled at me. "I got shot at. By a stinking droid."

"I'm sorry." He didn't seem that angry, though . . . "You heard them play."

He nodded grudgingly. "Yeah. They're pretty good."

"They're the best," I said softly. "And I think you know it."

He just snorted.

"About my fee."

"Yeah?"

"Free drinks for a year."

He snorted again. "Not bloody likely. We won't get a year out of this lot; they'll jump planet as soon as they can find some idiot to run the lines for them."

He had a point. Still—

"Their stay might be longer than that," I pointed out. "Jabba will want to keep them from leaving the planet. He might even want them back someday."

He actually smiled at me; I like him better scowling. "Seven free drinks a day as long as they keep playing. As soon as they sneak out of here, you pay again. You pay for every drink over seven anyway."

I grinned at him before I remembered myself, with the sharp teeth. "Deal." I got up and walked over to where Figrin was setting up with the band, and introduced myself.

I swear, Biths look contemptuous even when they're not trying to. The fellow had obviously heard of my reputation: Labria the drunk. The half bright, half sly, half sober. He barely glanced at me. "Oh, yes. Jabba's least favorite spy."

The fellow was a notorious gambler. "Interested in a

few hands of sabacc? The crowd doesn't start showing up here until later afternoon anyhow."

"I don't think so."

"Twenty-credit minimum bid."

His head swiveled as though it belonged to a droid. "Oh? Can you back that up?"

I gave him the sharp smile, on purpose. Bith *know* they're food. "Are you trying to insult me, Figrin Da'n?"

There may have been a deck somewhere, somewhen in the history of time colder than the one we used, but I wouldn't bet on it. Bith come from a warm, bright world. Devaronians, by the way, see farther into the infrared than practically anyone. It's useful to be able to see heat, when you evolve in the cold.

Buried in the black border along the edges of the cards were markers sensitive to low-spectrum infrared light. I knew every card he held, all that morning.

They were already broke. By the time we were done I owned their instruments, except for Doikk Na'ts's Fizzz.

And what a day *that* turned out to be.

For the life of me it seemed the universe had conspired to keep me from enjoying the music. First the band squabbled with each other, and then when they finally got going, with a nice upbeat rendition of "Mad About Me," some old fool chopped up another fool—with a lightsaber, of all frozen things—and interrupted it. That psychotic Solo actually showed his face in the cantina just after that, and then of course had to kill a miserable excuse for a bounty hunter named Greedo. If I'd had a blaster on me I might have shot Solo in the back as he left, but well, opportunities slip by.

Besides, it's best not to draw attention.

· · · ·

Afternoon slid into evening, and I nursed my drinks and watched them play. It took them a while to get into it; at first Figrin couldn't stand looking at me, and every time he saw me watching them it threw him out of his game. But it's hard to stay infuriated with someone who is knowledgeable about what you do, and appreciates it as I appreciated them. The music got darker as the day wore on, smokier and more intimate, and Figrin Da'n performed with his eyes closed, moving through the numbers, with Doikk Na'ts at his side; and they played with each other, building through the numbers together, playing off each other, feeding improvisations back upon improvisations, playing, for the first time in who knows how long, for an audience that could, and did, appreciate what they did. An audience of one.

They closed up with "Solitary World," an appropriate choice, I suppose, with the long intertwined sequences of Fizzz and Kloo, ending with one of the most difficult of the Kloo solos, and Doikk finished his piece, bowing out in recognition of genius: And the Bith stood there and played, Fiery Figrin Da'n in the midst of the music and I watched him wail away, safe, secure, surrounded by the sound, in that place that I would never know.

Swap Meet:
The Jawa's Tale

by Kevin J. Anderson

The sandcrawler labored up the long slope of golden sand that rippled with heat under the twin suns of Tatooine. The immense vehicle moved ahead at a moderate but inexorable rate. Its clanking tractor treads left parallel furrows on the virgin surface of the dune. Within a few hours, gusting sandwhirls would erase the tracks and return the Dune Sea to its pristine state. The desert resisted all permanent change.

Deep in the murky bowels of the sandcrawler, in the

cluttered engine rooms where throbbing power reactors pounded and echoed, Het Nkik labored with his Jawa clan members. From the depths of his hood, he sniffed the air, a veritable sauce of mingled odors. The engines smelled as if they were getting old again, lubricant spoiling, durasteel cogs wearing away.

Humans and many other sentient creatures loathed the way Jawas smelled, detecting only a stink that made them turn up their noses. But Jawas derived an incredible amount of information from such smells: the health of their companions, when and what they had last eaten, their identity, maturity, status of arousal, excitement, or boredom.

Het Nkik chittered his concern. At any other time the Jawas would have rushed to avert any potential breakdown—at least until they had unloaded their wares on a hapless customer. But today the Jawas paid him little heed, too preoccupied with the impending swap meet, the annual gathering of all clans. They pushed the engine to its maximum capacity as the sandcrawler toiled across the Dune Sea to the traditional meeting place of the Jawa people.

Het Nkik shook his head, his bright yellow eyes glowing in the dim shadows of his hood. The other Jawas would know he was annoyed and impatient from his scent.

Het Nkik had odd ideas for a Jawa, and he told them to any who would listen. He enjoyed watching his clan brothers scurry around, confused at the thoughts he placed in their heads—thoughts that perhaps the Jawas could do more than run and hide from persecution by the Sand People, by the human moisture farmers, or worst of all by the Imperial stormtroopers who had decided that helpless Jawa forts made good practice targets for desert assaults. He wondered if someone else among all the Jawas had realized that Jawas were only weak because they *chose* to be weak. None of his people wanted to listen.

Het Nkik turned back to the engines, tearing open an access panel and adjusting the delicate electronics.

He found it amazing that the Jawas could use all their skill and imagination in a desperate fight to keep this ancient machine running, yet they would do nothing to protect themselves or their property if some antagonist tried to take it.

With the sound of a grating alarm signal, the Jawas in the engine room squealed with delight. Cinching tight his pungent brown robe, Het Nkik scurried after the others as they rushed for the lift platforms to the bridge observation deck. The old elevators groaned, overloaded with jabbering creatures.

At the pinnacle of the great trapezoidal sandcrawler, fifteen Jawa crew members clustered around the long, high transparisteel window, standing on inverted spare-parts boxes to see. All during Tatooine's long double-day, Jawa lookouts stood atop makeshift stools, gazing out upon the baked sands, looking for any scrap of metal or signs of Sand People or Imperial storm-troopers or hostile smugglers. Upon glimpsing any potential threat, the pilot would swerve in a different direction and increase speed, locking down blast doors and shuddering with fear, hoping that the adversary would not pursue them. Het Nkik had never heard of even a krayt dragon striking something as big as a Jawa sandcrawler, but that did not stop the Jawas from living in terror.

Now the other small hooded forms looked down upon the broad bowl-shaped valley among the dunes. Het Nkik elbowed his way to one of the overturned metal boxes so he could step up and look out across the gathering place. Though this was his third season as an adult on the scavenger hunts, Het Nkik still found the swap-meet site breathtaking.

He stared across the dazzling sand as the twin suns shone down on a swarm of sandcrawlers like a herd of metallic beasts gathered in a circle. The vehicles looked similar, though over the decades Jawa mechanics had attached modifications, subtle differences in armor and patchwork.

Originally the sandcrawlers had been huge ore haulers brought to Tatooine by hopeful human miners who had expected to make a fortune exploiting the baked wastelands; but the mineral content of Tatooine's desert was as bleak and unappealing as the landscape itself. The miners had abandoned their ore haulers, and the rodentlike Jawa scavengers had seized them and put them to use, wandering the Dune Sea and the Jundland Wastes in search of salvageable debris. After more than a century, the sandcrawler hulls had been oxidized to a dull brown and pitted by the abrasive desert winds.

Their sandcrawler had arrived late, as Het Nkik had feared. Two days ago the pilot had taken them deep into a box-ended offshoot of Beggar's Canyon where the metal detectors had found a slight trace of something that might have been the framework of a crashed fighter's hull. But instead they had found only a few girders rusted away to flakes of powder. The oxidized debris was worthless, but before the Jawas could leave the narrow canyon, an early-season sandwhirl had whipped up, trapping them in a blinding cyclone of sand and wind. Strapped to the walls of their living cubicles, the Jawas had waited for the storm to blow over, and then used the powerful engines to plow through the drifted sand.

Though they had arrived at the swap meet late, there still seemed to be a bustling business. Far below, other Jawas scurried about like insects setting up the bazaar. Het Nkik hoped he could still find something worthwhile to trade.

Standing on their metal stools, the pilot and the chief lookout called across to each other, discussing the final sandcrawler count. Het Nkik calculated quickly with his darting yellow eyes and saw that they were not the last to arrive. One of the other vehicles was missing. Some of the Jawas around him speculated on what misfortune might have overtaken their brethren, while others consoled themselves by pointing out that even if the goods had already been picked over, they would have a new batch to inspect when the final vehicle arrived.

As the pilot guided the sandcrawler over the lip of the dunes in a switchback path down into the flat meeting area, the Jawas scurried back to their living cubicles to prep their own wares. His body wiry beneath the heavy robes, Het Nkik had no difficulty scrambling down fifteen decks to reach the stuffy cubicles.

Het Nkik slept in an empty upright shipping pod, rectangular and scarred with corrosion, barely large enough to step inside and turn around. During sleeping cycles he buckled himself to the wall and relaxed against the belt restraints where he could stare at his prized possessions stashed in pockets, magnetic drawers, and field jars. Now he grabbed the accumulated credit chips and barter notes he had earned during their great scavenger hunt and darted toward the main egress doors.

Faced with the magnitude of the great bazaar, the Jawas worked together as an efficient team. They had set up their merchandise dozens of times during their half-year trek, stopping at every moisture farmer's residence, every smuggler's den, even Jabba the Hutt's palace. Jawas didn't care where they sold their wares.

Down in the bowels of the sandcrawler, Het Nkik scurried among the merchandise, tweaking the barely functional droids and servo apparatus. Jawas had an instinctive feel for machinery and electronics, knowing how to get a piece of equipment functioning just well enough to sell it. Let the buyer beware.

The deserts of Tatooine were a veritable graveyard of junk. The harsh planet had been the site of many galactic battles over the centuries, and the dry climate preserved all manner of debris from crashed ships and lost expeditions.

Het Nkik loved to fix and recondition broken things, energized by his ability to bring wrecked machines back to life. He remembered when he and his clan mate and best friend Jek Nkik had stumbled upon a crashed fighter. The small fighter had blown up, leaving only fragments—nothing even a Jawa could salvage. But digging deeper, they had found the burned and tangled components of a droid—an E522-model assassin droid that had seemed hopelessly damaged, but he and Jek Nkik vowed to fix it, secretly scrounging spare parts from the storehouse in the Jawa fortress.

Their clan leader Wimateeka had suspected the two young boys were up to something and watched them closely, but that only made them more determined to succeed. Het Nkik and his friend had spent months in a secret hideaway deep in the badlands, piecing together tiny components and servomotors, adding new instruction sets. Finally the assassin droid stood emasculated of murderous programming, purged of all hunter-seeker weapons and all initiative to cause violence. The E522 functioned perfectly, but as little more than an extremely powerful messenger droid.

Het and Jek Nkik had proudly displayed their triumph to Wimateeka, who scolded the boys for such folly; no one would want to buy a reprogrammed assassin droid, he said. But Het Nkik could tell from the not-quite-controlled rush of scent that Wimateeka also admired the young Jawas' brashness. Never again had Het Nkik believed common wisdom about what Jawas could not do.

He and Jek Nkik had surprised themselves by selling the repaired assassin droid to the tusk-faced Lady Valarian, Jabba the Hutt's chief rival on Tatooine—a very risky trade that brought them even more scolding from Wimateeka. Lady Valarian was a tough customer; and the one time she had felt cheated, the only remains of the hapless Jawa traders were a few tattered brown cloaks found in the Great Pit of Carkoon where the voracious Sarlacc waited to devour anything that came within reach. Het Nkik had no idea what had happened to their reprogrammed assassin droid, but since Lady Valarian had not come after them, he presumed the huge Whiphid smuggler queen must have been satisfied.

Two years ago, Het and Jek Nkik had been separated

upon reaching their age of adulthood, sent out to do
scavenger duty away from the Jawa fortress. In a few
years, sandcrawler crews would swap clan groupings
and arrange marriages; but for the time being Het
Nkik saw his friend only during the annual swap meets.

Now he had credit chips in his barter pouch, he had
merchandise to trade—and he looked forward to seeing Jek Nkik.

The sandcrawler ground to a halt in the demarcated
area set aside for their clan subunit. When the cargo
doors opened, Jawa teams scurried to haul out the repaired droids, scraps of polished hull-metal plates, ap-
pliances, and primitive weapons they had found
among the sands. The Jawas' motto was not to look for
uses in a salvaged piece of garbage, but rather to imagine someone else who might find a use for it.

Jawas bustled about setting up tables, awnings, credit
display readers. Others gave a last burnish to the exo-
skeletons of clanking mechanical servants. A few tried
to look nondescript, hiding emergency repair kits inside their cloaks in the event that their wares unexpectedly stopped functioning before a sale could be
confirmed.

Power droids lumbered down a ramp, little more
than boxlike batteries walking on two accordioned
legs. Harvester droids and 'vaporator components
were set up and displayed; Jawa salesmen took their
positions proclaiming the quality of their wares. A few
lucky ones rushed off to be the first to snoop among
the items for sale or trade by other clans.

Around the perimeter of the rendezvous flat, Jawa
sentries stood with image enhancers and macrobinoculars, searching for any sign of approaching threat. At
the slightest suspicious sign, the Jawa clans would pack
up their wares in a flash to vanish into the endless
dune wilderness.

Het Nkik looked around but could not locate Jek's
sandcrawler.

After finishing setup procedures, he took his turn to look at the other wares. In the bustling melee, he smelled the stinging sweet scents of hundreds of Jawas keyed up with excitement. He felt the baking suns' heat on his brown cloak, he heard the cacophony of squeaking voices, the rumble of sandcrawler engines. Electronic motors ratcheted and choked, missing beats until Jawa mechanics effected quick fixes in hopes that none of the potential customers would notice. He wandered among the huckster tables, his excitement soured by the fact that Jek's sandcrawler was not there.

Het Nkik saw his clan leader, old Wimateeka, discussing something in hushed tones with the clan leader from an outlying Jawa fortress near the human settlement of Bestine. Het Nkik could smell the concern, the fear, the indecision. Wimateeka was so alarmed he didn't even try to mask his odors.

Het Nkik sensed bad news. Wimateeka was whispering, for fear of sending the rest of the Jawas in a panicked flight. With a feeling of dread, Het Nkik drove back his impulse to run back to the security of the sandcrawler and pushed forward to interrupt Wimateeka. "What is it, clan leader?" he asked. "Do you have news of the last sandcrawler?"

Wimateeka looked at him in surprise, and the other clan leader chittered in annoyance. Normal protocol among Jawas held that younger members did not approach their clan leaders directly, but went through a labyrinth of family connections, passing a message up through higher and higher relations until finally it reached its target; answers came back down through a similarly circuitous route. But Het Nkik had a reputation for sidestepping the rules.

"Clan leader Eet Ptaa was telling me of a Tusken attack on his clan's fortress," Wimateeka said. "The Sand People broke in and attacked before the Jawas managed to flee. Our brethren will never return to their ancestral home. They lost all possessions except what they could throw into the sandcrawler."

Het Nkik was appalled. "If the Jawas were inside

their fortress, did they not fight? Why did they just flee?"

"Jawas do not fight," Wimateeka said. "We are too weak."

"Because they don't try," Het Nkik said, feeling his temper rise. His body scent carried his anger to both clan leaders.

"We would have been slaughtered!" Eet Ptaa insisted.

"Jawas are too small," Wimateeka said. "Sand People are too warlike." The old clan leader turned to the other, dismissing Het Nkik. "This young one has a reputation for speaking without thinking. We can only hope his wisdom will grow with age."

Het Nkik swallowed his outrage and pushed for an answer to the question that concerned him most. "What about my clan brother Jek Nkik? Where is the last sandcrawler?"

Wimateeka shook his head so that his hood jerked from side to side. "We have lost all contact with them. They sent no explanation of their delay. We are concerned. Perhaps the Sand People attacked them, too."

Het Nkik scowled. "We can't simply run and hide all the time, especially now that the Imperials are growing more aggressive. We could all work together. Many small ones can make one large force. Now that the Jawas have gathered for the swap meet, clan leader, will you discuss my ideas with them?"

Wimateeka and Eet Ptaa tittered with nervous laughter. Wimateeka said, "Now you're sounding like one particular human moisture farmer I know! He wants Jawas and humans and Sand People to work together and draw maps separating our territories."

"Is that such a bad idea?" Het Nkik asked.

Wimateeka shrugged. "It is not the Jawa way."

Het Nkik felt as if he were talking to a droid with its power pack removed. Nothing would ever change until the Jawas saw how things might be different—until someone set an example.

He walked along between the tables, kicking up occasional billows of dust. The smell of roasted hubba gourd made his mouth water. Looking up, he searched the rim of the dunes for any sign of Jek Nkik's sand-crawler. As he passed a table from the Kkak clan, he heard a conspiratorial whisper, unlike the entreaties by other merchants.

"Het Nkik!" the Kkak clan member said, clicking the hard consonants and sharpening his name.

He turned and saw the other Jawa reach beneath his table to a private stash of wares. "Are you Het Nkik?" he repeated. "Of Wimateeka's clan, the one who is always talking about empowering the Jawas, about making us fight? Hrar Kkak salutes you and offers an exchange of wares."

Het Nkik felt a ribbon of cold inside him like a long drink of rare water. "I am Het Nkik," he said, letting suspicion curl through his body odor. It was good to let a salesman see healthy skepticism. "The opportunity for exchange is always welcome, and the time for opportunity is always now."

"I have something for you," the tradesman said. "Come closer."

Het Nkik took a step to the table, and now he was honor bound to listen to the sales pitch. The Kkak clansman looked around furtively and then hauled out a blaster rifle, scarred but magnificent. A Blastech DL-44 model, more power than Het Nkik had ever held in his own hands.

He took a step backward in alarm and then forward in fascination. "Jawas are forbidden such weapons," he said.

"I have heard rumors of such an Imperial decree from Mos Eisley, but I have received no confirmation of it," the salesman said. "We of the Kkak clan have been wandering the far fringes of the Dune Sea, and sometimes communication of such things takes a long time."

Het Nkik nodded in admiration of the smooth excuse. "Does it function? Where did you get it?"

"Never mind where I got it."

Het Nkik felt ashamed for his breach of Jawa proto-col. "If I'm going to purchase this . . ." He removed his pouch of barter credits, knowing instinctively that he *had* to have the weapon. He wanted it no matter what the consequences—and the salesman knew it, too. "I need to know if it works."

"Of course it functions." The salesman popped out the power pack. "You'll see that the charge is on three-quarters."

Het Nkik saw that it was a standard power pack of the type that could be used in many sorts of equip-ment. "Let me try it in that portable illuminator," he said, "just to make sure."

Both of them knew Het Nkik could not fire the blaster with all the other Jawas present. The Kkak sales-man slipped the power pack into the portable illumina-tor and switched it on. A bright beam stabbed skyward toward the two suns. "Satisfied?"

Het Nkik nodded. "My resources are meager, though my admiration of your wares is great."

The two haggled over price for an acceptable amount of time, though the price didn't change much. Het Nkik hurried away with only a few barter credits left to his name—but the proud owner of a highly ille-gal blaster hidden under his brown robes. For the first time in his life, he felt tall. Very tall.

He spent the rest of the swap meet looking for his comrade Jek Nkik, but the last sandcrawler never ar-rived.

After the swap meet disbanded, the sandcrawlers toiled across the Dune Sea in different directions, laden with new treasures each clan had obtained through hard bargaining.

After an hour of relentless jabbering, Het Nkik con-vinced the pilot to detour along the path Jek Nkik's vehicle might have taken, to see if they could discover what had befallen the missing Jawas. They headed toward the outlying moisture farms among which his clan mate's group often traded.

Het Nkik worked in the engine room, coaxing the faltering reactors to function for just a few more months until the storm season when the sandcrawlers would be parked next to Jawa fortresses in the badlands. Wimateeka's old mechanics would have to give the ion pumps and the reactors a full overhaul. Het Nkik's companions were much more focused on their tasks now that the swap meet was over.

At about midday, the lookout sounded an alarm. He had seen smoke. Normally the sight of burning wreckage made Jawas ecstatic at the possibility of a salvage claim, but Het Nkik felt a deep foreboding; none of the others noticed the change in his scent.

He left his post and took the lift platform to the bridge. In front of the wide viewport, he climbed on an overturned equipment box and stared. The smoke grew thick. His heart sank inside him as if he had just lost all his possessions in a bad trade.

He recognized the oxidized brown metal of an old ore hauler's hull, the trapezoidal shape. The sandcrawler had been assaulted, blasted with heavy-weapons fire, and destroyed.

Het Nkik knew his friend and clan brother was dead.

The lookout chittered in terror, expressing his fear that whatever had struck the sandcrawler might still be around to attack them. But the pilot, seeing the enormous wealth of unclaimed salvage, overcame his uneasiness. He used the comm unit to transmit a message to Wimateeka's fortress, establishing his salvage rights.

Greasy tatters of smoke curled up in the air as the sandcrawler descended toward the destroyed vehicle. Het Nkik felt a resurgence of anger bubble within him. He recalled how stormtroopers had assaulted Jawa fortresses for practice. He thought of Eet Ptaa's settlement raided by the Sand People. Yet again, someone bigger had attacked helpless Jawas, perhaps out of spite, or for sport, or for no reason at all.

The only thing Jawas ever did was take their beatings, flee, and accept their helplessness. Nothing would ever change until somebody showed them another way.

He thought of the blaster he had purchased at the swap meet.

The pilot brought the sandcrawler to a halt facing the best escape route if attackers reappeared. The hull doors clanked open, and the Jawas scrambled out, ducking low for cover but eager to dash toward the treasure trove of scrap. The pilot scrambled forward to apply a claim beacon to the ruined sandcrawler, warning away other scavengers. Jawas swarmed into the half-open door of the wreck, scurrying to see what treasures had been left undamaged.

Several Jawas squealed as they realized they were not alone by the damaged sandcrawler. A bearded old human in worn but flowing robes stood off in the shade beside two droids that he seemed to have claimed for himself. He had built a small, crackling pyre. Het Nkik sniffed, smelled burning flesh; the old man had already begun the ritual disposal of Jawa carcasses in the purging flames.

The human raised his hands in a placating gesture. Some of Het Nkik's cousins speculated that the old human had killed the other Jawas, but Het Nkik saw this was obviously absurd.

A protocol droid walked stiffly beside the old man. Its gold plating was a bit scratched, and it had a dent in the top of its head; but all in all the droid seemed to be in good functioning order. The other droid, a barrel-shaped model, hung back and bleeped in alarm at seeing the Jawas. Het Nkik automatically began to assess how much he could get in trade for the droids.

The protocol droid said, "I offer my services as an interpreter, sir. I am fluent in over six million forms of communication."

The old man looked calmly at the droid and made a dismissive gesture. "Your services won't be needed. I've lived in these deserts far too long not to understand a little of the Jawas' speech. Greetings!" the old man said in clear Jawa words. "May you trade well, though I sorrow for your tragedy here today."

Three Jawas bent close to the rock-strewn ground and spotted bantha tracks. They set up a wail of panic, suddenly convinced that the Sand People had declared an all-out war.

But something did not seem right to Het Nkik. He looked at the tracks, at the crude weapons fire that had struck the most crucial spots on the enormous ore hauler. He sniffed the air, sorting through layers of scent from molten and hardened metal to the burning stench of bodies, to the heated sand. He detected an undertone of plasteel armor, fresh lubricants, a mechanized attack, but he could find none of the musty smells of the Tusken Raiders or the dusty, peppery scent of their banthas.

Het Nkik pointed this out, and the other Jawas snapped at him, impatient, as usual, with his contradictory views. But the old man spoke up for him. "Your little brother is right. This was an Imperial attack, not a strike by the Sand People."

The others chittered in disbelief, but the old man continued. "The Imperial occupying forces would like nothing better than to see a war among Sand People and Jawas and human moisture farmers. You must not allow yourselves to believe their deceptions."

"Who are you?" Het Nkik asked him. "How do you know our funeral customs, and why have you claimed no salvage for yourself?"

The old man said, "I know of your customs because I try to understand the other people who share my desert home. I know the Jawas believe that all their possessions are forfeit to the clan at death, but your bodies are borrowed from the womb of the sands, and their elements must return to pay the debt you owe for your temporary life."

Some of the Jawas gasped at his eloquent recital of their own intensely private beliefs.

"If you understand us so well," Het Nkik · said brashly, "then you know that no Jawa would ever strike back at a Tusken Raider, even for such a blatant assault as this. The Jawas are all cowards. Nothing will make them fight."

The old man smiled indulgently, and his pale blue eyes seemed to bore through Het Nkik's robe, seeing deep into the hooded shadow of his face. "Perhaps a coward is only a fighter who has not yet been pushed far enough—or one who has not been shown the way."

"General Kenobi," the golden droid interrupted, "Master Luke has been gone far too long. He should have had ample time to get to his home and back by now."

The old man turned to the Jawas. "Your salvage claim is safe here, but you must warn the others of the tricks the Imperials are playing. The garrison in Mos Eisley has just been reinforced with many more stormtroopers. They are searching . . . for something they will not find."

The two droids stood huddled together.

"But the Prefect and the Imperial Governor will continue to foster turmoil between the Jawas and the Tusken Raiders." Then the human turned and looked directly at Het Nkik. "The Jawas are not powerless—if they do not wish to be."

Het Nkik felt a lance of fear and realization strike through him. A memory returned to him like a stun bolt. He recalled with the vividness of a double desert sunset a time—less than a year before his coming of age—when he had scanned a crashed T-16 speeder out in the rocky twists of an unnamed canyon. Wanting to claim the salvage for himself, Het Nkik had not asked for Jawa assistance, not even from Jek Nkik.

When he found the ruined vehicle, he spotted a young human male sprawled dead on the rocks, thrown there by the crash. Apparently, the T-16's repulsorlifts had been unable to counteract a sudden thermal updraft; the landspeeder had crashed and skidded, leaving a knotted tongue of smoke in the otherwise empty air.

Het Nkik had pawed at the mangled controls, ignoring the broken body that had already begun to attract moisture-seeking insects from crevices in the rocks. He had suddenly looked up to discover six young and vicious Tusken Raiders, their faces swaddled with rags, hissing through breath filters. They were angry, ready for a heroic adventure they could tell about around the story fires throughout their adulthood. The Sand People raised their sharpened gaffi sticks and uttered their ululating cries.

Het Nkik knew he was about to die. He could not possibly fight even one of the Sand People. He was unarmed. He was alone. He was small and defenseless —a weak, cowardly Jawa.

But as the Sand People attacked, Het Nkik had found the T-16's still-functioning security system, and triggered it. The sonic alarm sent out a pulsating screech loud enough to curdle dewback blood. Startled by the noise, the Raiders had fled.

Het Nkik had stood trembling in his brown robes, paralyzed with fear and astonishment. It took him many moments to realize that *he* alone had scared off the Tusken Raiders. A weak Jawa had driven back an attack by bloodthirsty Sand People!

It had been a warming revelation to him: Given the right equipment and the right attitude, Jawas could be different.

And now he had a blaster rifle.

"I know we are not powerless," Het Nkik said to the old man who continued to watch him, "but my clan members do not realize it."

"Perhaps they will," the old man said.

As the other Jawas scrambled over the wrecked sandcrawler, Het Nkik knew what he had to do. He went to the pilot and forfeited his entire share of salvage in exchange for a single functional vehicle that would take him alone across the desert to the human spaceport . . . where the Imperials were headquartered.

•　　•　　•

Het Nkik's sand vehicle broke down twice on his trek to the sprawling, squalid city of Mos Eisley. Standing under the pounding heat of the suns as the burning wind licked under his hood, he managed to use his skill and meager resources to get the vehicle limping along again over the rocky ground.

Inside his cloak the DL-44 blaster felt incredibly heavy, cold and hot at the same time. The weight inside his chest seemed even heavier, but burning anger drove him on.

On the dust-whipped streets of Mos Eisley, Het Nkik kept the sand vehicle functioning until he spotted another Jawa—a member of a distant clan who had been in town for some time—and offered the used-up vehicle for sale. Though he drove a poor bargain, Het Nkik did not expect to live long enough to spend the credits; but his nature forbade him giving anything away.

On foot, Het Nkik trudged through the rippling midday heat, clutching the blaster close to his chest, looking at languid creatures dozing in adobe doorways waiting for the day to cool. The streets were nearly deserted. He walked and walked, feeling his feet burn; the pale dust caked his garment.

He knew what he intended to do, but he didn't quite know how to go about it. He had a blaster. He had an obsession. But he had yet to find a target—the right target.

He noted an increased Imperial presence in the city, guards stationed by docking bays and the customs center; but no more than two at a time. Het Nkik knew that life was cheap in Mos Eisley, and killing a single Imperial trooper would not cause enough uproar. He had to go out in such a blaze of glory and heroism that the Jawas would sing of him for years to come.

In the town center he found the large wreck of the *Dowager Queen* spacecraft, a mess of tangled girders, falling-apart hull plates, and all manner of strange creatures, vagrants, and scavengers lurking inside the hull.

To Het Nkik it looked like the perfect place for an ambush.

His instincts told him to feel helpless, but he firmly squashed those thoughts. He had the strength, if only he could find the will to make an example of himself. It could change the lives of Jawas forever . . . or he could just get himself foolishly killed.

Panic welled up within him as he considered the folly of an insignificant Jawa planning something so preposterous. He wanted to hide in a shadowy alley. He could wait for darkness, scurry out of the city and find someplace where he could be *safe* and cower with the other Jawas, afraid of every threatening noise. Afraid to fight . . .

Bracing himself, Het Nkik slipped inside the bustling cantina right across the dirt thoroughfare from the wreck of the *Dowager Queen*. Conflicting scents overwhelmed him: strange smells of a thousand different patron species, chemicals that served as stimulants for an untold number of biochemistries, the smell of amorous intentions, of restrained violence, of anger and laughter, food and sweat. Strains of music drifted out, a mixture of noises chained to a melody.

He had credit chips. He could get a stimulant, something to help him focus his thoughts, brace up his courage.

Het Nkik moved with quick steps down the stairs, hugging the shadows, trying not to be noticed. Deep inside the folds of his garment he gripped the precious blaster. He placed a credit chit on the bar counter, straining to reach the high surface. He had to repeat his order three times before the harried human bartender understood what he wanted. Nursing his drink, Het Nkik hunched over a tiny private table, smelling rich volatile chemicals wafting from the surface of the liquid. The scent was just as intoxicating as the drink itself.

He tried to plan, but no thoughts came to him. Should he resort to a spontaneous action, an angry gesture, rather than a methodically orchestrated scenario? His plan required no finesse, merely a large number of targets and the element of surprise. He thought of the burning Jawa corpses at the wrecked sandcrawler and the old human hermit who had given him the courage.

He felt a warm rush of surprise as the old hermit entered the cantina with a young moisture farmer. The bartender made them leave their droids outside; at another time Het Nkik might have plotted a raid to steal the two unguarded droids, but not now. He had more important things on his mind.

The old hermit didn't notice him, but Het Nkik took his appearance as a sign, an omen of strength. He gulped his drink and sat up watching the old man talk to a spacer at the bar then to a Wookiee, and when the moisture-farmer boy got into trouble with one of the other patrons, the old man came to the rescue with the most spectacular weapon Het Nkik had ever seen, a glowing shaft of light that cut through flesh as if it were smoke.

Seeing the lightsaber made him suddenly doubt his mere blaster. He pulled out the weapon and held it on his lap under the table, touching the smooth metal curves, the deadly buttons, the power pack snapped into the end. He was startled by another creature joining him at his table: a furry, long-snouted Ranat who smelled of dust and eagerness to make a trade.

Jawas and Ranats often competed with each other in the streets of Mos Eisley. The Jawas tended to roam the empty areas of sand, while Ranats stayed within populated areas. They traded at times, but generally viewed each other with suspicion.

"Reegesk salutes Het Nkik and offers an exchange of tales or wares," the Ranat said in the formalized greeting.

Het Nkik was in no mood to talk, but he made the appropriate response. Sipping his drink, listening to the Ranat chatter about his wares, he tried to find a way to gather his own courage. But when the Ranat offered him a Tusken battle talisman, he suddenly sat up and listened.

The Sand People were great warriors; they fought creatures many times their size, slaughtered entire settlements, tamed wild banthas. Perhaps a Tusken charm could give him the advantage he needed after all. And what did he have to lose?

The Ranat seemed to realize how much he wanted the talisman, so Het Nkik offered a high price—provided he could pay a few credits now and the rest later—knowing full well that he would never be around for the second installment.

Against his better judgment, Het Nkik passed his blaster surreptitiously under the table so the Ranat could look at it. With the talisman in his hand and the blaster rifle under his fingertips, facing the burning intensity in the Ranat's eyes, Het Nkik felt inspiration return, felt his need for revenge. He thought again of his clan brother Jek Nkik, how the two of them had done the almost impossible, repairing the assassin droid—and then he remembered the smoking wreckage of the sandcrawler.

Imperials had done that. Imperials had attacked other Jawa fortresses. Imperials continued to tighten their grip on Tatooine. Perhaps his gesture would stir up not only the Jawas, but bring about a general revolution. Then the planet could be free again. That would be worth any sacrifice, would it not?

A loud explosion and a sudden commotion across the cantina startled him. He wanted to duck under the table, but he whirled to see a human sitting at a booth. Smoke curled up from a hole in the table in front of him and a strong-smelling Rodian lay slumped on the table. Het Nkik was paralyzed for a moment in terror, though the Ranat seemed amused at the Rodian's death. Het Nkik stared as the human slowly got up, avoiding the dead bounty hunter and tossing a coin at the bar.

Life was indeed cheap in Mos Eisley, but he wanted to sell his own for a high price. Other Jawas in the cantina scrambled to claim the corpse; at another time he too might have fought for his share of the remains, but he let his brothers take what they needed.

He looked down to see the Ranat fondling his DL-44 blaster, and Het Nkik snatched it away. He sensed determination and enthusiasm pouring through his muscles. The intoxicant buzzed through his brain. The weapon felt light and powerful in his hands.

He would never be more prepared.

Without saying good-bye to the Ranat, he took the blaster, squeezed the Tusken battle talisman, and scuttled out of the cantina, across the bright streets to the wreckage of the *Dowager Queen*.

As soon as he was there, Het Nkik knew he had been meant to do this. Pressing the blaster against his side, he scrambled up the hot metal hull plates of the wreck, finding handholds and footholds to get himself to a higher position, a good place to fire from.

His pulse pounded. His head sang. He knew this was his time. His entire life had been focused toward this moment. He found a shaded place. A good spot for his ambush.

A line of stormtroopers on patrol rounded the corner, marching toward the cantina as if searching for something. They marched in lockstep, crushing dust under their white heels, intent on their goal. Sunlight gleamed from their polished armor. Their weapons clicked and rattled as they walked, their helmets stared straight ahead. They walked quickly, coming closer and closer.

He counted eight in a row. Yes, eight of them. If he, a single weak Jawa, could mow down eight Imperial stormtroopers, that would be the stuff of legends. No Jawa could forget that their brother, Het Nkik, had struck such a blow against the Empire. If all Jawas could do the same thing, the Empire would flee from Tatooine.

He clutched the blaster. He bent down. He watched the stormtroopers approach. His glowing yellow eyes focused on them, and he tried to determine the best plan of attack. He would strike the leader first, then the ones in the middle, then behind, then back to the front in a sweeping motion. There would be a shower of blaster bolts. It would take them a moment to discover his location. For some of them, that would be a moment too long.

There was even the ridiculously small chance that he could kill them *all* before they managed a shot in his direction. In the ruined ship he had a bit of cover. Maybe he could survive this. He could live to strike again and again. Perhaps he could even become a Jawa leader, a warlord. Het Nkik, the great general!

Stormtroopers stepped in front of the ship, looking toward the cantina, not even seeing him. Arrogant and confident, they ignored the *Dowager Queen*.

Het Nkik gripped the blaster. His knees were ready to explode, springloaded, waiting, *waiting* until he couldn't stand it a moment, an instant longer—and uttered a chittering ululation of rage and revenge in a conscious imitation of a Tusken cry. In his life's single moment of glory, so close to the end, Het Nkik leaped up and swung the blaster rifle at his targets.

Before they could even turn in his direction, he squeezed the firing button—again, and again, and again.

Trade Wins:
The Ranat's Tale

by Rebecca Moesta

Dodging a pair of potentially meddlesome storm-troopers, Reegesk clutched his treasures and scurried with rodentlike efficiency into the narrow alley beside his favorite drinking establishment in Mos Eisley. Ah, yes, his favorite. Not because their drinks or performers were of superior quality, but because he could always find someone there who wanted—or needed—to make a trade. And in the small Ranat tribe that scratched out a larger place for itself each day on this arid outpost world, that was, after all, his job: Reegesk the Trader, Reegesk the Barterer, Reegesk the Procurement Specialist Par Excellence.

Whiskers twitching with satisfaction, he sat against a sun-washed wall, curled his whip-hard tail loosely around him, and opened his bundle to examine the day's prizes. An oven-hot breeze carried the not unpleasant scents of decaying garbage and animal droppings to Reegesk from farther down the alley. He had started the morning with little more than a handful of polished rocks and a few tidbits of information and had made a series of successful trades to collect the much more valuable items that he now spread out in the dust beside him. A small antenna, some fine cloth with very few holes in it, a bundle of wires for the tiny 'vaporator his tribe was secretly building. These he would keep.

But he had more bargaining to do yet. He still needed many things: a power source to complete the bootleg 'vaporator unit that could make his tribe less dependent on local moisture farmers, a length or two of rope, scraps of metal for making tools or weapons.

From his perspective, he always managed to trade up. Fortunately, he still had a few items left to trade from his most recent bargain: a cracked stormtrooper helmet, a packet of field rations, and a Tusken battle talisman carved from bantha horn. All this for only some day-old information and a discarded restraining bolt. He supposed the heat and dust could dull anyone's judgment. Perhaps the Imperial officer—a Lieutenant Alima, who was definitely not a local—should have paid more attention to the deal. Well, the officer had gotten what he wanted. Reegesk shrugged.

Of course, the old warning to buyers was valid: Always pay close attention during a trade. Less scrupulous traders tricked customers or tried to convince them to make useless purchases, but not Reegesk. This, despite the "semisentient" status the Empire had conferred on the Ranat race, had gained him a reputation on the streets of Mos Eisley for being shrewd but fair.

In fact, aside from the bothersome local storm-troopers, there were few potential customers in the port who would refuse a trade with Reegesk if he had just what they "needed."

Reegesk's furry snout quirked into a dry, incisor-baring smile. Well, he knew what *he* needed, and he knew where to conduct his next trade.

The interior of the cantina was relatively cool, and the dimness was a relief from the moisture-stealing intensity of Tatooine's twin suns. The air smelled of musky damp fur and baked scales, of nic-i-tain smoke, of space suits that had not been decontaminated in months, and of intoxicants from dozens of different worlds.

Reegesk stepped to the bar, ordered a cup of Rydan brew from Wuher the bartender, and scanned the room for a likely customer. A Devaronian? No, Reegesk had nothing to interest him. One of the Bith musicians who was just taking a break? Perhaps. Ah. Reegesk's glance fell on the familiar figure of a Jawa.

Perfect.

Reegesk pulled the hood of his cloak loosely over his head as he started toward the Jawa's small table. Jawas were private folk who believed in being fully covered, even indoors, and in Reegesk's experience, finding common ground with the customer always helped a trade. He was relieved to note by the scent as he approached the table that he knew the Jawa, Het Nkik, and had traded with him before.

When Reegesk saw the bandleader Figrin Da'n signaling an end to the musicians' break, he hurried to get Het Nkik's attention before the next song could begin. "Reegesk salutes Het Nkik and offers an exchange of tales or wares," he said, giving his most formal trader greeting to the Jawa, who seemed preoccupied and had not yet noticed Reegesk's presence.

Het Nkik did not react immediately, but when he

did look up, Reegesk thought he saw a look of relief, as if the Jawa were happy to be distracted from his thoughts. "The opportunity for exchange is always welcome, and the time for opportunity is always now," Het Nkik replied with equal formality, but the pitch of his voice was higher than usual and his eyes darted furtively about the room.

"May both traders receive the better bargain." Reegesk finished the ritual greeting with irony, knowing full well that Jawas were seldom concerned with whether their customers were satisfied. Well, that was not his way. Cunning as he was, Reegesk traded only with customers who needed (or believed they needed) what he had, and he bartered away only items the tribe did not need.

Reegesk's nose wrinkled briefly as he tried to identify the scent that hung about Het Nkik. Sensing what he could only interpret as impatience or anticipation, Reegesk decided against any further delay and swung smoothly into the trading process. He began with glowing descriptions of the bargains he had made that morning. Strangely, Het Nkik was not very enthusiastic as he spoke of his own trading and showed Reegesk a charged Blastech DL-44 blaster in excellent condition. Reegesk did not need to feign either admiration or jealousy over the trade; since it was still illegal to arm a Ranat in the Outer Rim Territories, it was difficult for Reegesk to bargain for anything that might be used as a weapon. And the DL-44 was a particularly fine weapon.

Seeming to take little notice of Reegesk's approval of his bartering, Het Nkik allowed the trading to move to an alternating exchange of increasingly valuable information. The two traders were so engrossed in their interchange that Reegesk did not notice the Rodian bounty hunter until he had bumped backward into their table. An obnoxious new arrival named Greedo. Reegesk made a grab for his brew and caught it as it teetered precariously at the edge of the table. He felt his nostrils contract in annoyance, as they would at an unpleasant odor.

Greedo turned, apparently ready to excuse himself for his mistake, but he stopped when he noticed the table's occupants. The greenish tinge of his skin deepened and the lips on his snout formed a sneer as he looked at Reegesk. "Womp!" he spat out, giving the table another sharp shove as he delivered the epithet, and then moved off in the general direction of the bar.

Reegesk bristled, hurling venomous thoughts after the sour-smelling green-skinned bounty hunter. The outrage of it! The insult. After all, Ranats were *no* relation whatsoever to the nonsentient Tatooine womp rats! Greedo was one person he would not mind seeing cheated in a trade.

When he was calm again, the trading moved to the next stage and Reegesk began discreetly displaying the items he was willing to trade. Het Nkik showed a mild interest in the stormtrooper helmet, but when Reegesk brought out the bantha horn carved in the shape of a Tusken battle talisman, Het Nkik's excitement was unmistakable. Reegesk, quickly searching his memory for anything he knew about such objects, managed to remember something of interest. The Sand People, he explained, believed a battle talisman brought them the physical strength of a bantha in battle and gave them the courage to face death, if need be. Het Nkik asked to hold the talisman, turning it over and over in his hands, uttering exclamations in a dialect Reegesk did not recognize.

Reegesk hid a triumphant smile. This would be almost too easy. It was unusual for a Jawa to show so much enthusiasm for an item being traded, since it might skew the bartering to indicate that the item had value to him. Reegesk closed in to begin the negotiation. "The talisman is indeed of great value. The exchange must measure up to its worth."

Het Nkik's reverent expression turned to one of chagrin. "I have little with me today that is suitable for this exchange."

Reegesk's heart began to beat rapidly as he smelled his chances improving. The Jawa definitely wanted to make a trade. Reegesk slyly lowered his eyes to indicate the blaster that Het Nkik held in his lap, hidden by the table. "The time for opportunity is always now."

The Jawa's hands clutched convulsively at the weapon, and for a moment he seemed at a loss. "I cannot meet such a high price," he answered carefully, ". . . today." His eyes did not meet Reegesk's. He negotiated for a while longer before finally agreeing to an amount far higher than Reegesk had expected to get.

"You know that I am a skilled trader," Het Nkik said. "Here are a few credits to show my good faith. If you will give me until morning, I will meet your price."

Success! But could the Jawa be trusted? Reegesk ordered himself to use caution. "Then I will bring you the talisman tomorrow morning," he said in a calm voice. He did not want to give away his own impatience, and he hoped the Jawa could not smell it.

But the Jawa was firm. "No. I must have the battle talisman today." Het Nkik's voice grew agitated as he spoke. "I will pay the rest in the morning, but I cannot wait until tomorrow." He stopped, as if searching for a way to convince Reegesk of his serious intentions. At last he said, "If you wait until morning, I will let you have the use of this blaster."

Reegesk could feel his eyes light with intensity at the very thought of having such a fine weapon.

Het Nkik's eyes burned into Reegesk's as he nodded to the weapon he held beneath the table. "Yes, I will let you hold it and use it. I am not afraid to arm a Ranat. Let me leave with the talisman today, and you will have what you need by morning."

Unable to pull away from the fervor of the Jawa's glowing gaze, Reegesk reached out one paw to touch the weapon. Did he dare take a risk on the honor of this Jawa? *Always pay close attention during a trade,* he reminded himself. Finally, he came to a decision.

At that moment, a commotion broke out across the cantina from them. Light and sparks filled the air, along with the sharp smell of singed flesh. When the air finally cleared, Reegesk was able to make out the form of Greedo the bounty hunter slumped over an otherwise deserted table.

Dead? Yes, definitely dead. This was indeed a lucky day for Reegesk. He felt a surge of excitement and his whiskers quivered with glee. "Yes. I accept the trade," he said to the Jawa, who was still staring at the scene across the room. "Keep the talisman for now. Bring me the price we agreed on by morning."

Het Nkik suddenly turned his attention back to Reegesk. Without a word, he pulled the blaster away from Reegesk's paw and stalked away.

"Both traders received the better bargain this day," Reegesk called after Het Nkik, but the Jawa did not seem to hear him.

Reegesk smiled as he watched Het Nkik walk with such confidence toward the entrance of the cantina. He was pleased to have made such a fair deal. The Jawa threw challenging glances around the room as he left with the DL-44 concealed beneath his cloak, one hand fingering the precious battle talisman.

Reegesk emptied the remaining brew from his cup and stood to leave, inhaling deeply. The smell of the scorched Rodian bounty hunter still hung in the air. *Very satisfactory,* he thought with a contented sigh.

Moments later, he stepped back out of the cantina into the parched streets of Mos Eisley. Reegesk patted the pocket inside his cloak that held the power pack he had slipped from Het Nkik's blaster. They had both gotten the trade they wanted today. He had paid very close attention.

And now Reegesk had the perfect power supply for the Ranat tribe's new 'vaporator.

When the Desert Wind Turns:
The Stormtrooper's Tale

by Doug Beason

It took Davin Felth all of thirty seconds on the military training planet Carida to decide that serving in the Emperor's armed forces was not as romantic as he had thought.

Davin hoisted his deep blue duffel bag containing his worldly possessions onto his back and queued up with the rest of the hundred and twenty other recruits. They filled the Gamma-class shuttle's narrow steel corridor. Davin was nearly overwhelmed by the diverse cut of clothes, colors, and unusual smells that wafted from the youths. Nervous chatter ran up and down the line of eighteen-year-olds, most of whom were away from home for the very first time. A blast of noise reverberated through the shuttle and the door to the outside sighed open.

Fresh air tumbled in, untouched by atmospheric scrubbers present on the ship; unfiltered light splashed against the gleaming deck, reflecting down the hallway, and for a glorious thirty seconds it seemed that all the hype and rumors about Carida, the planet used by the Emperor's own guard as a training base for his military, were suddenly magnified. This must be the most exciting place for a ship of eager eighteen-year-olds to begin their new lives.

And then the shouting started.

It was as if a bomb had exploded amidst the nervous group of draftees. Chaos, yelling, confusion, and a hundred thousand demands were suddenly thrust upon Davin from all directions. Officers in olive-gray uniforms or white stormtrooper armor swarmed all over them; the recruits stood at attention, rigidly trying to emulate statues as the officers moved to within millimeters of their faces, screaming demands.

Davin's only thought was to try and survive, to get out of this mess alive—he couldn't think, and every time he tried to answer a question that was screamed at him, someone else would thrust their face next to his and demand something else.

Davin started yelling, not caring what he said, or whom he was speaking to, but only reacting, attempting to look as though he were busy answering someone else's question. He raised his voice and shouted at the top of his lungs—and the ploy seemed to work. With all the confusion that surrounded him, with a stormtrooper major screaming in his face to try and disorient him, he succeeded in diverting attention from himself. But this was only the beginning of six months of hellish training that would mold Davin into one of the Emperor's own elite troops.

After what seemed hours, Davin and the rest of the recruits were led running down a pathway to the barracks. A huge prehistoric-looking man waved them to stand at one side of the passageway. The recruits scampered in fear. They lined up against the wall and snapped to attention. The burly man threw them supplies: generic dark uniforms, helmets, socks, underwear, handkerchiefs, emergency equipment, medpac kit, survival gear, and personal-cleansing equipment.

Davin accepted the supplies, but was too afraid to ask what he should do with them. One small voice, attached to a man who towered over the rest of the recruits like a solarflower grown in rich Gamorrean dirt, said meekly, "I . . . I can't take this anymore!"

Instantly, Imperial uniformed bodies swarmed over the man. A voice shouted, "You people—over here! Move it!"

Bending backward under his load of supplies, Davin staggered to join a line of recruits who looked like piles of crawling military storehouses. The group was led away, shown to their bunks. Davin deposited his blue duffel bag and armload of material on a cot. Two other recruits shared the room with him. Davin grinned tiredly and introduced himself. "Hi, I'm Davin Felth."

The first man shook his hand firmly. "Geoff f'Tuhns." He took a quick look around the corner and held out a bag of greasy-looking food. "Want a bite?"

Davin glanced in the bag and felt his stomach flip. "No, thanks."

Tall, big-boned, and sporting a head of flaming red hair, Geoff did not look as if he could ever fit inside stormtrooper armor. Looking once more around the corner, he sighed and stuffed a handful of food in his mouth. "If you brought any food, you'd better eat it now. I managed to hide this from them," he said, "but they threatened punishment if they caught me with any more food."

"Mychael Ologat," said the second man. "What do you think of all this?" As small as Geoff was tall, Mychael looked as though he could fit in Davin's duffel bag; but his muscles rippled underneath his taut skin.

Davin was still shell-shocked from the reception getting off the Gamma-class shuttle. They hadn't been on the military training planet for more than an hour, but with all the supplies he had been issued and the amount of ground they had covered, at Davin's normal pace it would have taken over a week to get these same things done. He shook his head. "They told me the military would change my life, but this is crazy. I expected to get some time to look around."

"Don't count on it," said Geoff, speaking around a mouthful of food. "We've been here since yesterday, and from what I've heard, this is only the welcoming committee. The really tough stuff comes later."

Mychael's eyes grew wide. He stood facing the door, and he managed to blurt out, "Uh-oh—here comes trouble."

Geoff dropped the bag of munchies and tried to kick it underneath his bed, but he slipped and the bag slid to the center of the room.

Davin turned to see one of the largest men he had ever seen in his life standing just outside the door. Dressed in antigrav shoes, black shorts, a white skinshirt, and wearing the ominous white helmet of an Imperial stormtrooper, the man looked like a massive pillar. He pointed at the bag of food. His voice had a tinny sound as it came over the speakers implanted in the side of the battle helmet.

"Your caloric intake is strictly regulated—whose contraband food is that?"

Davin heard Geoff gulp; from what he'd said, he couldn't afford to get caught. But no one had told *him* it was contraband! He spoke up. "It's mine."

The stormtrooper turned to face Davin. "You are new here."

"That's right."

"The correct response is 'yes, sir.' You will learn—or you will fail. Consider that your only warning." He smashed the bag with his foot, then turned to include the other two. "You sand slime have two minutes to change into your physical training gear and get out here with the rest of your squad—or your butt is mine. Now move!"

The three Imperial recruits scrambled over each other as clothing flew across the room.

"Thanks, Davin," Geoff gasped out as he struggled into a coverall.

Davin could only grunt as he hopped on one foot; he attempted to pull on thigh-high running boots. Despite the hectic pace, the next two minutes were Davin's last chance to relax during the six months of training.

Fifteen pounds lighter but immeasurably stronger, Davin adjusted to the breakneck training routine. The recruits spent less than five hours a night in their room, falling exhausted to sleep after day upon day of relentless training: physical fitness runs, daily expeditions via suborbital transport to the southern ice fields for winter training, a week-long expedition to the barren Forgofshar Desert for survival training, a three-day battle against nature in the equatorial rain forest . . . Davin soon lost track of the days.

He and his roommates soon learned to get up before their "wake-up call" came in the morning, when their Imperial stormtrooper sergeant would kick open their door and blast his sonic whistle. Davin would wake up a good half hour before reveille. He and the others would scurry about the small dorm room, cleaning and dressing, only to hop beneath their sheets for the early-morning wake-up ritual—they had seen what happened to the other recruits when they were caught out of their bunks before reveille.

Running out into the hallway, Davin would snap to attention, waiting to hear what the expedition of the day would entail. He never knew where he might be sent.

It was the morning Davin was in place in the hallway

nearly thirty seconds before the others that changed
his life. It didn't start out with a fanfare, simply:
"Davin, drive your butt over to the AT-AT detachment
at the end of the hall. The rest of you sandworms fall in
for inspection!"

As the rest of his squad stood at attention, Geoff
punched him in the side and whispered, "Good luck,
hotshot—we're going to miss you!"

Davin didn't have time to answer, as the Imperial
trooper in charge of the AT-AT detachment was already yelling for Davin to hurry up. "Twenty more seconds and we'll drop you off in a reactor core!"

Davin joined the group of recruits at the end of the
hall; he recognized several of his classmates as those
who had consistently finished near the top of the class
with him. They exchanged glances with one another,
but they were much too sharp to speak and bring down
the wrath of their drill instructor.

Lining up, they were marched out of the dorm area
to the parade field. Glass and syngranite buildings
soared above their heads; the parade field was surrounded by ultramodern buildings. Dozens of robot
observer eyes hovered overhead, keeping watch over
the military base. Situated in the middle of the circle of
classroom buildings, a sleek executive transport ship
squatted on the grass, its door open for boarding. The
recruits were hurried in as the all-clear signal alerted
the pilot for takeoff.

As Davin settled into his seat, a holo appeared in the
middle of the aisle. Tall and gaunt with sunken eyes,
the holographic image of the man was dressed in the
tight black uniform of a ground commander. The image spoke with forcefulness.

"I am Colonel Veers, commander of the Emperor's
AT-AT forces. You trooper candidates have been selected for your ability to learn quickly and put the re-
quirements of the mission over your personal needs.
No matter how superior our space forces may be, it is
the brilliance of the ground troops, ferreting out the
enemy from their dug-in encampments, that will win

this conflict. The ground forces are the true backbone needed for a total victory—and you have been selected to man the flagship of the ground troops: the All Terrain Armored Transport, the AT-AT!''

Colonel Veers's image was replaced by a four-legged metal behemoth, lumbering across rugged terrain. It moved in mere seconds distances that would have taken men on foot an hour to traverse. Twin blaster cannons fired laser pulses from the vehicle's metallic head; two uniformed crewmen could be seen in the command module in the AT-AT's head. The recruits in the executive transport drew in their breath in a collective gasp at the sight.

Colonel Veers's voice continued. "You will undergo six weeks of intensive training in the virtual reality simulators before being allowed in the AT-AT even as an observer. If you pass the qualifying phase of the test, you will be allowed to accompany the AT-AT in one of my combat battalions. Good luck to you all, but take a good look around you—fewer than one person in ten will successfully complete this arduous training." He scanned the room as though he could look into each recruit's face. Davin sat rigid in his seat and tried to meet the holo's eye, but the image dissolved from view.

A murmur ran through the ship. The recruits leaned over their seats and whispered excitedly to one another. The man next to Davin turned, his face flushed. "An AT-AT! Can you believe we've been picked for the chance to command one of them?"

The image of the monstrous vehicle stepping across the rocky terrain still burned in Davin's mind. Through all of his training experiences, nothing had sparked the fire in him as had the sight of the AT-AT. It was almost as if his destiny had been unfolded right inside the sleek executive transport.

"Yeah," whispered Davin, "and I'm going to make sure I'm not one of those nine recruits who washes out."

. . .

The AT-AT control room seemed large to Davin Felth. Multicolored touch-sensitive controls covered the walls and ceiling; the rectangular viewport at the front of the control room was as tall as Davin. Two swivel chairs sat at the front of the viewport, allowing the pilot and co-pilot access to all the controls, yet giving them a spectacular view of below. They were a good five hundred meters above the ground in the AT-AT control "head," docked at the training base.

Davin felt a shortness of breath, as if he had walked into some sacrosanct place; but it was more than that. He slowly stepped forward and ran a hand over the right-hand seat. He felt rich dewback leather—only the best for Colonel Veers's recruits!

"Do you like it?"

The voice startled Davin, and the past months of training made him cringe at the blast he knew was to come. "Yes, sir."

The instructor joined Davin and spoke quietly, as if not to disturb Davin's sense of awe. "I don't think I'll ever get used to the feeling I get when I climb aboard." He glanced at Davin. "And that's one of the attributes we look for in our recruits, Davin Felth. If they do not respect the AT-AT, then they approach their assignment as just another duty. They might as well stay in their virtual reality chamber, playing like children. We only want the best to pilot the AT-AT, because when something goes wrong that you can't fix by VR, then it's the best who survive."

He reached up and ran his fingers over an array of lights. A low sound thrummed through the floor as the instruments powered up. The instructor swung the chair around and flicked at the lights in front of him. "Do you want to take her out?"

"Yes, *sir*!" said Davin. He eagerly climbed into the copilot's seat and waited for instructions. When none came, he remembered the lessons he had been taught in the VR simulator, and quickly helped the instructor with the checklist. Within minutes they were ready to ease the AT-AT out of the docking bay.

Davin watched the screens inlaid above the viewport; he saw images broadcast from the docking area of the AT-AT from all different angles. In the seat next to Davin, the instructor effortlessly ran through the sequence to back the AT-AT away from its berth. Although the AT-AT was completely controlled by artificial intelligence, Davin appreciated for the first time the enormity of the task of running a machine that held nearly as many moving parts as the human body. The human presence on board served as a foolproof backup.

"Let's take her up into the hills," said the instructor. "I want to run through some target practice. I'll let Base know our call sign is Landkiller One."

The view outside of the viewport raced across the molecular-thick window as the AT-AT lumbered away from the base. They quickly left behind the syngranite buildings and roads and turned into the rugged hillside.

The ride was smooth. The AT-AT stepped across chasms so deep Davin couldn't see the bottom. They climbed the ridge and dropped down to the valley on the other side; boulders littered the hillside. They were in the middle of a barren wasteland. Sheer rock rose up on one side of them, and in the distance, Davin saw red and silver rock formations jutting into the air, looking like a forest of multicolored needles. Davin glanced at the clock—they had only left the base ten minutes before, but already they were out in the wilderness.

Little by little the instructor allowed Davin to take over the AT-AT controls. Piloting the AT-AT was just like using the virtual reality simulator, but Davin knew that any misjudgment would be disastrous. Davin devoted his entire attention to monitoring the myriad instruments.

"You're pretty good at this," said the instructor after a while. "Not many recruits are as comfortable as you."

"Thanks," said Davin, not breaking his concentration.

"Keep at this heading," said the instructor, pushing up from his seat. "I want to check the weapons cache. We're coming upon the target range and the terrain doesn't change any from here."

"Yes, sir."

"Just call out if anything goes wrong; I'll be right back. But don't leave the controls—no matter what happens."

"Yes, sir." Davin tried to keep his excitement in check. The AT-AT almost functioned on its own, but Davin still felt heady being in command, alone in the command center. Step by monstrous step, the AT-AT lumbered across the barren terrain. Looking out over the rugged land, Davin could imagine himself commanding a fleet of AT-AT's, massing against the Rebels—

Davin caught sight of something out of the corner of his eye. A dark speck, then suddenly three more, swooped down out of the sky. They headed straight for the AT-AT.

Davin glanced at his radar screen—nothing showed up. He punched up his scanning instruments and got the same response: nothing at all in the EM, gravitational, and neutrino spectrums.

Davin frowned and called out to his instructor, "I've got a visual on some fighter craft heading this way, but they don't show up on scanners. They're closing fast."

Davin didn't get an answer from his instructor, still back in the weapons cache. The only sound Davin heard was the muted rumbling of the AT-AT's power system, and the slight jarring that came over the electronically cushioned ride.

Davin turned in his seat. "Sir? Are you there?" The door to the weapons cache was sealed; Davin turned back to the front. The four fighter craft grew closer. He slapped at the intercom and broadcasted throughout the AT-AT. "Sergeant!" Still no answer.

The four ships split off in two pairs, each vessel turning sideways as they came directly for the AT-AT con-

trol chamber. Bright pops of blaster cannon erupted
from the fighters as they fired upon Davin's AT-AT.

"Hey!" Davin felt anger and fear surge through
him. "Sergeant, we're being attacked!" The vessels
thundered past the AT-AT, causing the giant war machine to sway slightly in the fighter's turbulence.
"What's going on? Are we in the target area or something?"

Still not getting a reply, Davin nearly unbuckled to
go look for the AT-AT instructor. What if something
had happened to the man? The instructor would know
what to do. This was crazy!

But when Davin saw the fighter craft swoop up again
in front of him, he sat frozen in his seat. The four
fighters were coming in for another strafing run. Davin
forced himself to grab at the communicator. He
flicked to the AT-AT Base frequency. "Distress, Distress
—this is Landkiller One! Attention, Base, we're under
attack. There must be some kind of mistake. I say
again, Distress!"

Only the sound of white noise came over the
speaker; even the emergency holo did not function.

Bright pinpoints of light once again erupted from
the head of the attacking fighter craft. Davin tensed
himself as the AT-AT was rocked with the impact of a
blaster cannon. A shrill alarm blasted above his head as
the acrid smell of oily smoke rolled throughout the
control room. "Sergeant—help me!" The warbling
sound of another alarm pierced the air; synthetic
voices announcing damage-control procedures came
from the rear of the control room. Twenty things
seemed to happen at once.

Throughout all the confusion, Davin spotted the
four fighter craft rolling up from upon high and diving down to make another . . . and perhaps their
last . . . strafing run.

Davin grew suddenly angry at all that had gone
wrong. Throughout his short career as an Imperial military man, he had been drilled that the only way to
survive was to follow procedures. But here was a situa-

tion that had not been covered in any textbook or testing sequence! He was out on his own, and as crazy as it seemed, somehow the Rebels must have found their way to the Imperial military training planet. How else could he explain the fighter vessels not showing up on radar?

Davin pushed all concern aside and armed the AT-AT fire controls. If he was going to be shot at, he wasn't going to go down without a fight. The automated fire-control system was of no use since the enemy craft did not show up on any of his scanning instruments.

Slaving the blaster cannon controls to follow his line of sight, he let loose a salvo of high-energy laser blasts. The bundles of energy shot past the attacking ships. Although his shots missed the fighter craft, the attacking ships split up. *Had they not expected him to fight back?*

The fighters flew past him, again coming so close that the AT-AT shuddered because of the passing crafts' shock wave. Davin slapped at the emergency beacon, sending out a continuous squawk over the airwaves. At the same time, he halted the AT-AT's forward motion, slaving the AT-AT's entire computer resources to fight the incoming attackers.

Since he had to rely on his eyesight and none of the instruments during the battle, Davin decided to put himself at the greatest advantage. He ordered the AT-AT to kneel, dropping as low to the ground as possible. Slowly, with jerky motions, the huge behemoth staggered to the ground.

Davin brought the war machine's head down flat with the body until there remained no part of the AT-AT that the fighters could fly under. By the time the four fighter craft came back around for another attack, Davin's AT-AT lay hunkered on the ground.

The fighters grouped together for a high-angle dive-bombing run. As they approached, Davin knew they could not fly under the AT-AT.

Davin forced them to make a suicide attempt on the control chamber.

Davin jammed his finger down on the firing control.

The AT-AT rocked with the recoil from the laser cannon. An explosion burst across the screen as he hit two of the fighters; a third fighter tried to steer away from the flying debris, but his wing clipped the ground and cartwheeled into a rocky cliff.

The remaining fighter bore down on him. He flew in low, wobbling in the hot layer of turbulent desert air. Davin waited until the fighter was nearly upon him before firing. The craft kept close to the ground, as if expecting Davin's AT-AT to rise and start shooting.

Seconds later, the last fighter plowed into a rock formation, erupting with a violent burst. Red-orange flames shot out, then quickly disappeared from view.

Davin sat in the sudden quiet. Moments ago the control room had been filled with a cacophony of alarms and the sight of four fighter craft attacking the AT-AT. But now, there was only the distant throb of the onboard power plant.

Davin felt drained, too tired even to call Base and report what had happened. But he knew that he must, for if these four Rebel craft had somehow managed to evade the Imperial defenses, then no telling how many of the dangerous vessels would be lurking in orbit.

He picked up the communicator when he heard a sound behind him. Davin turned. "Sergeant?" In the shock of battle, he had completely forgotten about his instructor being lost in the sealed weapons cache.

His instructor stood with his hands on his hips, grinning wolfishly. "Good job, Recruit Felth. You've got a command party landing on the AT-AT command module, so open up the top hatch."

"Yes, sir." Dazed and confused, Davin did as instructed. Once outside, he searched for the wreckage of the fighters that should have covered the landscape . . . but he was stunned to see nothing.

"You're the first recruit to bring down all four fighters, Davin Felth. This AT-AT was specially designed to simulate that battle—it was all projected via virtual reality into the control head." It was almost too much for Davin to comprehend.

Recovering from the fact that he had not been in an actual battle, Davin stood with his instructor on top of the AT-AT's sprawling metallic head. Davin squinted in the sunlight; the dry desert air smelled enthralling to him after the stuffiness of the damaged control room.

A dot appeared above them, dilating in size until Davin could make out the bottom of an Imperial command scout. Davin and his instructor stepped back. After the command scout landed, a door hissed open and a ramp extended to the surface.

Two white-armored Imperial stormtroopers marched out and stood at rigid attention on either side of the opening. Davin gasped as he recognized the man emerging from the ship. "Colonel Veers!" Davin snapped to attention and saluted.

Veers strode up and returned the salute. He looked Davin up and down. "Recruit Felth, is it?"

"Yes, sir," stammered Davin.

"This kneeling maneuver with the AT-AT—how did you come up with that idea, recruit?"

Davin opened his mouth but he was at a loss for words.

"Well," growled Veers. "Out with it, recruit!"

"I—I don't know, sir. It just seemed the logical thing to do. It was the only way to keep the fighters from finishing us off, by not allowing them underneath the AT-AT."

Veers sounded strangely cold. "And what would that do, recruit?"

Davin shrugged, thrown by Veers's line of questioning. *Why, he had fought off the fighters, hadn't he? And won!* "Well—"

"Address the colonel as sir!" corrected his instructor, embarrassed to be speaking in front of Veers.

"Thank you, Sergeant," said Veers. The colonel drew close to Davin and steered him away from the others. When they were some distance from the instructor and Imperial stormtroopers, the colonel spoke softly. "Now continue, recruit. What is so special about not allowing the fighters access to the AT-AT under-belly?"

Davin stiffened. "I lost track of them when they flew underneath. Once the fighters were under the AT-AT, they could have done just about anything they wanted."

Veers seemed about to lose his patience. "Such as—?"

Davin felt his face grow warm as he scrambled to think of something, anything to appease the colonel. "Such as . . . tying up the AT-AT legs, sir," Davin blurted out. "All they needed was some cable and they could have easily tripped the AT-AT."

A strange look came over Colonel Veers. The thin man smiled tightly and looked Davin over. "Very well. Thank you, recruit. That's very enlightening." He raised a finger to his lips. "Keep this classified until my battle staff can analyze the implications, understand?"

"Yes, sir!"

Veers turned to go. Raising his voice, he nodded at Davin's instructor as he spoke. "Have Recruit Felth report to Assignments when he returns. A man of his caliber deserves immediate recognition. My staff will have an assignment worthy of his talents ready when he returns."

"Yes, sir," said the instructor.

As an afterthought, Veers raised a finger. "And im-pound all the datacubes on this simulation. Have them sent to my command headquarters. Understood?"

"Yes, Colonel."

"And quickly. I have been dispatched for temporary duty as an advisor to the Emperor's new Death Star. I want this accomplished before I leave."

When the scout ship disappeared from view, Davin's instructor clapped him on the shoulder. "I don't know how you did it, recruit, but I have a feeling you've been marked for a one-in-a-million career!"

• • •

The familiar background hum of the starship didn't comfort Davin Felth. The sharp oil-on-metal smell, harsh lighting, and polished decks of the huge troop transport should have made Davin feel right at home—but ever since receiving the hush-hush orders from Colonel Veers's command section, he had been totally confused.

No one questioned the sealed orders when he reported to the Imperial troop transport, and no one explained exactly what he was supposed to do. All he knew was that now, two hundred light-years from Carida, he was assigned to a detachment of stormtroopers, setting off for some forsaken planet.

Stormtroopers!

He drew in a breath and tried to explain for the third time to the man staring at papers on the desk, ignoring him. "Captain Terrik, you just don't understand. I've spent the last day trying to find out what is going on, but no one has the authority to help me. I was told personally by Colonel Veers that I would receive an assignment worthy of my talents. I'm an AT-AT operator, not a . . . a foot soldier!"

The officer's smoothly shaven head snapped up so that Davin could see the man's eyes. Deep, penetrating, and utterly without fear, Captain Terrik bored his gaze into Davin like a lightsaber. "Stormtroopers are not *foot* soldiers!" He placed his hands on his desk and stood, barely holding back his trembling. "If it was up to me, you Jawa slime, I'd have spaced you when we first hit vacuum. I'm well aware of Colonel Veers's orders, and we're going to follow his directions to the micron!"

"Very well," said Davin, somewhat relieved. He straightened and looked smartly around the cabin. Headquarters for the small detachment of twenty stormtroopers on board the ship, Captain Terrik's cabin was decorated with battle streamers, plaques, paintings of battles against the Rebels, and a holo of Lord Vader. "You will show me to my correct assignment, then." He smiled at the captain. Terrik trembled more visibly and turned redder by the second.

"Stand at attention!" growled Captain Terrik. "Listen up, you mynock bait! It took me all day to confirm those orders, and Emperor only knows why Colonel Veers wants this. But you belong to me now, Felth! We've got another month of maneuvers before we get to Tatooine, and I intend to use that time whipping you into shape."

"Tatooine?" said Davin, his face growing white. "What's that? There must be some kind of mistake."

"Oh, no." Captain Terrik grinned wolfishly. He picked up Davin's orders lying on his desk and shook them under Davin's nose. "My detachment of stormtroopers is relieving the Thirty-seventh Detachment that has been stationed at Mos Eisley on Tatooine. We'll be assigned to the governor, but we're not in his chain of command—my superior is in the next sector, half a light-year away. In case you haven't noticed, we're not going directly to Tatooine, so I'll have a month to break in a young Jawa slime like you, turn you into a real stormtrooper. You'll learn pretty quick what it's like to be a *foot soldier*." Captain Terrik spat the words out of his mouth and grinned at Davin. "Any more questions, golden boy?"

Davin felt what hope he had left seep out of him. Standing at rigid attention just microns in front of Captain Terrik's face, Davin knew what it was like to jump from a crashing ship into a pit of burning fuel.

Davin Felth was in the best shape of his life when he prepared to land on Tatooine. But getting there on board the troop transport the past month had been pure hell.

The twenty stormtroopers in the detachment had all pitched in in some way or another, "helping" Davin get up to speed in the rigorous training. Their normal three-month period of disciplining, schooling, and physical fitness was compressed into a never-ending nightmare for Davin. The stormtroopers were not about to allow a mere AT-AT operator, although a graduate of Carida Basic Military Training, into their esteemed ranks without passing through a minimum of ritual.

Davin did not have the time to be homesick or lonely, although his thoughts sometimes drifted to his two roommates back at Carida. He wondered where they had been assigned.

Ten hours before landfall, Davin marched up to the quartermaster and collected his desert gear: heat-reflective armor, comlink, filtermask, blaster rifle, blaster pistol, temperature-control body glove, utility belt, energy source, and concussion grenade launcher. He staggered to his cabin under the load of equipment.

Davin donned his helmet with automatic polarized lenses. Fully outfitted in the desert-terrain gear, he clunked to the mirror in his small cabin and looked himself over. Like it or not, he was finally a stormtrooper.

He used his chin to click on his chinmike, activating the comlink. He tapped into stormtrooper radio traffic for the entire troop ship: "Access to AT-AT bay now open." "Cold assault and aquatic assault detachments reporting still in stasis." "Tatooine landing for refurbishment ready when ready."

A series of voices checked in. Davin thought he recognized some of the stormtroopers' voices.

There was a long pause of silence. Sounding irritated, Captain Terrik's voice came over the comlink. "Ten twenty-three? Are you up and ready?"

It took Davin a full two heartbeats to realize that Captain Terrik was speaking to *him*.

"Ten twenty-three ready, sir."

"Report to the landing craft, ten twenty-three. Prepare to disembark. Move it!"

"Yes, sir." His name stripped away, Davin had been assigned the emotionless number 1023 as part of his stormtrooper indoctrination. Their zealous devotion to duty demanded denial of the individual, pledging their allegiance only to the Emperor. Unwilling to make that commitment, Davin turned his thoughts to his family, his friends, as the training attempted to squeeze away his memories. His fellow stormtroopers reveled in the mystery that surrounded their existence, their lack of identity. With no one to turn to or confide in, Davin felt miserable.

It only took a moment to gather up his meager belongings. The clothes he had taken with him from home seemed useless now, but he kept them as a reminder of the life he used to have. He stuffed them in a sand-colored duffel bag and carried them with his weapons down to the landing craft. He kept to the side of the corridor as he walked, trying to keep out of people's way. A group of naval troopers double-timed around the corner.

The corridor widened to the immense landing bay. Stepping inside, he felt as if he were outdoors. Worker droids ran along scaffolding that reached higher than an AT-AT; the bay was so wide that he had trouble seeing to the opposite side. He set off for the landing craft, halfway across the immense bay, to join the contingent of stormtroopers.

"Ten twenty-three?"

Davin swung his gear down and faced Captain Terrik. "Present, sir."

"You're assigned to scout unit Zeta. Something came up. We're delaying reporting to the garrison, so pile your gear in the storage compartment with the rest of the detachment."

"Yes, sir."

Davin lined up and waited for Captain Terrik to finish his paperwork. Accepting a salute from the officer on deck, Captain Terrik faced the waiting stormtroopers. A warbling sound came over Davin's comlink, informing him that Captain Terrik was going to a secure communications mode, using frequency-jumping techniques known only to the stormtroopers' sensors. "Quickly now—change of orders. We're deploying to the surface, bypassing Mos Eisley to participate in a search-and-destroy mission."

Someone asked, "What are we searching for, sir?"

"An escape pod. It jettisoned from a Corellian Corvette evading Lord Vader's Star Destroyer and landed somewhere on Tatooine."

Breaking military silence, a gasp went up over the secure link. "Lord Vader—here?"

"That's right," said Captain Terrik grimly. "Now double-time on board the landing craft!"

Although Davin was the last to board the spacecraft, he was set into his station before all the other stormtroopers in his detachment. Lord Vader! The very thought of the Dark Lord being so close to the backwater planet sent a chill through Davin. He hadn't felt this strange since he had learned through the grapevine that Colonel Veers had never even mentioned Davin's "kneeling" defense for the AT-AT to his superiors. It was almost as if Colonel Veers didn't want anyone to know of the fatal flaw in the giant walker's design.

The stormtroopers sat mute as they left the troop transport, their home for the past month. Visual images of Tatooine flashed inside their helmets, transmitted from the intelligence network orbiting Tatooine. Computer-generated graphics pinpointed the most likely landing place of the small escape pod.

As part of scout unit Zeta, Davin was tasked with reconnoitering the rocky highlands. He gripped his blaster rifle and stole a glance at the rest of the stormtroopers waiting patiently in two rows beside him. Everyone studied the data dump from the mother ship. He wondered how the others could remain so calm when they were about to embark on a mission. And for Lord Vader at that! He just wondered why the pod was so important.

The scouting craft landed with a bump. The side yawned open, spilling in hot air and brilliant sunshine. Davin pushed out and joined the other stormtroopers, who quickly lined up in front of Captain Terrik. No one spoke over the comlink until Davin heard Captain Terrik's voice.

"Lord Vader's Star Destroyer is mapping the planet with a sensor scan, trying to locate the escape pod. It must have buried itself on landing, or was hidden by some Rebel sympathizers. We have a preliminary position on the pod from just before it impacted, so we'll spread out and sift through all the sand on this planet if necessary to find it."

"Why is the pod so important, sir?" Davin surprised himself by blurting out the question; he only hoped that Captain Terrik would be so busy that he wouldn't yell at him.

"It's carrying classified material, and that's all you need to know. The point is that we need to find it . . . or we'll have to explain to Lord Vader why a detachment of the Emperor's Own failed in their duty. Got it?"

"Yes, sir!"

"Then listen up. Alvien and Drax squads, cover the next quadrant. Zeta squad, come with me. Headquarters at Mos Eisley has grav-lifted in three dewbacks to aid in the search—they can cover more territory than we can and will lead us to the pod if they get a scent. Start a circular search pattern, move."

The desert terrain was featureless, ever-shifting. Davin crunched his way through the sand, not sure what he was looking for, but knowing that some kind of evidence from the escape pod's landing had to be present. He climbed a small hill. The desert spread out in every direction. They might as well have been the only ones on the planet.

Seeing a rise in the sand below him, he scooted down the ridge and poked his blaster into the ground. He struck something hard! He clicked on the comlink. "Captain Terrik, ten twenty-three reporting. I think I found the pod."

"Are you sure?"

"Yes, sir." Davin excitedly dug into the ground with his blaster butt . . . only to unearth a large rock.

Captain Terrik appeared over the ridge just as Davin made his discovery. "Ten twenty-three, what are you doing!"

"Sorry, sir." Discouraged, he trudged back up the small hill and joined the rest of his squad continuing the search.

After arriving from Mos Eisley, a giant lizardlike dewback was assigned to each squad. Davin was not given the opportunity to ride the monstrous reptilian beast, but that suited him fine. Every step the scaly animal took reverberated in the sand.

The search seemed to last forever. Davin lost count of the breaks he took, and per Imperial orders, they were forced to stay in their suits and drink the distilled water flown in from Mos Eisley with the dewback.

Setting out to cover another part of the quadrant, Davin spotted a glint out of the corner of his eye. There . . . whatever it was just caught the light from Tatooine's second sun.

He almost cried out, but clamped his mouth shut. Clutching his blaster, he bounded for the glint of light. Slowly, the object took shape. Half-buried in the sand, the object looked scorched. As he drew near, he made out the faint red and blue markings of an escape pod.

There was no doubt in his mind now. "Captain Terrik, ten twenty-three reporting. I've found the escape pod!"

"If this is another one of your daydreams, ten twenty-three—!"

"I'm positive, sir. It may not be what we're looking for, but it has Imperial markings."

Minutes later Captain Terrik joined Davin by the object. A stormtrooper riding a dewback appeared over the crest of a rise, waiting for a signal that it was the right pod.

Captain Terrik surveyed the site. "Someone was in the pod. The tracks go off in this direction."

Davin fished a mechanism from inside the escape pod. There was only one thing that used such a device

—an R2 unit. He held it up so all could see. "Look, sir, droids!"

"All right. Form up. I'll inform Lord Vader the pod wasn't destroyed. Now we've really got to move."

"Ten twenty-three reporting. They're not in the repair bay, sir," said Davin Felth. He stood in the middle of a bay full of droids, deep in the bowels of a Jawa sand-crawler. Cables drooped across the ceiling; tables with disassembled equipment were strewn across the floor.

"You've all searched the entire sandcrawler?"

"Affirmative," answered each stormtrooper, calling off their trooper numbers one by one.

"Form up outside."

Davin stepped across a Roche J9 worker droid lying on the metal floor. Two Jawas stood just outside of the repair bay and muttered between themselves, obviously displeased that the stormtroopers would search their ship. Davin scanned the room one last time before he left and counted off an Arakyd BT-16 perimeter droid, a demolition droid, an R4 agromech droid, a WED15 treadwell droid, and an EG-6 power droid—but there was no R2, or even a protocol unit that was often paired with an R2 droid.

A gaggle of Jawas followed him outside the cruiser. All Davin could see of the little aliens were their bright eyes, looking out of their flowing hooded brown robes. The rest of Zeta squad stood waiting for him, their blaster rifles held loosely by their sides. The stormtroopers kept their backs to one another, watching all sides for any possible attack.

As he joined the squad, Davin overheard Captain Terrik conversing with the head Jawa on the officer's suit speaker. "You are certain that the droids were sold to a moisture farmer at your last stop?" After a series of high-pitched chatters came from the Jawa, Captain Terrik turned and waved his arm back to Zeta squad; he switched to the secure stormtrooper frequency. "Form up with the rest of the detachment."

Zeta squad double-timed in the sand away from the Jawa sandcrawler to join the remainder of the storm-troopers. They kept guard over the sandcrawler on a rise just to the south. Three enormous hairy banthas airlifted in from somewhere, two converted GoCorp Arunskin 32 cargo skiffs, and a Ubrikkian HAVr A9 floating fortress with two heavy blaster cannons waited on the other side of the rise.

The Jawas yelled and shook their fists at the storm-troopers as they left. The little brown-robed aliens then scurried around the sandcrawler, preparing to con-tinue their journey.

Captain Terrik's voice came over Davin's helmet. "Floating fortress—fire when ready upon the Jawa sandcrawler. When it is destroyed, ride those banthas up to the wreckage and leave that material we confis-cated from the Sand People. We want people to think the Sand People attacked the sandcrawler. The rest of you, load up the cargo skiffs—we will find those droids at that moisture farmer's."

The floating fortress immediately wheeled off the ground, rising above the ridge in a banking turn. Climbing on board the bulky cargo skiff, Davin saw two bolts of blaster energy burst out of the floating fortress.

Over the whoops of joy from the other storm-troopers, Davin remained quiet. His thoughts were on the little Jawas, and how they were no more.

Davin lingered behind the rest, staying just far enough behind the other stormtroopers so that he didn't draw attention to himself. Zeta squad raced through the lower levels of the moisture farmer's house, overturn-ing tables, ripping doors off cabinets, smashing metal lockers with their blaster rifles until the containers popped open. One by one the stormtroopers checked in with Captain Terrik: "No sign of the droids, sir."

Davin watched the stormtrooper in front of him kick over a vat of oil before heading to the upper level. The moisture farmer's house was a shambles.

"Zeta squad check in and form up," said Captain Terrik, his words clipped and precise in Davin's helmet.

"Ten twenty-three," said Davin. He tried to control his breathing, but the thought of what was going to happen next nearly overwhelmed his senses. He trotted into the bright Tatooine double-sunshine and stood at attention with the rest of his squad. Captain Terrik stood in front of the moisture farmer and his wife, just outside of the house. The moisture farmer's face was bright red with anger; the woman cried, her head down. Davin flicked his outside audio sensor on with his chin and listened to the exchange.

". . . you men are nothing but criminals! I told you I haven't seen those droids since last night. And look what you've done to my house! The governor will pay for this."

"This nephew of yours," said Captain Terrik, his voice modulated by the speaker in his battlesuit, "one more time: Where did he take the Artoo unit?"

"Haven't you been listening?" The moisture farmer shook a fist in the air. "I don't know—and now I would not tell you even if I *did* know! You Imperial thugs are worse than I imagined." He stepped up to Captain Terrik's helmeted face and spat; spittle ran down the officer's helmet.

Captain Terrik made no attempt to remove the spittle. "Where is the boy?"

"I never did care much for the Rebel movement; but now I hope they find every one of you bantha slime and grill your carcasses!"

The moisture farmer turned and put an arm around his wife, drawing her near. The two turned away, back toward their home.

Without emotion, Captain Terrik nodded toward the stormtroopers. His voice came over the secure link. "There's only one place the boy could have taken the droids—into Mos Eisley, to escape offplanet. Zeta squad, load up. Floating fortress, this house needs to be left as a reminder of what happens when quarter is given to Rebels. Fire when ready."

Turning quickly for the cargo skiff, Davin Felth pushed aboard and kept his eyes averted from the blast on the house. A sour taste clawed up his throat. First they executed the Jawas, and now these humans. And over what—a couple of lousy droids? What could be so important that it deserved executing these people?

On his home planet, joining the military had seemed all fun and games, his chest swelling with pride as he had boarded the ship to transport him to Carida. But now, this was reality. People were dying, being indiscriminately killed.

The cargo skiff lifted off the ground, giving Davin a view of the carnage below. Smoke drifted up from the house. He could see the charred remains of two bodies lying in the scorched sand. As the skiff wheeled toward the desert city of Mos Eisley, Davin didn't know what he would do if he was ordered to kill.

Landing on the outskirts of Mos Eisley, the storm-troopers marched off the cargo skiff. They spent hours digging through the databases at the port authority, interrogating charter-ship owners, and searching repair shops before Captain Terrik gave up in disgust and ordered a methodical search of the streets.

The smells of the rich food, dirty bodies, and fuel permeated even their battle suits as they gathered around Captain Terrik. "All right, listen up," he said. "Alvien squad, set up checkpoints on every road coming into the city. You'll supplement the detachment already there. Drax and Zeta squads, run a patrol through the city, check door-to-door for those droids. There's only one way for those droids and that kid to get offplanet, and it's got to be through this hellhole of a city. Move out."

Davin joined the rest of the squad as they double-timed away from the detachment. Mos Eisley yawned open in front of them, a collection of dusty, low-slung brown buildings that looked as if they had been scattered by a juri-juice addict. Creatures in long flowing robes moved quietly through the dirt streets; Davin hadn't seen this many aliens in one place since the galactic olympics on the holovid.

Every door was sealed tight, supposedly closed against the sand, but Davin suspected it was to ensure the privacy of the unsavory characters he saw stepping back into the shadows.

They marched into the heart of the city, passing Lup's general store, the marketplace, Gap's grill, and the spaceport express. A potpourri of jabbering sounds and sharp smells invaded Davin's senses, mixed together with the ever-present sand. After his initial exposure to Tatooine by being dumped in the middle of the desert with his detachment, Davin realized that he really hadn't had a chance to sit back and savor this strange new world to which he had been assigned. But then again, he bitterly realized it might be a long time before he ever got offplanet.

His thoughts were shattered by a scream, then several shouts coming from an old blockhouse. Davin remembered the briefings on the landing craft—several buildings had been originally designed as a shelter against Tusken Raiders. This certainly looked like one of them.

No one else in Zeta squad seemed to hear the commotion.

Looking for a chance to get away from the craziness for a while, Davin clicked on his comlink. "Ten twenty-three, checking out a disturbance at a blockhouse."

"Permission granted," said Captain Terrik. "Ten forty-seven, back him up."

Davin gripped his rifle and peeled off from the squad. Creatures in every form of dress moved aside for Davin and his backup. A nondescript sign with faint lettering read: Mos Eisley Cantina.

A 2.8-meter-high green insectoid crawled from the cantina as they arrived. It sported bulbous eyes atop a

slender stalk, with four legs supporting a slender thorax and abdomen. It chattered at Davin.

"I am taking my spice trade elsewhere if I cannot be
assured of my own safety!"

Davin turned to his backup, 1047. "Sounds like trouble."

"These places don't serve droids," said 1047.
"We're needed elsewhere."

Wanting to keep away from the droid hunt, Davin
ignored him and pushed on inside the dark cantina.
Davin's solid-state visor immediately compensated for
the low light level. He stood on an elevated entranceway, just inside the door. It looked like a place where
smugglers, bounty hunters, and other low-class types
would hang out.

Davin spotted two people in the back, a boy and an
old man, get up from a booth and walk quickly toward
a back hallway. He ignored them and stepped up to
the bartender.

Davin clicked on his outside speaker. "I understand
there's been some trouble here."

"Nothing out of the ordinary," said the bartender,
nodding to the rear of his establishment. "Just having
a little fun. You can look around if you like."

"All right—we'll check it out."

Davin kept a grip on his rifle and walked slowly
through the cantina. He passed two slender human
women and a sharp-smelling Rodian standing by the
bar; a horned Devaronian nodded curtly and stepped
back, out of the way. Reaching the booth where Davin
had spotted the boy and old man heading for the back
hallway, he found an athletic-looking human who
stared sullenly at the table, ignoring him.

Davin turned to 1047, his backup. "You're right—
there's nothing here."

"Let's join the others."

Davin merely grunted. He was in no hurry to witness
another senseless killing. But what else could he do?

They stepped into the brilliant Tatooine sunlight,
leaving the shady cantina behind. Davin started to sug-

gest they continue the search for the missing droids on their own instead of joining the rest of the detachment, when the rest of Zeta squad marched around the corner in lockstep, completing their circuit of the perimeter.

Before Davin could say anything into his helmet microphone, he heard a shrill yell. It sounded like an outraged Jawa! How could he forget the high-pitched chatter from the little creatures that they had brutally executed?

Davin instantly crouched into a combat position, pulling up his rifle. A long-robed Jawa leaped from a hiding place in the middle of some space wreckage crashed in the middle of the square. The Jawa struggled with an oversized blaster, the weapon dwarfing the ridiculous-looking creature.

Finally aiming the blaster rifle at Zeta squad, the Jawa cut loose with one last shrill yell and squeezed the firing button—

Nothing happened. The Jawa howled with anger and surprise. He kept pushing the button. Everything happened so fast that Davin didn't react.

Or maybe his instincts kept him from reacting, with all of the senseless killings he had witnessed . . .

"Crazy Jawa," muttered 1047. The stormtrooper pulled out his blaster and flipped off a shot at the Jawa, still struggling with the weapon. The shot's momentum sent the Jawa flying back against the wreckage. It slid to the dirt. "One less Jawa slime to bother us," said 1047 as he holstered his blaster.

Davin stepped back in shock. *What have we become?* He had almost excused the Imperial stormtroopers for the way they indiscriminately killed the Jawas in their sandcrawler because of this so-called threat to the Emperor. But the moisture farmer, and now this latest act of violence . . . Davin couldn't reconcile it. The only answer to these actions kept coming up the same, time after time: The Empire was basically evil. And he didn't fit in.

But I can't resign, he thought. *So what can I do?*

•   •   •

He seemed to walk forever in a daze with Zeta squad, when he heard a voice in his helmet speaker. "Trouble at Docking Bay Ninety-four—we've located the droids! All personnel, converge and assist!"

"Come on, Ten twenty-three!" said 1047. "Follow me!"

Davin clutched his blaster rifle and trotted after the white-armored man. His time on Tatooine had seemed like a dream—he didn't know how long he had been onplanet, but he had been surviving off his suit rations and supplements for longer than he imagined it would be possible.

Captain Terrik's voice came inside his helmet. "Capture the droids! The Rebels have them—don't let them get away!"

Sounds of laser blasts ricocheted down the narrow streets. A crowd had gathered outside the docking bay; several peered over the crowd and tried to get a glimpse of what was going on.

1047 switched to his outside speaker: "Move aside—now!"

Davin blindly followed his backup, more confused than ever. Rebels? Why would the Rebel force be so blatant and try to escape now?

Running down the alley, they rounded a corner and came upon the firefight. A modified light freighter cruiser sat in the middle of the docking bay, its back hatch open. Davin caught a glimpse of a boy running up the ramp into the ship. A volley of laser blasts peppered the area.

A score of stormtroopers were scattered around, firing upon the light freighter. The air was filled with the searing sounds of laser blasts.

Davin was stunned to see that an athletic-looking man held the stormtroopers at bay—he fought at twenty-to-one odds! Was this man one of the mysterious Rebels that dared to rise against the Emperor? *It was the same man Davin had seen at the cantina!* So this was the one who had kept two detachments of storm-troopers on the run!

Mesmerized by the very thought that so few could accomplish so much, Davin felt a rush of solidarity—he felt an empathy with the Rebels, fighting against such overwhelming odds . . . and surviving. He hadn't felt this much emotion since the day he left for Carida . . .

The noise and confusion were overwhelming. Smoke sprang from stray laser blasts that ignited building material. Stormtroopers shouted conflicting orders.

Directly in front of Davin, Captain Terrik knelt on one knee and took careful aim at the athletic-looking man who was still holding off the Emperor's finest. Captain Terrik waited for the precise moment before slowly squeezing his blaster rifle to take out the Rebel—

Davin glanced quickly around. No one was behind him . . . and more importantly, no one was watching him.

Without hesitation, Davin pulled up his blaster and shot Captain Terrik in the back.

The officer slumped to the ground, unnoticed by the others.

The athletic-looking Rebel scrambled safely up the access ramp as it closed, sealing off the starship. An earsplitting wail came inside his helmet over the storm-trooper's frequency: "Clear the area, the Rebel's lifting off! Clear the area!"

Defeated, the stormtroopers scrambled back. Anyone left in the docking bay would be irradiated by the starship's exhaust. Someone's voice came over the secure frequency: "Where's Captain Terrik?"

"Leave him," came another voice. "He's dead. Killed in the crossfire."

Cursing filled the stormtroopers' airways. Several threw their blasters against the wall in disgust.

But as Davin pulled back with the rest, a new sense of purpose swept over him, like a cool wind cutting

through the endless heat. He felt a kinship with the
Rebels and almost wanted to join their cause.

But how?

Maybe he could warn them of the AT-AT's vulnerability. Or maybe he could work as a "deep plant," passing along vital information . . .

A spy? Maybe *that* was it. He'd have something to live
for, something to believe in. He felt heady, as things
suddenly fell in place.

As the stormtroopers formed up, Davin knew that he
could help the Rebels best by staying in the belly of the
beast.

Soup's On: The Pipe Smoker's Tale

by Jennifer Roberson

Pain/pleasure . . . pleasure/pain. Inseparable. Indescribable. Ineluctable.

—come closer, a little closer—

Tatooine. Mos Eisley. A cesspit planet, a cesspit spaceport, offering little to the undiscerning save perhaps the loss of coin, of limb, of life, but rich to others in risk, in Chance, in Luck, in the endless mirage of hope—illicit, illegal, wholly intoxicating.

—closer, if you will—

To me, as to blood-bred crèche-mates, Tatooine and Mos Eisley are richer still in potential: of the flesh, of the blood, of the viscera, of the overwhelming promise of risks already taken and risks *to* be taken; in the ineffable indefinable we of my race call soup.

Pleasure/pain . . . pain/pleasure. Deep in flesh-molded pockets beside my nostrils, hidden by subtle flaps in otherwise humanoid features, proboscii quiver.

—closer yet—yet—

This is what I live for, what I fish for, what I hunt. The scent of soup, then the soup itself, running hot and fast and sweet in the confines of the veins, the vessels, the brain. In the confines of the flesh.

It lends us to legend. It makes of us myth. It shapes

of us demons of dreams: Don't misbehave or an Anzat will catch you and suck all your blood away.

But it is not blood at all.

—nearly within reach—

In the bloated brilliance of Tatooine's unyielding high noon there are no such things as shadows. Only the boldness of the day, the magnified munificence of double suns, and the still brighter blazing of the glory of my need.

—it has been long, too long—

Mos Eisley is never uncrowded, but those who understand Tatooine's uncowed character understand also its malignance, its maleficent intent: to bake, to broil, to sear. And so they flee, those who know, into the sullen succor of sand-scoured, sun-flayed shelters.

What need have I of shadows when the daylight itself will do, and the heedless, headlong haste of a man fleeing it?

—three more steps—

Humanoid. I can smell him—*taste* him, there, just *there;* measured in all the ways we measure: a tint, a hue, a whisper, a kiss . . . a *soupçon,* if you will, of minor excrescence, the steam off body-boiled soup, undetectable to all humanoid races save my own.

—two more—

He is not a fool, not completely; fools die long before meeting those such as I, which saves us some little trouble. Better by far to let life handle the screening process. By the time folk come to Tatooine, the true fools are already dead. Those who have survived to come have some small measure of wit, talent, ability, of significant physical prowess—and a greater portion of Luck.

An intangible, is Luck; an attribute one can neither buy, steal, nor manufacture. But it is finite, and wholly fickle. Only you never know it.

Only I know it. I am Dannik Jerriko, and I am the Eater of Luck.

—one more step—

—YES—

He is good. He is fast. But I am better, and faster.

An image only; I am too lost, too hungry: the black-blind glaze of shock in his eyes, naked and obscene to those who understand; but he does not understand, he comprehends nothing. He knows neither who nor what I am, only *that* I am—and someone who has clapped hands across his ears and grasped his skull to hold it face-to-face in an avid embrace.

—*hot, sweet soup*—

He would fight, given leave, extended invitation. And I give leave, extend invitation—outright terror curdles the soup—briefly, oh so briefly, to make him think he is better than I; that Chance is his confidant and Luck remains his lover. It isn't fear I want, nor cowardice, but courage. The blatant willingness to step off the edge with a life at risk, *your* life, trusting skill and Luck and Chance to spread the safety net.

He is good, is fast, is willing to step off the edge; and so he does step: leaping, lunging, lurching . . . but no one is better or faster than I, and I have unraveled the net. Chance and Luck, thus mated, are dismissed in my presence: I am after all Anzati.

It is simply and quickly done with the manifest efficiency of my kind: prehensile proboscii uncoiled from cheek pockets, first inserted, then insinuated through nostrils into brain. It paralyzes instantly.

I eat his Luck. I drink his soup. I let the body fall.

They will not know when they find him; they never know at first. That comes later, after, and only if someone cares enough to run a scan on him. I knit my own nightmare, make my own mythos. A quick, clean kill; no fuss, no muss.

But assassins by trade have no friends, and no one to care enough. This is why I kill the killers.

Exterminator. Terminator. Assassin's assassin.

Soup is soup is soup, but sweeter from the container sitting longest on the shelf.

—*oh—it is sweet*—

But sweet—like Luck, like Chance—is finite. Always.

And so the cycle begins, ends, begins again, and ends; but there is always another beginning.

I am Anzat, of the Anzati. You know me now as Dannik Jerriko, but I have many names.

You knew them all as children, forgot them as adults. Legend is fiction, myth unreal; it is easier to set aside childish things in the false illumination of adulthood, because the fears of childhood are always formed of truths. Some truths are harder than others. Some folktales far more frightening.

Let there be no fear. Fear is not what I crave, neither what I desire. It is corrosive to the palate, like vinegar in place of wine.

Let there be courage, not cowardice; let there be arrogance aplenty. Self-confidence, not self-doubt; security in one's skills. And the willingness, the restlessness, the boundless physicality of the *only* constant: the testing of one's limitations. Assumption of risk, not reticence. The challenge of Chance.

Make me no predictions. Write me no prophecy. Permit me to take what is best of you, what is best *in* you.

Let me liberate it. In me you will live forever.

It is not that I *want* to kill beings.

Yes, I know—you have heard the tales. But this is a truth of the heart, if you can believe I have one: Beings embellish.

I am not crazed; I do not skulk; I don't drink blood. I take pride in appearances, pride in my heritage, pride in my work. It is serious to me, such work; there is no room at all for error, no latitude for a bad attitude.

Given a legitimate and efficacious way out, I would stop the killing . . . but I have tried joydrugs, and they are not effective; the rush is temporary and counterproductive. Synthetic derivatives and recreations are utterly useless; in fact, such half-measures make me ill. Which leaves me only one answer, the answer for all Anzati: the soup in its purest form, freshly exuded and as freshly extracted. It rots outside of the body.

Which means there must *be* a body.

It is a mother lode, Mos Eisley, a powerful concentration of entities of all gender, gathering on private business that now is also mine. Between jobs, it is vacation, holiday, opportunity to hunt for myself. To track and find the vessel most capable of satisfying my palate. Call me gourmet, if you will; I see no reason not to please myself between those assignments that, in their completions, in the method of their completions, serve to please my employers.

I have time. I have wealth. I am in fact quite rich, though I say nothing of it; credits are a wholly vulgar topic. If you cannot afford to hire me, you do not even know I exist.

Only one employer, my first, complained about my prices. He was a hollow man of small imagination . . . I drank his soup for it, but he left me unsatisfied; the entities who hire me are usually cowards themselves, incapable of anything beyond the desire for power and financial reward, and their soup is dilute. But it served, that death; no one ever again complained.

Loyalty, like Luck, cannot be purchased, only *borrowed* for a precontracted space of time in which I serve myself even as I serve others in furthering the ambitions—or settling the petty squabbles—of myriad entities. It is altogether a wholly satisfactory arrangement: My employers have the pleasure of knowing a certain "annoyance" will no longer annoy, I drink the soup of the fallen foe, and my employers pay me for it.

But what the entities do not realize is how transitory my bondage: It is only the soup to which I am loyal, and the purposes of extraction.

Other Anzati bind themselves to small lives, lives wholly focused on hunting. But there is more, so much more; one need only have the imagination to see what lies out there, and to find a way to take it.

Let them bind themselves. Let them live their small

lives, drinking soup from unworthy vessels. Let *me* take the best instead. A heady brew, such soup, far more intoxicating—and therefore longer-lasting—than the temporary measures that other Anzati rely on.

And meanwhile I am *paid* to do what I must do.

Yes. Oh, yes. The best of all the worlds.

It is always the spaceports, always the bars. I suppose one might equally suggest the brothels serve much the same purpose, but in those places an entirely different sort of business is conducted, transitory in nature and without much risk taken save in choice of partner and, perhaps, of mechanics. In bars they drink, they gamble, they deal. They come here first when a run is completed, seeking such vice and spice and entertainments as might be purchased in the cantina; and they come here looking for work. Space pirates, blockade runners, hired assassins, bounty hunters, even a handful of those involved in the Rebel Alliance. The Empire has driven the latter out of such places as they might prefer, altering good-hearted, once-innocent entities into souls as desperate as others, but with a vision pure and argent as the double suns of Tatooine, wholly unadulterated by the harsh realities of the times.

When one believes firmly enough, when conviction is absolute, one is undaunted by odds. Their soup is very sweet.

Sand chokes. It is an entity of itself, at once coy and pervasive. It dulls boots, befilths fabric, insinuates itself into the creases of the flesh. It drives even Anzati to seek relief, and thus I go indoors, out of the heat of the double suns; and I pause there—remembering one day many years before, and a corpulent, unforgiving Hutt —eyes closed to adjust more quickly to wan, ocherous light, thick and rancid as bantha butter.

It is too much to hope the cantina owner might install more lights, or improve his Queblux Power Train, identifiable by its lamentable lack of efficiency and a low, almost inaudible whine. Such repairs would be at odds with Chalmun's nature, which is dictated by distrust; deals are done at dusk, not under the fixed, unmitigated glare of Tatoo I and Tatoo II, conflagrations of eyes in the countenance of a galaxy that is, much as the Emperor's face, shrouded within a cowled hood.

Ah, but there is more here, inside, than relief from sand, from heat. There is the scent, the promise of satiation.

—*soup*—

It is thick, so *thick*—at first I am overwhelmed; this is better than I remembered: so many layers and tastes, the hues, the tints, the whispers . . . here I may drink for endless days, replete with satisfaction.

Ahh.

So many entities, so many flavors, so much Luck to eat. Chance is corporeal here, variety infinite. It is a symphony of soup running hot and fast and wet, like blood ever on the boil beneath the fragile tissue of flesh.

I am not droid, the detector says; I am welcome in Chalmun's cantina. And I laugh in the privacy of my mind, because Chalmun, contented by his bias, doesn't know there are things in the world more detestable than droids, which are on the whole inoffensive, unassuming, and more than a little convenient. But leave a man his bigotry; if they were all like the Rebel Alliance, so intransigent in honor, the soup would be weak as gruel.

—*soup*—

In cheek pockets, proboscii quiver. For an instant, only an instant, they extrude a millimeter, overcome by the heady aroma detectable only to Anzati; the others, despite races and genders, are in all ways unaware. But nothing is earned without anticipation; it is a fillip wholly invigorating, and worth the self-denial.

Accordingly proboscii withdraw, if resentfully, coiling back into the pockets beside my nostrils. I brush a film of sand from my sleeves, tug the jacket into place, and walk down the four steps into the belly of the bar.

Soup here is plentiful.
Patience will be rewarded.

He is at first disbelieving. A sour, sullen, mud-faced
man, doughy-pale despite double suns, somewhat
lumpy and misshapen as if he were unfinished, or perhaps unmade later in the small hostilities of his life. A
long blob of a swollen nose downturned above a loose-
lipped mouth. His clothing is unkempt, his hair lank
and stringy. He does not remember me.

Courtesy is nonexistent; in Mos Eisley, in Chalmun's
cantina from Chalmun's bartender, none is expected.
"You want *what?*"

"Water," I repeat.

Dark eyes narrow minutely. "You know where you
are?"

"Oh," I say, smiling, "indeed."

He jerks a spatulate thumb beyond his shoulder. "I
got a computer back there that mixes sixteen hundred
varieties of spirits."

"Oh, indeed, so I would imagine. But I want the one
it can't mix."

He scowls. "Ain't cheap, is it? This is *Tatooine.* Got
the credits for it?"

His soup is slow, and weak, its scent barely discern-
ible. He is servant, not the served, not one who ac-
knowledges edges or assumes risks beyond setting a
glass before a patron; he would offer little pleasure,
and less satisfaction.

But there are those who would. And all of them are
here.

I withdraw from a pocket a single flat coin. It glints
in wan light: clean, ruddy gold. It is not precisely a
credit chip, but it will nonetheless buy my water. On
Tatooine, they know it. In Mos Eisley they know to fear
it.

The bartender moistens his lips. Eyes slide aside,
busying themselves with glaring at a tiny Chadra-Fan
coming up to ask for libation. "Jabba's marker ain't

any good here," he mutters, and reaches beneath the bar into his hidden reserve to bring forth an ice-rimed crystal container of costly chilled water.

I leave the coin on the bar. It tells him many things, and will tell others also; Jabba pays well, and those who work for him—or work for others who work for him—recognize the tangible evidence of the Hutt's favor.

It has been a long time. There have been countless other employers in all sectors of the galaxy, but Jabba is . . . memorable. Perhaps it is time I sought a second assignment; there are always failed assassins the Hutt wants killed. He does not suffer incompetence.

I consider for a moment what it would be like to drink *his* soup . . . but Jabba is well guarded, and even an Anzat might find it difficult to locate within the massy corpulence the proper orifices into which to insert proboscii.

I shut my hand upon the glass and feel the bite of ice. On Tatooine, such is luxury. It is not soup, in no way, but worth anticipation. Even as the bartender turns away to bellow rudely at two droid-accompanied humans stopped by the detector, I sip slowly, savoring the water.

Spirits muddle the mind, slow the body, nourish nothing but weakness. Anzati avoid such things, even as we avoid joydrugs and synthetics. What is natural is best, even to the soup. There is strength in what is pure.

There is weakness in vice—and I, after all, should know. In the freedom of my lifestyle there is also captivity. There are no bars, no mesh, no energy fields, no containment capsules. There is instead an imprisonment more insidious than such things, and as distasteful to an Anzat as soup drunk from a coward.

I drank tainted soup from a tainted man, and assimilated his vice: the daily need for a proscribed but oftsmuggled offworld substance known as nic-i-tain, its vector named t'bac.

I am Dannik Jerikko. Anzat, of the Anzati, and Eater of Luck.

But I never said I was perfect.

It blows up quickly enough—a Tatooine sandstorm from the heart of the Dune Sea—as bar confrontations do. I pay it no attention beyond air-scenting for promise; it is there, but muted. I take my time preparing my pipe—there is comfort in ritual, satisfaction in preliminaries—set the mouthpiece between my teeth, then draw in t'bac smoke deeply. It is a despicable habit, but one that even I have been unable to break.

Behind me, music wails. Chalmun has hired a band since my last visit. It is appropriate music for a cantina dim as desert dusk. Through the malodorous fug of smoke and sweat, the whining melody waxes and wanes, insidious as dune dust.

—soup—

I turn, exhaling evenly; in cheek pockets, proboscii twitch.

—soup—

A flare, abrupt and unshielded, wholly raw and unrefined. It takes me but an instant to mark it, to mark the entity: human, and young. Fear, defiance, apprehension; a trace of brittle courage—ah, but he is too young, too inexperienced. Despite the stubborn jut of his jaw, the flash of defiance in blue eyes, he has not lived long enough to know what he risked. He is as yet unripe.

The young know nothing of life, nothing of its dangers, its small and large hostilities. They know only of the moment, blind to possibilities; it is not courage in the young, only the folly of youth. In males it is worse: a bantha-headed intransigence mixed with hormonal imbalance. Their soup is immature and wholly unsatisfying. It is better to let them ripen.

I draw in smoke, hold it, exhale. In the small moment of such activity the confrontation worsens. Two entities now challenge the boy: human and Aqualish. It

is bar belligerence, born of drink and insecurity; a foolish attempt to establish dominance over a raw boy
whose inexperience promises shallow entertainment
for those amused by such things. A scuffle ensues, as
always; the boy is swiped away to crash against a table.

Behind it the music stops, cut off in mid-wail. It tells
me much of the band members: Clearly they are unaccustomed to such places as Chalmun's cantina, or they
would know never to stop. Experienced musicians
would play a counterpoint to the shouts, the shrieks,
the squalls, using the cacophony, no matter how ato-
nal, to build a new melody.

Then a wholly unexpected sound is born, a sound
such as I have not heard for a hundred years: the low-
pitched, throbbing hum of an unsheathed and triggered lightsaber.

  —*soup*—

I turn instantly, seeking . . . proboscii quiver, extrude, withdraw reluctantly at my insistence. But they
know it even as I know it: Somewhere in Chalmun's
cantina is the vessel I need.

It is a quick, decisive battle, a skirmish soon ended.
With but a single stroke of the lightsaber, the Aqualish
is—well, unarmed. *One*-armed, if you will.

The boy hangs back. I scent him again, wild and
uncontrolled. But there is more here now, far more
than expected, hovering at the edges, tantalizing me
with its presence, with the repression of its power . . .
and then I see the old man quietly putting away the
lightsaber, and I realize what he is.

A Master despite his reticence, seeking no battles in
word or deed; Master of what is, in such times, left
wholly unspoken, lest the Emperor suspect. But I know
what he is: Jedi. I could not *but* know. He is too disciplined, too well shielded against such intrusions as
Anzati probing, and in that very shielding the truth, to
me, is obvious.

I leave it its due: unspoken. I see no need to speak it.
Let him be what he is; no one else will suspect. He is
safe a while longer.

The boy has earned my study. If they have true business together it is information worth knowing. If the old man has taken a pupil there is indeed cause to fear —*if* you are part of the Empire, and recall the old ways.

If not, as I am not—save I recall the old days, the even older ways—it matters not at all. Unless you care to count the coin Jabba would pay, or others, including Darth Vader.

Including the Emperor.

Braggadocio. It is a staple of such places, the ritual boasting of entity to entity to save face, or to build face; to request a place in the world, or to make a place; an attempt to create of oneself something *more* than what one is.

There are those who are indeed more—as Anzat I am far more than anyone might suspect (or comfortably imagine)—but only rarely do they resort to braggadocio, because everyone else knows who they are and what they have done. To say anything at all is redundancy, which dilutes the deeds.

But even those most skilled, even those most notorious may well be pressed to resort to braggadocio in the implacable face of a Jedi Master dubious of those deeds. Such entities as the old man can reduce the strongest to crèche-born, and with little said or done.

The band has recovered itself, or is under pain of reduced payment if the musicians do not immediately resume playing. The music, less strident now, mutes all conversations but those closest to me, but I need not rely on words and tone for information. In braggadocio is often borne the scent of soup.

I exhale, feel proboscii quiver, turn slowly to take my measure of the cantina. The direction is easily gained, and as I mark it I cannot help but smile; the old man and his pupil have gone into one of the cubicles. It is not them I scent now, but those with whom they speak: a hulking Wookiee, and a humanoid male.

—*soup*—

It boils up quickly, powerfully, so quickly and so powerfully I cannot help but mark it. It leaves me breathless.

Not the old Jedi, who is disciplined, and shielded. Not the boy, who is young and unripe. Not the Wookiee, who is passive in all but loyalty. The humanoid. The Corellian.

Anzati are long-lived. Memory abides.

A curl of smoke winds its way from my pipe. Through the wreath of it I smile. He is wanted, as is the Wookiee, but all entities in Chalmun's cantina are wanted somewhere. Even *I* am wanted, or would be; no one knows who or what I am, or what I am wanted for, and in that there is continuance.

I am careful in the hunt, always meticulous in those details others ignore, and too often die of; I require confirmation. I commit nothing until I am certain.

In this instance confirmation and certainty need little time and less patience. The Jedi and his pupil depart, but are immediately replaced by a Rodian. He is nervous. His soup is so insubstantial as to be nonexistent; he is servant, not served.

He is coward. He is fool. He is incompetent. He is slow to commit himself. And thus he is dead in a burst of contraband blaster in the hand of a wholly committed and consummate pirate.

—*soup*—

I exult even as proboscii twitch expectantly. It is here, *here*—and now, right now, *this moment* . . . the hue, the tint, the whisper, the shout, the evanescence of soup incarnate, enfleshed and unshielded, and rich, so *rich*—

I need only to go and to get it, to drink it, to embrace as Anzati embrace, to dance the dance with the Corellian whose soup is thick, and hot, and sweet, sweeter by far than any I have tasted for too long a time—

Now.

Now.

But haste dilutes fulfillment. Let there be time, and patience.

—*such soup*—

The band wails on. There is the sharp scent of smoke; the acrid tang of sweat; the smut-dusty stench of dune sand, of city sand; the blatancy of blaster death but newly encountered, redolent of the Rodian's cowardice and stupidity. It was a poor death worth no comment; he will not be mourned even by the entity who hired him.

He is—*was*—the Hutt's, of course. Need you ask? There is none other who would dare to hire assassins in Mos Eisley, on Tatooine.

None but Lord Vader, and the Emperor.

But they are not here. Only Jabba.

The Hutt is in all things; is of *himself* all things, and everywhere, on Tatooine, in Mos Eisley, in Chalmun's cantina.

—*such soup*—

A final inhalation of t'bac, sucked deep inside and savored, as is the moment, the knowledge, the need itself savored. A brief glare of searing sunlight illuminates the interior as the Corellian pirate and his Wookiee companion depart with alacrity Chalmun's premises, wary of Imperial repercussions. It is Jabba's spaceport in all but name, and that name is the Emperor's, who need know nothing of such dealings as the Hutt's; or who knows, and does not care.

It is dusk again inside. They will clear the body away; and someone will report to Jabba that his hireling is dead.

Has reported; he knows it by now, and by whose hand it was done.

—*such soup*—

But what sense in paying for it of my own pocket? Jabba's is deeper.

Indeed, the Hutt will pay well. But it is *I* who will drink the soup.

—*such soup*—

Proboscii quiver as I exhale the twinned smoke-stream slowly, steadily, with quiet satisfaction and the frisson of my own soup as it leaps in anticipation.

—*Han Solo's soup*—

Ah, but it will be a hunt worth the hunting . . . and soup such as I—even Dannik Jerriko, Anzat of the Anzati, Eater of Luck, of Chance—have never, ever known.

At the Crossroads: The Spacer's Tale

by Jerry Oltion

The *Infinity* was hot in more ways than one. BoShek smiled as he prepared to drop out of hyperspace over Tatooine. He'd just beat Solo's time on the Kessel run.

Of course he was running empty, bringing in just the ship to have its transponder codes altered, but even so, it would be fun to tell the braggart Corellian and his furry sidekick he'd broken their record.

The cockpit fit like a glove around him. He could reach all the controls from the single pilot's chair, and everything was right where instinct made him reach first. The windows wrapped around to give him almost a full circle of view, and a heads-up holo filled in the gap to the rear. In his three years of piloting smugglers' ships for the monastery-cum-forging operation, BoShek had never flown one so well designed as this.

The computer counted down the last few seconds, then automatically switched to the sublight engines. Elongated starlines snapped back to points of light, and high to the left the bright yellow-white disk of Tatooine swelled into being. Holy bantha breath, it was close! Another second in hyper and he'd have popped out underground.

He swung around so the navcomputer could get a

straight shot at the orbiting beacons, but he was willing
to bet it already knew where they were. Sure enough,
within seconds the planetary image in the navscreen
filled with longitude and latitude lines, then showed a
sparse dotting of oases and settlements across the desert planet.

Mos Eisley was about a third of an orbit away.
BoShek was just about to accelerate toward it when the
navcomputer buzzed a warning and two bright white
wedges slid into view from around the curve of the
planet. Imperial Star Destroyers. BoShek glanced out
the windows and shuddered. They were so big he could
actually see them with the naked eye.

Where had they come from? Tatooine was so far off
the beaten track, the Empire hardly ever sent a tax
collector, much less a pair of warships. Somebody must
have caused some major trouble while he was gone.

And now their trouble was his too, because the *Infinity* was still running under hot transponder codes. If
the Imperials bothered to scan for its engines' unique
emission signature—and they no doubt would—then
they would know it was a smuggler's ship, wanted
throughout the galaxy for tariff violation, tax evasion,
gun-running, and dozens of other crimes. The fact that
BoShek was merely piloting it to Tatooine for someone
else wouldn't save him in a trial. If he ever *got* a trial.

For that matter, neither the monastery nor the *Infinity*'s owners would be happy with him if he let the Empire confiscate the ship. His job was to bring it in
undetected so the monastery's technicians could alter
its codes and give it a clean record, not to lose it to the
first patrol that happened along.

Without hesitation, he aimed straight down and ac-
celerated hard. In space he wouldn't stand a chance
against the destroyers' short-range TIE fighters, but
down in the atmosphere, with the planet to help con-
fuse their sensors, he might be able to lose them.

Tatooine grew from a sphere to a close, mottled wall.
The *Infinity* began rocking gently as it reached the top
of the atmosphere, then a bright flash came from the

starboard side and the ship suddenly lurched to port. The destroyers had opened fire.

BoShek kept the *Infinity* aimed straight down, diving deep before he leveled out, knowing that the more air he put between him and the destroyers, the more shielding he would have from their turbolasers. His passage left a glowing, ionized wake behind him, but when he slowed to just a few times the speed of sound he left no trace.

He wasn't free yet, though. Four TIE fighters from the warships arced into the atmosphere after him, and their closer range made up for the air's energy absorption. The *Infinity* once again shuddered under Imperial fire.

Fortunately, they weren't trying to kill him yet. Confident that he couldn't get away, they were just trying to disable the ship and force him down. They were probably even trying to contact him by radio, but BoShek left the receiver switched off. Any transmission he could make would only give them his voiceprint; as it was, if he could lose them he might remain anonymous.

He shoved the throttles forward again, at the same time corkscrewing down and underneath the fighters to skim the sand. He was over the vast Dune Sea, far to the west of civilization; the wavelike dunefield erupted into clouds of roiling sand as his shock wave passed over it.

Lining up directly behind him for another salvo, the flat-winged fighters plowed straight through the clouds, the airborne particles etching away their instruments and control surfaces and pitting their windows. They immediately rose up above the billowing sand, but BoShek chose that moment to pull back on the throttles, letting them overshoot him. He banked left, waited until they had committed to a left turn, then banked hard right and shoved the throttles down again, racing for the Jundland Wastes to the east.

The TIE fighters were catching up again by the time the jagged canyonland slid toward him over the horizon. BoShek dodged a few last energy bolts, then dived into the first canyon he reached and wove his way up it at top speed. The *Infinity* handled like a dream, hugging the ground as if on rails, but the TIE fighters were just as maneuverable. Only the damage they'd taken in the sand cloud kept them from catching him.

Then one of them made a mistake. Closing in for a crippling shot, it crossed into the *Infinity*'s shock wave, and the turbulence against its wide vertical wings tossed it like a leaf into the side of the canyon. The explosion sent another fighter into the ground, leaving only two to follow him.

Losing half their number had changed the rules, though. Now they weren't shooting just to cripple; they were out for blood. BoShek frowned as he tried to think of a way to take them out first, but the *Infinity* was built for speed, not fighting.

Fleetingly, he thought of calling upon the Force, of trying to use its ancient mystical powers to throw his pursuers off, but he knew it would be useless. He'd been meditating and concentrating on the Force ever since he'd heard of it from one of the few real monks at the monastery in Mos Eisley, but he'd never yet gotten any indication that it even existed, other than a faint awareness of other people's presence from time to time. The old Jedi might have been able to draw from it to subdue their enemies a long time ago, but the Force hadn't protected them from the advancing Empire. No, he needed something more concrete, something physical he could do to escape.

Then he remembered a story Solo had told him once, about how he'd faked out a bounty hunter in an asteroid belt. Yeah. The same thing might work here.

He led the fighters deeper and deeper into the canyon, until its high walls boxed them in on either side. The *Infinity* shuddered under more and more impacts, and a flashing light on the instrument board warned of a shield about to fail, but instead of speeding up, BoShek intentionally slowed down. He rested his finger on the emergency escape-pod launch button, and just as he rounded a sharp bend, he hit it. The escape pod blew free and continued straight into the canyon wall, where its fuel supply exploded in a spectacular fireball. BoShek kept his eye on the heads-up rearview, but neither of the TIE fighters emerged from the flames. Either they'd been swallowed up in the explosion, or they'd pulled up and were circling around to examine what they no doubt assumed was the wreckage of the entire *Infinity*.

Smiling, BoShek pulled up out of the canyon, aimed straight east, then cut his engines completely. He had enough velocity to fly ballistic all the way to Mos Eisley if he had to, and with his engines dead the TIE fighters would never spot him.

"Solo," he said aloud in the close control cabin, "I owe you a drink."

BoShek knew right where to find him, too. Whenever the *Millennium Falcon* was onplanet, either Solo or Chewbacca—and sometimes both—would be at the Mos Eisley Cantina, trying to drum up business. After he'd dropped off the *Infinity* at the monastery, leaving instructions for the mechanics to modify its engine transponders immediately, BoShek headed straight there, not even taking the time to change out of his flight suit first. The monastery was south of the city's center; he stopped for a moment at the ancient wreckage of the first colony ship, the *Dowager Queen*, to pass a sealed note from the abbot to one of the street preachers there, then hurried on.

The streets were lousy with stormtroopers, but they didn't seem to be looking for BoShek. He saw four of them hassling an old hermit and a kid and two droids in a beat-up old landspeeder, but they evidently weren't too interested in them either, because they let them go after just a few questions. BoShek ducked into the cantina before the stormtroopers could take an interest in him.

It took his eyes a minute to adjust to the dark interior, but Chewbacca was easy to spot, towering above the other beings at the bar the way he did. BoShek wove his way through the crowd and leaned up against the bar next to him.

"I beat your record," he said without preamble.

Chewbacca grunted the Wookiee equivalent of "Get lost," but then BoShek's voice registered and he turned his head to ask what record BoShek meant.

"The Kessel run," BoShek said, grinning. "I beat your time by a tenth, and I had to take out four TIE fighters when I got here to boot."

Chewbacca growled appreciatively. He howled a long, ululating phrase that BoShek translated as "You'd better not let the customers catch you wringing out their ships, or they'll start taking their business elsewhere."

"Hey, we're the best there is, and you know it," BoShek told him. He waved at the bartender, who shot him a surly look and turned away. "So how's the *Falcon* holding up? You need another code job yet?"

The Wookiee shook his shaggy head, then hooted in laughter. He howled another phrase that BoShek tentatively translated as: "After what you charged us last time, we've been keeping our noses clean. It's cheaper."

"Think of it as life insurance," BoShek said, echoing the abbot's favorite sales pitch. He was about to shout at the bartender when he felt an unmistakable awareness of someone behind him. It was the strongest presence he'd ever felt.

He turned as casually as he could and saw the old hermit and the boy in the doorway. The hermit's eyes met his, and just a hint of a smile showed on his grizzled face. Leaving the boy with their droids, he walked straight up to BoShek and said in an astonishingly rich voice, "May the Force be with you, my friend."

The *Force*? Had he really felt it just now? "I—uh—thanks," BoShek stuttered. "How did you know . . . ?"

"Your struggles are as plain as words for someone who is trained to see them. I could teach you much, but I fear my time here is short. I need passage off the planet. However, since I believe you have a ship, perhaps we could further both our quests at once.''

BoShek could hardly believe what he was hearing. This old guy was practically reading his mind. BoShek had never told anyone about his fascination with the Force, yet here came this complete stranger who picked up on it immediately. But he'd gotten part of BoShek's story wrong. "I wish I *did* have a ship," he said. "But I'm just a pilot."

"Ah, that's a pity," said the hermit. "Perhaps when I return we can discuss the Force anyway."

"Yeah, maybe we can."

Chewbacca growled softly, and BoShek took the hint. "I do know someone with a ship who might be willing to take on passengers, though," he said, nodding toward the Wookiee.

"I see. Thank you." The hermit glanced toward Chewbacca, then looked back at BoShek and said, "I'll leave you with one piece of advice: Beware the dark side. Your role here on the edge of society has put you in a very ambiguous position, one that you must resolve before you can continue in your journey. Only the pure of heart can ever hope to wield the Force's power with any success."

"Thanks, I think," BoShek said.

"You're welcome."

It was clearly a dismissal, so BoShek bowed out with a nod to Chewbacca, letting them discuss business while he went around to the other side of the bar to get the bartender's attention.

He'd finally managed to get a drink and was casting about to see if he could spot Solo when the old man pulled a lightsaber on a walrus-faced Aqualish and an even worse looking human, and BoShek got knocked over in the rush to give them room. The Aqualish lost an arm in the fight, and the old man gained a wide zone of respect, but BoShek didn't care about either one of them at the moment, being occupied with wiping a pint of bitter off the front of his flight suit.

Bloody brawls were nothing new in the cantina, and aside from the old man's lightsaber this one was nothing special, but enough of the other bar patrons had spilled their drinks that it took BoShek another ten minutes to get served again. By then he'd spotted Solo, but the Corellian was already deep in conversation with the old man and the boy, so he sat back down at the bar and waited his turn. Maybe he could learn something more from Solo about the old guy after they were done.

While he waited, he tried asking around to find out what all the stormtroopers were doing in town, but nobody would admit to knowing. The Imperial troops had simply swooped down from their Star Destroyers a couple of days ago and set up roadblocks all over town, and in most of the other towns surrounding the Jundland Wastes as well. They were looking for something, but nobody knew what.

A couple of them came into the cantina, shining conspicuously in their white body armor. BoShek looked over to see how the hermit and the kid would react to their presence, but they were already gone. He stood up to go take their place at Solo's table, but first the stormtroopers, then a long-nosed, green-skinned Rodian, beat him to it. Solo was a popular guy today.

The Rodian held a blaster pointed straight at Solo's chest. BoShek slipped his own blaster out of its holster, ready to help if it looked as though Solo needed it, but then he saw something that made him reholster his weapon and watch with amusement. Slowly, almost imperceptibly, Solo was drawing his own blaster under the table.

Sure enough, when he got it free of its holster, he gave a little shrug as if to say "So long, sucker," and fired right through the table at the Rodian, who collapsed forward on the smoking remains.

Solo stood up, flipped a couple of credits to the bartender, and stalked out before BoShek could catch his attention. He downed his drink and followed him out, but he had barely made it out the door when he felt someone grab his arm and an authoritative voice said, "All right, hold it right there, spaceman."

He turned slowly to see a local cop pointing a blaster at him. "What's the problem?" he asked, keeping his voice as unconfrontational as he could manage.

The cop scowled. "The problem is, a wanted starship ran an Imperial blockade, dusted four interceptors in the process, and landed here in town just a little while ago. Darth Vader's on one of the battleships and wants somebody's head for it, and yours looks about the right size to me. You're still suited up; how 'bout you and me have a little chat down at the station?"

Only his years of practice at talking his way through customs allowed BoShek to keep his expression neutral. Inside, he was close to panic. If they got him under a mind-probe, they'd know for sure he'd done it, and there was a good chance he'd blow the monastery's cover as well. Either way, he was dead.

Forcing himself to sound calm, he shrugged and said, "You've got the wrong pilot, I'm afraid, and there's a whole bar full of people in there who can prove it. I've been here all afternoon."

The cop hesitated, looking into the dark doorway, and when he squinted to see inside, BoShek lashed out with a foot and kicked the blaster out of his hands. He followed with a punch to the side of the head, putting all his weight behind it, and the cop collapsed like a shorted droid.

The blaster clattered to the ground a few steps away. BoShek lunged for it but lost the race to a pair of Jawas, who scurried away with their prize and quickly disappeared among the dozens of taller aliens on the street. BoShek didn't particularly care; he had his own blaster if it came to that, and as long as the cop *didn't*, he was happy. He turned and walked nonchalantly— but quickly—away from the cantina toward the city's central plaza and the thickest crowds.

He had only made it across the street and down half

a block to the wrecked *Dowager Queen* when he heard a shout behind him. Few of the street's inhabitants even looked up, since shouts from the cantina were a regular thing, but BoShek quickened his stride toward the old colony ship's rusted hulk.

Twisted girders arched out over the packed dirt, awnings tied between some of them providing shade for the crowds gathered to listen to the street preachers pontificating from the upper levels. Ruptures in the hull and busted portholes provided glimpses into the ship's dark interior, from which the red glow of Jawa eyes peered outward.

BoShek ducked inside the sagging cargo lock. The hold smelled strongly of Jawas, but he didn't care. The more the merrier, in fact. He stepped over vagrants and preachers resting in the shade, pushing past them until he was well hidden from the street. In the dim light filtering in through holes in the hull, he stripped off his flight suit and flung it farther into the darkness, keeping only the tool belt with all his personal belongings. A chorus of growls and high-pitched chattering erupted as the wreck's inhabitants quarreled over their new prize.

His gray suit liner was a little less of a beacon for the police, but it still wasn't very good camouflage. BoShek knelt down beside one of the vagrants and said, "Ten credits for your cloak." That was far more than it was worth, and they both knew it. Without a word the vagrant tugged off his rough brown robe and handed it over. BoShek paid him and wrapped himself up in the noxious-smelling garment, then pushed back toward the door.

He had underestimated the cop's tenacity. He had evidently seen BoShek slip into the wreckage, and was now standing at the edge of the crowd with a small boot-top blaster in his hand. The crowd had thinned considerably under the policeman's glare; BoShek didn't think he'd be able to hide among the few people left.

He turned and reentered the ship. There had to be

another way out of it. He stumbled over more bodies, circumnavigating the cargo hold, but all he found was a ramp leading up a level. Thinking maybe there would be a stairway back down over the outer hull, he climbed the ramp, but it only led to the observation deck from which half a dozen preachers harangued the crowd below.

From his new vantage, BoShek saw reinforcements coming to the first cop's aid. He was trapped. They obviously weren't going to drop it, not with the Empire breathing down their necks. They needed a sacrificial suspect to deliver to the stormtroopers, and they weren't about to let him get away now. Which meant they wouldn't rest until they'd swept through the entire ship. BoShek looked around frantically, but there was no place to hide. The observation deck was even more open than the cargo hold. It had been gutted of everything that could be unbolted or torn loose, leaving just an empty floor with blasted-out windows spaced evenly around it. All but one of the window frames had a preacher standing before it, facing outward toward the people on the street below. None of the preachers were from the monastery; BoShek wondered why until he remembered the note he'd dropped off here on his way to the cantina. The abbot must have called them in for some kind of conference.

With no place to hide and no friends to help him, he could see only one possibility. He bent down and smeared his hands along the floor near the wall, then wiped the grimy black goo he gathered there on his cheeks and forehead, darkening his complexion and making his face fit his clothing. Then he stepped to the window and said in a quavering voice he hoped sounded old and wizened, "Brothers, sisters, friends, and aliens; beware the dark side of the Force!"

A few of the people below him looked up, squinting into the sun, and BoShek realized why this particular window was empty. Tatooine's twin suns were directly behind him from the vantage of anyone below; not a good location for a preacher interested in gathering a following. It was perfect for BoShek, though. He pulled his hood over his head so nobody could get a good look at him from the side, then he cleared his throat and began his sermon.

Despite living at a monastery, he knew almost nothing about the religion they preached. He spent his time in the underground ship-alteration complex, not in the cathedral the monks had set up to establish their cover. He knew their doctrine was all based on the divinity of banthas or some such crock, and had been borrowed from a group of true believers who lived out in the wilderness, but he had no idea how it all tied together. Far better, he thought, to preach something he at least knew a little about, though he didn't suppose it really mattered. Who listened to street preachers, anyway?

Remembering what the old man in the cantina had told him, he said, "Only the pure of heart can ever hope to achieve true mastery of the Force." A few more faces looked up, then away. BoShek spread his arms wide. "You must open yourselves up to salvation. You must cleanse yourselves, make peace with your inner natures, and accept the Force as your guiding principle."

The preacher to his right had stopped his own sermon to listen. BoShek smiled nervously at him, then went on. "When you surrender yourselves to the Force, you deliver your lives unto the greatest power in the universe. With it you can move mountains, see the future, and find eternal life." Hah, he thought, this preaching stuff wasn't that hard. Just string all the buzzwords together, and you had it.

Another of the preachers fell silent. BoShek wasn't sure he liked their attention, but the cops had moved to surround the ship, and he could hear the commotion in the cargo hold as they began their search. And now, attracted to a scene of trouble like flying insects to light, a stormtrooper patrol was also heading toward the ship.

BoShek pulled his robe closer about him and leaned farther out the window, saying, "Repent! Dig deep into your hearts, and the truth shall set you free!"

"Be silent," the priest on his right hissed. BoShek noted that he wore a robe considerably cleaner than his own, and his fingers and wrists were spangled with gold rings and bracelets. Preaching was evidently good business.

"Be silent yourself," BoShek told him. He could hear the cops ascending the ramp now. "On second thought, don't be. Preach, or we're both going to be saying our prayers in jail." He turned back to the window and said to the crowd below, "There are disbelievers among you, people who deny the existence of the Force, or say that it's weakened with time and no longer useful in these modern days, but I say to you, every living creature that is born increases the power of the Force."

The preacher who had shushed him glanced warily down the ramp, then turned back to his window and picked up where he'd left off, saying in a voice loud enough to drown out BoShek completely, "Consider the banthas of the dunefields. They quail not; neither do they sting. They are the holiest of beasts . . ."

Oh, boy. This guy was the real item. BoShek was glad he hadn't tried to fake the monastery religion, although the preacher didn't seem too thrilled to be hearing a competing doctrine, either. Well, it couldn't be helped; BoShek was committed now.

The other preacher resumed his spiel too, offering to heal anyone who tossed him money.

BoShek gladly let them drown him out, babbling on about the Force merely to keep up his cover. He could sense the cops behind him, three of them sweeping blast rifles around the observation deck. He closed his eyes and wished for a miracle, wished that they would just turn around and march back down the ramp and go away.

A high-pitched Jawa voice chittered angrily from below. The unmistakable crack of blaster fire made BoShek nearly leap out the window, but he realized just in time that the shooting had come from outside, too. He leaned out and peered around the curve of the hull, and could just see the Jawa lying in a smoking heap on the ground. The patrol squad of white-armored stormtroopers stood in the middle of the square, waving their blast rifles around menacingly, but no one else fired.

The cops behind BoShek rushed back down the ramp to investigate. BoShek leaned against the window frame for support, his legs suddenly weak. Whatever the Jawa had done, its noisy death had distracted the cops long enough for him to escape.

He turned to go, only to meet a gold-ringed fist with his face. He staggered back and landed hard on the floor. "Mock us, will you?" the preacher snarled at him, aiming a kick at his ribs that BoShek barely dodged.

The other preachers quickly joined the first in kicking and hitting him. "Here's for trying to make people laugh at us!" one of them said as he nearly wrenched BoShek's arm from its socket. "And here's for leading the militia up here," another said.

BoShek scrambled to his feet, trying to explain. "No, wait, I didn't mean to—" But they weren't interested in excuses. Under continual pummeling, he covered his head and dived for the ramp, rolled halfway down it, and came up running. He thought the preachers would leave it at that, but two of them chased him right out of the wreck and out into the plaza, where the police, gathered around the Jawa's corpse, turned to see what this new commotion was.

"That's him!" the cop he'd knocked down shouted, and he snapped off a blaster shot that just missed BoShek's head, blowing a rusty attitude jet off the side of the wreck instead. BoShek leaped over the jet and dashed around the curve of the hull; then when he had its bulk between him and his pursuers, he sprinted

straight down the street toward the thickest crowd he
could see: the buyers and sellers in front of the Jawa
trading center.

The preachers were still hot on his tail, which was
the only thing that kept him from getting a blaster bolt
in the back. The police were evidently reluctant to
shoot a bona fide religious leader, even by accident,
probably fearing the trouble their followers would
cause in retribution.

Taking advantage of their hesitation, BoShek ran
past the traders and on down the street toward the
used-landspeeder lot. He thought briefly of dodging
through the speeders and trying to lose his pursuers
that way, but as he drew closer he saw the triangular-
headed Arconan dealer gloating over a deal he had
just made, and he realized his salvation was at hand.

Running up to the speeder the Arconan had bought
—a battered XP-38A with two engines on the side and
a third up on a fin in back—he tossed a fistful of credits at the surprised alien, then leaped into the driver's
seat and shouted over his shoulder, "I'm taking it for a
test drive!"

"No, wait! What do you think you're—" the Arconan wailed, but BoShek didn't stick around to argue.
The engines were still running; he jammed the accelerator on full and zoomed away, nearly running over a
cylindrical droid before he swerved the speeder farther
out into the street.

The cops took a couple of wild shots at him, but the
energy bolts only succeeded in making the people in
the street dive for cover. BoShek zoomed down the
clear avenue, took the corner at the end of the block at
full speed, and continued on.

Two blocks farther, he slowed for another corner,
then proceeded at a more normal speed to the next
corner, where he turned again and tried to blend into
what little vehicle traffic there was. His zigzag course
was leading him in a loop around Docking Bay 94.
Good. The jumbled streets dead-ending at the bay

would keep the police busy for a long time, if they even bothered to look for him anymore.

He was thinking about ditching the speeder and heading back to the monastery when he turned another corner and found himself gliding toward a patrol of four stormtroopers who stood blocking the street. One of the troopers raised a hand with his palm out, indicating that BoShek should stop.

They didn't have their rifles drawn, which meant they were probably just stopping everyone on the street for questioning. Even so, there was no way BoShek could get past them or turn around and flee before they could unsling their blasters and take him out. He forced himself to let up on the accelerator and drift to a stop before the troopers, all the while frantically trying to think of a way out of this latest predicament.

"What's your business here?" the patrol leader asked him. His voice was distorted by the full battle helmet he wore, and the bubble lenses of his visor kept BoShek from seeing where he was looking.

"I'm, uh, just headed down to the cantina," BoShek told him.

"I see. Is this your landspeeder?"

"I'm test-driving it," BoShek said.

"A likely story. Let's see your—" The stormtrooper's words were drowned out by the roar of a ship taking off under full thrust. BoShek winced at the blast as the ship cleared the rooftops, then did a double take when he recognized its outline. It was the *Millennium Falcon*.

Looks like the old man must have made it, he thought. Too bad, in a way; he could have used a little bit of his luck right now.

But it wasn't luck, was it? The guy knew about the Force, and by the way he talked and the way he handled a lightsaber, he was a master at it. He'd probably used its power to manipulate his way past all the obstacles. A little roadblock like this would hardly make him sweat.

Well, BoShek was sweating plenty. The stormtroopers had all turned to watch the ship blast free, but they would be bringing their attention back to him soon enough.

Go check out the docking bay, BoShek thought at them. *Go bother somebody else. Whatever, just let me go.*

What had the old man told him about the Force? "Beware the dark side," he'd said. "Only the pure of heart can ever hope to wield the Force's power with any success." And he'd told BoShek he'd have to resolve his role here on the edge of society before he could continue his journey.

Great. Stealing the landspeeder had probably nixed whatever chance he'd ever had at using the Force.

But he hadn't actually stolen it, now had he? He'd tossed the Arconan who'd bought it at least fifty credits, and while it was true that he'd only been hoping to keep the landspeeder dealer from raising the alarm for a few minutes, he *could* still take it back.

All right, he thought, directing his thoughts out into the vastness of space where he imagined the Force accumulated. *I'll take the speeder back just as soon as I get free, and I'll quit running hot ships for smugglers and I'll clean up the rest of my act, as long as you get me out of this mess.*

He didn't really expect it to work. The Force wasn't some judgmental god deciding a person's fate; like the old man had implied, the Force just *was.* It didn't care what BoShek promised. The power to manipulate it came from within, and BoShek wasn't foolish enough to believe he had reached internal harmony in the last few seconds. But maybe, just maybe, he had changed enough to make a difference.

He concentrated all his effort on the stormtroopers, willing them to let him go, and he was almost sure he felt something, a twinge of awareness directed toward them. An answering sensation came back, as if they too possessed some rudiments of the Force, or had once been exposed to it. They seemed to feel his touch; all four of them turned in unison to regard the landspeeder again.

BoShek could hardly breathe. *Fog your brains,* he thought at them. *Forget I'm here.*

"How long have you had these droids?" the storm-trooper captain asked.

"Huh?" BoShek turned his head toward the passenger seat, wondering how he could have missed seeing a droid there, but save for himself the speeder was empty.

"I—" he said, but the trooper cut him off.

"Let me see your identification."

Here we go, BoShek thought. He reached slowly for his belt, wondering if he could grab his blaster and take out all four troopers, but the captain's next words stopped him cold.

"We don't need to see his identification," he said to the others. "These aren't the droids we're looking for."

Bewildered, BoShek could only say, "That's . . . uh, that's good."

"You can go about your business," the trooper said. He waved his arms in dismissal. "Move along."

BoShek's field of vision was shot full of tracers from the sudden rush of relief. He had to take a deep breath to keep from fainting, but he managed to urge the landspeeder forward and around the corner before he pulled it to a stop and collapsed back against the seat.

He had no idea what had just happened, except for one thing: The Force was real, and he had somehow manipulated the stormtroopers with it.

But not without a price. He imagined the old man, probably half a light-year away by now, still watching over him somehow, waiting to see if he would follow through on his promise.

Would he? It was hardly a question. BoShek had been given a glimpse of something vast, something at once wonderful and terrifying. Beware the dark side, the old man had told him, and BoShek knew the warning was sincere. He could use this newfound power of his for good or for evil, but once he made the choice, there would be no going back. He was standing at a crossroads, and whatever decision he made now would affect the rest of his life.

Smiling for the first time in what seemed like hours, he started the landspeeder and began driving it back to its rightful owner.

Doctor Death:
The Tale of Dr. Evazan
and Ponda Baba

by Kenneth C. Flint

The odd scraping sound could be heard even above the distant rumble of thunder.

One of the two figures seated at the dining table twisted around, cocking its head to listen.

"What's that?" a gruff voice demanded. "Rover, go check!"

Something shifted in a shadowed corner. A mass slid forward with a wet, sucking sound, coming into the light. It was a gelatinous form, a mucuslike mass of

313

greasily shining bile-green that humped and slithered itself over the floor as a ring of slender, bulb-tipped stalks wavered atop the rounded mass. It oozed on across the width of the long dining room toward one of the arched window openings in the far wall.

"I wouldn't have believed a Meduza could be trained at all," the second figure at the table remarked with some surprise.

The first man turned back to the guest seated across the dining table from him. "On the contrary, Senator. It's quite easy to train. One of the most malleable species I've found, in fact. I wish there were more like it."

The man's face was obscured by a massive scar disfiguring the right side, leaving the right eye a slit in the sagging flesh and flattening out the nose, giving him a piggish look.

"I can unfortunately imagine what things you wish for, Dr. Evazan," the Aqualish senator replied with a shudder of revulsion. Generally humanoid, he had walruslike features, with large, liquid black eyes and thick, incurving tusks. Short bristling whiskers lined the stubby snout that was split by a wide, thin mouth.

The senator lifted a hand to clutch the glass before him. The hand was finlike, fingerless, but with an opposable thumb. It marked him as a member of the more prominent of the two Aqualish races, and thus belonging to their ruling classes. He drank deeply of the dark green Andoan ale within the glass as he watched Rover nervously.

The gelatinous creature had by now reached one of the window openings. Heaving itself into a higher peak, it poised a moment, its bulbed stalks jerking about as if sniffing the air.

Beyond the opening, the vast sea of the water planet of Ando stretched away to a gray-black horizon. In the boiling storm clouds that hung there, spectacular lightning flickered and flared to light the towering thunderheads.

The deep boom of thunder rolled across the gale-churned waves to rebound from the sheer stone walls of the spired castle perched high upon the cliffs. Hundreds of meters below the castle window, fists of massive waves slammed themselves against the base of the rocky isle, splaying to white fingers that grabbed futilely upward.

The full magnificence of the wild scene was somewhat obscured by a shimmering scrim of light created by the energy shield that formed a screen across each opening.

The bloblike creature sank back down. Its pod-tipped stalks turned toward Evazan at once and waved to him, as if in urgent signal.

Dr. Evazan cocked the remaining eyebrow above his left eye. His half-blasted face expressed no other sign of emotion.

"You might just want to drop down under the table now," he told his guest in a quite matter-of-fact voice.

The Aqualish senator stared in astonishment as one of Evazan's hands appeared from under the table clutching a blaster pistol. The other hand lifted to punch one button on a small tabletop console, and then a second.

All the lights went out.

Simultaneously a sizzling sound came from beyond the windows, and the energy screens of three openings were punctured inward as three forms dived through them from outside.

The senator gave a shrill honk of terror and dived beneath the thick tabletop.

The three forms hit the floor, rolled, and came instantly to their feet. A flicker of distant lightning illuminated three humanoid shapes as they lifted blaster rifles to fire.

Evazan was already rolling from his chair toward the shelter of a conform lounge. He fired as he went, his bolt striking one of the three forms squarely.

The attacker let out a grunt of pain as he staggered and went down. The other two dived for cover. Bolts from opposing weapons crisscrossed the dark room, cracking into stone walls and ripping through furnishings.

One of the attackers was so intent on hitting Evazan, he was not aware of something creeping up—not until a liquid sound made him whip about just as Rover lunged.

The intruder had no chance for defense as the Meduza's stalks all shot forward, touching their pod ends to the other's face and chest. Each pod flared brightly, and the victim's form stiffened, shuddering as if an electric shock coursed through it, then collapsed.

Evazan's twisted mouth lifted in a grotesque smile. "Good boy, Rover," he muttered. But the smile vanished as he looked toward the room's door, adding in an irked tone, "But where in hell are you, Ponda?"

He moved out from his cover, crawling about the dark room, angling for a shot at the last foe. As Evazan lifted up to take aim at the last place he had seen the other, that final invader drew a bead on the doctor's shadowy form.

The door of the room burst inward and a new figure plunged through. A quick, well-aimed blaster bolt skewered Evazan's attacker, barely saving the doctor from a fatal shot.

The last body thudded to the floor. Evazan climbed to his feet, brushing himself off. "About time, Ponda," he told the new arrival, stepping to the table to switch the lights back on.

The returning illumination revealed another Aqualish male clutching a freshly fired blaster. But Ponda Baba's left hand was the hairy, talon-fingered hand of one of the lesser Aqualish race. The right hand and the forearm to which it was fixed were artificial, and of a rather crude mechanical type, their skeletal metal frame uncovered by bioflesh.

"You're lucky," Ponda replied in a growl, shoving his blaster back into a holster. "I almost left you to take them all yourself."

With that he turned and clomped out of the room. The Andoan senator was just rising from beneath the dining table. Evazan holstered his own weapon and looked to his guest apologetically.

"Sorry. In the old days, Ponda Baba would have been in here like a shot. A real team we were then."

"He . . . ah . . . works for you?" the senator said, still recovering from shock.

"We were partners," the doctor tersely explained.

The senator seemed dismayed by that. "You know, he is of the lowest caste here on Ando. Its people have dubious morals and most violent habits. They are treated with so much contempt that few of them stay on our planet. They go off and often become galactic criminals."

"Well, Ponda couldn't have been a better pal to me," Evazan said, pouring out stiff drinks for them both. "That is, until one day on Tatooine. Had a run-in at the Mos Eisley Cantina there. An old man with a Jedi lightsaber took off Ponda's right arm for helping me. After that we had a kind of falling-out."

"He's here now," the senator pointed out. "And it does seem he just saved your life."

"Well, I still owe him an arm," the doctor explained. "He's had trouble raising enough credits for a good bionic replacement. So we've set up an uneasy alliance until I can help him out. I supply an arm, he works as my bodyguard . . . supposedly." He took a deep draft of his ale.

"What about them?" asked the senator, looking toward the downed attackers.

"Them?" said Evazan, shrugging carelessly. "Just more bounty hunters. Must have climbed all the way up here."

He set down his glass and walked toward one of the bodies. It was clad in a gray jumpsuit and helmet, like the other two, with an equipment belt around the waist. He rolled it over with a foot, revealing the staring, slack-jawed face of a human male, swarthy of complexion, lean and sharp of feature.

Evazan eyed a small device attached at the man's waist.

"They used individual field disrupters to get through the screens," he said thoughtfully. "Looks like a new type. I'll have to boost shield power." He looked around to the Aqualish, adding testily, "Senator, I shouldn't have to worry about this kind of thing at all. You're supposed to be protecting me, making sure no one can even get near here with equipment like that."

"We can't screen and search everyone who comes to the planet," the senator said defensively. "The security we've provided for you is already very great and incredibly expensive."

Evazan shook his head. "Still not enough. This is the third attempt on my life here. They get better every time."

"We had rather assumed that hiding you in such a fortress on such an isolated isle would be protection enough," the senator returned with an indignant tone. "Of course, we didn't know then that half the galaxy was trying to hunt you down."

Evazan stepped back toward him. "Are you saying I'm not worth it?" he demanded.

"It is that very point about which I'm here," was the stern reply.

"All right," the doctor assented. "We'll talk about it." He waved at the dining table. "Do you want to finish our meal first?"

The senator looked at their plates still filled with food. "Eat?" he said, then looked toward the bodies. "What about them?"

"Oh, Rover will take care of it," said Evazan.

The blob had already crawled up to one of the dead men. drawing its viscous mass over the form, engulfing and hiding it. The creature began to quiver in excitement and gave forth a slurping noise.

"He cleans up all leftovers," Evazan said. "It's part of why I've been able to train him with such ease. He's so well fed here."

"I'm really not very hungry anymore," the Aqualish said. He sat down and took a very deep gulp of ale.

"Let's just get on to the point of my visit, shall we? I don't want to . . . I mean, I don't have much time to stay here."

"Fine," said the doctor, taking a seat, too. "What's your problem?"

"Credits," the senator replied bluntly. "This whole project has gotten out of hand. Supplying this place and your laboratory facilities was costly enough. And now there's security. This incident only underscores the problem. It's costing our government a fortune!"

"And well worth one," Evazan returned, leaning forward on the table to speak with intensity. "For decades now you've been all but slaves of the Empire, living by its orders. You've lost your pride and your identity to survive. Just how much are you willing to pay to get loose from your chains?"

Rover had finished ingesting the first body. Leaving only a man-shaped wet spot on the stone, it crawled to a second form.

"No amount would be too great to be free of the Empire," the senator admitted, trying not to watch the creature's grisly work. "Still, my appropriations subcommittee needs reassurance to continue your financing. Our present budget squeeze—"

"Your budget be scorched!" Evazan shouted. "When I finish my research, you'll have a secret so valuable to the Empire that they'll give you your freedom and anything else you'd want."

"Yes, yes, so you assure us," the senator replied. "But we've had little evidence of late to support your claims for some great medical breakthrough. Perhaps if you give me some proofs of your progress, something solid I can take back, then I can convince them to go on."

"Fair enough," the doctor conceded. "I'll show you how very close to total success I am. It's already been tested several different ways. In fact, I only need one last thing to prove my breakthrough works. I have to find a specimen of a human male—a young, strong, healthy, perfectly formed one."

The senator's large eyes narrowed in curiosity. "Why?"

"You'll see for yourself." Evazan got to his feet. "I'll take you down to the laboratory right now."

The senator looked up at him. "To your . . . laboratory?" he said with clear misgivings. "Is that really necessary, Doctor? Surely some other evidence would suffice. Research data, perhaps, or—"

"I insist," Evazan said. "You have to see what I've done here for yourself!"

The Aqualish sighed and, with great reluctance, got to his feet.

"This way, Senator," said the doctor, ushering him from the room.

Behind them the Meduza noisily finished its second meal and moved on to the final course. The third dead man lay curled halfway on his side. A small comlink unit attached to his belt was partly visible. The tiny green "power on" indicator light was aglow . . .

Outside the castle, not far above the windows, a single figure clung to the sheer stone wall—a man of slender build and dark complexion, with hawkish features, deep brown eyes, and a black mustache. He was clad like the three dead men.

Both his feet and one hand were wedged in narrow cracks to hold him in the precarious spot, his body pressed tight to the wall against the tearing wind. His free hand held his own comlink close to one ear.

He had listened in on the conversation between Evazan and the senator. He had heard the two depart. Now he listened to the grotesque squooshing sound as the creature enveloped his last comrade.

With a crackling of shorted power the comlink channel went dead, and the man's face tightened into a grim expression.

Hanging his comlink back on his belt, he clambered up the castle wall with great dexterity, onto a slanting section of roof. A long-range comlink unit in backpack form was fastened to the smooth slate by suction-support webbing. Cramming his body into a corner between the roof and a spire to secure himself against the wind, he pulled the comlink headset from the pack and spoke urgently into its mouthpiece.

"Hello, Mother? It's Gurion. Do you copy?" He looked up to the clouded sky with some concern. "Are you still up there?"

"Still in orbit, Gur," came a reply. "What's the report?"

"All dead," Gurion answered bluntly. "All but me. Evazan must have some heavy protection inside there. They were the best."

After a heavy silence, the voice came again, carrying a tone of sorrow not fully masked. "That's it, then. You get off there, Gur. Right now. We'll pick you up."

"No. Not me," he said firmly. "I'm going to go inside, get close to him. It's the only way to be sure of nailing him."

"By yourself?" said the voice in surprise. "That's suicide!"

"If it has to be. I don't care," Gurion said fiercely. "I mean to get to him, and I think I know how!"

Within the castle, Evazan and guest descended a long spiraling stairway. The deeper they went into the mysterious lower sanctums of the doctor's lair, the more apologetic the Andoan senator became.

"For my part, there's never been a question of your integrity," the alien explained in a voice pitched ever higher by his rising concern. "It's my Senate colleagues who have been picking up rumors. Some are saying you have the death sentence on ten systems."

"Twelve, actually," Evazan said carelessly. "It may be more by now. I haven't checked."

"Really?" said the senator, his voice rising a bit more. "And then there have been tales of some of your . . . ah . . . medical practices."

"I won't deny there's some truth to them, too," the doctor admitted. "I don't apologize for what I've done. It was all to a good end."

They reached the bottom of the stairwell. Evazan unlocked and opened a massive metal door. It creaked back on its hinges, and they both passed through.

Beyond, a single space took up all the huge castle's basement area. Squat pillars and heavy arches of stone held up the high ceiling. Stretching into the far shadows, bank after bank of large glass cylinders glowed faintly, filled with gold liquid . . . and something else.

The senator stepped forward, staring in shock. Each cylinder appeared to contain some type of being.

He walked farther forward, looking down a row of creatures floating in amber fluid. There were giant Wookiees and diminutive Jawas, skeletonlike Givins and one-eyed Abbyssins. There were horned humanoids from Devaron and insectlike creatures of the Kibnon race, along with countless other species from planets all across the galaxy.

"Are they . . . dead?" the senator nervously inquired, peering into the cylinder of a reptilian Arcona who stared back with blank, jewellike eyes.

"Unfortunately," said Evazan. "Preserved in my special embalming fluid. They're some of my patients who didn't survive my surgical attempts to help them. But the medical work I did on them has still been of great value to me."

The senator looked at the corpses again, more closely. All had been worked upon in a manner that might loosely have been termed "surgical," though the word "butchery" might better have been applied. Most were mutilated, their bodies slashed open, various limb parts or organs missing. In some cases the beings' own elements had been replaced with things quite clearly alien.

"I say they've helped me," Evazan went on, walking down a row of his "patients." "Mostly by showing where my research had reached a dead end"—he cast the senator a ghastly smile—"if you'll pardon the expression."

"You experimented on them?" the senator said in horror.

Evazan waved the idea away. "Of course not. I meant

to help them through my creative techniques. I intended to give them greater health and longer life. In theory, at least."

He touched the cylinder holding the eviscerated form of a rodentlike Ranat. "I've devoted my whole life to helping others. They've called me a madman, a criminal, for my pains. But no one's understood. I was only using my skills to re-form life in various ways, trying to create something better." He sighed and looked back to the Aqualish. "But it wasn't enough."

The senator looked up and down the long ranks of the doctor's victims. "Not enough?"

"Physical alteration wasn't enough."

The doctor moved on to the next cylinder. Within was a particularly hideous specimen. It was a creature that had been constructed of parts scavenged from dozens of different beings, stitched and stapled together to form a patchwork monstrosity.

"As you see, even cutting and splicing together the best of the galaxy's body parts couldn't achieve the effect I wanted." He lifted a hand to touch the scarred right side of his skull. "No, it was the *mind* that was the key. That's why my research took a new direction. Come over here."

He led the way along the cylinder rows and into a large area in the middle of the room. Here a complex assemblage of electronic equipment towered to the ceiling in a rather precarious way. Its various systems, rigged together with tangled festoons of wire, crackled and sizzled uneasily even with the minimal power input now running through them.

The key feature of this haphazard but high-tech pile was two platforms set with operating tables. Straps clearly meant to restrain subjects added to their sinister look. Above each an odd, sievelike device dangled by a dozen wires from a pivoting boom. More wires connected these to the central machine.

"This is my transfer instrument," Evazan said proudly. "The main components were modified from advanced Imperial transmogrification units originally intended to alter droid programming. Ponda and I managed to 'liberate' this equipment from an Imperial research facility. But I've adapted it to use on living beings.''

The senator had been staring with mixed awe and skepticism at the dubious-appearing mass. Now he looked at Evazan in disbelief. "Living beings?"

"Living brains also store their gained knowledge electronically, much like a recording. That record can be altered, erased . . . or moved. The means to do it is now sitting before you."

"To what end?"

"To have something no one has ever had before," said the doctor grandly. "I'm finally on the brink of creating a practical form of immortality!"

The senator's disbelieving look grew more pronounced. "You are joking, Doctor."

"No joke at all," said the other. He moved closer, speaking with sober intensity. "Just think of it! Not even the greatest of the Jedi Masters with all their powers over matter have achieved a real immortality. They may be able to prolong life to some extent, but they still decay and die eventually. My method will transfer the higher levels of a being's intelligence into a fresh, new body whenever needed, just by the flick of a switch. Think how valuable *that* would be to the Empire. Their greatest rulers, their finest military minds could live on forever, gathering even more knowledge with each lifetime.''

"I suppose that *is* something the Empire would pay almost anything for," said the Aqualish, but with grave misgivings in his tone. "*If* the thing works."

"It'll work," Evazan said confidently, "and I'll soon be able to prove it." He grinned in sardonic delight. "Ironic, isn't it, that Evazan, the one they've called Dr. Death, will be the one to create such eternal life!"

A nearby intercom console beeped an alert to an incoming transmission. Evazan turned to see the face of Ponda Baba appear in its tiny viewscreen as a voice came with some urgency from the speaker.

"Evazan, someone is at our door!"

"Our door?" the doctor repeated.

"At the sea gate below the castle. Says his aqua-speeder just broke down. Wants to call for a lift from here."

"So he says," Evazan replied. "Let's see him."

Ponda punched at his own console and the picture on the screen shifted to show a view of the sea gate area. A small ocean-going repulsorlift craft sat at the castle's single dock. At the massive gate stood a most impressive-looking human male.

He was quite large, with a strapping build, as was evidenced by the body-hugging suit he wore. His chiseled features were handsome, and a thatch of blond hair waved about his well-formed head.

Evazan gazed with great interest upon the man, then he punched console buttons, bringing Ponda's image back.

"Let him come up," he ordered. "But only into the foyer. Keep a watch on him."

"Are you sure that's smart, Doc?" Ponda inquired.

"Just do it!" Evazan snapped the intercom off and turned to the senator. "You may get to see more than you'd hoped," he said excitedly. "Today could be the climax of my research!"

He rushed up from the laboratory, the nonplussed senator following. They entered the castle's huge entrance hall. In the wall beside its main door was set a control panel with a surveillance screen. Ponda Baba was already there, staring at a view of the room beyond the door.

In a small, bare antechamber to the entrance hall, their blond-haired visitor stood waiting patiently.

Evazan peered over Ponda's shoulder at the man. His eyes lit with an eager glow.

"This one will be perfect!" he said. "What a piece of incredible luck!"

He reached past Ponda to flick a switch on the panel. From the ceiling light in the anteroom a crim-

son beam shot down, striking the blond man's head.
He went limp instantly, crumpling to the floor.

"You killed him?" the Andoan senator said, aghast.

"Just stunned him," the doctor replied. He looked
to Ponda. "Help me take him downstairs."

He took hold of the door handle, but a hairy paw
came down on his hand to stop him.

"Hold on, Doc," came Ponda's harsh voice. "You're
gonna make the transfer to him, aren't you?"

"He looks as good as any I've ever seen," Evazan
admitted. "Why not?"

"No, Doc," Ponda barked at him. "Me first!"

Evazan regarded his erstwhile partner. "What do you
mean?"

"You promised I'd go first. You promised I'd get a
body with a good arm. I brought you to my planet,
helped you set this up, kept you alive for just that one
thing. You cost me my arm on Tatooine. You owe me.
It's time to pay up."

"How can I do that, Ponda?" he reasoned. "My perfect subject just showed up at my door. He's here right
now!"

"We're both lucky then, Doc," Ponda answered.
"You got yours. I've got mine."

Realization dawned in the doctor's face. As one,
both of them turned toward the Aqualish senator.

The senator had listened to their dialogue with
growing alarm. As they looked to him, his expression
grew taut with horror.

"He's not young," Evazan commented critically.

"He's one of the ruling class, though," Ponda replied. "I get an arm, and I get power, too."

"You . . . you can't mean what I think," the senator gasped.

"We do," said the doctor, pulling out his blaster.
"Congratulations. You'll be helping to make a great
step for science." He gestured with the gun. "Get going, please."

"You can't do this!" the senator cried as they

marched him downstairs to the lab. "What about your financing? Your protection?"

"I won't need either anymore," the doctor replied. "I'll finally be able to acquire a whole new identity. Be free of this scarred face. I can go out of here safe from bounty hunters, and with a secret that can change the galaxy."

"That's what you intended from the start, isn't it?" the other guessed. "Just to help yourself!"

"What else?" said Evazan, laughing cruelly. He shoved the senator through the doorway into the lab. "Now, go get onto that left table. Quick."

He and Ponda hustled the hapless senator to the table and strapped him upon its top. Evazan pulled the left-hand boom down closer, and fastened its dangling metal helmet over the dome of the captive's head.

Ponda swiftly took a place on the other table. Evazan repeated the process of buckling restraints and fitting the other Aqualish with the second weird headpiece. Then he stepped away to a bank of controls.

He pulled levers, rotated dials, and watched readout screens indicating the surge of power. The machine sizzled loudly now, alive with enormous energy. The great pile of its parts shuddered visibly, threatening to tumble down.

As the indicators showed he'd reached maximum power, he threw a red double-handled switch. Blue-white sparks like tiny lightning bolts flickered downward along the wires, into the metal helmets on the two heads. The strapped-down bodies both jerked spasmodically.

Evazan watched a pair of dials right beneath the red switch. As the indicator on the left moved one way, its counterpart on the right moved the other. In only seconds the two needles had buried themselves on opposite sides of their dials.

With a cackle of glee the doctor slapped the power levers to Off. The flickering lights quickly faded, and the crackling of energy died away.

"It's done! It's worked!" Evazan chortled, running

to the table holding the elder Andoan's body. "Ponda! I've done it!" he said, undoing the straps. "How do you feel?"

But the Aqualish who had once been the senator lay quite still, apparently unconscious.

"It's okay," Evazan assured, patting the being. "You'll be fine soon. Just rest there. I've got to see to my own new body!"

He left the laboratory, all but running back up to the main hall. His eyes gleamed with a wild look of nearly overwhelming anticipation. He threw open the door to the anteroom and charged in. His splendid specimen still lay motionless.

He knelt beside the man, gloating over his perfect body. "All I've wanted," he said. "Youth, strength . . . and an unmarked face! I hope he's unharmed."

He put out a hand to lay on the man's heart.

The hand vanished down through the massive chest as if the flesh had opened to swallow it!

He jerked his hand back, staring in astonishment. "A holoshroud!" he gasped.

His hand shot to grip the butt of his blaster. But the other man sat suddenly upright, swiftly striking out. A fist thrust forward to slam into Evazan's face. The blow knocked him backward, sprawling at full length, stunned.

Before the doctor could recover, the blond man was on his feet. The image of his large form wavered, faded, and vanished completely, revealing the figure of a thin and hawkfaced man of dark complexion with a black mustache. One hand rested on the belt control for the holographic disguise, the other hand held the grenadelike shape of a powerful thermal detonator. Its thumb guard was already pushed back, and the man's thumb rested on the detonator button.

"Toss the gun away, Evazan," the man grated out, "or we'll both go up together."

Evazan drew out his blaster gingerly and heaved it far away. "Who are you?" he demanded.

"Gurion's the name. I've been trying to get you for a long, long time. Get on your feet."

"Pretty smart of you to use that disguise," Evazan told him, climbing up. "You'd never have gotten in here otherwise."

"That's just what I figured. Now, get moving, you butchering monster. Take me to the roof. Some friends'll be picking us up there." Gurion gestured meaningfully with the bomb. "I said, move!"

Evazan readily complied. They went into the main entry hall and up a broad staircase.

As they turned the corner on the first landing to start up a second flight, Evazan glanced down to see a shimmering first bit of Rover ooze through a doorway into the hall below. He smiled to himself.

"Look here," he told his captor, intent on keeping the man's attention on him, "this is crazy. I'm going to be a very rich man. I don't know how much bounty you're after, but I can pay you a lot more."

"I'm not after bounty," Gurion shot back. "My family name is Silizzar. Sound familiar?"

Evazan blanched at the name. "I—I may have had a-a patient or two—" he stammered.

Gurion cut him off. "You treated my whole family. For a stomach disorder caused by a poison you gave them as medicine! You gutted them one by one like so many fish. Seven people! None of them survived. No, I don't want money for you. This is purely for revenge!"

Several flights higher they reached a small door that opened onto a flat area of the roof. A brisk wind from the sea tugged sharply at their clothes as they came out. The distant lightning flickered eerily on the scene, and the deep growling of the far thunder made a constant, ominous background sound.

Gurion directed Evazan around the roof's edge, close to the spot where his backpack comlink was secured.

"Just stand there like stone," Gurion warned. He lifted the bomb. "Remember, if I push this button, we've both only got a few seconds to live. I'd rather take you back to stand trial for all the other beings you've murdered. But I won't hesitate to finish it right here!"

"I'm a statue," Evazan readily agreed.

Gurion fetched his backpack and crouched beside it to take out the comlink's headset. He kept an eye on the doctor as he spoke into the mouthpiece.

"Mother, it's Gurion. Do you still copy me?"

"Still here, my friend. What's happened?"

"I've got our baby here, alive. I'm up on the roof. Can you come get us?"

"On our way!" the voice said jubilantly. "Mother out."

Out of the corner of one eye, Evazan saw the door onto the roof push open. One bulb-tipped stalk poked cautiously out around it, sensing the air ahead.

"There'll be a shuttle here for us in a few minutes," said Gurion as he put his comlink headset away.

The doctor took a couple of casual steps around him to get Gurion's back to the door.

"You've really got to listen to me," Evazan said pleadingly. "I've got a secret. Right here. An invention. A very big thing. Too valuable for anyone to turn down."

"Not for me," the other said flatly, his hard gaze fixed unwaveringly on his foe.

The shining mass of Rover squeezed through the door. The creature began to slither forward slowly, noiselessly. Flickering lightning glinted from its gelatinous form.

"But with it I can make you live forever," the doctor argued on. "Real immortality. Everybody wants that."

"Do you actually think giving me more lifetimes can make up for all the lives you stole?" Gurion said in disbelief. "You're even more demented than I thought."

Rover was now only meters behind the crouching man. The creature began to hump up higher, its stalks shifting forward to strike out.

In the tiny mirrors of Evazan's eyes Gurion saw the

Meduza's twin reflections as a brighter lightning flare gleamed from its surface. He sprang upright, wheeling around to see the thing nearly on him.

Rover struck just as he jumped back away from it. Only a single bulb's tip managed to graze Gurion's knee with a sharp crackle of power.

The man cried out at the stinging pain and staggered. The arm holding the bomb dropped down.

Evazan leaped instantly for the arm. His two hands clenched tight on Gurion's wrist and he shook hard. The untriggered detonator came loose and bounced away across the flat roof, coming to rest before the door.

With his captor disarmed, Evazan tried to break away to let Rover finish things. But Gurion grappled tight with him, his hands going for the doctor's throat.

"I'll kill you with my bare hands!" he snarled.

Evazan stumbled backward as he fought wildly to break loose. Gurion hung on with a strength born of his rage.

The back of the doctor's foot hit the roof's edge. Desperately he swung about, dragging Gurion off balance and out into space. The man fell.

Gurion's own weight tore his hands free from the doctor's throat. But the last downward jerk overbalanced Evazan also.

For a moment the doctor teetered on the brink, flailing out with his arms for balance. When that failed, he twisted his body violently around, grabbing out for the roof's edge as he went over it.

His agility saved him. He hung on fiercely, dangling at arm's length against the sheer stone face. Below him, Gurion's form plunged downward, striking the jagged cliffs at several spots.

Evazan glanced down to see the body make the final crash into a surging wave. He then turned his attention to ensuring his own safety, but he quickly found this was not so easy a task. His arms alone weren't strong enough to pull him up. His scrabbling feet could find no holds in the smooth stone.

A noise came from above him. He looked up as the toes of boots appeared over the edge just inches from his face. His gaze moved on up the body to see that it was Ponda Baba who stood there, staring down at him.

"P-Ponda!" he gasped out, at first with great relief. But a new realization swiftly turned relief to surprise. "But . . . how! You here? The—the transfer . . . it didn't work?"

"Oh, it worked, Doctor," came a voice no longer like that of his old friend. "But it worked backward."

"Backward?" he echoed.

"That's right. And so you've condemned me to the loathsome form of one of my people's lowest breed of scum." The Aqualish lifted the hairy arm that marked him as a social pariah on his own planet. "You've destroyed my life as a senator, Doctor. So now I am going to destroy yours!"

The mechanical arm lifted. In its jointed fingers was clutched the thermal detonator. The metal thumb rested on the triggering button.

"No!" cried Evazan. "No, no, wait! You can't!"

"Good-bye, Doc!" the new Ponda Baba said simply.

He pushed the button, dropped the bomb, turned, and strode away.

"No, no!" Evazan screamed out as the bomb's timer ticked down.

With the strength of desperation he hauled himself up. His eyes cleared the edge. He glimpsed the ticking bomb, and just beyond it the Meduza's form.

"Rover!" he shouted to it. "Hellllp meeee!"

Far above, a small shuttle skimmed down through the atmosphere, flashing high across the waves. The rocky isle with the towering castle lay straight ahead. Two men of Gurion's lean build and swarthy complexion sat at the controls.

"There it is," one said. He looked to his companion. "Get ready to hover above the roof, while I get out the boarding—"

A great flash of light from ahead interrupted him. An explosion enveloped the entire castle top.

Both men stared with astonishment as the upper half of the structure disintegrated in the initial blast. A cloud of fine debris billowed up while larger pieces showered out and down. Then the lower half of the shattered castle collapsed inward, becoming in seconds a vast rubble pile.

"Poor Gurion," the first man said, looking down at the broken remains as they soared overhead.

"That blast probably attracted Andoan security," said the other. "We'd better get well away from here."

He turned the ship, heading upward again.

"At least Gurion got his revenge on that lunatic Evazan," the first man said as they left the ruins behind . . .

Far below, halfway down one rugged side of the castle's high cliffs, a large bile-green mound of goo lay motionless on a ledge. From its splattered edges a thick yellow oil ran, dripping in greasy, fat globules over the edge.

Then the gellike mass heaved and quivered, bulging upward. Out of the largest lump of its center an arm suddenly shot forth, followed by another, and then by the head of Dr. Evazan. He took a great shuddering breath as he broke the surface, like a swimmer who'd been long under the sea.

With some difficulty he extricated himself from the blob that had once been his pet. Though the loyal creature had saved him by cushioning his fall, their hard impact together had squashed the Meduza's life from it.

"Thanks, Rover," he said, plucking a last clinging streamer of the slime off his shirt. He bent and patted the ruptured mass. "Sorry, boy."

He looked upward to the blasted castle.

"Backward," he said regretfully. "Damn!" Then he shrugged. "Oh, well. Maybe I'll get it right next time."

And with that he began the long climb downward to the sea.

Drawing the Maps of Peace:
The Moisture Farmer's Tale

by M. Shayne Bell

Day 1: A New Calendar

I thought: This is it. I won't get out of this one. I topped a dune in my landspeeder—going fast, always fast—and saw eight Sand People standing around the vaporator I'd come out to fix. I had seconds, then, to decide what to do: Plunge ahead over the last dunes to save a malfunctioning vaporator whose output I needed, or turn around and speed back to the defenses of my house and two droids. I gunned the speeder ahead.

The Sand People scattered and ran, and I watched where they ran so I'd know where they might attack from. *All for .5 liter of water,* I thought. I was risking my life for .5 liters of water. The vaporator's production was down thirty percent to maybe one liter a day, and I had to get its production up to the standard 1.5 and keep it there, the farm was that close to the edge, so close that every vaporator had to work at maximum or I'd lose the farm.

In seconds I was at the vaporator, stopped in a cloud of dust and sand my speeder raised. I couldn't see the Sand People, though their musky scent lingered around the vaporator in the heat at the end of the day.

The shadows of the canyon walls were lengthening across the dunes on the valley floor.

It would soon be dark, and I was in a canyon where Sand People had come, far from home.

Human technology scared the Sand People—my speeder certainly had—but they wouldn't stay scared for long. I grabbed my blaster and jumped out of the speeder to see what damage they had done to the vaporator.

A smashed power indicator. One cracked solar cell. Scratches around the door to the water reservoir, as if they had been trying to get to the water. The damage was minimal.

But what to do now? I couldn't guard all of my far-flung vaporators. I had ten of them, each placed in a half kilometer of sand and rock, not the standard quarter kilometer—I was so close to the Dune Sea that a vaporator needed twice the land to pull the 1.5 liters of water worth harvesting out of the air. If the Sand People had figured out that vaporators held water and if they were determined to get into them, my farm would be ruined. I could replace power displays and solar cells. I couldn't guard vaporators kilometers apart from Sand People who wanted water.

I heard a low grunt over a dune to the north, and I immediately crouched down against the vaporator and scanned the horizon. The grunt sounded like a wild bantha waking from the heat of day, but I knew it wasn't bantha. The Sand People were coming back.

They were determined to get this water.

And why shouldn't they, I suddenly wondered? Before I came, the water collected inside my vaporator would have been their water, distilled out of the air in the morning dew, not pulled out at all hours of the day by a machine. They must have been desperate for water to have come up to a human machine, to have touched it, to have tried to open it. What were they suffering to drive them to this?

I heard more "bantha" grunting south of me, over the dunes, then to the east and west, and finally to the north again. I was surrounded, and an attack would come in minutes.

Suddenly I realized what I had to do. "Go ahead and waste your profits," Eyvind, who owned the farm closest to mine three valleys over, would say, "waste your profits so I can buy your farm cheap from your creditors when they force you off the land." But I wouldn't listen to Eyvind's voice in my head, and I wouldn't have listened to him if he'd been with me then. I spoke to the vaporator, and a panel slid back from in front of the controls. I punched in the number sequence I'd programmed, and I heard the vaporator sealing the pouch of water in the reservoir. When it finished, the door in front of the reservoir slid open. I pulled out the pouch and set it on the sand west of the vaporator, in shade out of the light from the second setting sun. I took out my knife and made a tiny slit in the top, where the air was, so the Sand People could smell the water and get to it.

I punched in the command to close the door to the reservoir, then told the vaporator to close the door over its controls, ran to my speeder, and flew it to the top of a dune southwest of the vaporator. I could see no Sand People, but I knew they were masters at blending into a terrain and surprising the unwary. I'd heard plenty of stories about just how quick—and deadly— they could be with their gaffi sticks, the double-bladed axlike weapons they made from scavenged metal off the Tatooine wastes. I sat low in my speeder and tried to watch for any movement—I did not dare fly farther away: They were all around me and they would surely throw their axes if I tried to run, and I did not fancy being beheaded in my own landspeeder. Besides, I hoped they would recognize what I had done: that I had given them water. I did not know, then, if I could hope it would buy my life and their trust and thus my farm.

I saw movement: one of the Sand People, coming from the north, slowly, low over the sand toward the vaporator and the water. When he reached the water pouch in the shadow of the vaporator, he knelt in the sand and smelled the bag: smelled the water inside it. He lifted his head slowly and gave out one keening cry that echoed through the canyon. Soon I counted eight Sand People—no, ten—hurrying toward the water, from all directions, four making a wide berth around my speeder.

Only one of them, a small one—young?—took a drink. Two others poured the rest of the water in a thin pouch of animal skin to take with them, and they did not spill any water. When they finished, the one who had first smelled the water looked at me. Then they all looked at me. They did not speak or make any noise, and they did not run. The one who had smelled the water suddenly raised his right arm and held up a clenched fist.

I jumped from the speeder, walked a few steps from it, and raised my right arm and clenched my fist in return. We stood like that, looking at each other, for some time. I had never been so close to them before. I wondered if they had ever been so close to a human. A light breeze from the east down the canyon blew over us and cooled us, and abruptly all the Sand People turned and disappeared in the dunes.

They did not destroy my vaporator. They did not try to kill me. They left the vaporator alone after I gave them the water, and they left me alone. They had accepted my gift.

I pledged, then, to leave them the water from this vaporator. I would miss selling the water, I knew that— I needed to sell it—but it seemed a small price to pay if by giving them a few liters they would then not ruin my vaporators. I could make do with the output of the other nine vaporators for a short time—and meanwhile buy two of Eyvind's old second-generation vaporators to fix. When *they* came on-line, my output would be back to the minimum I'd need to survive.

All this effort seemed a small price to pay to be able to live near the Sand People in peace.

I counted the days of my farm from that day.

Day 2: A Farm on the Edge

Eyvind had told me I was crazy to come out this far. "No one has gone that far," he said. "I can't believe the moisture patterns consistently flow up those canyons—you're only a handful of kilometers from the Dune Sea!"

But I had tested the moisture patterns: There was water to be had there. Not a lot. It would not be a rich farm, like those outside Bestine, but one morning when I was camped in what I thought of then as a far canyon, I woke on the blanket I'd laid out on the sand, and it was damp from the dew. My clothes were damp. My hair was damp. I pulled the instruments from my speeder and set them up and they all read one thing: water. Harvestable water. Somehow it blew over the mountains and settled here before evaporating in the wastes of the Dune Sea farther west, and it did it day after day for the two weeks I spent in that canyon running tests. Over the course of a year, I tested that canyon and the surrounding canyons twenty-nine more times—I had to have that much detailed data to prove that this farm could work so I could borrow the start-up money. But I'd known from that first day when I woke up with damp hair that I could have a farm here.

I spent months filling out Homestead Act forms and waiting for a grant of land, then months filling out loan applications and waiting for replies, all the while listening to other farmers tell me I was crazy. But I had the undeniable facts of my readings to hand anyone who could authorize my homestead or loan me the start-up money or even just listen and offer advice, and finally the manager at the Zygian branch bank did listen—and he read my reports, checked my background to see whether I knew anything about moisture farming, which I did, and whether I would keep my word, which I would. He loaned me the money.

He gave me ten thousand days to pay him back.

Ten thousand days was enough time to make any dream come true, I thought.

I lay on my bed in the dark at the end of a hard day, after leaving the Sand People the water I'd pledged them, remembering all this, remembering how badly I'd wanted to come out here, how hard I'd worked to get my homestead and the loan and then to set up my farm. Not once had I thought about who might already be out here, depending on this land I called *my* farm.

I rolled over and asked the computer to display the holomap I'd made of my farm and this region.

"The files you have requested can only be accessed after a user-specified security clearance," it said. "Please prepare for retinal scan."

I stared for a few seconds into a bright, white light that suddenly shone out of the monitor. I had to guard my map. I'd made the map myself—after a year of surveying and taking photographs that I fed into the computer and working from notes and memory—and if the wrong people knew I was making maps it could be dangerous. I programmed the computer to display the maps only to me and to never reference them when working with other files; they were not cross-referenced or indexed. When asked if such files existed, it would say no to anyone's voice but my own. If asked to access them, it would respond and proceed with the security clearance only if it heard my voice.

"Retinal scan complete," the computer said. "Hello, Ariq Joanson. I will display the requested files."

Part of the wall I kept blank and white just for this projection suddenly became the canyons of my farm seen from the air: my house, marked in blue; the vaporators, smaller dots of green, widely separated; the canyons and mountains and dunes all in natural colors. A red dot far up Bildor's Canyon northeast of my farm marked a Jawa fortress. White dots marked the houses of the farms closest to mine—and none of those dots were very close. "You'll be three canyons and kilometers away from me—and I've been the farthest one out for two years!" Eyvind had warned. Over all the canyons and mountains and dunes I'd had the computer draw in black lines for the boundaries of the farms.

The land lay spread out over my wall in the darkness, and the dots for houses and vaporators gleamed like jewels behind their black lines. Except for the red Jawa dot, all of them represented human houses or machines. I'd never thought of putting in dots for the nomadic Sand People—or of drawing boundaries for them and the Jawas.

"Computer," I said. "Draw in a boundary line from the northeast border of my farm in Bildor's Canyon, along the ridges on both sides of the canyon to a distance of one kilometer above the Jawa fortress."

"Drawn as requested," the computer responded, and it was. The lines appeared.

"Label the space inside those new lines 'Jawa Preserve.'"

"Labeled as requested."

The words appeared, but I didn't like them. "Relabel the Jawa Preserve, the 'Jawa—'" What? Land? Reservation? Protectorate? "Just label it 'Jawa,'" I said.

"Labeled as requested."

The word "Preserve" disappeared from the map, and the word "Jawa" centered below the red dot.

"Now draw borders west from the northwest boundary of my farm to the Dune Sea and west from the northernmost boundary of the Jawa land also to the Dune Sea."

"Drawn as requested."

"Label that 'Sand People.'"

The words appeared over the land. "Have the Jawas and Sand People acquired rights to this land?" the computer asked.

"No," I said. "I'm only daydreaming."

"Do you wish these changes saved?"

I considered that. "No," I said finally. "It is a fiction. Erase the changes and shut down."

It did so.

I lay back on my bed. What I had told the computer to draw was worse than a fiction. I had asked two successive Imperial Governors to commission a mapping project of this region, with the same response: "We just don't have the money." Translate that: "We have too many people here who don't want accurate maps made of what lies beyond the known settlements and farms, and if you want to live to bring your next water harvest to Mos Eisley, quit asking for such things."

So I'd quit asking for them. But it wasn't criminals who needed to hide places of illegal activity who threatened my life or livelihood, yet. It was Sand People violence and Jawa dishonesty and manipulation—all caused in part, I was coming to realize, by constant encroachments into what had no doubt been traditional Jawa and Sand People territories. Maps would be the first step to a secure peace for the farmers and Jawas and Sand People—if you could get them all to draw in negotiated boundaries on those maps and honor them. Without such agreements, farmers faced the equivalent of blundering around in the dark—setting up farms in areas where maybe no one should go, living in places that could—and did—get decent people killed. I wanted the killing to stop.

But for that, we needed a map. The government would not draw it.

So I drew it.

And I decided, that night, to take my map to the Jawas near my farm and talk to them about how to take it to the Sand People. If we agreed among ourselves on how to live together in these mountains and canyons, maybe someday the government would make our agreements official.

I looked at the monitor for another inevitable retina scan. "Computer," I said, "redisplay the map I just requested and redraw the boundaries I had you erase. Copy this file to the portable holo-display unit."

Day 3: In the Jawa Fortress

I knew these Jawas. I had been to the gates of their fortress many times, especially during the year I spent measuring the moisture in the canyons of my farm: They would come out to trade water for trash I'd found in the desert and for information about the Empire and its cities and the systems that made them work and the alien races and how to deal with them. I tried to be good to the Jawas, and fair. If they got the better of me in a few deals, I'd come out ahead in a few others, and the tally remained about even. Some of the Jawas even became my friends—the old ones, the ones I could learn from who had the patience to teach me their language, the uses of native plants, geographic lore.

Their thick-walled fortress blended into the walls of the canyon, but I knew how to fly straight to its closed and hidden gates. I stepped out of my speeder and held up the holo-display unit. "Oh, Jawas!" I called out. "I come to you with information and to barter."

The gates opened at once—the word "barter" would always open their gates—and eight Jawas rushed out. I tried again to see inside, but could not in the darkness there. They had never invited me in. I had no idea what lay inside. This was a new family fortress, maybe only a hundred years old, with, I guessed, fifteen clans—four hundred Jawas. They were jealous of any secrets and wary of any alien, but they would talk to me and barter with me and spend hours outside on the sand.

The first Jawa to reach me was my old friend Wimateeka. He began chittering at me in Jawa, slowly, so I could understand.

"Do you still come here asking for water now that you farm it yourself?" he chittered, and they all laughed.

"No," I said. "But I have brought you a gift of water to thank you for your generosity to me in the past."

I set a pouch of water in Wimateeka's arms, and he could barely hold it up alone. The others crowded around to help him set it on the sand and to touch it, to feel the water move inside it.

"What else have you brought us?" Wimateeka asked.

"The knowledge of maps," I said, "and how the Empire uses them to decide questions about land. We can use them in the same way."

I set the holo-display unit on the level sand outside the fortress, sand beat down and compacted by the comings and goings of Jawa crawlers, and I asked the unit to display my map close above the sand. The Jawas shrieked and rushed back, but not Wimateeka. He would not leave the water pouch: He kept his hands on it.

"What is this that you have brought, Ariq?" he asked.

A map, I explained. I told them what maps are and the purpose of them, how all the mountains and valleys and sand plains around us were represented here with small replicas, and they began to recognize and point out familiar features, marvel that at this scale their fortress was as small as the red dot.

I explained boundaries to them and what they could mean to us: How if they agreed to respect the boundary of the land grant the government had given me, I would not go to the government to claim land farther up the canyon toward their fortress—I would, in fact, help them fill out the forms to claim the land themselves. I suggested that they buy and put out vaporators of their own, all down the valley, to the border of my farm. Even if they didn't do this, the imaginary line between their land and mine would give them some protection, and I told them how I hoped the Empire would come to accept the lines we agreed on and keep other humans from making farms in their valley.

When I finished, the Jawas hurried inside the fortress to discuss my information and proposal. They took the water. I asked Wimateeka to stay outside with me for a short time. We sat in the shade of my landspeeder to watch the sunsets while we talked.

"Can you teach me a Sand People greeting?" I asked him.

He looked up at me, surprised. After a moment, he said: "Koroghh gahgt takt. 'Blessed be your going out from us.' "

"No, a greeting," I said. "Not a farewell." I thought

I had mispronounced the Jawa word for "greeting" the first time I asked.

"That is a greeting," he said. "The most polite. They greet each other like this because they are always traveling. They will seldom stay long in one place."

Not even long enough to develop greetings, I thought, only hasty blessings because they left each other so soon.

"Say it again," I asked, and Wimateeka did, and I repeated it till I could say it.

"Why do you want to learn this greeting?" Wimateeka asked me.

I explained to him about the Sand People and the water and my questions about the land—their land.

Wimateeka was quiet for a time, looking at me. "The young Sand People are dangerous in the days that come and for a time," he said. He explained that this was the time when the adolescents had to perform some great deed to earn adulthood, deeds that often included acts of mayhem against non–Sand People races.

"All our crawlers are coming home to wait here through this time," he said. "You should take your fellow humans to Mos Eisley and do the same."

He told me how a vast army of young Sand People had once attacked a Jawa fortress south of us and slaughtered the inhabitants. That fortress was still an empty, burned ruin that Wimateeka had once visited. I was lucky the Sand People around my vaporator had not been adolescents out to earn adulthood.

Wimateeka asked me how to operate the holo unit, and I told it to obey Wimateeka's voice when he asked it to display the map, nothing more. He displayed the map three times, then asked if he could take it to the discussions in the fortress.

"This is not a trade," I said. "I want this holo unit back, unharmed."

"I will bring it to you personally," he said. He abruptly snatched up the holo unit and hurried into the fortress.

I ate the supper I'd brought with me. After the last sunset, I laid blankets out on the sand. I expected to sleep there, blaster in hand—especially after Wimateeka's story about the young Sand People's rite of passage—in the relative safety outside the Jawa gates. But in the night, the Jawas came out to me, with torches.

Wimateeka led them. "You have honored us," he said. He set the holo unit in front of me. "Extend our boundaries to include the valley west of us to the Dune Sea, and we will accept your proposal."

I displayed the map and told the holo unit to make the boundary changes. The Jawas chittered softly when their black lines moved to include the valley they asked for. It was a valley their crawlers traveled through to get to the Dune Sea to scavenge. Everyone would agree that they needed that valley.

"It is not safe out here on the sand," Wimateeka said. "Bring your blankets, your speeder, and your holo unit and come inside to spend the rest of the night with us."

I hadn't expected this. I got up at once and folded my blankets and stowed them and the holo unit in my speeder and walked the speeder through their gates.

We did not sleep. The Jawas took me to a great room, and in the heart of their fortress we talked by torchlight about maps and water and the Sand People and how to talk to them about maps.

Day 5: A Greeting

Eyvind and I sat openly in front of our speeders on the dune southwest of the vaporator and my day's gift of water to the Sand People.

"So they come here for this water?" Eyvind asked.

"Every day."

"And they don't break into your other vaporators?"

"No."

"I still don't like this. Your farm's the farthest out, and you're separated from the rest of us—so maybe you have to deal with the Sand People—but my farm's the second farthest out and I don't want to do anything to encourage Sand People to come around it. I won't give them any water—but how long before they show up on my farm expecting it?"

"There—I can see one of them. Watch the dunes to the northwest. They come most often from that direction. They must camp somewhere to the northwest."

"And you're luring them down *here*."

I didn't answer that. We'd argued about this again and again over the last few days. I was not going to argue with Eyvind when Sand People were so close to us. To give Eyvind credit, he stopped arguing, too. The canyon was utterly still, then. No wind blew. I could not hear the Sand People moving. It was the first time I'd brought anyone else to see the Sand People take my gift of water.

I stood and put my hand on Eyvind's shoulder. I did not believe that the Sand People would harm me. I hoped that if they saw me physically close to Eyvind they would learn not to harm him or ever want to. I'd made decisions, and I meant to stick by them—but I realized my decisions had moved the boundaries of racial interchange for everyone out here, I hoped for the good, that's what I hoped.

Suddenly one of the Sand People stood in the shadow of the vaporator, near the water pouch. I hadn't seen him come up. He was just suddenly there. I raised my arm and clenched my fist in greeting, but he would not raise his fist in return.

"Maybe this wasn't a good idea," Eyvind whispered. "Should I leave?"

"Not yet," I said. I kept my arm up and my fist clenched. "Koroghh gahgt takt," I called out.

The Sand Person stepped back, out of the shadow and into the sunlight, almost as if he were going to run.

"Koroghh gahgt takt!" I called again. I hoped I was pronouncing the words right—that Wimateeka had learned the greeting right to begin with before teaching it to me, that I wasn't challenging the Sand People to a fight or cursing their mothers.

Slowly, the Sand Person began to raise his arm and clench his fist. "Koroghh gahgt takt!" he shouted back.

So I had it right, I thought. This was working.

I heard the greeting shouted at me from somewhere over the dunes to the east—then from all directions and from the canyon walls, again and again the same greeting: Koroghh gahgt takt.

Eyvind stood up. "They are all around us!" he said.

But we could see only one of them. That one picked up the water pouch and disappeared into the dunes.

Eyvind and I took our speeders and got out of there and saw no more of the Sand People that day. We went to my house and talked late into the night.

I'd sent Wimateeka's warning about the Sand People's rite of passage to all the other farmers in this region, and everyone agreed that we couldn't run to Mos Eisley. If we did, we could never expect to stay out here at all. But to stay, we had to have peace, and most farmers felt that could only be guaranteed with blasters and maybe Imperial protection. A few listened to my ideas about maps and good neighbors. Not Eyvind.

Never once did Eyvind tell me about his wedding plans.

Day 15: Eyvind and Ariela

I took my speeder to Eyvind's farm to pick up one of his old broken-down vaporators, and he walked out of his house with a beautiful girl.

"This is Ariela, my fiancée," he said. "We're getting married in five weeks."

As simple as that. Eyvind hadn't told anyone about this, not even me. I hadn't known he'd kept boundaries like this between our friendship.

"I'm pleased to meet you," I told Ariela. "And congratulations to both of you."

"You're the farmer with the big plans for us all," she said.

Eyvind looked closely at me. "Can you understand now why I don't want Sand People coming around my farm?" he said.

The arguing wouldn't stop. I'd barely met Ariela—I'd barely been told about their wedding—and already the three of us were arguing. "Look," I said. "I just believe that none of us can survive out here if we can't make peace with the Sand People and the Jawas. At any rate, I'm sure the two of you don't want to argue with me five weeks before your wedding. Sell me that old vaporator, Eyvind, and I'll go."

"But I think you're doing the right thing, Ariq," Ariela said, and that stopped me, fast. I didn't know what to say.

"I think we should help you—and I believe I know the way to start. Would your Jawa friends come to our wedding? Would you invite them for us? As neighbors, they should be part of the important things in our lives."

"She's never smelled them," Eyvind said.

"They'll come," I said. "I'll go today to invite them."

And I did. I dropped the old vaporator off at my house, packed up provisions for a night in Bildor's Canyon, and set off. I reached the Jawa fortress before the sunsets.

"You have honored us again!" Wimateeka chittered after I extended the invitation. "But what of presents? We should take something, but we can spare so little! Our gifts will seem cheap and tawdry."

"They will honor whatever you give them," I said.

They took me, again, inside their gates to the great council chamber. We talked late into the night about wedding gifts—of rock salt, which they thought might make a good gift; of water, which they couldn't spare; of cloth, which was never in adequate supply; of reconditioned droids, which would make elegant but prohibitively expensive gifts.

"Offer to teach them your language," I said. "That would make a fine gift."

But they liked best the idea of rock salt.

We did not resolve the question that night.

Day 32: Some Neighbors Pay Me a Visit

I finished installing the second old vaporator I'd bought from Eyvind just after dark, and if the diagnostics I'd run on it were accurate it would be a decent producer—maybe as much as 1.3 liters a day. My farm would be producing one to two liters above my old average, so I knew I was definitely not going to miss the water I was giving the Sand People.

I packed my tools in the landspeeder and headed slowly back toward my house and supper. I went slowly because it was dark and there were things out here to be wary of. At least I didn't have to worry about the Sand People as I had before. At least there was that.

I dropped down into the canyon where I'd built my house, and there were lights around my house—a lot of lights. I sped up then.

"It's him!" I heard people shouting when I stopped. What had happened?

It was Eyvind and Ariela, the Jensens, who'd homesteaded next to Eyvind, the Clays, the Bjornsons—and six or eight others.

"What's wrong?" I asked.

Eyvind stepped forward. "We've come to ask you, as your neighbors, to stop giving water to the Sand People. You don't know what you're doing."

I'd imagined Imperial trouble of some kind—maybe the razing of Mos Eisley to stamp out corruption and the need to house refugees—trouble on that level to bring people out here to my farm. Not this. "Have the Sand People hurt any of you since I started giving them water?" I asked.

"They killed my son five years ago," Mrs. Bjornson said.

"You don't know that," Ariela said quietly.

"I found him dead in the canyon north of us! Who else is out there chopping people apart with axes? The Imperial investigators *said* Sand People killed my son."

No one said anything for a minute. No one wanted to point out that so many people could have been out there, not just the Sand People. No one wanted to say that Imperial investigators might have wanted to fix blame on suspects who could never be brought to trial.

"They destroyed five of my vaporators," Mr. Jensen said.

"They broke into my storage shed and tore it apart," Mr. Clay said.

"One of them threw a gaffi stick that lodged in a rear stabilizer when I was driving into Mos Eisley," Mrs. Sigurd said. "I barely made it to the city."

Ariela stopped them. "So bad things happened out here, and all of you jumped to blame the Sand People."

Mr. Olafsen cut her off. "It's outsiders like you, coming here from where was it—Alderaan?—with your ideas of how we should start living, it's outsiders like you—and this Ariq, here—who cause the most trouble."

"I'm not an outsider," I said, but that was not the point. My ideas *were* new. There could be trouble before they worked, before we could all live in peace. It looked as if all the trouble wouldn't come from the Sand People.

"So you worked on a moisture farm as a kid," Eyvind said to me, "so you've made this farm of yours turn a profit—does that mean you can appoint yourself diplomat for the rest of us and negotiate with the Sand People and Jawas?"

"The Sand People would have ruined my farm, Eyvind, you know that. I have to find a way to live with them. You know that, too."

"Most people out here are against what you're doing, Ariq."

"Is that so? The McPhersons, the Jonsons, and the Jacques all support me, and I don't see any of them here. What about Owen and Beru? Have you talked to them? Or the Darklighters? Where do they stand?''

''In two days we have a chance to see firsthand how Ariq's plans are working,'' Ariela said. ''Eyvind and I asked him to invite the Jawas to our wedding, and they are coming as our guests.''

That announcement started more arguing amongst these people than I had ever heard. Eyvind did not look happy to have had her say that.

''The Jawas were honored to be invited,'' I said. ''We can live with them—you'll see. Maybe we can come to live with the Sand People.''

But no one listened to me. Ariela looked at me, and she looked worried. I could imagine plenty of reasons for her to be worried. It was clear she didn't support Eyvind's ideas about my ideas. I was sorry to be the cause of what was probably their first argument.

''We'll take this to Mos Eisley—we'll even take this to Bestine,'' Eyvind said when everybody started to leave.

I walked my speeder into the shed and locked things down for the night. When I came back out, Ariela was still standing there.

''What are you going to do?'' she asked me.

I wanted to ask her the same question. ''I don't know,'' I said. We sat on the sand in front of my house and were quiet for a time.

''Are you really from Alderaan?'' I asked her.

''Yes.''

''Don't you miss it?''

''Not really,'' she said. ''I'm in love, and that makes up for it. But I do miss the water—we're so wasteful with it there!''

''I can't imagine such a place. I'm used to guarding every drop.''

''Not there. If I could take you and Eyvind to Alderaan you'd get fat on the water.''

''I'd swim in it all day.''

''You could take an hour-long shower and no one would care.''

''I'd keep plants in my house and water them.''

She looked at me and smiled. After a minute she stood up. "I won't let Eyvind cause trouble for you in Mos Eisley or Bestine. I can't answer for the rest."

"Thank you," I said. After she left to catch up to the others, I went inside. I didn't have the stomach to eat. It was hot in the house, so I took the holo-display unit and walked outside onto a ridge overlooking my house and sheds. I'd shut down all the lights, so the compound was dark. I displayed the map, and it shone out brightly above the rocks. The rocks around the map looked like the mountains around my farm. The stars shone brightly, and I lay back on the rock to look at them.

I do not look up often enough. I am so busy all the time and so tired after dark that I do not look up often enough at the stars.

I wondered how all of this would turn out.

Day 50: Jawa Gifts, and the Wedding

Thirty-one Jawas came to the wedding, and they brought sacks of rock salt, a liter of water, a bolt of their brown cloth—and a diagnostic droid so small it could fit in the palm of my hand. They couldn't decide on one gift, so they brought some of everything we'd talked about.

The diagnostic droid spoke the binary language of vaporators. The Jawas had polished it so finely that it hurt to look at it lying in the sun with the other gifts.

People just stood and stared at their rich gifts and wondered at the pleasure the Jawas had in being invited to this wedding.

Eyvind hurried up to me and asked me to come translate for him and Ariela. They wanted to thank the Jawas. I was standing by the punch bowl with the Jensens and Ariela's mother and sister, who had come out from Alderaan for the wedding. Mrs. Jensen stopped me before I could leave. "Maybe you're right about all this," Mrs. Jensen said. "Maybe you are."

I smiled at her and hurried off to translate. The

Jawas all bowed to me, and I bowed back. I translated for Eyvind and Ariela, then started answering the Jawas' questions about this human ceremony: Yes, the humans crowded here were all potential customers of their wares and, yes, the tiny diagnostic droid impressed everyone; no, Eyvind and Ariela would not consummate their marriage in public; yes, everyone hoped Eyvind and Ariela would have children; yes, the humans brought special foods to the wedding to make the day memorable. "Try the spiced juice," I said. "You'll love it. It's better than plain water."

I wondered what they would think of the spice. They followed me to the punch table, and I poured Wimateeka a cup of spiced juice and gave it to him.

He just held the cup and looked into it. "The cup is so cold!" he said.

"We usually serve cold drinks at important occasions," I said.

"Why is it red? Does it have blood in it?"

"No—we don't drink blood!"

Wimateeka looked up at me oddly, and I suddenly wondered if the Jawas drank blood at their weddings. I would probably find out soon enough. Wimateeka still hadn't tasted the drink. "It's quite good," I assured him. "At least, we think so."

"How much does this cost?" he asked, finally.

So he thought he'd have to pay for this. They'd all no doubt worried about having enough to pay for food and drinks—especially if they were pressed to try certain things. "Everything here is a gift to the guests of the wedding," I said.

Wimateeka smiled then, and lifted the cup to his lips. His eyes went wide when he tasted the spiced juice —and I wondered if he would spit it out, but he didn't, and soon he took another drink. I served the rest of the Jawas, and they all loved the spiced juice and asked me for more and I served Jawas for fifteen minutes straight.

Eyvind came up to me, nervous and anxious. "I want

to get started," he said, "but Owen and Beru aren't here yet, and they were sure to come."

"Who knows what's kept them?" I said, while I handed a Jawa another cup of spiced juice. "But you'd better start soon or I'll have all thirty-one Jawas drunk *before* the wedding."

Eyvind laughed.

And the shooting started.

From over by the landspeeders. Everyone had parked west of Eyvind's house, and the commotion came from there: Two or three men were shouting and firing at the landspeeders. I wondered *why* they would do such a stupid thing—and then I saw the Sand People.

The adolescents, I thought. They'd taken it into their heads to steal a landspeeder or two while we were busy with the wedding.

The Sand People fought back with their gaffi sticks, and threw a few with deadly aim, and people screamed and ran for cover, and Eyvind ran off to start shooting or to stop the shooting, I didn't know which. I ran after him, but lost him in the crowd, and when I broke through I almost stumbled over Ariela holding something on the ground.

Eyvind. I knelt next to her. She was holding Eyvind with blood all over him, and there was shooting all around us, and then Sand People. I stood up and held on to Ariela so maybe they would recognize me and not kill me and Ariela, and some of them did step back when they saw me—

But something hit me in the back and sent me sprawling—a backhanded slap from the broad, flat face of a gaffi stick—and I couldn't breathe for a minute, though I never blacked out. I heard screams, and I heard Ariela scream, and I couldn't move, I could only see, for a minute, the feet of Sand People rushing around me, and then human feet, and a human pulled me up and leered into my face.

"This is your fault!" he shouted. "This comes from giving them water."

He shoved me back down onto the sand, but I could breathe now and get up on my own, and they were carrying Eyvind away.

"He's dead," someone shouted at me, and the words hit me almost as hard as the gaffi stick had hit me. I couldn't breathe again.

"They've taken Ariela," someone else shouted. "They dragged her away from Eyvind and took her."

Ariela's mother grabbed hold of my arm. "You've got to save her," she said. "The others are going after the Sand People to shoot them, and the Sand People will surely kill my daughter before she can be rescued. You've got to save her."

"I'll take Wimateeka," I said. "He can translate for me."

And that eventually became our plan: I had twelve hours to find the Sand People and convince them to turn Ariela over to me. In the meantime, everyone else would organize a well-equipped posse. If I wasn't back in twelve hours, they would come looking.

And they would come out to kill the Sand People.

I found Wimateeka and the other Jawas huddled in their crawler. I explained what I had to do, and I asked Wimateeka to come with me. He started shaking, but he got up and walked with me to my speeder. He was still shaking when I lifted him in.

After I'd started off, I wondered why I wasn't shaking.

Day 50, Early Afternoon: I Wait by the Vaporator with a Last Gift of Water

I waited by the vaporator because I thought the Sand People would take Ariela to their main camp, somewhere northwest of here. I could travel faster than the adolescents in my landspeeder, so I was ahead of them and they would pass by me. They would probably stop to see if I had left some water.

And I had worked out what I would tell them. These were adolescents who needed to prove themselves worthy to be adults. I could offer them a way to be remembered forever in tales and gain an adulthood always honored: negotiate with the Jawas and me to secure the boundaries of their land and thus their nomadic way of life. I knew their adults would have to be consulted, but the adolescents could start the process and convince them of the necessity of it.

I hoped they would agree with me. I hoped they wouldn't behead me first. I hoped they would agree that Ariela was a trifling matter compared to this and that the water and cloth Wimateeka and I had brought from my house to trade for her would buy her back.

So we waited on the sand, with our water and cloth, and the holo-display unit and my map.

And they came to us, suddenly. All at once we were surrounded by young Sand People, each armed with a gaffi stick, glistening sharp-edged in the harsh sunlight. The dunes were covered with Sand People. I looked for Ariela, but could not see her at first.

I stood and raised my arm and clenched my fist and greeted them: "Koroghh gahgt takt."

They were all quiet. None of them spoke or raised their arms. That's when I saw Ariela: bound and gagged and guarded on top of a dune south of me. "Tell the Sand People what I say," I asked Wimateeka, and I knew I had to speak quickly and well to save her life, and probably Wimateeka's and my own.

I told them we could stop trouble like we had gone through today. I knew a way. I told them my plan, and my hope that the Empire would come to recognize what we had done, and what this would mean for their people and mine.

Wimateeka had trouble explaining the map, and I didn't know if they could understand what a map was. Wimateeka and I smoothed out a flat space in the sand, and I set up the holo-display unit and displayed my map. Some of the Sand People rushed back, startled, but others soon crowded forward, and it began to make sense to them.

But I would not negotiate till they had freed Ariela.

"What we are about to do is better than more killing," I said. "I want you to free your captive—release her to me. She is my friend. Accept this water and cloth as compensation for the trouble you've had in caring for her till now."

They argued about that, but eventually they took the water and cloth and passed it back into the crowd somewhere, and they cut Ariela free and let her walk up to me.

She came slowly through the throng of Sand People. They would barely move aside for her. But she was taller than all of them, so she kept her eyes on me and Wimateeka and eventually got to us. I hugged her, and she hugged me and Wimateeka.

And we started to haggle and negotiate and draw the lines on my map.

It was working.

I thought of all the generations of anthropologists who would have wanted to be here with the Sand People. The day was bright with sunlight, and I could feel the tension ebb away from among us. My map had never looked so beautiful, I thought, as it did then shining out flat above the sand and divided by the black lines of boundaries.

We finished negotiating, six hours before my deadline.

Ariela and Wimateeka and I packed up.

The Sand People stood up and watched us, then started to move off into the dunes, heading northwest to their camp.

Ariela climbed into my landspeeder.

I handed Wimateeka to her and climbed in.

And the dune west of us exploded in flame. My vaporator blew apart, and steam rushed up from it like smoke. Explosions ripped the air—and the young Sand People were screaming and running.

Six hours before our deadline—after everything we had worked for had come to pass. I *had* to stop the shooting.

I flew straight to where the shots were coming from

—a rocky rise south of us—and we were not hit. A path through the fire opened up for us.

Stormtroopers. There were Imperial stormtroopers in the rocks. The farmers who opposed me had called them in, that was all I could think. I slammed the landspeeder to a stop and rushed up into the rock. "Stop shooting!" I shouted. "Those aren't even adults you're killing!"

But no one listened or stopped firing. I pushed into the stormtroopers and shoved their guns up to make them stop—and I was grabbed from behind and slammed into the rock.

"Stop it!" someone shouted at me.

It was the other farmers who had me, eight or ten of them.

"The stormtroopers will kill you," someone hissed in my ear. "Live through this day and we'll talk later about what happened."

I tried to break free, and they shoved me back.

"The Empire would never let your plan work," someone else hissed in my ear, then Ariela was in front of me, her face white and tear-streaked.

"Don't you see?" she said. "They want trouble on all the worlds so the majority will welcome their presence to keep the peace. If you make peace here, our real enemies would become clear—and what then?"

I should have seen this. I should have known this would happen from the day the Imperial Governors first refused to map this region.

The firing stopped. The other farmers thanked the stormtroopers for "rescuing" Ariela and Wimateeka and me.

"You'll have to evacuate from your farm for a time," a stormtrooper told me. "It won't be safe to stay in your house, isolated as it is."

I wouldn't just have to evacuate for a time. This could be the end of my farm. The Sand People would want to kill me for sure—unless I could find a way to convince them I hadn't betrayed them, unless I could find a way to convince them just who had betrayed them.

"We'll escort the Jawa home," another stormtrooper said.

"No," I said. "I'm taking him myself."

And I did. I would not let them take him alone. I thought they might kill him if they got him alone—to anger the Jawas and to drive a wedge between them and the farmers. So a stormtrooper contingent escorted us to the Jawa fortress.

I lifted Wimateeka out of my speeder, near the gates of his fortress, and he rushed inside without saying a word to me.

Day 50, Night: I Become a Rebel

The Imperial commander ordered me into Mos Eisley to make a deposition, and I had to go. Ariela asked me to take her mother and sister to the spaceport. She stayed with the other farmers to prepare for the Sand People's onslaught of revenge.

"Eyvind left me his farm," Ariela told me. "I'd like you to help me run it after this is over—when we can go back to it."

So I had that to think about on my way into Mos Eisley.

I left Ariela's mother and sister at the spaceport. In a short time, they would be safe on Alderaan. I made my deposition, and the Imperials confiscated my map and let me go.

I wondered for how long.

In the meantime, my farm was abandoned.

My hopes for making peace with the Jawas and the Sand People were ruined.

The Sand People would surely feel betrayed and kill innocent people.

My maps, my dreams, my successful negotiations meant nothing to the Empire.

All because the Empire did not want us to have peace. All because the Empire did not care about the safety and the work and the lives of its citizens. We were pawns to be used and discarded—our efforts channeled as long as possible into "approved" paths.

I stopped at the cantina for a drink. I could not go straight back.

I sat in a dark corner and watched the people around me—people from all corners of the Empire. Representatives of peoples who had each, in their own way, been oppressed by the Empire. We had all endured it.

But there was another way. I knew there was another way.

There was the Rebellion.

The Empire had driven *me* into rebellion.

I took another drink and looked around. I didn't know how to find the Rebellion. I didn't know how to join. But this cantina would be the place to find out, I thought. If I asked a few judicious questions, maybe I'd find out. I decided to ask the Ithorian a few tables down.

I took another drink, for courage, but before I could move, Owen and Beru's nephew, Luke, walked in with somebody I didn't know and two droids that got ordered out.

Where were Luke's aunt and uncle? I wondered. And that started me thinking. Owen and Beru's farm was quite far from mine and Ariela's. Maybe they could use an extra hand or two till things settled down and it would be safe for Ariela and me to go back to our farms.

Then we could start our work for the Rebellion.

Ariela would follow me into the Rebellion. Most of the other farmers probably would too after what had happened today. The Jawas would help. In time, maybe even the Sand People might come to understand what had happened to them—and that restoring the Republic would stop Imperial atrocities. Farmers like me, in an odd alliance with Jawas and maybe Sand People, would have to fight for our right to live in peace on the world we called home.

After I thought this through, something told me I'd find the Rebellion just fine, out in the mountains and valleys of the water farms of Tatooine.

Something told me things were going to change on Tatooine, in ways the Imperials never imagined or wanted.

Something told me that, in the end, someday, somehow, there would be peace here.

We would draw the maps of peace.

One Last Night In the Mos Eisley Cantina: The Tale of the Wolfman and the Lamproid

by Judith and Garfield Reeves-Stevens

Instants after the jump from lightspeed, the situation became as simple as the balance between predator and prey. Despite the secrets bought with Bothan blood, the half-finished Death Star above the forest moon of Endor was ready for what was supposed to have been an unexpected assault. The Rebel fleet was doomed.

Sivrak punched the controls of his X-wing fighter even as Admiral Ackbar gave the order for evasive maneuvers. But that would buy only a few moments of life. The Imperial fleet already advanced from Sector 47— Star Destroyers, Cruisers, waves of TIE fighters—and Sivrak knew it was a trap. It had always been a trap.

The fur rose on his face and his fangs flashed in the reflexive grimace of attack. In the common tongue of the Alliance, Sivrak was a Shistavanen Wolfman, and he faced his death with all the primal rage that evolution and unknown genetic engineers had encoded in his cells.

The TIE fighters surged ahead of their fleet, as if the Star Destroyers were not needed in this final battle. Already space blossomed with deadly flowers of exploding spacecraft. Sivrak heard his orders through the static of Imperial interference and the cries of the dying: Protect the fleet no matter what the risk.

Sivrak howled at the challenge. He *had* nothing more to risk. All that had given his life meaning was now ash scattered across the icy wastes of Hoth.

His lips glistened with anticipation of the hunt as he switched his weapons to manual and wrenched his craft onto a collision course with a trio of TIE fighters. Over his helmet communicator, he heard the medical frigate was under attack. But it was too late to alter his trajectory. His course was as set now as it had been the day he had first met *her*.

Endor's moon spiraled before Sivrak. The three TIE fighters converged as they changed course to meet him. His weapons carved space like blazing gouts of blood released by the stab of his fangs. The Imperial ships fired back, closing faster than even a perfect hunter's eye could track.

But Sivrak throttled forward, faster still, and his fighter's engines shrieked behind him. His full-throated voice joined theirs as he shouted out *her* name as his battle cry. The all-encompassing roar swept to a thundering crescendo as charged particles from the Imperial fighters resonated against his own fighter's canopy. Space distorted, wrapping him in red destruction. He embraced the end of his existence, the beginning of nothingness. Yet somewhere inside that senseless maelstrom, Sivrak heard faint strains of music. Music he had heard before. Long ago. The day he had first—

—walked into the Mos Eisley Cantina, boots heavy with the dust of Tatooine, burning with the heat of streets scorched by two blazing suns. He wiped a paw against his mouth, feeling the scrape of grit and sand against his fangs, letting his eyes adjust to the dimmer light.

For a moment, he experienced a slight wave of vertigo, as if his body had not expected to be back in a natural gravity well so soon after . . . after . . . he couldn't remember what. He closed his eyes and a green world spun before him. Something about a deflector shield. Something about a . . . Death Star? He shook his head to dispel his confusion, then walked down the stairs by the droid detector, heading for the bar.

Without prompting, the bartender served Sivrak his regular order—a mug of crushed Gilden, organ tendrils still writhing, attesting to their freshness. Sivrak lapped at it, trying to remember how this drink could be his regular when he had never been in this cantina before. He was a rim scout, or had been, until the Empire had closed off the Outer Rim Territories to new exploration. Now he was just another displaced being, on the run from the Empire and all political entanglements. And Mos Eisley had too many Imperial stormtroopers for his liking. He knew he'd leave as soon as he had the necessary credits. He . . . moved to the side an instant before a Jawa scuttled past him, rushing up the stairs for the door.

Sivrak felt a shock of recognition. He had *expected* the Jawa to run past him. He had known what the Jawa would do. Exactly what the Jawa had done that first time he had stepped in here and met . . .

Sivrak stared past the bar, into the gloom on the side of the cantina opposite the band.

And he saw her again. Just as he had seen her that first time.

He stood by her table, savoring the unmistakable pheromones that identified her as female, admiring the sinuous twists of the muscular coils she draped over her chair, all the more sensual for the strength they contained, able to squeeze the skull from a bantha. She turned to him, her loose-hinged coral jaws revealing rings of glittering fangs, with the outermost the length of Sivrak's claws. Her light sensors bristled as they shifted toward him, seeing in wavelengths beyond those even the Wolfman's glowing eyes could perceive.

Sivrak had heard of such beings before—Florn lamproids—the sole intelligence born on a world of such dangers it meant instant death to any who set foot on it without hyperaccelerated nerve implants.

"Buy you a drink?" the lamproid hissed seductively. Her inflection of the predator's tongue was intensely personal, as if they had hunted and shared blood a thousand times.

Sivrak felt the temperature of the cantina increase and he shrugged off his jacket and sat down across from her just as he had the first time.

But this *was* the first time, wasn't it? How could two beings meet for the first time except for the first time?

"Lak Sivrak," she breathed, and Sivrak growled to acknowledge that somehow, incredibly, she knew even his litter name.

"Dice Ibegon," he replied, disturbed that he knew her name in turn, the moment he spoke it aloud, as if he had always known it.

"You are troubled," Dice said.

"We've met before." Sivrak had said those words in a hundred other cantinas on a dozen other worlds, but this time he meant them. Though how could he, a perfect hunter, forget having met such a perfect killer?

"Are you certain?" the lamproid asked. She trailed the exquisite tip of her lethal tail through the shimmering translucence of a snifter of clarified bantha blood. The reflective surface of the liquid made Sivrak think of force-field emanations. Wasn't there something else he should be doing? Someplace else he was supposed to be?

"At the bar, I knew a Jawa was going to bump into me," he said.

"Jawas often do."

Sivrak concentrated. A new memory came to him. "A golden droid will enter soon."

Dice brought a single drop of bantha blood to Sivrak's muzzle. The liquid trembled on the tip of her tail. "Their kind is not served here," she said. Her voice was inviting, distracting.

Sivrak drew a single, razor-sharp claw against the cool pink flesh of Dice's tail tip, transfixed by her light sensors and her scarlet mouth and its endless rings of needle teeth. "The farm boy with the droid will talk to it."

Dice's voice dropped in tone, sharing secrets. "And the golden droid will leave."

Sivrak's rough-rasped tongue flicked out and captured the teardrop of blood from the lamproid's tail. His claws tightened around the sweet, boneless flesh, feeling the steel cords of her muscles flex in response.

"Tell me what is happening," Sivrak said.

"Only that which has happened," the lamproid answered. A single light sensor shifted to the left. Sivrak glanced in that direction and saw a horned Devaronian sitting against the wall, nodding dreamily in time to the music of the cantina's band as he watched the main entrance.

Sivrak looked over to the entrance to see what the Devaronian saw—an old man in desert robes, a farm boy, an Artoo unit.

And the golden droid.

The old man hurried ahead to the bar. Without knowing how, Sivrak was aware of what lay hidden beneath the old man's robes—an antique lightsaber. There was an Aqualish pirate at the bar who would soon be short an arm.

Sivrak released the lamproid's tail and began to rise

from his chair. But Dice's coils snaked out to bind him tight, keeping him in his place across from her.

"Hey! We don't serve their kind here!" the bartender shouted.

"Tell me," Sivrak demanded.

"What you already know?" Dice replied.

The farm boy spoke to the golden droid. The golden droid and the Artoo unit left. The farm boy joined the old man by the bar. Sivrak struggled—not against the lamproid, but against hidden knowledge that was somewhere inside him.

There could be only one answer, yet it made no sense.

"Is it the Force that binds us to this place?"

"The Force binds all, if you would believe in it."

"I believe only in the hunt."

The lamproid's teeth shifted in amusement—the Florn equivalent of a smile. "That's not what you said when we first met here. You were most eloquent then, my romantic Wolfman."

Sivrak's eyes narrowed. Was she teasing him? "Is there a price to be paid?" he asked stiffly. An altercation began at the bar. "To understand why everything is familiar yet new at the same time?"

"Poor Wolfman," Dice said. "You still don't understand the promise I made you. So for now the price of your understanding is the same price it was the first time we met here."

Sivrak searched his memory for events yet to happen. He cast back to predict what he had already seen. On the other side of the bar the farm boy was thrown into a table. Despite Dice's hold on him, Sivrak leaned forward threateningly. "You're a member of the Alliance, aren't you?"

A lightsaber thrummed into life. The Aqualish pirate screamed. Sivrak's nostrils flared at the scent of fresh blood exploding through the smoke-filled air. The lamproid's tail tip fluttered as she scented it, too. A severed arm fell to the floor of the cantina.

"I *am* a member of the Alliance," she said. "Just as you chose to be, that first time."

But the heady wash of the blood scent pushed Sivrak beyond understanding, and Dice swiftly released the pheromones that would guide the Wolfman to the one state he could achieve without endangering bystanders.

Sivrak arched in her deadly grip, and with a powerful undulation, Dice uncoiled the rest of her body and slithered across the table toward him. Then perfect killer met perfect hunter as their fangs clashed, then locked in the lethal kiss of predators. Sivrak's senses were overwhelmed. He felt the floor of the cantina shift beneath him, gaining momentum as it spun faster and faster, just as if he rode an—

—X-wing fighter spinning through space. A storm of debris rattled against his fighter's skin as Sivrak fought to stabilize the craft. His tactical display showed that two of the TIE fighters had survived his headlong strike. The third was a vapor of incandescent particles dispersing in vacuum. He turned to Dice to make certain she was safe and growled when he saw only the reflection of his own glowing eyes in the canopy. The cantina had been a hallucination, a dream of what had been . . . what might have been . . . he couldn't be sure.

A second sun flared over Endor's moon and Sivrak was torn from his memories by a lance of unthinkable energy that burst from the Death Star to claim a Rebel frigate. The communicator channels were flooded with transmissions of shock and confusion. The Death Star was operational.

Admiral Ackbar ordered a retreat—all fighters were to return to base. General Calrissian countermanded the retreat—all fighters were to engage the Star Destroyers at point-blank range. And every other Rebel voice asked about General Solo's strike team on the moon's surface. Would they destroy the force-field generator? Had they already tried and failed?

Sivrak pulled back on the controls to bring his X-wing on course to the nearest Star Destroyer. There were many ways to die in space. He would find one soon enough, he knew.

The X-wing did not respond.

Sivrak activated the diagnostics, rechanneled auxiliary power, and closed his wings for increased etheric stability.

But the X-wing continued its fall toward the forest moon, and nothing he could do would change its course.

One thought and one thought alone flooded through him: He was going to live.

Once in the moon's atmosphere, Sivrak knew he could use the fighter's control surfaces—useless in vacuum—to bring his craft to a soft landing. A whole forest world waited for him. The Alliance and the Empire would fall from his consciousness as he stalked its prey and returned to what he knew and understood—the hunt. Perhaps, in time, he might even forget Dice Ibegon, and things would be as they had always been. Simple. Balanced. The pure equation of life and death, free of the pain of love and duty.

The raging space battle receded behind him. He watched it diminish in a cockpit display. It appeared his damaged X-wing was no longer a target worthy of the Empire.

He focused on the forest moon, closing fast, bringing him a new life. Another life.

As if any life could have meaning without her.

Rebel craft exploded on the battle display. Sivrak knew that meant the force-field generator on the moon's surface still protected the Death Star. Perhaps his battle wasn't over yet.

He touched the atmospheric controls of his fighter, searching for the first sign of resistance from the wispy upper reaches of the atmosphere he plunged into. To change course one way was to land in safety. The other way, Rebel tacticians had set the odds of a successful atmospheric attack on the generator at a million to one. Standard Imperial ground defenses were too strong.

Sivrak's claws tapped the control yoke as he considered his choice. One way or another. And then his fighter yawed violently as an Imperial particle beam sliced through a rear stabilizer. His tactical display showed two TIE fighters closing behind him, hiding in his propulsion wake—the same two he had faced before. For whatever reason, perhaps to avenge the death of their wingman, Sivrak was still at least a worthy target to them.

The Wolfman felt relieved the choice had been taken from him. There was now no need to plan, no need to decide. There was only the fight. The balance. The reassuring enormity of *now*.

Unable to change his fighter's course in space, he threw it into a spiraling roll, releasing all his decoys and mines in an expanding cloud of sensor-opaque, carbon-fiber chaff. Then he locked his rear sights onto the cloud's dark center, daring one or both of the TIE fighters to survive the cloud's perils. Sivrak calculated he would have time for at least two shots before the Imperial pilots could target him. Perhaps those shots would be enough. Perhaps they wouldn't. Sivrak did not care either way.

He glanced ahead at the rushing disk of the moon, colors smearing as he wildly spun. At last, he felt the first tremors of atmospheric resistance fight his craft's roll. With fierce satisfaction, he pictured his X-wing tearing itself into pieces, raining down on the moon like a comet come to die. It was a good image. A fitting image. A hunter's death.

The tactical display flashed as the mines he had deployed erupted behind him. At least one of the fighters had vanished. But then the display glowed as a piercing beam of brilliant energy shot from the defensive carbon cloud, blinding his rear sensors with a wash of static-filled white that enveloped Sivrak like a smothering snowdrift—

.   .   .

—carved by the icy winds of Hoth.

Sivrak dove for the trench before him as an energy bolt from an Imperial walker obliterated a nearby gun emplacement. Echo Station—the Rebel base's lone outpost on the north ridge—was a charnel house. The awkward dead lay all around him as he pushed himself to his feet and shook the snow and ice from his matted fur. It was so achingly cold he could not even scent the blood of the dying. But then he caught the scent of *her*.

The ground shook with the thunder of approaching walkers and the constant firing of the ion cannon as desperate Rebels tried to clear the way for the retreating transports. But Sivrak was aware of only one sensation—she was close.

He ran to her, dodging the other troops in the slippery, ice-lined trench, his brilliant orange flight suit startling amongst their white Hoth camouflage. The main communicator channel crackled with the call to evacuate all ground crew. The command center had been hit. All troops in Sector 12 were to report to the south post to protect the fighters. But Sivrak was beyond the reach of orders now. He collapsed in the snow at Dice's side.

It was stained with the rich purple of her blood.

Sivrak spoke her name and touched her face, afraid to disturb the ragged shard of metal that had sliced through her insulated suit and cut deeply into her upper thorax. Purple drops of frozen blood shone there, as if, for her, time had stopped.

Her eye sensors trembled and stiffened and she looked up at him.

"Go," she said.

"How can I?" he answered. "I have sworn allegiance to the Princess and the return of the Republic."

The lamproid's teeth shifted in amusement, even as her gasp of pain formed mist in the icy air.

"You never meant to wear the uniform of a Rebel. That day in the cantina, when we first met, you only accepted my offer to join the Alliance as a way to wrap yourself in my coils.''

She was right, of course. The first time in the cantina —the *real* first time—he had made much of his Rebel sympathies, sensing it might make him a more acceptable companion to her. But in time, he had come to believe in what the Alliance stood for. He had become a proud and willing warrior in its cause. But now Dice was dying and the past no longer mattered.

"What *is* the past?" Dice asked, reading his mind again.

Sivrak tore the med-kit from his belt, somehow knowing that another battle was being fought above a world of forests. He stared blankly at the contents of the kit. Most of its salves and ointments were for his species. He had no idea how they would react with Florn biology. But he had to do something.

"You have done something," Dice said soothingly. Her voice was calm, almost peaceful. She fixed her light sensors on the clear blue sky.

"We *are* alike," she continued, "as you have always known. The hunter and the killer know the sick and diseased must be culled from the herd—and the Empire is rotten with corruption. That is why you must leave me, to continue our fight until its end."

The vials and tubes from the med-kit spilled into the snow from Sivrak's rigid paws. "Dice, no. I can't."

"I know you can't. In time, I know you won't. But for now, my love, you *must.* Alliance and Empire. Predator and prey."

Sivrak's communicator sounded the evacuation code sound. A terse voice announced that Imperial troops had entered the base.

"I will die with you here," Sivrak said.

He cradled her head close against his warm body.

"What is death compared to love?" Dice asked, her voice fading.

Sivrak could not move. He was losing her.

"What you must do," she whispered, "is believe in the Force."

"If you wish me to," Sivrak said thickly, unwilling to argue with the old religion if that is what brought her peace at this time. He felt the mourning cry rise in his chest.

"Not because I wish you to, but because there is no other choice you can make."

Before Sivrak could answer, the lamproid's body shivered, then quietened. He stared down at Dice as one by one her light sensors drooped, losing focus, losing contact. And then, amid the sounds of battle light-years removed from the moment that they shared, Dice blessed him with the Force, willing it to remain with him, forever.

Sivrak held her body until a walker destroyed the main generator and the fall-back lines finally fell. Energy beams cut through the air like falling stars. Sivrak's communicator relayed a final evacuation alert. The roar of departing transports, now launching two at a time, was continuous.

But as if he were on a different world, one that knew no war or conflict, Sivrak arose and moved with a slowness and surety that set him apart from the chaos around him.

He heard no explosions as he laid Dice upon the snow, sheltering her in an alcove of the trench. He felt no walker's footfall as he arranged her fur-trimmed hood around her serene, unmoving face, and caressed her ringed teeth that were never again to know the bliss of shredded flesh.

A human Rebel slipped to a near halt in the trench and pulled on Sivrak's arm to urge him to the evacuation point. But Sivrak's snarl sent the human on alone.

Then Sivrak stood over his beloved and took his blaster from his holster. He had heard the stories of what the Imperial biogeneticists did with the bodies of the Rebel dead. How parts could be cloned and kept alive for unspeakable research, or Imperial sport. He set the blaster for full immolation.

"May your Force be with you," he said in the most

intimate inflection of the predator's tongue, and his breath swirled into the frozen air to join with hers.

He would make it to the evacuation point or he would not. There was no reason to hurry.

Sivrak activated the blaster.

Dice's body shimmered with the disassociative energy of the beam. She became fiery, incandescent, and somehow, Sivrak thought, she might have appreciated that transformation. And then the fire that consumed her reached out for Sivrak, engulfing him too as—

—a single TIE fighter emerged from the carbon cloud with all weapons firing blindly. Blinking with surprise, Sivrak felt the chill of Hoth still pulsing through him as he instinctively switched from his etheric rudder to full atmospheric controls, and dodged the killing strands of the TIE fighter's beams until his rear sights locked and he fired.

The TIE fighter flew apart as Sivrak's beam tore open its skin and the moon of Endor's atmosphere instantly ripped the Imperial craft to dust-sized fragments. The hunt was over.

But now the Endor moon filled his canopy. Sivrak slammed at the atmospheric controls, fighting to reduce the X-wing's roll. The navigation display showed his two possible courses. One to safety. One to the generator. The rear display showed the Death Star firing at will. The X-wing shook as it tore through the thickening atmosphere. Sivrak's claws dug into the yoke. He was less than thirty heartbeats from the point of no return. Again, he had to decide. He couldn't decide. The atmosphere sang to him. Like music. Like music from—

—the cantina. Sivrak leaned against the wall inside the doorway, trying to understand what he heard outside on the streets of Mos Eisley. Fighting. Rioting. Speeders rushing. Detonations from the direction of the spaceport.

He stumbled down the stairs to the bar, breathless, feeling the panic of time running out.

It was night. The cantina was deserted. The music was recorded. Something was wrong.

Sivrak slumped against the bar, feeling it shudder as if it coursed through atmosphere.

"Jabba is dead," Dice said.

Sivrak looked up from the bar to find the lamproid close beside him, studying the reflections in her snifter of clarified blood.

"How . . . ?" Sivrak rasped. His question took in everything that had happened but Dice heard it in only one way.

"Strangled on his sand ship," Dice said. "A human slave girl, of all things. Used her own chains."

From somewhere outside, there was an explosion, much closer than the spaceport. The bottles and glasses stacked up behind the bar rattled.

Dice picked up her snifter. "Mos Eisley is in flames. No one knows who is in control." She unrolled her drinking tongue into the blood and ingested.

Sivrak smoothed the fur around his muzzle in agitation. He knew there was something he had to do, but he couldn't work it out. He *had* to discover what was out of place here.

"If Jabba is dead," he began uncertainly, "then Hoth . . . Hoth has already been evacuated."

Dice put the snifter back on the bartop. "That's right," she said.

Sivrak felt the fur lift along his spine. "But then," he said, "you're dead."

Dice slid the tip of her tail across Sivrak's forearm. "Do I *feel* dead?" she asked.

The Wolfman closed his claws over the tail tip, focusing only on the magic of her improbable presence. He heard other sounds now. Shuffling. Voices. Boots grinding sand into the floor. He looked up at Dice.

They were sitting at the table in the corner, the horned Devaronian nodding to the music behind them. Now the cantina was full, bustling. As it had been, long ago.

"The golden droid will come in soon," Sivrak said. He wasn't sure how, but he was beginning to understand what was happening, the choice he must make. "And then the golden droid will leave again."

Dice's light sensors were unfathomable, as deep as a gravity well. "And what of you, this time?" she asked, as if she had read his mind. "Will you choose to leave as well?"

"The Force," Sivrak said with wonder as understanding finally welled within him. "The Force *is* with me, isn't it?"

Dice smiled, an irksome habit in those who knew the Force so well. "The Force is within everything," she said.

"But here and now, in this cantina"—Sivrak's voice rose as all that had happened, all that would happen, all that *might* happen, converged on him at once—"in the trenches of Hoth, or falling toward some nameless moon of Endor—the Force binds it *all*."

His pulse hammered, his lungs strained for air. A flicker of light by the entrance showed that someone had entered the cantina. The Devaronian glanced over to see who it was.

"Of course," Dice said, as if she had heard every word he had spoken uncounted lifetimes ago.

The farm boy appeared on the stairs as the old man hurried ahead. The Artoo unit and the golden droid followed behind.

"This time, when the golden droid leaves, I can leave too, can't I?" Sivrak asked.

"That choice was yours when we first met," Dice said. "Nothing has changed."

Sivrak felt the worldlines converge, then pull apart, not on this one place and time, but on this one feeling, this one experience that transcended all else.

He now knew that through some trick of the Force,

he *could* follow the golden droid back onto the streets of Mos Eisley, and all would be as it had been before he had met Dice Ibegon.

The same choice but a second chance.

In love, Dice had given him this way out.

"Hey," the bartender growled from behind the bar. "We don't serve their kind here."

Sivrak watched intently. The farm boy talked with his droids. Only heartbeats remained. The time between one decision and another. One direction or the other.

"I don't want to leave you," Sivrak said to Dice.

"Knowing all that you know?" she asked. "Knowing with certainty what lies ahead?"

Sivrak didn't answer. He simply reached out to her, to gather her coils close around him for one timeless moment that would last, had lasted, forever.

The golden droid left the cantina. The music played. Sivrak waited for the hum of the old man's lightsaber to drown out all other noise.

"Sometimes choice is an illusion," Sivrak said, at last knowing that all choices were the same choice, and had been from the instant he had set foot into this cantina and seen Dice Ibegon, waiting as she had always waited to join him.

He forced his eyes shut, knowing all that would happen. The old man reached into his cloak and pulled out his antique lightsaber. The glow of its beam sparkled from the glasses on the bar. The Aqualish pirate screamed. The cantina shuddered—

—under the withering assault of the Endor moon's atmosphere.

Sivrak bayed at that moon as he lifted the nose of the X-wing to make it skip through the turbulence, riding his own sonic compression wave, shedding just enough speed to bring his velocity below the X-wing's critical stress load. This time he reached the point of no return and knew at once he had always lived his life precisely at this moment. The enormity of *now*. His movements were instinctual, no thought required, no decision possible. He pulled on the control yoke to bring his course around to intersect with the ground generator's coordinates.

His X-wing screamed through the atmosphere, the forward deflector shields blazing red like a dying star. His tactical display remained silent—no Imperial ground defenses tracked him. Standard defenses were unbreachable, but perhaps, with the space battle in progress above, these weren't standard times.

The navigation display confirmed his trajectory. Over-the-horizon scanners locked him onto the generator's transmission antenna. The X-wing bucked like a crazed tauntaun. Everything Sivrak saw blurred before him, blending in with the cacophony of his communicator: a burst of static, then Ackbar's exultant voice—"The shield is down! Commence attack on the Death Star's main reactor!"

The moon's forest streaked below Sivrak's X-wing as he saw a plume of smoke and fire rush for him, the remains of the transmission antenna already destroyed. Solo's strike team had succeeded after all.

General Calrissian's voice broke up with static. "We're on our way!" Raw cheering voices. Human and Bothan. Mon Calamari and Bith. Even a droid who announced it had always wanted to do this.

It was the frenzy of a successful hunt, Sivrak knew, even as he understood that no power in the universe could stay the streaking course of his fighter, because it had already been set by the strongest power.

The flaming ruins of the Imperial base came at him with the speed of destiny. Calmly, Sivrak took his claws from the controls—

—and walked the forest of Endor's moon.

It was night. The breeze was cool. His nostrils were aflame with the scents of a multitude of prey and smoky woodfires. The fires' distant crackling was punctuated by rhythmic drumbeats and excited voices lifted in triumphant song.

Sivrak drew in the clean air, flushing the last stale traces of recycled fighter oxygen from his lungs. This time, he did not try to remember what had happened. He knew, in time, all answers would come.

"Those are the Ewoks singing," Dice said behind him, as he knew she must.

He turned to face her, gasping at the ethereal wonder of her lamproid form as she glowed with the inner light she had always carried. The dark trees of the forest basked in her radiance.

"They celebrate the death of the Emperor," she said.

"Then the battle of Endor's moon . . . ?" Sivrak began.

"Has been won. Our fight is at its end."

Sivrak lifted his paw to touch her, and was not surprised when he saw that his own arm shone as did Dice's body.

She wound her tail tip around his paw. "We are luminous beings," she said, "and always have been. True love can never be denied."

For long moments, Sivrak stood silent in that forest, united at last in such a way that he knew he would never be alone again—a balance even simpler than that between predator and prey, the joining of all things in the Force. But blended in the Ewoks' chorus, he heard the strains of a different music, from a different time.

"The cantina," Dice explained without him having to ask.

"I know," Sivrak said. "But there is no need to return there."

"There never was," she said.

And then, tail in paw, their hearts and souls entwined forever, Dice led Sivrak through the forest of Endor's moon, to a special place near an Ewok village where three friends waited, as they had always waited, as they always would wait, for all who would join them, bound by the Force.

And behind them in the forest, the music from the cantina softly faded, and was never heard again.

Contributor Biographies

KEVIN J. ANDERSON has spent a lot of time in a galaxy far, far away. He is the author of the STAR WARS: The Jedi Academy trilogy and the forthcoming STAR WARS novel, *Darksaber,* due in December 1995— as well as the science fiction novels *Climbing Olympus, Resurrection, Inc.,* and several others with Doug Beason. He is currently editing two other STAR WARS anthologies, *Tales from Jabba's Palace* and *Tales of the Bounty Hunters.* He has worked for ten years as a technical writer at the Lawrence Livermore National Laboratory. He is married to writer Rebecca Moesta.

Author of eight books—five with *Cantina* editor Kevin J. Anderson and three on his own—DOUG BEASON is an accomplished short-story writer, appearing in such publications as *Analog, Amazing, Full Spectrum, SF Age,* and others. A PhD physicist, Doug has served on a presidential commission with astronaut Tom Stafford to develop plans for the United States to return to the Moon and go on to Mars. He worked at the White House for the President's Science Advisor under both the Bush and Clinton administrations. As a lieutenant colonel in the USAF, he is currently an associate professor and director of research at the

United States Air Force Academy in Colorado Springs, Colorado.

M. SHAYNE BELL grew up on a ranch in Idaho. His first novel, *Nicoji,* was released in 1991 by Baen Books. His short fiction has appeared in *Asimov's Science Fiction, The Magazine of Fantasy and Science Fiction, Amazing Stories,* and anthologies including *Simulations: Fifteen Tales of Virtual Reality, Hotel Andromeda,* and *Under African Skies.* He also just completed editing an anthology of stories set in Utah by all the SF writers from or living in Utah, *Washed by a Wave of Wind.* His poetry was nominated for the 1989 Science Fiction Poetry Association Rhysling Award. He writes medical software documentation. In 1987 he was awarded first place in the Writers of the Future Contest. In 1991 he received a Creative Writing Fellowship from the National Endowment for the Arts.

He lived in Brazil for two years in the 1970s, where he first saw *Star Wars* in a crowded theater in Campinas —the only movie he saw during the entire two years. He could not understand the English through the bad sound system and had to resort to reading the Portuguese subtitles.

DAVID BISCHOFF is the author of over forty SF/ horror/fantasy and mystery novels and several dozen short stories. His most recent efforts include *The Judas Cross,* with Charles Sheffield (Warner/Aspect), *Dr. Dimension,* with John de Chancie (ROC Books), and the *New York Times* bestselling *Star Trek: The Next Generation* novel, *Grounded.* He lives in Eugene, Oregon.

A. C. CRISPIN is the author of three *Star Trek* novels: *Yesterday's Son,* its sequel, *Time for Yesterday* (classic *Trek*), and *The Eyes of the Beholders (Next Generation).* She is the creator, author, and co-author of the *StarBridge* series: *Starbridge, Silent Dances, Shadow World, Serpent's Gift,* and *Silent Songs* (ACE Books). In addition, she has coauthored two fantasy novels with Andre Norton: *Gryphon's Eyrie* and *Songsmith* (TOR Books).

Ms. Crispin is a frequent guest at *Star Trek* and science fiction conventions, where she often teaches writers' workshops. She currently serves as the Eastern regional director of the Science Fiction and Fantasy Writers of America. A Maryland resident, she lives with her teenage son Jason, two horses, and three cats. In her spare time (what's that?) she enjoys trail riding, swimming, sailing, hiking, and reading.

KENNETH C. FLINT of Omaha, Nebraska, is to date the author of fifteen novels for Bantam Doubleday Dell Books. All are works of adventure/fantasy, many of which are based upon ancient Celtic legends and myths.

From her earliest years BARBARA HAMBLY found fantasy and science fiction far more interesting than reality in the modest California town where she grew up. She attended college at the University of California in Riverside and spent one year at the University of Bordeaux in France. After obtaining a master's degree in medieval history, she held a variety of jobs: model, clerk, high school teacher, karate instructor (she holds a black belt in Shotokan Karate), technical writer, mostly in quest of a job that would leave her with enough time to write. Finally, in 1982 her first novel was published by Ballantine/Del Rey.

Her novels are mostly sword-and-sorcery fantasy, though she has also written a historical whodunit, a vampire novel, and novels and novelizations from television shows, notably *Beauty and the Beast* and *Star Trek*. She is currently editing an anthology of original vampire stories, *Sisters of the Night,* and her STAR WARS novel, *Children of the Jedi,* was released in April 1995. Her interests besides writing include dancing, painting, historical and fantasy costuming, and occasionally carpentry. She resides in a big, ugly house in Los Angeles with the two cutest Pekingese in the world.

REBECCA MOESTA is the co-author, with Kevin J. Anderson, of the upcoming series of STAR WARS adventures for young readers, *Young Jedi Knights*. She is currently the co-editor of the Science Fiction and Fantasy Writers of America *Forum*. She holds a master of science degree in business administration from Boston University and works as a technical writer and editor at Lawrence Livermore National Laboratory.

DANIEL KEYS MORAN claims he has never done anything or been anywhere interesting. He is the author of the wildly popular *Tales of the Continuing Time*, and does in fact very much resemble the character Trent from those books, except that he is handsomer, wittier, and a much better basketball player. The most recent novel in the series, *The Last Dancer*, was published in 1993 from Bantam Books.

He is extremely pleased to have named, six years after the fact, the Cantina Bar song from *Star Wars*. It's now called, of course, "Mad About Me."

JERRY OLTION has published stories in most of the major science fiction magazines and various anthologies. His story "The Love Song of Laura Morrison" won the *Analog* reader's choice award for best short story of 1987. His novels include *Frame of Reference* (Questar 1987) and two books, *Alliance* and *Humanity*, in the *Isaac Asimov's Robot City* series. His short-story collection, *Love Songs of a Mad Scientist*, was recently published by Hypatia Press. He is also the originator of the Jerry Oltion Really Good Story Award for achievement in science fiction and fantasy.

JUDITH and **GARFIELD REEVES-STEVENS** have been a writing team since 1986. In education, they are authors of a series of science and technology textbooks for children, as well as interactive reading and writing computer programs. In fiction, they have written two *Star Trek* novels, the first novel in the *Alien Nation* series, and have created their own action-adventure fantasy series in *The Chronicles of Galen Sword*. Their other writing credits range from comic books to episodes of *Beyond Reality*, *The Legend of Prince Valiant*, and *Batman: The Animated Series*. For the 1994–95 television season, the Reeves-Stevenses have helped develop and are executive story editors for the new animated science fiction series *Phantom 2040*, a futuristic updating of Lee Falk's classic costumed hero.

In 1977, at age twenty-three, JENNIFER ROBERSON spent her entire summer in a movie theater. The ritual was simple: She and a friend would find a "rookie," haul him or her off to the theater, and relive vicariously the thrill of viewing *Star Wars* for the first time. This ritual served two purposes: It provided a fix for Roberson's addiction, and it got others hooked as well.

Seven years later DAW Books published her fantasy novel, *Shapechangers*, the first volume in an eight-book series titled *Chronicles of the Cheysuli*. Roberson has also published the four-volume *Sword-Dancer* saga as well as short fiction in magazines, anthologies, and collections, and a bestselling historical reinterpretation of the Robin Hood legend emphasizing Marian's point of view, titled *Lady of the Forest*. Her upcoming projects include a hardcover political intrigue–fantasy trilogy, *Shade and Shadow*, and a historical novel set in seventeenth-century Scotland.

Intending to target the young-adult market, KATHY TYERS started writing science fiction in 1983. Bantam Books asked her to rewrite her space adventure *Firebird* as an adult release in 1986. Her other books include *Fusion Fire* (1988), *Crystal Witness* (1989), *Shivering World* (1991), *Exploring the Northern Rockies* (1991), and, forthcoming, *The Springhill Aliens*. The 1994 release of

STAR WARS: *The Truce at Bakura* marked her return to space opera for all ages.

A flutist and Irish harper, Kathy performs and records semiprofessionally with her husband, Mark. They have one son and live in Bozeman, Montana.

MARTHA VEITCH is a writer and stained-glass artist.

TOM VEITCH wrote STAR WARS: *Dark Empire* and STAR WARS: *Tales of the Jedi* for Dark Horse Comics. He is currently collaborating with Kevin J. Anderson on STAR WARS: *Dark Lords of the Sith*, a series continuing the saga of the ancient Jedi begun in *Tales of the Jedi*.

DAVE WOLVERTON is the author of several novels, including STAR WARS: *The Courtship of Princess Leia*, *Serpent Catch, Path of the Hero,* and *On My Way to Paradise*. In 1986 he won the grand prize for the Writers of the Future contest. He has worked as a prison guard, missionary, business manager, editor, and technical writer.

TIMOTHY ZAHN grew up near Chicago, studied physics in college and grad school, and spent the first forty years of his life in the Midwest. With such a background, it was practically inevitable that he would settle placidly into a standard respectable middle-class profession and standard respectable middle-class life.

Somewhere along the way, he took an unlikely off-ramp.

Writing science fiction as a hobby to relax from long bouts of work on his doctoral-thesis project probably would have stayed a hobby—except that in 1979 his advisor suddenly died, leaving him with a project that wasn't going anywhere. So in 1980 he took a deep breath and set off on a full-time writing career.

Since then he has published thirteen novels and over fifty short stories, including the Hugo-winning novella "Cascade Point." The publication of his three STAR WARS novels altered his life from one of comfortable obscurity to one of international bemusement. It also permitted him to exchange the corn fields of Illinois for the ocean beaches of Oregon. He is currently at work on *Conquerors' Legacy,* the third book of the *Conquerors* trilogy.

The World of
STAR WARS Novels

In May 1991, *Star Wars* caused a sensation in the publishing industry with the Bantam Spectra release of Timothy Zahn's novel *Heir to the Empire*. For the first time, Lucasfilm Ltd. had authorized new novels that *continued* the famous story told in George Lucas's three blockbuster motion pictures: *Star Wars, The Empire Strikes Back,* and *Return of the Jedi.* Reader reaction was immediate and tumultuous: *Heir* reached #1 on the *New York Times* bestseller list and demonstrated that *Star Wars* lovers were eager for exciting new stories set in this universe, written by leading science fiction authors who shared their passion. Since then, each Bantam *Star Wars* novel has been an instant national bestseller.

Lucasfilm and Bantam decided that future novels in the series would be interconnected: that is, events in one novel would have consequences in the others. You might say that each Bantam *Star Wars* novel, enjoyable on its own, is also part of a much larger tale beginning immediately after the last *Star Wars* film, *Return of the Jedi.*

Here is a special look at Bantam's *Star Wars* books, along with excerpts from these thrilling novels. Each one is available now wherever Bantam Books are sold.

THE TRUCE AT BAKURA by Kathy Tyers
Setting: Immediately after *Return of the Jedi*

The day after his climactic battle with Emperor Palpatine and the sacrifice of his father, Darth Vader, who died saving his life, Luke Skywalker helps recover an Imperial drone ship bearing a startling message intended for the Emperor. It is a distress signal from the far-off Imperial outpost of Bakura, which is under attack by an alien invasion force, the Ssi-ruuk. Leia sees a rescue mission as an opportunity to achieve a diplomatic victory for the Rebel Alliance, even if it means fighting alongside former Imperials. But Luke receives a vision from Obi-Wan Kenobi revealing that the stakes are even higher: the invasion at Bakura threatens everything the Rebels have won at such great cost.

Here is a scene showing the extent of the alien menace:

On an outer deck of a vast battle cruiser called the *Shriwirr*, Dev Sibwarra rested his slim brown hand on a prisoner's left shoulder. "It'll be all right," he said softly. The other human's fear beat at his mind like a three-tailed lash. "There's no pain. You have a wonderful surprise ahead of you." Wonderful indeed, a life without hunger, cold, or selfish desire.

The prisoner, an Imperial of much lighter complexion than Dev, slumped in the entenchment chair. He'd given up protesting, and his breath came in gasps. Pliable bands secured his forelimbs, neck, and knees—but only for balance. With his nervous system deionized at the shoulders, he couldn't struggle. A slender intravenous tube dripped pale blue magnetizing solution into each of his carotid arteries while tiny servopumps hummed. It only took a few mils of magsol to attune the tiny, fluctuating electromagnetic fields of human brain waves to the Ssi-ruuvi entenchment apparatus.

Behind Dev, Master Firwirrung trilled a question in Ssi-ruuvi. "Is it calmed yet?"

Dev sketched a bow to his master and switched from human speech to Ssi-ruuvi. "Calm enough," he sang back. "He's almost ready."

Sleek, russet scales protected Firwirrung's two-meter length from beaked muzzle to muscular tail tip, and a prominent black **V** crest marked his forehead. Not large for a Ssi-ruu, he was still growing, with only a few age-scores where scales had begun to separate on his handsome chest. Firwirrung swung a broad, glowing white metal catchment arc down to cover the prisoner from midchest to nose. Dev could just peer over it and watch the man's pupils dilate. At any moment . . .

"Now," Dev announced.

Firwirrung touched a control. His muscular tail twitched with pleasure. The fleet's capture had been good today. Alongside his master, Dev would work far into the night. Before entenchment, prisoners were noisy and dangerous. Afterward, their life energies powered droids of Ssi-ruuvi choosing.

The catchment arc hummed up to pitch. Dev backed away. Inside that round human skull, a magsol-drugged brain was losing control. Though Master Firwirrung assured him that the transfer of incorporeal energy was painless, every prisoner screamed.

As did this one, when Firwirrung threw the catchment arc switch. The arc boomed out a sympathetic vibration, as brain energy leaped to an electromagnet perfectly attuned to magsol. Through the Force rippled an ululation of indescribable anguish.

Dev staggered and clung to the knowledge his masters had given him: The prisoners only thought they felt pain. *He* only thought he sensed their pain. By the time the body screamed, all of a subject's energies had jumped to the catchment arc. The screaming body already was dead.

THE COURTSHIP OF PRINCESS LEIA
by Dave Wolverton
Setting: Four years after *Return of the Jedi*

One of the most interesting developments in Bantam's Star Wars *novels is that in their storyline, Han Solo and Princess Leia start a family. This tale reveals how the couple originally got together. Wishing to strengthen the fledgling New Republic by bringing in powerful allies, Leia opens talks with the Hapes consortium of more than sixty worlds. But the consortium is ruled by the Queen Mother, who, to Han's dismay, wants Leia to marry her son, Prince Isolder. Before this action-packed story is over, Luke will join forces with Isolder against a group of Force-trained "witches" and face a deadly foe.*

In this scene, Luke is searching for Jedi lore and finds more than he bargained for:

Luke popped the cylinder into Artoo, and almost immediately Artoo caught a signal. Images flashed in the air before the droid: an ancient throne room where, one by one, Jedi came before their high master to give reports. Yet the holo was fragmented, so thoroughly erased that Luke got only bits and pieces—a blue-skinned man describing details of a grueling space battle against pirateers; a yellow-eyed Twi'lek with lashing headtails who told of discovering a plot to kill an ambassador. A date and time flashed on the holo vid before each report. The report was nearly four hundred standard years old.

Then Yoda appeared on the video, gazing up at the throne. His color was more vibrantly green than Luke remembered, and he did not use his walking stick. At middle age, Yoda had looked almost perky, carefree—not the bent, troubled old Jedi Luke had known. Most of the audio was erased, but through the background hiss Yoda clearly said, "We tried to free the Chu'unthor from Dathomir, but were repulsed by the witches . . . skirmish, with Masters Gra'aton and Vulatan. . . . Fourteen acolytes killed . . . go back to retrieve . . ." The audio hissed away, and soon the holo image dissolved to blue static with popping lights.

They went up topside, found that night had fallen while they worked underground. Their Whiphid guide soon returned, dragging the body of a gutted snow demon. The demon's white talons curled in the air, and its long purple tongue snaked out from between its massive fangs. Luke was amazed that the Whiphid could haul such a monster, yet the Whiphid held the demon's long hairy tail in one hand and managed to pull it back to camp.

There, Luke stayed the night with the Whiphids in a huge shelter made from the rib cage of a motmot, covered over with hides to keep out the wind. The Whiphids built a bonfire and roasted the snow demon, and the young danced while the elders played their claw harps. As Luke sat, watching the writhing flames and listening to the twang of harps, he meditated. "The future you will see, and the past. Old friends long forgotten . . ." Those were the words Yoda had said long ago while training Luke to peer beyond the mists of time.

Luke looked up at the rib bones of the motmot. The Whiphids had carved stick letters into the bone, ten and twelve meters in the air, giving the lineage of their ancestors. Luke could not read the letters, but they seemed to dance in the firelight, as if they were sticks and stones falling from the sky. The rib bones curved toward him, and Luke followed the curve of bones with his eyes. The tumbling sticks and boulders seemed to gyrate, all of them falling toward him as if they would crush him. He could see boulders hurtling through the air, too, smashing toward him. Luke's nostrils flared, and even Toola's chill could not keep a thin film of perspiration from dotting his forehead. A vision came to Luke then.

Luke stood in a mountain fortress of stone, looking over a plain with a sea of dark forested hills beyond, and a storm rose—a magnificent wind that brought with it towering walls of black clouds and dust, trees hurtling toward him and twisting through the sky. The clouds thundered overhead, filled with purple flames, obliterating all sunlight, and Luke could feel a malevolence hidden in those clouds and knew that they had been raised through the power of the dark side of the Force.

Dust and stones whistled through the air like autumn leaves. Luke tried to hold on to the stone parapet overlooking the plain to keep from being swept from the fortress walls. Winds pounded in his ears like the roar of an ocean, howling.

It was as if a storm of pure dark Force raged over the countryside, and suddenly, amid the towering clouds of darkness that thundered toward him, Luke could hear laughing, the sweet sound of women laughing. He looked above into the dark clouds, and saw the women borne through the air along with the rocks and debris, like motes of dust, laughing. A voice seemed to whisper, "the witches of Dathomir."

HEIR TO THE EMPIRE
DARK FORCE RISING
THE LAST COMMAND
by Timothy Zahn
Setting: Five years after *Return of the Jedi*

This #1 bestselling trilogy introduces two legendary forces of evil into the Star Wars *literary pantheon. Grand Admiral Thrawn has taken control of the Imperial fleet in the years since the destruction of the Death Star, and the mysterious Joruus C'baoth is a fearsome Jedi Master who has been seduced by the dark side. Han and Leia have now been married for about a year, and as the story begins, she is pregnant with twins. Thrawn's plan is to crush the Rebellion and resurrect the Empire's New Order with C'baoth's help—and in return, the Dark Master will get Han and Leia's Jedi children to mold as he wishes. For as readers of this magnificent trilogy will see, Luke Skywalker is not the last of the old Jedi. He is the first of the new.*

In this scene from Heir to the Empire, *Thrawn and C'baoth meet for the first time:*

For a long moment the old man continued to stare at Thrawn, a dozen strange expressions flicking in quick succession across his face. "Come. We will talk."

"Thank you," Thrawn said, inclining his head slightly. "May I ask who we have the honor of addressing?"

"Of course." The old man's face was abruptly regal again, and when he spoke his foice rang out in the silence of the crypt. "I am the Jedi Master Joruus C'baoth."

Pellaeon inhaled sharply, a cold shiver running up his back. "Joruus C'baoth?" he breathed. "But—"

He broke off. C'baoth looked at him, much as Pellaeon himself might look at a junior officer who has spoken out of turn. "Come," he repeated, turning back to Thrawn. "We will talk."

He led the way out of the crypt and back into the sunshine. Several small knots of people had gathered in the square in their absence, huddling well back from both the crypt and the shuttle as they whispered nervously together.

With one exception. Standing directly in their path a few meters away was one of the two guards C'baoth had ordered out of the crypt. On his face was an expression of barely controlled fury; in his hands, cocked and ready, was his crossbow. "You destroyed his home," C'baoth said, almost conversationally. "Doubtless he would like to exact vengeance."

The words were barely out of his mouth when the guard suddenly snapped the crossbow up and fired. Instinctively, Pellaeon ducked, raising his blaster—

And three meters from the Imperials the bolt came to an abrupt halt in midair.

Pellaeon stared at the hovering piece of wood and metal, his brain only slowly catching up with what had just happened. "They are our guests," C'baoth told the guard in a voice clearly intended to reach everyone in the square. "They will be treated accordingly."

With a crackle of splintering wood, the crossbow bolt shattered, the pieces dropping to the ground. Slowly, reluctantly, the guard lowered his crossbow, his eyes still burning with a now impotent rage. Thrawn let him stand there another second like that, then gestured to Rukh. The Noghri raised his blaster and fired—

And in a blur of motion almost too fast to see, a flat stone detached itself from the ground and hurled itself directly into the path of the shot, shattering spectacularly as the blast hit it.

Thrawn spun to face C'baoth, his face a mirror of surprise and anger. "C'baoth—!"

"These are *my* people, Grand Admiral Thrawn," the other cut him off, his voice forged from quiet steel. "Not yours; mine. If there is punishment to be dealt out, *I* will do it."

For a long moment the two men again locked eyes. Then, with an obvious effort, Thrawn regained his composure. "Of course, Master C'baoth," he said. "Forgive me."

C'baoth nodded. "Better. Much better." He looked past Thrawn, dismissed the guard with a nod. "Come," he said, looking back at the Grand Admiral. "We will talk."

The Jedi Academy Trilogy:
JEDI SEARCH
DARK APPRENTICE
CHAMPIONS OF THE FORCE
by Kevin J. Anderson
Setting: Seven years after *Return of the Jedi*

In order to assure the continuation of the Jedi Knights, Luke Skywalker has decided to start a training facility: a Jedi Academy. He will gather Force-sensitive students who show potential as prospective Jedi and serve as their mentor, as Jedi Masters Obi-Wan Kenobi and Yoda did for him. Han and Leia's twins are now toddlers, and there is a third Jedi child: the infant Anakin, named after Luke and Leia's father. In this trilogy, we discover the existence of a powerful Imperial doomsday weapon, the horrifying Sun Crusher—which will soon become the centerpiece of a titanic struggle between Luke Skywalker and his most brilliant Jedi Academy student, who is delving dangerously into the dark side.

In this scene from the first novel, Jedi Search, *Luke vocalizes his concept of a new Jedi order to a distinguished assembly of New Republic leaders:*

As he descended the long ramp, Luke felt all eyes turn toward him. A hush fell over the assembly. Luke Skywalker, the lone remaining Jedi Master, almost never took part in governmental proceedings.

"I have an important matter to address," he said. For a moment he was reminded of when he had walked alone into the dank corridors of Jabba the Hutt's palace—but this time there were no piglike Gamorrean guards that he could manipulate with a twist of his fingers and a touch of the Force.

Mon Mothma gave him a soft, mysterious smile and gestured for him to take a central position. "The words of a Jedi Knight are always welcome to the New Republic," she said.

Luke tried not to look pleased. She had provided the perfect opening for him. "In the Old Republic," he said, "Jedi Knights were the protectors and guardians of all. For a thousand generations the Jedi used the powers of the Force to guide, defend, and provide support for the rightful government of worlds—before the dark days of the Empire came, and the Jedi Knights were killed."

He let his words hang, then took another breath. "Now we have a New Republic. The Empire appears to be defeated. We have founded a new government based upon the old, but let us hope we learn from our mistakes. Before, an entire order of Jedi watched over the Republic, offering strength. Now I am the only Jedi Master who remains.

"Without that order of protectors to provide a backbone of strength for the New Republic, can we survive? Will we be able to weather the storms and the difficulties of forging a new union? Until now we have suffered severe struggles—but in the future they will be seen as nothing more than birth pangs."

Before the other senators could disagree with that, Luke continued. "Our people had a common foe in the Empire, and we must not let our defenses lapse just because we have internal problems. More to the point, what will happen when we begin squabbling among ourselves over petty matters? The old Jedi helped to mediate many types of disputes. What if there are no Jedi Knights to protect us in the difficult times ahead?"

Luke moved under the diffracting rainbow colors from the crystal light overhead. He took his time to fix his gaze on all the senators present; he turned his attention to Leia last. Her eyes were wide but supportive. He had not discussed his idea with her beforehand.

"My sister is undergoing Jedi training. She has a great

deal of skill in the Force. Her three children are also likely candidates to be trained as young Jedi. In recent years I have come to know a woman named Mara Jade, who is now unifying the smugglers—the former smugglers," he amended, "into an organization that can support the needs of the New Republic. She also has a talent for the Force. I have encountered others in my travels."

Another pause. The audience was listening so far. "But are these the only ones? We already know that the ability to use the Force is passed from generation to generation. Most of the Jedi were killed in the Emperor's purge—but could he possibly have eradicated all of the descendants of those Knights? I myself was unaware of the potential power within me until Obi-Wan Kenobi taught me how to use it. My sister Leia was similarly unaware.

"How many people are abroad in this galaxy who have a comparable strength in the Force, who are potential members of a new order of Jedi Knights, but are unaware of who they are?"

Luke looked at them again. "In my brief search I have already discovered that there are indeed some descendants of former Jedi. I have come here to ask"—he turned to gesture toward Mon Mothma, swept his hands across the people gathered there in the chamber—"for two things.

"First, that the New Republic officially sanction my search for those with a hidden talent for the Force, to seek them out and try to bring them to our service. For this I will need some help."

Admiral Ackbar interrupted, blinking his huge fish eyes and turning his head. "But if you yourself did not know your power when you were young, how will these other people know? How will you find them, Jedi Skywalker?"

Luke folded his hands in front of him. "Several ways. First, with the help of two dedicated droids who will spend their days searching through the Imperial City databases, we may find likely candidates, people who have experienced miraculous strokes of luck, whose lives seem filled with incredible coincidences. We could look for people who seem unusually charismatic or those whom legend credits with working miracles. These could all be unconscious manifestations of a skill with the Force."

Luke held up another finger. "As well, the droids could search the database for forgotten descendants of known Jedi

Knights from the Old Republic days. We should turnup a few leads."

"And what will you yourself be doing?" Mon Mothma asked, shifting in her robes.

"I've already found several candidates I wish to investigate. All I ask right now is that you agree this is something we should pursue, that the search for Jedi be conducted by others and not just myself."

Mon Mothma sat up straighter in her central sea. "I think we can agree to that without further discussion." She looked around to the other senators, seeing them now agreement. "Tell us your second request."

Luke stood taller. This was most important to him. He saw Leia stiffen.

"If sufficient candidates are found who have potential for using the Force, I wish to be allowed—with the New Republic's blessing—to establish in some appropriate place an intensive training center, a Jedi academy, if you will. Under my direction we can help these students discover their abilities, to focus and strengthen their power. Ultimately, this academy would provide a core group that could allow us to restore the Jedi Knights as protectors of the New Republic."

CHILDREN OF THE JEDI
by Barbara Hambly
Setting: Eight years after *Return of the Jedi*

The Star Wars *characters face a menace from the glory days of the Empire when a thirty-year-old automated Imperial Dreadnaught comes to life and begins its grim mission: to gather forces and annihilate a long-forgotten stronghold of Jedi children. When Luke is whisked onboard, he begins to communicate with the brave Jedi Knight who paralyzed the ship decades ago, and gave her life in the process. Now she is part of the vessel, existing in its artificial intelligence core, and guiding Luke through one of the most unusual adventures he has ever had.*

In this scene, Luke discovers that an evil presence is gathering, one that will force him to join the battle:

Like See-Threepio, Nichos Marr sat in the outer room of the suite to which Cray had been assigned, in the power-down mode that was the droid equivalent of rest. Like Threepio, at the sound of Luke's almost noiseless tread he turned his head, aware of his presence.

"Luke?" Cray had equipped him with the most sensitive vocal modulators, and the word was calibrated to a whisper no louder than the rustle of the blueleafs massed outside the windows. He rose, and crossed to where Luke stood, the dull silver of his arms and shoulders a phantom gleam in the stray flickers of light. "What is it?"

"I don't know." They retreated to the small dining area where Luke had earlier probed his mind, and Luke stretched up to pin back a corner of the lamp-sheathe, letting a slim triangle of butter-colored light fall on the purple of the vulwood tabletop. "A dream. A premonition, maybe." It was on his lips to ask, *Do you dream?* but he remembered the ghastly, imageless darkness in Nichos's mind, and didn't. He wasn't sure if his pupil was aware of the difference from his human perception and knowledge, aware of just exactly what he'd lost when his consciousness, his self, had been transferred.

In the morning Luke excused himself from the expedition Tomla El had organized with Nichos and Cray to the Falls of Dessiar, one of the places on Ithor most renowned for its beauty and peace. When they left he sought out Umwaw Moolis, and the tall herd leader listened gravely to his less than logical request and promised to put matters in train to fulfill it. Then Luke descended to the House of the Healers, where Drub McKumb lay, sedated far beyond pain but with all the perceptions of agony and nightmare still howling in his mind.

"Kill you!" He heaved himself at the restraints, blue eyes glaring furiously as he groped and scrabbled at Luke with his clawed hands. "It's all poison! I see you! I see the dark light all around you! You're him! You're him!" His back bent like a bow; the sound of his shrieking was like something being ground out of him by an infernal mangle.

Luke had been through the darkest places of the universe and of his own mind, had done and experienced greater evil than perhaps any man had known on the road the Force had dragged him . . . Still, it was hard not to turn away.

"We even tried yarrock on him last night," explained the Healer in charge, a slightly built Ithorian beautifully tabby-striped green and yellow under her simple tabard of purple linen. "But apparently the earlier doses that brought him enough lucidity to reach here from his point of origin oversensitized his system. We'll try again in four or five days."

Luke gazed down into the contorted, grimacing face.

"As you can see," the Healer said, "the internal perception of pain and fear is slowly lessening. It's down to ninety-three percent of what it was when he was first brought in. Not much, I know, but something."

"Him! *Him! HIM!*" Foam spattered the old man's stained gray beard.

Who?

"I wouldn't advise attempting any kind of mindlink until it's at least down to fifty percent, Master Skywalker."

"No," said Luke softly.

Kill you all. And, *They are gathering . . .*

"Do you have recordings of everything he's said?"

"Oh, yes." The big coppery eyes blinked assent. "The transcript is available through the monitor cubicle down the hall. We could make nothing of them. Perhaps they will mean something to you."

They didn't. Luke listened to them all, the incoherent groans and screams, the chewed fragments of words that could be only guessed at, and now and again the clear disjointed cries: "Solo! Solo! Can you hear me? Children . . . Evil . . . Gathering here . . . Kill you all!"

THE CRYSTAL STAR
by Vonda N. McIntyre
Setting: Ten years after *Return of the Jedi*

Leia's three children have been kidnapped. That horrible fact is made worse by Leia's realization that she can no longer sense her children through the Force! While she, Artoo-Detoo, and Chewbacca trail the kidnappers, Luke and Han discover a planet that is suffering strange quantum effects from a nearby star. Slowly freezing into a perfect crystal and disrupting the Force, the star is blunting Luke's power and crippling the Millennium Falcon. *These strands converge in an apocalyptic threat not only to the fate of the New Republic, but to the universe itself.*

Here is Luke and Han's initial approach to the crystal star:

Han piloted the *Millennium Falcon* through the strangest star system he had ever approached. An ancient, dying, crystallizing white dwarf star orbited a black hole in a wildly eccentric elliptical path.

Eons ago, in this place, a small and ordinary yellow star peacefully orbited an immense blue-white supergiant. The blue star aged, and collapsed.

The blue star went supernova, blasting light and radiation and debris out into space.

Its light still traveled through the universe, a furious explosion visible from distant galaxies.

Over time, the remains of the supergiant's core collapsed under the force of its own gravity. The result was degenerate mass: a black hole.

The violence of the supernova disrupted the orbit of the nova's companion, the yellow star. Over time, the yellow star's orbit decayed.

The yellow star fell toward the unimaginably dense body of the black hole. The black hole sucked up anything, even light, that came within its grasp. And when it captured matter —even an entire yellow star—it ripped the atoms apart into a glowing accretion disk. Subatomic particles imploded downward into the singularity's equator, emitting great bursts of radiation. The accretion disk spun at a fantastic speed, glowing with fantastic heat, creating a funeral pyre for the destroyed yellow companion.

The plasma spiraled in a raging pinwheel, circling so fast and heating so intensely that it blasted X rays out into space. Then, finally, the glowing gas fell toward the invisible black hole, approaching it closer and closer, appearing to fall more and more slowly as relativity influenced it.

It was lost forever to this universe.

That was the fate of the small yellow star.

The system contained a third star: the dying white dwarf, which shone with ancient heat even as it froze into a quantum crystal. Now, as the *Millennium Falcon* entered the system, the white dwarf was falling toward the black hole, on the inward curve of its eccentric elliptical orbit.

"Will you look at that," Han said. "Quite a show."

"Indeed it is, Master Han," Threepio said, "but it is merely a shadow of what will occur when the black hole captures the crystal star."

Luke gazed silently into the maelstrom of the black hole.

Han waited.

"Hey, kid! Snap out of it."

Luke started. "What?"

"I don't know where you were, but you weren't here."

"Just thinking about the Jedi Academy. I hate to leave my students, even for a few days. But if I *do* find other trained Jedi, it'll make a big difference. To the Academy. To the New Republic . . ."

"I think we're getting along pretty well already," Han said, irked. He had spent years maintaining the peace with ordinary people. In his opinion, Jedi Knights could cause more trouble than they were worth. "And what if these are all using the dark side?"

Luke did not reply.

Han seldom admitted his nightmares, but he had nightmares about what could happen to his children if they were tempted to the dark side.

Right now they were safe, with Leia on a planetary tour of remote and peaceful worlds of the New Republic. By this time they must have reached Munto Codru. They would be visiting the beautiful mountains of the world's temperate zone. Han smiled, imagining his princess and his children being welcomed to one of Munto Codru's mysterious, ancient, fairy-tale castles.

Solar prominences flared from the white dwarf's surface. The *Falcon* passed it, heading toward the more perilous region of the black hole.

The Corellian Trilogy:
AMBUSH AT CORELLIA
ASSAULT AT SELONIA
SHOWDOWN AT CENTERPOINT
by Roger MacBride Allen
Setting: Fourteen years after *Return of the Jedi*

This trilogy takes us to Corellia, Han Solo's home world, which Han has not visited in quite some time. A trade summit brings Han, Leia, and the children—now developing their own clear personalities and instinctively learning more about their innate skills in the Force—into the middle of a situation that most closely resembles a burning fuse. The Corellian system is on the brink of civil war, there are New Republic intelligence agents on a mysterious mission which even Han does not understand, and worst of all, a fanatical rebel leader has his hands on a superweapon of unimaginable power—and just wait until you find out who that leader is!

Here is an early scene from Ambush *that gives you a wonderful look at the growing Solo children (the twins are Jacen and Jaina, and their little brother is Anakin):*

Anakin plugged the board into the innards of the droid and pressed a button. The droid's black, boxy body shuddered awake, it drew in its wheels to stand up a bit taller, its status lights lit, and it made a sort of triple beep. "That's good," he said, and pushed the button again. The droid's status lights went out, and its body slumped down again. Anakin picked up the next piece, a motivation actuator. He frowned at it as he turned it over in his hands. He shook his head. "That's *not* good," he announced.

"What's not good?" Jaina asked.

"This thing," Anakin said, handing her the actuator. "Can't you *tell?* The insides part is all melty."

Jaina and Jacen exchanged a look. "The outside looks okay," Jaina said, giving the part to her brother. "How can he tell what the *inside* of it looks like? It's sealed shut when they make it."

Jacen shrugged. "How can he do any of this stuff? But we need that actuator. That was the toughest part to dig up. I must have gone around half the city looking for one that would fit this droid." He turned toward his little brother. "Anakin, we don't have another one of these. Can you make it better? Can you make the insides less melty?"

Anakin frowned. "I can make it *some* better. Not all the way better. A *little* less melty. *Maybe* it'll be okay."

Jacen handed the actuator back to Anakin. "Okay, try it."

Anakin, still sitting on the floor, took the device from his brother and frowned at it again. He turned it over and over in his hands, and then held it over his head and looked at it as if he were holding it up to the light. "There," he said, pointing a chubby finger at one point on the unmarked surface. "In there is the bad part." He rearranged himself to sit cross-legged, put the actuator in his lap, and put his right index finger over the "bad" part. "Fix," he said. "Fix." The dark brown outer case of the actuator seemed to glow for a second with an odd blue-red light, but then the glow sputtered out and Anakin pulled his finger away quickly and stuck it in his mouth, as if he had burned it on something.

"Better now?" Jaina asked.

"Some better," Anakin said, pulling his finger out of his mouth. "Not *all* better." He took the actuator in his hand and

stood up. He opened the access panel on the broken droid and plugged in the actuator. He closed the door and looked expectantly at his older brother and sister.

"Done?" Jaina asked.

"Done," Anakin agreed. "But *I'm* not going to push the button." He backed well away from the droid, sat down on the floor, and folded his arms.

Jacen looked at his sister.

"Not me," she said. "This was your idea."

Jacen stepped forward to the droid, reached out to push the power button from as far away as he could, and then stepped hurriedly back.

Once again, the droid shuddered awake, rattling a bit this time as it did so. It pulled its wheels in, lit its panel lights, and made the same triple beep. But then its camera eye viewlens wobbled back and forth, and its panel lights dimmed and flared. It rolled backward just a bit, and then recovered itself.

"Good morning, young mistress and masters," it said. "How may I surge you?"

Well, one word wrong, but so what? Jacen grinned and clapped his hands and rubbed them together eagerly. "Good day, droid," he said. They had done it! But what to ask for first? "First tidy up this room," he said. A simple task, and one that ought to serve as a good test of what this droid could do.

Suddenly the droid's overhead access door blew off and there was a flash of light from its interior. A thin plume of smoke drifted out of the droid. Its panel lights flared again, and then the work arm sagged downward. The droid's body, softened by heat, sagged in on itself and drooped to the floor. The floor and walls and ceilings of the playroom were supposed to be fireproof, but nonetheless the floor under the droid darkened a bit, and the ceiling turned black. The ventilators kicked on high automatically, and drew the smoke out of the room. After a moment they shut themselves off, and the room was silent.

The three children stood, every bit as frozen to the spot as the droid was, absolutely stunned. It was Anakin who recovered first. He walked cautiously toward the droid and looked at it carefully, being sure not to get too close or touch it. *"Really* melty now," he announced, and then wandered off to the other side of the room to play with his blocks.

The twins looked at the droid, and then at each other.

"We're dead," Jacen announced, surveying the wreckage.